THE HERD

EMILY EDWARDS

PENGUIN BOOKS

TRANSWORLD PUBLISHERS
Penguin Random House, One Embassy Gardens,
8 Viaduct Gardens, London SW11 7BW
www.penguin.co.uk

Transworld is part of the Penguin Random House group of companies
whose addresses can be found at global.penguinrandomhouse.com

Penguin
Random House
UK

First published in Great Britain in 2022 by Bantam Press
an imprint of Transworld Publishers
Penguin paperback edition published 2022

A CIP catalogue record for this book
is available from the British Library.

ISBN 9781529176919

Typeset in 12.02/14.25pt Garamond MT Std by Jouve (UK), Milton Keynes.
Printed and bound in Great Britain by Clays Ltd, Elcograf S.p.A.

The authorized representative in the EEA is Penguin Random House Ireland,
Morrison Chambers, 32 Nassau Street, Dublin D02 YH68.

Penguin Random House is committed to a sustainable
future for our business, our readers and our planet. This book
is made from Forest Stewardship Council® certified paper.

For James

If it's not viral or bacterial, it must be maternal.

Janna Malamud Smith

Farley County Court

December 2019

They arrive in court separately. Bry first, early, perhaps to avoid the worst of the demonstrations outside. She keeps her dark, hollow eyes fixed right ahead of her, her head bowed as if in prayer, Ash's arm around her, before she crumples into her seat just in front of the judge's bench.

The last time I saw Bry or Elizabeth was months ago at the now infamous party. I remember watching them and feeling – as I always did when it came to those two – a tug of envy, like a great hook in my abdomen, pulling. It wasn't what they said or did, quite the opposite in fact; it was the absence of explanation. There was a calmness between them, a knowing, because each was absolutely confident of the other. Their friendship made them seem untouchable somehow. I've never had that with anyone.

It's a few minutes before the doors open again. The whole court shifts, sits more upright, as Elizabeth walks into the large, serious room, Jack a couple of paces behind. Her eyes cast about, scanning to see who is there to support them. She nods at a couple of people. Her gaze lands for just a beat on Bry and Ash. Her expression doesn't even flicker before she moves on. Her composure is impressive, silently letting us all know she is blameless, unafraid. She takes her place on the other side of the court to Bry. Her solicitor leans forward to whisper something and Elizabeth nods in agreement, careful not to smile.

1

Next to me, a woman I recognise from the school gates says quietly, 'It's so sad, so sad, isn't it?'

She sighs, then she finishes whatever she was doing on her phone before dropping it into her coat pocket and turning back to me.

'I always found their friendship a bit weird, to be honest. I mean, they were so different, weren't they?'

I nod and wonder whether she feels it too. This sense of something lacking – the hook, pulling – that behind all the gossip, all the bullshit chat about school plays and football teams, we are starving for each other, for connection. Is she, like me, desperate to see and truly be seen by another woman?

'I heard Elizabeth was almost assaulted by one of those anti-vax demonstrators yesterday.'

Her voice is light, bouncy with glee. Her phone buzzes and she snatches it out of her pocket. I turn back to face the court. And I think, 'No, not her, she doesn't feel it.'

Now, sitting here, I realise it was stupid of me, stupid to be jealous of Bry and Elizabeth, because if this court case is the cost of true friendship – families devastated, lives destroyed – then it can't be worth it. Maybe women like us are the lucky ones after all, maybe our distance from each other keeps us safe, helps us to hide our wounds, our fears, so we can't be injured by others, lone wolves making our own way as best we can.

1 July 2019

For once, Bry isn't late. She is waiting outside the Nettlestone Primary School gates at exactly 3.30 p.m. She'd tiptoed out of her vinyasa flow class a little early, been stern with herself when she was tempted to nip into a shop on the short walk to her goddaughter's school, Elizabeth's request in her ears: *Please don't be too late, Clem panics if she thinks she's been forgotten.* Bry has to admit it feels kind of leisurely being early, to be one of the first at the school gates, simply waiting, the afternoon sun warm on her face. It's a relief not to feel a flood of panic rising in her; not to run. *So this is how it feels to be Elizabeth.* More parents start to gather, a few faces Bry recognises from around town, parents she knows are friends with Elizabeth, but no one Bry knows well enough to say hello to. They acknowledge her vaguely and turn back to their conversations. Bry can see why Elizabeth fits in perfectly here, leading the chats about school trips and nit treatments.

Suddenly the school doors open and there's a rush of noise: small, high voices shrieking, laughing; a couple of teachers' voices lower, louder, warning, 'Slow down!' A fast-moving cloud of children fills the little playground, all clamouring towards the gates. Bry sees Clemmie immediately.

3

Her red hair, the same colour as Jack's, makes her easy to spot. Today it's plaited, the plait moving side to side like a fox's tail as Clemmie runs. Her rucksack is too big and full for her small six-year-old frame; it moves awkwardly on her back, out of time with her run, but she's laughing, her blue eyes and freckled face creased in joy. Clemmie's not laughing at anything in particular; she's laughing at the feeling of release, the novelty of Auntie Bry collecting her from school, the chaotic speed of her running. Bry bends, opens her arms, and laughs too. Clemmie runs into her with a gentle thud. Her hair smells of pencil shavings and strawberry lip balm.

'Auntie Bry!'

Bry holds her and closes her eyes briefly. Clemmie wiggles away before Bry is ready. She wipes a few strands of hair from her face with her palm and says, 'My class did the song today in assembly, we did.' Her rucksack starts falling off her shoulders. Bry lifts it on to her own back and reaches for her goddaughter's hand. Clemmie starts singing a song, presumably the one she sang in assembly, about baking a cake for her friend. She looks up at Bry, dimples showing as she beams. Bry swings their held hands so Clemmie knows she loves her song as they start the short walk through the narrow, hilly old streets of Farley, towards Saint's Road, where both their families – the Chamberlains and the Kohlis – live. She gives Clemmie a two-pound coin, which she drops into the cap of a man busking on the cobbled bridge.

'Cheers, girls,' he says with a wink, and they both wave to a friend who works in the health food shop.

'Bry! Yoo-hoo! Bry, Clemmie, wait for us!' Bry turns, slow and reluctant, as her friend Row, still in her yoga leggings, steams up the tree-lined pavement behind them, her daughter Lily tinkling along by her side.

'Told you you didn't have to leave yoga early,' Row says as she catches up with them. Clemmie peels away from Bry and greets Lily enthusiastically, before the two girls run ahead a couple of paces.

'But I guess Elizabeth would have killed you if you'd been late,' Row adds, her bangles jingling as she loops her arm through Bry's. 'Where is she anyway?'

'She has a meeting with the council about that petition she got everyone to sign, about reducing the speed limit on Saint's Road to twenty.'

'Oh yeah, right. I was wondering what was going on with that,' Row says, her tone slightly tinted with disdain, as though Elizabeth has been sloppy letting the issue slide when Elizabeth does more for the whole community than anyone else, a fact that people seem to admire yet also pisses them off in equal measure. Bry is used to Elizabeth being divisive. She understands it – sometimes Elizabeth pisses her off too – but she still bristles slightly at Row's tone. Like a sibling, she feels that she is justified in highlighting Elizabeth's failings – how uptight and controlling she can be – but she can't abide anyone else doing so, even her own husband, Ash.

'Lil, shoelace!' Row calls to her daughter, and the four of them stop so Lily can retie her lace before Row continues, 'So, does it feel weird doing school pick-up? Alba will be here in September, won't she?'

Bry tries to picture her four-year-old daughter not in her usual choice of outfit – yellow wellies and pink tutu, perhaps – but wearing the same blue gingham dress and

5

black shoes as Lily and Clemmie. She imagines Alba shaking her little brown head and saying, 'Not wearing it, Mumma.'

It makes her heart flood and break simultaneously.

'God, don't. It's such a weird thought.'

'I know, I know. But everyone feels like that, trust me. I cried and cried after I dropped Lil off the first time. But then, you know, suddenly you have all this time and it's amazing, so . . .'

Bry nods; she does this a lot when she's with Row.

Loves giving advice, whether you ask for it or not, doesn't she? Elizabeth said about her once.

'Clemmie, what do you think about Alba coming to Nettlestone after the summer holidays?' Bry asks.

Clemmie's head shoots up from her hushed conversation with Lily and she says, 'Baby Alba's coming to my school?'

Bry nods, smiles, and Clemmie jumps up and down a couple of times. From her kneeling position on the pavement, Lily watches Clemmie, confused.

'Why do you like her so much?' she asks.

'Baby Alba is like my little sister,' Clemmie explains patiently, still celebrating. 'Isn't she, Auntie Bry?'

Bry leans forward, kisses Clemmie on the top of her head, and says, 'Oh, that's a lovely thing to say, Clem, so nice for Alba to have a big sister . . . Just make sure she doesn't hear you call her Baby Alba,' she adds with a wink, as though it's their secret how cross Alba gets when people do that.

Clemmie turns to Lily and says seriously, 'Alba *hates* being called a baby.'

The girls start to skip on and Row's about to take Bry's arm again when Bry notices the corner shop on the other side of the road is open.

'Actually, Row, I think we'll leave you here. I've got to pick up a few bits.'

'Oh, OK,' Row says, pulling her arm away. 'See you on Saturday then?'

'Saturday?'

Row laughs at Bry, her eyes widening in genuine surprise as Bry adds quickly, trying to cover up her forgetfulness, 'Oh yeah, yeah, Elizabeth's barbecue.' She lifts her eyebrows, to show that she exasperates herself sometimes, before calling to Clemmie, holding her small hand in her own as they cross the quiet road.

'Bye, Lily, bye, Row!' Clemmie waves; Lily waves back and Row blows them a kiss before taking her phone out of her pocket as she shoos Lily on.

In the shop, Bry heads straight to the ice cream fridge.

'Choose whatever you like.'

'Anything?'

'Anything.'

They spend the next five minutes agonising over whether Clemmie would like chocolate with sprinkles or strawberry ice cream more, before she decides to have the same multi-coloured ice lolly as Bry.

Bry pays, forgetting the bread and milk Ash said they needed at home, and the two of them leave hand in hand, their ice lollies already melting in the afternoon sun, a medley of red, orange and yellow creeping down their wrists.

'There you are!'

Elizabeth is standing, hands on hips, outside the Chamberlain family home, a Victorian house, the sun casting dappled shadows through the magnolia tree in the small front garden. She looks like a mother from the past in her red striped apron, her dark blonde bob held back from her face by two clips, and she's wearing proper make-up – eye-liner and lipstick – presumably for her meeting. She's also holding a bottle of white wine Bry immediately recognises as the Sancerre Ash buys in bulk.

'Mummy!' Clemmie skips towards her, presses her lips to Elizabeth's.

Elizabeth takes her hand and says, 'Poppet, you're so sticky!'

'Auntie Bry and me had lollies,' she says, sticking out her colourful tongue as evidence.

'Auntie Bry *and I*, pops, and yuck, I don't want to see your tongue, thank you,' Elizabeth adds in mock horror over Clemmie's head to Bry, 'Lollies *before* supper, Auntie Bry?'

Bry shrugs. 'Godmother's privilege,' she says, showing Elizabeth her own coloured tongue before kissing her friend's cheek.

'I'll remember that when I return the favour,' Elizabeth replies, picking a bit of leaf out of Bry's dark hair. 'I've just been over to yours. Ash and Alba are coming over in a bit. The meeting finished earlier than I thought, so I had a few minutes to make a fish pie.'

Bry thinks about the can of baked beans she'd planned for Alba's supper and the bread she suddenly remembers she didn't buy, and feels simultaneously grateful to Elizabeth and ashamed of her own forgetfulness. But it doesn't last long because Clemmie takes Bry's sticky hand in her own and says, 'Yay! Baby Alba is coming for supper!' and Elizabeth and Bry smile at each other and say at the same time, 'Don't call her Baby Alba!' before they head into the familiar warmth of Number 10 Saint's Road.

*

Summer is already in full swing in Elizabeth and Jack's garden. Max and Charlie have set up their cricket stumps at the end of the lawn, their gloves, pads and bat left on the grass waiting for their return from school. Clemmie's pink paddling pool sits a strategic distance away at the other end, half full of water. The lawn, recently mown, is emerald, and the apple and pear trees at the bottom of the garden next to the wall that leads to the woods beyond are in full leaf. Max and Charlie will be home soon; the kids always eat together at 5 p.m., so Clemmie skips upstairs to change out of her uniform, and Elizabeth steps out of the kitchen French doors and gestures to Bry to join her at the garden table in front of the knobbled flint wall that is covered in creeping jasmine.

'I know it's early, but it's your husband's fault . . .' She hands Bry a glass of the Sancerre.

'He is such a bad influence,' Bry agrees.

Bry closes her eyes, feeling the July sun pour over her skin like warm cream while Elizabeth starts to tell Bry about her 'meeting from hell', and Bry thinks, *Yes, yes, this is what the long winter wait was for, these simple, beautiful pleasures.*

For Bry, being with Elizabeth is the easiest, most natural thing in the world. But it hasn't always been this way. When they'd first met at university, Elizabeth had been dating a friend of Bry's called Adam. No one in Bry's friendship group understood why laid-back, crumpled Adam was dating this tall, statuesque blonde who looked Norwegian but was actually from Essex. She was organised, cynical, and hated recreational drugs and excessive drinking, which made her – in Bry's misted view – an uptight pain in the arse.

It wasn't until Adam dumped her and Bry heard Elizabeth

crying in the next-door cubicle in the pub toilets (*I'm only upset because* he *got there first*) that Bry started to like her. She passed her loo roll under the cubicle door and after that they'd got steadily and thoroughly pissed together. It revolutionised Bry's life. She discovered in Elizabeth a relationship where there was no room for competition, for comparisons or envy, simply because they were so different. They weren't exactly chalk and cheese; more like cheese and pineapple – a weird, unexpected pairing that just worked. She'd never met someone her own age who was like Elizabeth: she was into politics, wasn't ashamed to say she wanted to make money, but she laughed easily and cared more about others than anyone Bry had ever met. Whereas Bry wanted to be an artist, was in love with all things bohemian and hated politics. Bry wore a hemp scarf wrapped around her head and Elizabeth carried a little black handbag, which held her phone, a book, a fold-up hair-brush and her perfectly organised wallet. Elizabeth kept all her receipts; Bry stored fivers in her bra. Bry held her hands in the air, swaying her whole body when she danced, while Elizabeth sidestepped, buttocks clenched hard as a walnut, and kept a close eye on her watch. It was as if each was dis-covering a fascinating new country in the other, a place they'd never choose to live but somewhere they knew they could always seek refuge when their own world was shaking.

'Bry, you're not even listening to me!'

Bry opens her eyes. Elizabeth has her phone in front of her and is pecking away at her calendar with one finger.

'So obviously, it's July already, and with the fete, barbecue, Clemmie's birthday and end-of-term stuff, there aren't any free weekends left. So how about we organise your birthday camping trip early August – say, the weekend of the third?'

Bry had suggested way back in the safety of February that perhaps a camping weekend would be the best way to celebrate the fucking appalling fact that she was turning forty, and Elizabeth, of course, hasn't forgotten. Bry flushes, hot and uncomfortable.

'Can we talk about it another time?' she groans. 'Preferably never.'

Elizabeth puts her phone down, keeps her blue eyes on her friend as she takes a sip of wine, and says, 'Look, Bry, I know you won't believe me, but you're actually in very good shape for forty.'

'I'm telling you, it's all the yoga.'

'Bollocks to yoga. I mean, you're married to a great man you love who just happens to be very rich; you have a brilliant daughter, you live in an amazing house in an amazing town opposite your amazing friend, and when your brilliant daughter goes to school you're going to find a new career – some arty, hippie nonsense that I won't get but you'll make a huge success of, so you know, I just don't think there's any cause to freak out. Your life is on track.'

'You freaked out when you turned forty.'

'I did not!'

'Yes, you did; I just wasn't allowed to say anything about it. Remember when I came over the night before your birthday and you were ironing the kids' pants?'

Elizabeth grimaces.

'Oh yeah, now you mention it, that was a bit of a low point . . .' Elizabeth takes another sip of wine, changes tack. 'Fine. Freak out if you want, but let's confirm this date first so I can figure out . . .' Her eye is drawn to a streak of bright pink and yellow as a small red-headed bird flaps her arms across the grass towards the paddling pool.

'Clem, really? Now?' Elizabeth calls to her daughter, who has changed into her swimsuit, her bare skin the colour of milk.

But Clemmie isn't listening; she's stopped dead by the edge of the pool and is staring down at something in the water. At the same time, there's a shout from inside the house: 'Mum! We're home!' The boys are back and Elizabeth goes to them in the kitchen, like a first responder ready to take on the triumphs and challenges of their day.

Bry goes to kneel next to Clemmie, who is now cupping her hands in the pool and saying softly, 'Poor baby ladybird, poor ladybaby.'

Inside her hands, swirling in the water with its stocky legs waving absurdly in the air, is a ladybird.

'She's drowning, Auntie Bry, she's drowning!' Clemmie's voice lifts in panic, tears close.

'No, look, we can save her.' Bry flips the insect over like a tiddlywink and lifts Clemmie's hand towards the flailing legs. The ladybird immediately starts trudging up Clemmie's wrist as though nothing at all has happened, leaving tiny puddles of water as it goes.

Clemmie giggles and says, 'Tickles!'

'Well done for spotting her just in time, Clem.'

'Do you think she's hungry, Auntie Bry?'

The two of them gather daisies and leaves to make a nest for the rescued ladybird. Clemmie calls her Dandelion, and they're just about to introduce Dandelion to her new home when Bry spots Alba running across the grass towards them. Her daughter's little chest is puffed out with effort, her chubby legs pumping away as fast as they can, her brown hair a chaos of curls around her – she's like a lovely typhoon. She's grinning widely, her eyes fixed on Clemmie, laughing in anticipation of her joke, her fingers already together and straight, just like her dad showed her. She clatters to a stop and lands both prepared hands over Clemmie's eyes. This might not go well.

'Guess who, 'lemmie?' Alba squeals, breathing hard.

But Clemmie twists easily away and says, 'No, Alba, you have to shh. Look, we're showing Dandelion her new house and all her new things.'

Alba squats on her haunches next to Clemmie, like a stout mechanic checking over a vehicle. She looks from Clemmie to the bundle of leaves and back to Clemmie again.

'Ohhh,' she says before her face twists in confusion. 'But beetles have wings, not things!'

Elizabeth brings out the fish pie a few minutes later, and Max and Charlie follow with plates and cutlery, shoelaces flapping, their uniforms crumpled and askew after the school day. Charlie calls, 'Hi, Auntie Bry,' and Max waves. Ash arrives soon after. He holds Bry's shoulder as he gives her a kiss, before topping up Bry and Elizabeth's glasses and pouring himself a large one. Bry opens a bag of vegetable crisps for the adults to share, and Clemmie hides Dandelion on her lap under the table while Elizabeth's busy getting water.

'How was yoga?' Ash asks, sitting next to his wife as Elizabeth settles Alba on a cushion. Max and Charlie start arguing about some cricket match in the West Indies, and the girls pass secret little pieces of mashed potato to Dandelion.

'Was mad old Emma there leading the oms?' Elizabeth

asks, pulling her apron over her head and adding, 'Elbows off the table, please, Max.' Max rolls his eyes and hovers his elbow just above the table. Charlie giggles and looks nervously towards Elizabeth, who, having taken her seat opposite Bry and Ash, only needs to raise her eyebrows at her eldest son for him to submit and lower his elbows off the table.

'No, no, she wasn't, actually. Apparently she's been a bit unwell.'

One side of Elizabeth's mouth curls up and she raises her wine glass as she says, 'Aw, is one of her chakras playing up again? That woman is not in my good books – she offered to do some research into local traffic-calming initiatives and has completely flaked out on me; not that I'm surprised.'

'When was she ever in your good books, Elizabeth?' Bry counters, trying not to get defensive. Ash and Elizabeth love nothing more than taking the piss out of Bry's hippie friends.

Elizabeth nods in agreement. 'Yes, that's fair.'

'I saw her in Waitrose yesterday,' Ash says, leaning forward for a crisp. 'I was at the cheese counter and heard her beads and bells and whatever clanking together all the way over from the vegan bit. I tried to pretend I hadn't seen her, but she caught me.'

'Clemmie, eat some fish, please,' Elizabeth interjects before turning to Ash and continuing, 'I fear for you, Ashy, there is no escape in Farley.' Only Elizabeth gets away with calling Ash 'Ashy'.

'Don't I bloody know it,' he says. Elizabeth frowns briefly at his swearing in front of the kids, but neither Ash nor the kids notice. 'I'll never get used to bumping into people. I just don't understand why anyone would want to have a bollocks, awkward conversation in the street about nothing when we could just nod or wave or something. Seriously, if I want to see you, I'll message and arrange to meet up, but why do we have to stop and talk about the weather just because we happen to live close to each other and be walking down the same bit of pavement at the same time? I don't get it.'

Elizabeth is frowning openly at Ash now, before she shakes her head and says, 'It's called community, Ashy.'

'No, it's not; it's called a waste of bloody time.'

Elizabeth keeps talking, ignoring Ash.

'It's called getting to know your neighbours, being responsible, caring for one another.'

Ash wrinkles his nose in mock distaste.

'Nope. Not for me.'

'Honestly, you can take the boy out of North London but you can't take North London out of the boy.'

'Amen to that.'

They'd moved to Farley two years ago, leaving Ash's beloved North London, where his elderly parents have lived ever since they moved to Britain from New Delhi fifty years ago. Ash had lived every one of his first forty-five years in London but he left willingly because Bry promised clean air for their daughter, less stress for Ash, and more like-minded people. Ash's suits have been replaced with shorts and flip-flops; he's grown a beard which is more grey than black, and he seems to have his old Ray-Bans welded to the top of his head. Before they moved, he'd sold the online digital marketing company he'd spent over a decade building, a company that cost him his first marriage and means he can only talk about his two sons' early years in a vague way, like a kindly uncle and not their dad. When everything broke down with his first wife Linette, Ash had pretty much sworn his life away, decided he'd marry his work. He'd make a lot of money, buy all the best shit and intimidate his employees. He'd live in Zone 1 and date women to make other men jealous. It would be a cold existence but it would be reliable. But then all this had gone to hell when Bry, with her long, dark hair and chocolate eyes, bounced into his life at a work event. He promised Bry – actually swore and cried – that he'd never, ever let work take priority over everything else again. So he didn't take too much convincing to move to Farley – a town they knew they both liked after visiting the Chamberlains for weekend breaks from London.

The Chamberlain kids have all finished their fish pie, but they know they have to wait for Alba to finish before getting the fruit salad that's waiting for them in the kitchen. Three sets of eyes watch as Alba crams the last forkful of smudgy potato and fish into her mouth before clattering her fork down and clapping.

Charlie clears all the plates into the kitchen before coming back out with the fruit salad, and punches Max on the arm when his elder brother starts spooning their pudding into the waiting bowls – 'Max knows it's my favourite job!' he wails to his mum.

With an aggravated sigh, Elizabeth says, 'Max, you know the one who clears the table gets to serve pudding. Stop upsetting your brother.'

Once peace is restored and the kids are bent over their bowls again, a large figure fills the French doors to the kitchen, and Jack calls out, 'Surprise!'

There are cries of 'Daddy!' from around the table before Jack Chamberlain makes loud smacking noises as he kisses all four of the kids, pausing to be introduced surreptitiously to Dandelion as Elizabeth says, glancing at her watch, 'You finished early!'

Jack's cheeks redden slightly, but he doesn't say anything. Once he's done with the kids, he makes a show of kissing all the adults too – even Ash on both cheeks – making Charlie and Max laugh. Ash pours his friend some wine and Jack tugs his tie, loosening it from around his neck. He's not ready to sit down, not yet, the energy from the city still quickening through him. Bry offers him some crisps but Jack shakes his head and pats his only slightly domed stomach.

'No thanks. Big lunch.' Jack works for a Chinese property developer in London, something that Bry always finds incongruous with his foppish, affable nature. Ash reckons that's why the Chinese hired him in the first place (*They fucking love him, he's their ginger Hugh Grant*).

'Busy day?' Elizabeth asks, taking a crisp herself.

'Always,' Jack says, without meeting his wife's eye. 'So, is this what you lovely lot get up to, drinking wine in the sun while I'm slogging away at work?'

'Pretty much, mate, pretty much,' says Ash, leaning back on the bench, tipping his sunglasses down from his forehead as he drapes an arm over Bry's shoulders.

Elizabeth laughs as if Jack's suggestion is the most ridiculous thing she's ever heard, and she launches into the story about her meeting at the council. 'So apparently we need to fill out yet another application that no one ever mentioned before today's meeting, which is just typical . . .'

While Elizabeth talks, Bry feels Ash's warm hand on her shoulder and tries to remember the last time she came home energised and buzzing from a day's work. When she met Ash, she had been a documentary producer, working on what Ash called 'medium-brow social commentaries', which was a nice way of saying 'fairly shit fly-on-the-wall stuff'. She made behind-the-scenes series about hospital wards and prison blocks, and had just set up her own company with a director colleague of hers when she discovered she was pregnant. Her colleagues didn't find out until Bry burst into tears after refusing a glass of champagne in celebration of their first commission – a documentary slated for a 3 p.m. Sunday slot about people who work on the Underground. Bry was nearly eight months pregnant when they started filming, and eight months and one week when she finally accepted she wasn't going to finish the film. She would have gone back to it if they'd stayed in London, but now Pool Productions is flying, Bry seamlessly replaced by someone else.

In the beginning, Bry's life had been absorbed by her relationship with Ash – their move out of London, visits from Theo and Bran (his two sons with Linette), Alba, the house renovations. When they'd been in Farley a few months, she'd tried putting Alba into a nursery, stating she was going to train to be a yoga teacher. But Alba cried when Bry did her best to cheerfully wave goodbye and she would spend the day a tight ball of anxiety, trying to learn about yogic breathing and meditation while all she could see was Alba red-faced and wailing, ignored by staff in a lonely corner of the nursery. She decided yoga could wait; she'd focus on transforming herself into a brilliant mum. She'd keep Alba at home and focus on learning how to bake, imaginative play and curtain patterns. But the transformation she imagined hadn't happened, not yet at least.

And now this last year, especially with Alba in preschool, the extra time in her life has seemed more of a hindrance than a blessing. Bry has noticed how it seems to take her at least three times as long as Elizabeth to complete a simple task, such as making sandwiches or paying a bill. Time seems to spill around her, messy and uncontainable. She sees the same thing in Ash. How life sags around him like excess skin. True, Ash does a couple of days' consultancy work a week from home, and he did oversee the renovations of their new home, but still, they see too much of each other. That's their problem.

Ash lifts his arm away from Bry and tugs at his short, grey beard, which means he's uncomfortable about something; perhaps he senses what she's thinking. He gets up from the table and Alba laughs as she stands on her chair to spoon fruit salad into his mouth. Clemmie asks Elizabeth's permission to get down before she runs over to sit in her dad's lap. Max kicks Charlie on the bottom as they carry the empty bowls inside, laughing, and then run, shouting, all the way to their cricket stumps. After the boys have left, Alba asks for some more, and after batting Ash away she sits quietly, nodding seriously and singing a made-up song between mouthfuls of orange and banana. Bry sees Elizabeth cast a quick glance at Alba. If she was one of Elizabeth's kids she'd be told not to sing with her mouth full, but Bry catches her eye, reminds her silently about their agreement to respect their different ways of parenting. They've done this for twenty years, after all – recognised a difference between them, talked about it as much as they could bear and then, like respectful warriors, put their swords down and quietly backed away from each other.

'Quick, Auntie Bry, quick, Baby Alba! Come and look – Dandelion has a family!' Clemmie calls from the apple tree at the bottom of the garden. Alba puffs out her chest, makes her hands into fists and steams into her fastest run, Bry following behind, her toes cool in the grass and a warmth in her chest.

Yes, this is it, she thinks, *this is my happiness*, and her whole life suddenly feels like one long joyful moment.

2 July 2019

It's 12.23 a.m. and Elizabeth can't sleep. As usual, she's done everything she's read she should do to help herself drift off – she'd not looked at a screen for an hour before bed, she'd sprayed her pillow with lavender, made a list of all the stuff she has to do tomorrow so it doesn't swirl around her head – but still she is wide awake, blinking in the pitch black.

The end of term is always crazy: Elizabeth has to attend all the sports days and school plays as Jack is at work or travelling back from work during the week, and in addition there's Clemmie's birthday party to organise the day after the end of term. At times like these especially, Elizabeth's life feels like an endless to-do list, one which she's constantly adding to even while she's trying to get to sleep.

Each one of Jack's rhythmic snores feels to Elizabeth like a little brag about how pleasurable his sleep is, how fucking free his mind is. She knows it's not his fault, knows she should be happy that one of them isn't going to be cranky in the morning; she just wishes for once it could be her. With an irritable groan she gets out of bed. It feels like she's giving up somehow. The bedroom door closes behind her with a sharp click, but it doesn't matter. Jack sleeps through everything.

Downstairs, Elizabeth makes herself a camomile tea and sits heavily at the old oak kitchen table, moving bowls and spoons out of the way: she always sets the table ready for breakfast before she goes to bed. The kitchen looks better at night when the chips in the cabinetry paintwork and the mildew around the sink are less visible. Jack tells her there's no point in refurbing while the kids are still small, but Max is almost a teenager and the skirting boards are still decorated with his toddler scrawls, despite Elizabeth scrubbing them. It's a money thing: apart from her voluntary stuff, Elizabeth hasn't worked since having Clemmie and Jack hasn't had a pay rise in nearly four years. They only managed to buy the house thanks to the money she inherited when Elizabeth's dad died without warning from an aneurysm seven years ago.

She needs to speak to Jack again, and not let him get away with mumbling something about the long-term effects of the recession and then make an excuse to get away from her. Sometimes, when she can't sleep, Elizabeth fantasises about how much money she'd be making if she'd been the one to stay at work and Jack looked after the kids. She used to be a solicitor representing media companies; she'd probably be a senior partner by now on a very healthy six-figure salary.

But she doesn't want to go back; the media landscape has changed dramatically in the seven years since she left, and besides, she was miserable when she worked after having Charlie. Commuting to London, constantly leaving work early, full of apologies, because of stomach bugs and unreliable childcare. She was exhausted at work and exhausted at home.

She felt like she was failing at being both a mother and a professional – a familiar story for so many, she knew, but for Elizabeth failing was anathema. It went against everything she believed to be true about herself. It was, if she was totally honest, part of the reason they had a third kid. Clemmie gave her a reason, the best reason, to stay at home. Thanks to Clemmie, giving up work didn't feel like a failure; Elizabeth simply reframed it to herself as the honourable, loving thing to do. Then, when Clemmie started having fits when she was just a few weeks old, it was more proof of how much Elizabeth was needed. Until she was almost three, Elizabeth struggled to leave Clemmie even with Jack for a few minutes, convinced that if she peeled herself away, that was when Clemmie's eyes would roll back and her little doll body would start to shake so unnaturally. Her skin would burn a bright red and foam would bubble from her mouth like a chemical reaction. It saddens Elizabeth that she doesn't have many happy memories from Clemmie's first few months. She just remembers the fear; the crushing, suffocating fear she felt for herself and her baby.

Elizabeth opens up her laptop to the BBC homepage and types the name of Charlie's tennis camp into the search bar to pay the deposit for his place (yet another thing she forgot to write on her list), when a news headline catches her eye. The photo is of a baby grinning, all gums and cheeks. Elizabeth's heart clenches as she reads the text above: *Don't let Rosie's death be for nothing.*

She knows she shouldn't, but also knows there's no way she won't click on the article and read the whole thing. It was written by the baby's father, Mark Clancy, and describes how Rosie died of meningitis a few weeks before her scheduled

MMR. Rosie went to bed with a slight temperature, so her mum gave her Calpol. She slept for thirteen hours straight. And then she woke up screaming. They amputated all her limbs but that still wasn't enough to save her.

Elizabeth lifts a hand to cover her mouth and starts biting her forefinger as she reads. *Her little red coat is still hanging on its hook by the door. I don't think I'll ever be able to pack it away.*

After the piece, there's another article link below she doesn't need to read – there are so many lately and they all say roughly the same thing: vaccination rates falling below what is required for herd immunity, the rising dangers to the immunosuppressed and the elderly, the question around whether vaccines in schools should be mandatory.

Elizabeth stares at the picture of Rosie again; Clemmie has dimples just like her. Her heart curls tighter around itself, like a fist. Before Clemmie started school, Elizabeth would interview any childminder or playgroup leader, ask them to ensure the other children were vaccinated because Clemmie couldn't be due to her fits. Most of them understood, but some of them refused and others prickled, as if it was as offensive for Elizabeth even to raise the issue as it would be to ask them how much money they had in their bank account. Knowing the vaccination rates were especially low around Farley, when Clemmie started at Nettlestone Elizabeth met with Mr Paterson, the headmaster, and although he made it clear he couldn't enforce anything, he did send an email to all parents asking them to 'act with serious consideration and foresight' on the vaccination issue. It's part of the reason Elizabeth is so involved in everything to do with the school and the community – if her family are known and hopefully liked by others, surely people will be more willing to do the right thing?

Clemmie hasn't had a fit in years: she can run faster and handle knocks better than any other almost-seven-year-old, probably in no small part thanks to Max and Charlie. She is an energetic, happy little girl and so Elizabeth has become lax, as though her daughter has reached some unknown goal and is now safe. But the article about Rosie reminds Elizabeth that Clemmie isn't safe. She isn't safe unless Elizabeth makes her safe. And in the dim light of early morning, she opens up a new email.

Hi Everyone!

We're so excited to have you over for the first day of the summer holiday and to celebrate Clemmie's seventh birthday on 18th July. The plan is for all the kids to eat loads of sugar and throw themselves about on the bouncy castle all afternoon, and for the adults to drink wine and join them.

She adds 'until someone's sick' at the end and immediately deletes it. It comes across badly.

So as you all know, Clemmie had a lot of seizures and was very unwell when she was a baby. Because of this, Clemmie cannot be vaccinated, which means we have to be extra careful, especially with all the scary stuff being reported in the news recently. As parents of Clemmie's good friends, it would be great if you could confirm that your child is up to date with their vaccination schedule. If you have chosen not to vaccinate your child, then we respect your decision but, with regret, we think it's best if you don't attend Clemmie's party, and we'd appreciate it if we could limit future close contact.

Please do respond and let us know.

With love & thanks, Jack and Elizabeth.

They're usually an 'Elizabeth and Jack' couple, but Elizabeth thinks it sounds better on this occasion if it's 'Jack and Elizabeth'. She forwards the email, including a link to the article about Rosie, to Jack with a quick note at the top:

Love – Please read this article. It reminded me we've got a bit soft about the vaccination thing – can you let me know what you think of my email below? I'd like to send it out ASAP. x

As she presses send, Elizabeth feels the fist in her chest uncurl; her daughter is a little bit safer. Clemmie comes into contact daily with her friends and other children at school, of course, and in the many clubs she attends, but having a group of them here at the house makes a difference somehow, and it's the perfect opportunity to ask the parents directly. Elizabeth finishes her tea and pays the deposit for Charlie's tennis camp before she opens up another search bar and starts researching residential traffic speed zones. Outside, the morning washes the sky a light blue, as though all of yesterday's stains have been cleaned and carried away with the vanishing night.

By 7 a.m. Elizabeth hasn't yet had a chance to register how shit she feels. Jack leaves the house every weekday at 6.30 a.m. for the 6.45 a.m. train to London, so it's up to Elizabeth to make the mornings run as smoothly as possible. There's a rota for which child is cleaning up after breakfast, she makes sure the kids have packed whatever they need for school the evening before, and she writes herself another list to ensure nothing is forgotten. She's forever chasing the future – a future full of muddy boots and unemptied dishwashers. Yet no matter how hard she tries, stuff still goes wrong. This morning Max can't find his bike helmet, Charlie stays in bed a full fifteen minutes longer than he should, while Clemmie can't decide which clip feels right in her hair. Elizabeth feels these delays, these slips, like a finger poking some internal bruise. They feel like her fault, her failings as a mother, as a human. She hears her own mother tutting. Elizabeth can't breathe properly until they're all out of the door on time – fed, clean and prepared for the day ahead. Which of course, under Elizabeth's eye, they always are.

Max cycles to his secondary school on his own now, while Charlie walks a few paces ahead of Elizabeth and Clemmie, who rides on her pink scooter. This is the best bit of Elizabeth's morning. Walking the quaint Farley streets, sipping her coffee from her reusable cup as she watches her children – neat and ready – ahead of her. She's done it, another morning. Finally, she can breathe.

'Elizabeth! Wait for us!' Bry calls, coming out of the Kohlis' gate at Number 9, their vast double-fronted house – the largest on the street – looming behind her. For the last few months, Alba's been going to the Nettlestone preschool a couple of mornings a week to help her settle when she starts school in September. Elizabeth likes walking with them, when Bry's got her shit together, but one glance at Bry tells her this is not one of those mornings. Bry's carrying Alba, a sweet, shoeless bundle of messy hair, toast and a large pink flamingo, in one arm, and her handbag and a hessian shopping bag in the other.

'Charlie, Clemmie, wait a minute, please!' Elizabeth calls to the kids, and crosses over Saint's Road to meet her friend just outside her gate; Bry's left the front door open. She finds it extraordinary (and privately a bit unfair) that Bry and Ash have so much money – Bry told her confidentially that Ash's company sold for close to two million – and yet they still both dress like students. She knows Jack isn't much better but he doesn't have two million quid.

Bry's wearing the navy cotton jumpsuit she seems to wear every morning (Elizabeth will have to find the right moment to tell her to ditch the thing). A pair of stripy pink tights pokes out of one of her top pockets and there's a hairbrush in the other; both – hopefully – for Alba, who is now nuzzling into her mum's chest. Elizabeth pretends not to see. They had a drunken, tense conversation only a few months ago about women who continue to breastfeed. Elizabeth thinks it's weird once the child can walk but Bry said Elizabeth was blinded by patriarchy.

'Sorry, Elizabeth, this one didn't wake up until ten minutes ago – totally go on without us if you want.'

Elizabeth is momentarily tempted to stride into the clear air of the morning, to get her kids to school on time, but she knows she won't.

Bry jostles Alba into a more comfortable position in her arms. Alba squeals.

'Here, I'll take her,' Elizabeth says, as Bry untangles her arm from her bag and passes over Alba, who opens both arms and legs, like a monkey flying through the air, ready to land, before she clamps on to her godmother.

'Say 'ello to Fred,' Alba says, thrusting the flamingo into Elizabeth's face. Fred's fur is slightly crusty against Elizabeth's cheek and she smells dried saliva, sour milk and Sudocrem. Elizabeth kisses the air, with a loud smacking noise, just in front of Fred's nose.

Bry starts pulling the pink tights from her pocket on to her daughter's legs. 'Thanks, Elizabeth. Sorry – Ash left really early to meet the plumber about something and I just totally lost track of time . . .' Bry glances up at Elizabeth. 'Yeah, I know, I know – no need to look at me like that. I know that's what Jack does every morning, but we can't all be super mum.'

Bry stops talking as a large rented van signals and turns into Saint's Road. As it gets closer Elizabeth sees the van is being driven by a slim, attractive older woman, a blue scarf tied around her head. She's laughing, presumably at something said to her by the absurdly beautiful dark-haired young man next to her, his bare feet resting on the dashboard. The woman raises a hand to them both as they rumble past. She's not sure why, but the gesture feels patronizing to Elizabeth. The van stops abruptly just beyond Elizabeth's own house.

'Oh, they must be the new people renting Number 8,' Bry says, twisting around so she can watch the van.

'Who is Number 8?' Alba asks.

'It's the house next to Auntie Elizabeth's,' Bry answers, her voice small, as if she's far away.

'The man who lived there went to 'eaven,' Alba says solemnly. Bry turns to her daughter but Alba fixes her eyes on to Elizabeth. This is a serious question and she needs a serious answer.

'Yes, that's right, Albs.'

Oh, how Elizabeth misses this. Maybe they should have a fourth – she could always pretend it was an accident.

'We should go and say hello,' Bry says, and as she pulls the tights over Alba's bottom, Elizabeth lowers Alba to the ground, still holding her hand.

'Bry, we can't go now – the kids . . .'

Bry glances at them; Charlie is tickling his sister with a stick.

'Oh yeah, of course; they get in trouble if they're late, don't they . . .'

But even Elizabeth forgets about the kids for a moment as the two doors to the van slam shut and the woman skip-jumps in front of the house, throwing her arms open towards the beautiful man, as though the house is a wonderful old friend she's introducing to her . . . what? Son? Nephew maybe? He hooks his thumbs into the back pockets of his jeans and, taking in the tired-looking building before him, says something in what sounds like rapid Italian before following her, with a little run, into the house.

Elizabeth raises an eyebrow. 'Well, they don't seem particularly interested in saying hello to us, I have to say.'

'They waved!' Bry says, defensive on behalf of these people she doesn't even know, before adding, 'You are going to be nice to them, aren't you, Elizabeth?'

Elizabeth feels hot suddenly.

'I'm always nice,' she says, disproportionately pissed off. She wants to know what the fuck Bry is talking about, *nice*, but Alba tugs at Elizabeth's arm before worming her hand away.

'Come on!' she shouts, before she refastens the long-suffering Fred under her arm and skips off across the road towards Charlie and Clemmie, and both Elizabeth and Bry call out, 'Road!' but Alba ignores them, because she's four and she doesn't yet know anything about danger.

Farley County Court

December 2019

The court goes quiet as she pulls the photo out of the envelope, like when a car slows down to view a crash. We all want to see the girl, but it still feels wrong, this urge to look. I only see her for a second; no one cares what the court usher sees or doesn't see, but now I wish I'd kept my head down.

Her face is blown up like a balloon; her lips are blistered with sores, a pink flamingo on the pillow next to her. They've blurred her eyes in an attempt at anonymity, so I imagine them red and swollen shut. It hurts to look at her. She looks dead already. I think of my kids and have to clear my throat. I fold my hands over my black court robes, shift my weight from left to right and back again, hold my head higher. My kids are safe. We've taken them to the nurse, rolled up their sleeves every time we were told. No question.

The female prosecutor smooths her hair behind her ear. She has to clear her throat, have a sip of water before she says, 'When you look at this photo, what do you see?' She pauses again. A couple of folks in the public gallery are shaking their heads, and the old lady I help to her seat every morning has a hand over her mouth.

'I'll tell you what I see. I see a child in abject agony and terror. Wait, no, I see something far worse. I see a child in abject agony and terror that could easily have been avoided.' She says the last bit as if it's breaking her heart – perhaps it is – and at the same moment, the protestors

outside take up their chant again. Their voices are muffled; we can only just hear them. I wouldn't have known what they were saying if I hadn't heard them all damn morning: 'My child, my choice! My child, my choice!'

They don't know it, but their timing, their chant, is playing right into the prosecutor's hands. She pauses, lets them have their moment, making sure the whole court hears them while they're staring at the photo of the dying girl. She's smart; she knows how to play a room. She doesn't need to say anything. She lets the court make the connection themselves. If I wasn't here under oath, representing Queen and Country, I'd be tempted to applaud.

'My child, my choice!'

It's as if they're chanting for agony, demanding to protect their right to let their kids suffer. I'm not normally one for swearing, but what a fucked-up logic.

I clear my throat again. But my kids are safe, *I remind myself again,* my kids are safe.

6 July 2019

Ash opens his front door at 7 a.m. on Saturday morning to find Jack running on the spot in shorts and a lightweight top, his Fitbit glinting on his wrist: a present from Elizabeth for his birthday in March, and also roughly the last time Jack and Ash went running together.

'Morning!' Jack grins at his mate.

Ash, who is wearing tracksuit bottoms he's had since uni and a Radiohead T-shirt, closes his eyes and says, 'This is a nightmare. I will wake up. It's just a nightmare.'

Jack snorts and starts stretching his legs on the front step.

'Afraid not, fatty. Get your trainers on.'

Three miles later the two are jogging side by side, deep in the woods that start at the back of Saint's Road, their feet in step and the early-morning summer air cool in their lungs. It's a beautiful morning, the sky pastel, the colours blending gently into each other. Moments like this – no matter how brief – are, for Jack, a balm, soothing him from the crushing boredom of his working week. He glances over at Ash: his face is reddening already. Jack's not feeling the strain yet, but he slows just enough that Ash won't do himself an injury, though not so much that it bruises his friend's ego. It was on this same run, about a year ago, that Ash told Jack about his fear of fucking things up with Bry, like he fucked things up with his ex, Linette. His confession had formed an unspoken rule to their morning jogs – if they talk, they talk about real shit; otherwise they run in companionable silence. Jack keeps his eyes fixed on the dappled light falling through the young oak trees, casting golden pebbles on the grassy track ahead. They might not have properly talked in a few months, but he reminds himself there is no risk in confiding in Ash. What is said on a jog stays on the jog. In the past, they've talked about their wives, about the fears they have for their kids – fuck, on one rainy November day Ash even talked about his fear of death. Anything can be opened up here on this path, together, so why not this?

Jack clears his throat. 'Work's getting pretty bad, mate.'

He feels Ash look at him but Jack keeps his eyes fixed forward. He'd mentioned that he wasn't enjoying work to Ash over a few pints just after the New Year. The truth is that from the second he leaves the house he craves being home again, imagines that moment when a little hand slips into his as he walks through the front door. He thinks about how Max's English lesson is going while he's sitting in an acquisitions meeting. He'll urge Charlie on during a swimming race while he shows a foreign investor the plans for another block of flats.

'Go on,' Ash encourages.

'The thing is that I've lost all my motivation.' Jack doesn't tell Ash how he's taken to putting fake meetings in his calendar and going to sit on his own in art galleries and churches – places where he can stare into space and not look like a freak.

'Your heart's not in it, mate, I can see that,' says Ash.

Jack doesn't tell Ash that people he hired have now been promoted ahead of him.

'Yeah, I mean, I'm literally selling London off to rich foreign businessmen. It feels really shitty.'

'You mentioned before you'd always fancied teaching . . .' But Jack shakes his head, cutting Ash off.

'Money, mate. A teaching job would be like a third of what I'm on now, and we're only just getting by as it is, and now Elizabeth keeps going on about doing the house up, which is your fault by the way . . .' Ash spent almost two hundred grand renovating their place. Elizabeth was more involved in the plans than Bry, emailing Ash links entitled 'My dream door handles' and 'The best tiles bar none'. But Ash knows better than to offer Jack financial support; he did so once before and the offer had left a strained atmosphere between them for a few days.

'What about Elizabeth?' Ash puffs. 'Now Clemmie's at school, could she go back to work part-time and at least help with the bills, give you a bit of breathing space?'

Jack nods. 'Yeah, I was thinking about talking to her. It's a good idea.'

But Elizabeth has never been part-time at anything in her life, and she'd been so stressed when she went back to work after having Charlie that she gave herself hives.

Jack glances over at Ash, who is tiring quickly, puffing hard and pitching his upper body forward as though trying to trick his legs into keeping moving, his trainers scuffing the ground. Ash raises his hand and points at his leg to show he needs to stretch – Jack knows it's an excuse for a breather. Ash drops his head as he holds on to a tree, winces as he grabs hold of his foot to stretch out his quad. Once his breathing is more under control, he says, 'Look, I know a guy who works in recruitment – all corporate stuff but with new, interesting start-ups – he found me most of my team at the company. Anyway, I could give him a call. I'm sure he'd be interested in meeting up, having a chat.' Ash drops his foot and picks up the other.

'Mate, that would be great, I'd really appreciate that.'

Jack feels a little bit lighter. Ash pats him on the back once, smiles and says, 'C'mon then,' and the pair start running again, but a few minutes in, Jack clears his throat.

'Bit more advice needed.' Next to him, Ash nods. 'Elizabeth wants to send an email to all the parents with kids coming to Clem's party in a couple of weeks.'

'Huh?' Ash's response is an expulsion of air. They're on an incline; he can't manage a word just now, but it's enough to let Jack know he should keep talking.

'I don't know how to reply because in it she's asking people . . . erm, she wants to know if people have vaccinated their kids – the kids who are coming to the party, I mean.'

Jack sneaks a look at Ash, who keeps his eyes fixed straight ahead. Is he frowning? Or is it the strain of the run making him tense his forehead? Ash must feel his friend looking; he manages a nod. Ash is one of the few – possibly the only one – of Jack's mates who seems to understand why he married Elizabeth. His other mates shrivel up around her, as if someone's intimidating mother has just walked into the room. Jack met Elizabeth when he almost spilt a drink on her in a pub seventeen years ago – Elizabeth a newly qualified solicitor and Jack a junior but promising property surveyor for a huge global medical charity. Unlike other girls he'd dated, Elizabeth seemed to know exactly who she was; she wouldn't bend or change to fit others' ideas of who she should be. She wasn't interested in being 'cool'; she just wanted to be herself. Her self-possession, her clarity, made Jack feel safe. He felt confident in Elizabeth when he couldn't feel confident in himself. But that wasn't all he loved about her – Elizabeth was funny, clever, and she loved the handful of people she kept close with an unparalleled ferocity.

Next to him, Ash rolls his hand for Jack to get on with whatever he needs to say.

'So the thing is, the thing is that . . .' Jack breathes out deeply. Is he being disloyal? No, no, he's just talking honestly, something Elizabeth is always advocating. 'If any of the kids we've invited aren't vaccinated, she's telling them they can't come to the party, and more than that, she's basically saying they can't be friends with Clem.'

Ash stops running this time. Jack slows and stops a few paces further down the track and turns to his friend, who has one hand on his waist and has turned his face towards the clear sky, eyes closed, breathing hard, but his feet still moving as though they haven't got the message they can stop yet.

Ash has aged in the months since they last ran together, his stomach creeping out before him, his legs skinny. When Bry had excitedly introduced Ash to Jack five years ago on a weekend visit from London, Ash's age, at five years older than Jack, had seemed exotic in the way teenagers seem awesome to Jack's kids. Ash Kohli was impeccable then, 'well groomed', Elizabeth said, which Jack joked made Ash sound like a gym-khana pony. In quiet moments, Jack used to worry that Elizabeth fancied Ash. He was rich, knew about wine, had silver hair and just enough of a dark past to make him mysterious – and of course, there was the grooming. Jack, on the other hand, suffered from a perfectly blessed past. No one he loved had died unexpectedly, his parents lived in Surrey, the only cashmere jumper he could ever afford he'd shrunk on the first wash, and he still chose wine based on whether he liked the label design. But then, Clemmie got sick.

After a couple of minutes, Ash walks up to Jack, pats him on the back.

'Sorry, mate.'

'You sure you're OK?'

'Yeah, I think I'm coming down with something – Albs has a cold so . . .' The words come out wispy and unconvincing.

Ash starts jogging, small, careful steps, looking like one of those octogenarians who run marathons. After a couple of minutes, they go through a gate into a field with a gentle downward slope. Farley in miniature is laid out in front of them; it looks so perfect from up here, nestled in the green hills, a protected, innocent egg of a town. Jack's eyes are drawn to the landmarks he always spots – the medieval castle in the centre of town, the ugly council block, the sports centre where his kids play football – all padded out by cafes, community buildings, independent shops and the obligatory Waitrose. There's no sprawl to their little town, surrounded as it is by national park land, which is what keeps the house prices high and the locals pissed off with all the rich London émigrés. Ash seems comfortable, his breathing steady thanks to the downward slope, so Jack tentatively resumes their conversation.

'Yeah, so this email, I can't figure out whether it's excessive or not. I mean, I get that she's just trying to look after Clemmie, but saying that Clem can't be friends with unvaccinated kids is a bit extreme, don't you think? It's like we're choosing who our daughter can be friends with based on whether their parents' values align with our own.'

'So, the way I see it' – Ash keeps his eyes fixed straight ahead as he talks – 'is that you guys aren't the kind of parents to suffocate Clemmie, wrap her up in cotton wool, right? You want her to live her life. Which means you're going to have to let her take risks. Letting her go to school, ride a bike, cross the bloody road . . . there's risk in everything, probably more risk in all those things than there is of her contracting polio, or whatever. So I suppose you have to figure out how great the risk is that Clemmie could catch one of these, you know, viruses and if she did catch something, how great is the risk that it could make her really sick? I mean, when was the last time you heard of someone we know getting TB? Honestly, I think the risk is pretty marginal, mate, I really do.'

Jack doesn't know what to say. He wasn't expecting this. He thought Ash, with his left-wing, community-centred politics and his subscription to *New Scientist*, would be waving the flag as hard as he could for vaccines. But then, for Ash this is all theory. And of course, Ash hadn't been around six years ago when Clemmie had been really sick, when Jack would come home from work and Elizabeth would be shaking and wild-eyed. Those terrible nights when he'd wake to find Elizabeth sobbing, clutching Clemmie fast asleep in her arms. Bry had been worried about her friend, had tried to talk to Jack about it, but he'd reassured her; of course Elizabeth felt overwhelmed from time to time – she had two energetic young boys and a tiny baby. Who wouldn't feel like they couldn't cope occasionally? Bry and Ash had only just started dating when Clemmie was ill, so Ash hadn't seen their toughest time.

Ash didn't know the horror of watching his tiny little girl turn blue and struggle to breathe. He wasn't there when Elizabeth didn't sleep for two weeks, terrified that if she closed her eyes for a moment her baby would fit to death. He didn't have to pick her up from the kitchen floor. He wasn't there for the trips to A&E; he didn't know that the fear had sent them to therapy, Clemmie with them even then, cooing in her car seat under Elizabeth's constant, watchful eye. Ash didn't know how it felt not to be trusted by your wife to look after your own child.

Ash slows as they approach the gate that will take them on to Neville Road, which leads in one direction to the cemetery then into town, and in the other, home to Saint's Road.

'So what I think you should do, mate, is say that you don't mind sending an email but perhaps word it differently, so it's like: *As you know, Clemmie isn't vaccinated blah, blah, so we'd appreciate it if your child has any signs of an infection or illness to please give this one party a miss*, or something like that?'

Jack bridles. 'It's not that she *isn't* vaccinated, mate, it's that she *can't* be vaccinated.'

'OK, sorry, but it's basically the same thing, right?'

Jack hangs back, letting Ash go through the gate first.

It's fucking not the same thing, not at all, he thinks.

'Yeah, yeah, I guess so; good idea, mate. Thanks.'

Ash smiles, pleased he's solved another of his friend's problems, and he starts to run, spritely now, towards home. Jack hangs back, wishing he'd never started talking about the email, wishing he'd left it alone. His mood is heavy, lead throughout his body. It's not until he's home and in the shower that Jack replays the conversation and realises that it isn't what Ash said exactly that troubles him; it's that he had everything so well rehearsed, almost as if he was anticipating this chat, as if it had been weighing on his mind as well.

Jack eats a bowl of muesli while Elizabeth does the online shop next to him. Clemmie, bless her, is trying to join in with the boys' cricket practice outside. The ball cracks against the bat and Clemmie shouts 'I'll get it!' for the third time.

He winces for her, calls, 'Good running, Clemmie!' but he knows the boys will be laughing at her – her red, determined face, her knock-kneed run – and that they'll soon grow weary of watching her try her best, their amusement hardening to irritation. He'd skimmed the article about the baby girl who died from meningitis after his shower. What the fuck was he doing, chatting to Ash, worrying about what other people think? His first job, his *only* job of any real importance, is to protect those he loves, and he loves his little girl more than life itself.

'Sweetheart, I think that draft email you sent is perfect by the way.'

His wife looks up from her computer screen, lifts her glasses off her face and says, 'Oh, good. You're OK for me to send it now then?'

'Absolutely,' he says, getting up. She tilts her long neck back as he kisses her on the lips. 'The sooner the better.'

By 5 p.m., Ash has been sitting in Jack and Elizabeth's garden drinking wine for an hour. He's feeling peaceful, wonderfully numb already. After the run this morning, the wine seems to be taking quick, pleasing effect. Jack – poor Jack – took the three Chamberlain kids to the Nettlestone School fete just after he arrived. Ash had waved him off, delighted to have

41

the excuse of firing up the barbecue – as requested by Elizabeth. He'd enjoyed watching Elizabeth work around him. She was so utterly unflappable. She was like a swan swimming serenely down a river, powerful legs constantly in motion. Busy, but calm and in control. It was admirable. He'd watched her smoothing (ironed) white tablecloths on the outside tables and placing the finishing touches on the salads she'd prepared the night before – lentil, sweet potato, green bean and mixed lettuce, all garnished with herbs and delicate little flowers from the garden.

She can be a bit uptight though. Ash remembers the email Jack talked about on their run. Sometimes it's like she actually wants to piss people off. But he doesn't want to think about that email now, what it means, so instead he watches Elizabeth as she steps on tiptoes into a flower bed and starts cutting flowers. She is unruffled and looks pretty good in a light blue dress that shows off her smooth, pale skin, but also homely, comforting in her flour-stained denim apron. It took him a year or two to warm to her sharp ways, but now Ash loves being able to appreciate her qualities without coveting her. It feels quite wonderful to love her but not want her.

'You are remarkable, you know, Lizzie,' Ash says from his deckchair next to the barbecue. She wrinkles her nose at him; she hates it when people call her Lizzie.

'What's that, Ashy?' she asks, gathering her shoulder-length hair into a ponytail before she surveys a rose bush in full bloom in front of her. Ash can see she's smiling slightly, and guesses she heard him but she wants to hear more nice things, and he wants to please her.

'You. You're completely remarkable. A pro. You just seem

to know how to make everything beautiful, how to make people feel welcome.'

The muscles in Elizabeth's toned legs flex as she stands, a rose now in hand, and she smiles at Ash, appreciating the compliment before she says carefully, 'Hmm, that's not what your wife thinks . . .'

'What? Don't be silly, of course she does.'

Ash tries not to let his surprise at this rare moment of vulnerability show – Elizabeth would spot it and retreat back into herself. He keeps his tone light as he asks, 'Why'd you say that?'

Elizabeth places a hand on her lower back and bends slightly to relieve some pressure that must have gathered there.

'Oh, just something she said the other day, when the new woman at Number 8 waved to us.'

'What did she say?' Ash asks, in the same wary tone he'd use if he was talking about Alba when she'd done something naughty.

'She told me to be "nice" to her.'

Ash can't help but let out a small, surprised laugh.

'Don't laugh, Ash! I found it really annoying.' Elizabeth walks carefully out of the flower bed, takes his wine glass off him and has a couple of sips before handing it back and continuing.

'She was basically implying that I'm not nice to people. Or that people don't think I'm nice. I mean, I know I'm not to everybody's taste, especially Bry's hippie mates, but frankly, they're not to mine, so I don't care.'

By 'hippie mates', Ash knows she's talking about Row and Emma.

'I'm sure she didn't mean anything by it, Elizabeth. Bry loves you like a sister.'

Elizabeth nods; she knows.

'Have you said anything to her about it?'

Elizabeth scrunches up her nose again and says, 'No, no,' before she smiles. She looks just like Clemmie with a secret. 'I went one better and invited Rosalyn, our new neighbour, to the barbecue.'

Ash laughs again, offers his wine to Elizabeth for another sip, but she shakes her head before he asks, 'Does she seem all right?'

Elizabeth nods, shrugs her shoulders. 'Hmm, not sure yet. Suspect from her clothes and the fact she's an artist that she's a massive hippie – she definitely had a joss stick burning somewhere in the house – but I'm trying to be *nice* and reserve judgement.'

Ash salutes her before asking, 'So, who else is coming?' He pokes the glowing charcoal in the barbecue as Elizabeth picks up her secateurs again and starts snipping at a lavender bush.

'I've kept it mostly to Saint's Road people this year. You guys, obviously. My old school friend Charlotte is driving down from London; think you've met her a few times.' Ash nods and remembers a stout, conservatively dressed woman who talked loudly about horse racing.

'Then the usual suspects – Chris and Gerald, Jane – and then of course there's this new lady, Rosalyn. Oh, and Clemmie mentioned it to Lily before I could intervene, so Row and Lily are coming over. Steve's got some catering job on apparently, which is a relief.'

Elizabeth walks over to the table and starts arranging the delicate summer sprays.

'Jack's dropping the boys at a sleepover straight after the

fete, which is also a bit of a relief.' Ash feels, as he always does when Max and Charlie are mentioned, a familiar twist in his stomach for his own boys. Theo and Bran come to stay with Ash and Bry every other weekend but it doesn't feel like enough to Ash. It's never felt like enough, but for some reason he can't put his finger on, he's always shied away from broaching the topic with Bry. To give her credit, and despite Linette's best efforts, the boys like Bry, and she likes them in turn. But he once overheard Bry describing herself to Elizabeth as their 'part-time parent' and he knew, without ever having to ask, that her 'like' for them would never grow into love.

'How's the barbecue looking?' Elizabeth asks, peering at the bright orange coals. Ash gives them another judicious poke to show he's on it.

'All totally under control, ready to go in twenty minutes as requested.' Ash smiles up at her.

'Perfect. I'll get the meat out of the fridge just before everyone arrives, then.'

She casts her eye round the garden and says, 'What next? Ahh, cushions for chairs, and let me get you an ice bucket for your wine, and then I think we're almost there.'

As Elizabeth walks into the kitchen, Ash leans back in his chair and lets the sun land on his face, and thinks, *Yep, life is good.*

'Daddy!' Alba comes skipping out of the kitchen, down the grassy slope into the sunshine, and Ash makes an exaggerated 'ouff!' sound as she buries her head in his stomach. Her face has been painted at the fete; the black stripes and orange fading to white make him think she must be a tiger. It was a pretty good attempt, but she's managed to lick away all the paint around her mouth, a round circle of exposed skin showing exactly how far her tongue could reach. Maybe that was why she'd done it.

Ash kisses her dark, curly head and then Alba skips away from him to walk her new brontosaurus toy on the table. He becomes aware of voices talking over each other in the house: Bry and Elizabeth. Bry's voice sounds higher than normal. She's apologising, probably about Ash.

'I don't know what you're talking about – it looks gorgeous, beautiful as always,' Bry says to Elizabeth, as she steps out from the kitchen into the garden. She's wearing an old dress, white with a delicate flower pattern, that Ash used to love but is now looking a bit worn. Bry hardly ever wears make-up but she's put some on today. The mascara is slightly smudged underneath her dark eyes; she probably forgot she had it on. She's carrying her handbag, Alba's cardigan, Alba's pink flamingo Fred, a drink for Alba and a bucket full of ice. She looks totally unbalanced, as if she's about to drop everything and unravel right there on the lawn. The chaos of his lovely wife, the tension in her face, suddenly makes Ash feel stressed, which is annoying – he was having such a nice time. Bry raises one eyebrow at him. It tells him everything he needs to know. That he shouldn't be sitting there watching her, that he shouldn't be drinking wine, and that she's had a stressful time at the fete. He gets up rather ungracefully from his deckchair, which makes him seem drunker than he actually is, and goes over to her.

'Take the ice bucket, my fingers are fucking freezing,' she says through a stiff jaw. Ash waits a beat too long and she repeats 'Ice bucket!' louder before he snaps into action, grabs the ice bucket and puts it on the table along with Alba's drink.

46

'Bry, don't forget your wine!' Elizabeth calls from the kitchen, as the front doorbell rings.

Before he says hello to anyone, Ash dashes upstairs to use the loo as the route to the one downstairs by the front door is blocked by arriving guests. The family bathroom is pristine, the tub glistening white like a bathroom-detergent advert, bath toys neatly stacked in a wicker basket. Ash holds on to the side of the sink as he takes a piss. A small, sensible voice that sounds like his wife tells him now would be the time to slow down on the wine, but he doesn't want to slow down and he doesn't want any water. He doesn't want to worry about Bry and . . . *shit*, he splashes the rim of the toilet as he pees. He looks down and sees poking out of a neatly stacked pile of *National Geographic*s a piece of A4 paper, the words *Mark Clancy, whose one-year-old daughter Rosie* . . . He wipes the rim of the toilet and pulls up his zip. He knows that name – he can't figure out where from, but he knows he knows the name Mark Clancy. He pulls the old silver chain to flush the toilet and takes out the paper. There are a few sheets stapled together; it's a BBC article. There's a photo of a baby girl laughing at the camera. He reads the headline: *Don't let Rosie's death be for nothing.*

Ash grips the sink again. Mark. Mark Clancy . . . And suddenly his blurry memory brightens into focus. He used to work with Mark. Yes . . . Mark was a project manager at Schwartz, the Swiss company where Ash was a partner before he left to set up on his own. He remembers a nice bloke, solid, hard-working, moving through his life with a smile, blissfully unaware of the tragedy waiting for him in the future. The article isn't long, just a few hundred words, but a quick skim tells

Ash that each and every one is a tiny bomb of agony, of regret. An internal wail rips through his whole being. He stares at Rosie's beautiful face and feels the horrifying lightness of her coffin. He holds the sink tighter and then suddenly the doorknob rattles, spinning left and right, against the lock.

'Daddy! Daddy, wha' doing in there?'

He drops like a stone back into the sparkly white bathroom and opens the door in one fluid movement. Before Alba can even squeal, she's in his arms and he's hugging her as hard and close as he can without hurting her. 'I love you, Alba, I love you so much.'

Alba somehow knows he needs her. She wraps her arms around his neck and says, as though he's one of her teddies that needs soothing, the words she's heard so many times. 'Is 'kay, darling. I'm here. I'm here.'

6 July 2019

'Hello, sweetheart.' Gerald's short grey beard clings to his face like a small animal. He's wearing one of his trademark bright waistcoats, yellow today, and holding a fedora. He kisses Bry with plump lips carefully on both cheeks and says, 'I saw that naughty man of yours come over here with a whole box of that lovely Sancerre.'

'He's in the garden with most of it now, waiting for you, Gerald,' Bry replies, as Gerald cuffs her hand and raises a dramatic finger to his lips while pointing towards his partner Chris, who is waiting to say hello.

Chris is younger than Gerald by about ten years. He smells warm, like expensive woodsmoke, and as he kisses Bry's cheek he says, 'Bry, you look very lovely.' Bry squeezes Chris's hand. She feels very unlovely. She's had a queasy, dull ache in her lower abdomen all morning and she knows it can only mean one thing.

As Jack appears in the hallway from the kitchen, Gerald opens his arms and says loudly, 'Here's Red!' giving Bry the chance to slip away upstairs. Elizabeth has kept her tampons in the same little padded wallet for as long as Bry's known her. It'll be under the sink in their bathroom.

She sits heavily on the toilet. Yes, she was right. Her knickers will have to be thrown away, and why the fuck did she choose today to wear a white dress? Ash doesn't know Bry stopped taking her pill a couple of months ago. Bry told herself it would just be better if she got pregnant 'as a surprise'. She didn't want to talk to Ash about it because she didn't want to hear his answer out loud. She knew it already – he was forty-seven, he already had three kids, four was environmentally and socially irresponsible. These were rational, sane reasons. Bry's reasons were pure emotion. It would be wonderful for Alba to have a sibling, a proper sibling, not two sullen half-brothers who still look at her as if she stole their father.

It's fine, she tells herself, *at least you can have a few drinks now. Relax, it's fine.* She opens her eyes, sniffs and cleans herself up, wrapping her knickers in toilet paper before hiding them at the bottom of the swing bin. She pinches a couple of tampons for her bag – she didn't buy any on the weekly shop because, you know, positive thinking. As she stands to wash her hands, the printed photo of a beautiful baby catches her eye, as if some shitty higher power has planted it there for a laugh.

'Great,' she mutters, before picking up the article. She reads the headline and immediately feels like a selfish dick for being so consumed with her own momentary, very minor loss. Tears fill her eyes as she stares at Rosie's dimpled, chubby face. She can't read the full piece; she is supposed to be at a barbecue after all. Instead she skims to the factual section about meningitis and her tears disappear. No, no, the BBC should have more responsible reporting than this bullshit. The way the article is written makes it sound as though Rosie wouldn't have died if she'd had the vaccine – but it doesn't say what strain of meningitis she had. Bry tries to remember the facts from *Vaccines: The Hidden Truth*, the book her mum Sara sent her when she was pregnant with Alba. Sara had highlighted whole paragraphs for Bry, and one fluorescent yellow passage said the meningitis vaccine only protects against one strain of the infection – so even if Rosie had had the vaccine, she could still have got meningitis. This is just the sort of negligent journalism Sara had warned Bry about.

Laughter trickles into the bathroom through the window, which is open slightly to the garden. Bry shouldn't let herself get worked up about an article now. She puts it back where she found it and moves towards the window, just enough so she can peek out. Elizabeth is sitting at the table with that god-awful Charlotte. Charlotte looks hot and sweaty already in tight jeans and a fitted, stripy suit jacket. Even from up here, Bry can see she's got that smug smile fixed to her face, as though she's constantly having to restrain herself from bursting into laughter at their small, provincial lives. Elizabeth looks around and beckons to Jack, who reluctantly leaves everyone else laughing around the barbecue to kiss Charlotte hello. Their elderly neighbour Jane, resplendent in peacock blue, has swapped sun hats with Gerald. He's wearing her straw hat, decorated with colourful little flowers, and she's got his fedora on her white head at a jaunty angle. Alba tries to help Ash carry a chair over for Jane, who bends down arthritically to say something to Alba. Everyone turns towards Row and Lily as they arrive. Elizabeth looks at them and whispers something to Charlotte that makes Charlotte put her hand over her mouth and her shoulders shake, her mirth getting the better of her for a moment. Bry frowns at Elizabeth; it's not like her to be bitchy.

No one glances up and sees her through the window. She washes her hands and gazes a little further out of the window, over the wall into the garden at Number 8. During the growing season it's become a sharp swamp of brambles. The woman they saw in the van is in the garden staring at the brambles. She's wearing a beautiful coral silk kaftan. Her hair looks like it was once blonde but it's now silver and clasped on top of her head in a large clip. Her neck and arms glint with colourful, exotic-looking jewellery, and even from up here Bry can see she's striking. The woman turns sharply, as though responding to a noise, and the beautiful young man walks out to stand next to her. He has mop-like, curly hair, the kind of hair most people grow out of or have cut off. He looks broad and agile as a pup, his skin a deep, many-layered brown suggesting season upon season in the sun. The woman motions towards the tangled garden, and the young man nods along with whatever she's saying, not taking his eyes off her for a second, and then she says something that makes him throw his head back, his shoulders shake. The woman turns to watch him – seeing him happy makes her smile – and the two of them look at each other, and even from so far away Bry sees a spark pass between them.

Bry leans in, her breath clouding the windowpane.

The small space between them closes as the young man moves behind the silver-haired woman. Bry feels his muscles against her own back, the strength of him. She runs her hands lightly along the dark forearms that snake around her waist. She bends her neck towards him – an invitation and a request – and he kisses her slowly, with reverence and confidence; he knows exactly where he's going.

Bry feels a flash between her own legs.

The woman turns around to the young man, her fingers lost in his hair. She's still smiling as her hand drops from his head to hold his hand, and as she leads him away, into the house, she looks up, directly at Bry, and she smiles.

'So anyway, the upshot is that I'm taking her to the *seriously* lux place in Cornwall instead, but you know, it is her fortieth after all.' Bry has somehow been trapped with Charlotte in the kitchen for the last ten minutes. Charlotte is thrashing around insisting on making her own salad dressing, waving away the fact that Elizabeth made one earlier. Even salad dressing can be a competition, apparently. Charlotte is a vision of what Bry likes to think she and Jack rescued Elizabeth from becoming. Charlotte is head of HR for some big corporation Bry has never heard of, lives in Chelsea, and is divorced with two kids who grew up calling for their nanny at night rather than their mum. Bry fades Charlotte out, instead imagining what could be happening right now just next door, white legs wrapped around dark torso.

'So yours must be coming up, no?' Charlotte asks, turning the lid tightly on the jam jar she's using for the dressing.

'Sorry, my what?' Bry asks, reluctantly turning back to Charlotte. Charlotte rolls her eyes.

'Your fortieth, Bry. Is Ash going to throw you a big party? I'd love to come.'

'Oh, I, um, I don't really like having parties, so . . .'

'What?' Charlotte starts shaking the jam jar, her teeth gritted with effort. 'That's so boring of you!' she shrieks.

Since Bry married Ash and became unexpectedly rich, Charlotte has made more effort with her than she ever has before, texting her occasionally, even inviting Bry to her own recent birthday party – which Bry flatly declined despite Elizabeth's pleas.

While Charlotte launches into a story about her own *flamboyant* party, the Victorian glass in the front door rattles a warning as someone unfamiliar with these old houses closes the door too forcefully.

Here's the excuse Bry's been looking for.

'Sorry, Charlotte, I didn't think we were expecting anyone else . . .' Bry walks quickly into the hall where, moving towards Bry, her silk kaftan flowing either side as if she's swimming, weightless, through the air, is the woman from next door.

'Hi,' she says, 'I'm Rosalyn.'

For a beat Bry thinks Rosalyn's here to tell her to mind her own fucking business and stop spying on her, but then she sees that Rosalyn is holding a bottle of red wine. She's here for the party.

'Elizabeth invited me? I hope that's OK?'

Bry shakes her head. 'No, I mean, yes! Great!' She shakes her head again, at herself this time. 'Sorry, I was just preoccupied with something else. I . . . I'm Bryony – Bry.' She puts her hand out towards Rosalyn. Rosalyn holds Bry's hand rather than shaking it. She feels warm and she moves forward, kisses Bry on both cheeks. Rosalyn smells of lemons and faintly – or does Bry just imagine it? – the electric tang of sex.

Still holding on to Bry's hand, Rosalyn asks, 'Didn't we see you the other morning, when Rafe and I pulled up in the van?'

'Oh yes, sorry I didn't come and say hello,' Bry replies, her hand now released from Rosalyn's. 'I had to get my daughter to school – well, preschool, she's only four – so we were all a bit frantic.'

'Don't worry at all! We were totally preoccupied anyway.'

There are so many things Bry could ask, but all she says is, 'Ahh yes. You looked busy.'

Rosalyn smiles and Bry blushes. There's something alluring about this woman, something that makes Bry want to learn everything about her. Bry's drawn to her at a deep, subtle level she can't find a word for.

'Sorry, Rosalyn, come in, come in.'

Bry leads the way into the kitchen where Charlotte is now bright red, still vigorously shaking her dressing.

'Hi.' Charlotte swaps the dressing to her left hand so she can hold her right out towards Rosalyn. 'Charlotte.' Her hand is rigid, fingers like soldiers standing to attention, her legs slightly apart, braced.

Charlotte looks startled as Rosalyn kisses her on both cheeks and, smiling, looks Charlotte in the eye as she says, 'I'm Rosalyn. I just moved in next door.' Charlotte nods as though she's in a business meeting and this was exactly the news she wanted from an employee.

'Do you live in Farley, Charlotte?'

Charlotte snorts and starts shaking her dressing again.

'God, no. Chelsea. Far too quiet for me down here. I come every year for Elizabeth's barbecue, don't I, Bry? Old school friends, you see.'

Bry is about to point out that Charlotte means she and Elizabeth are old school friends, not Bry and Charlotte, but Rosalyn moves into the garden and introduces herself to Gerald, who says, 'The sculptress!' and immediately starts trying to talk in clumsy-sounding Italian. Rosalyn laughs along with him as though he's an old, dear friend.

Suddenly, a high-pitched scream followed by a loud cry makes Bry rush further out into the garden. She knows from the pitch it's not Alba, but she still needs to see her to be able to relax. She exhales when she spots her there at the end of the garden, crawling under the rotting garden bench, pretending to be a puppy.

Row is powering up the garden with Lily in her arms, Clemmie trotting along by her side trying to explain what happened. Elizabeth leaps up from the table and rushes over to Row and Lily, who is curled and crying in her mother's arms. Elizabeth looks first at Clemmie – like Bry, she needs to know her own little one is safe – before she turns to look at Lily's bare foot. Lily's howls grow louder and Elizabeth steams ahead of them, striding towards the kitchen.

'First aid kit,' Elizabeth says to the kitchen as she enters, making her way to the utility room and coming back a second later with a green plastic box as if she's playing doctors and nurses.

'Bry, can you make Lily an elderflower cordial and give her a meringue from the fridge? The sugar will help with the shock.'

'Yes, yes, of course.' Bry, relieved to have a job, heads to the small larder for the bottle of elderflower. Row and Lily make it to the kitchen. Lily's face is pressed firmly away from the world, into Row's neck; Row is whispering in her daughter's ear and holding her foot firmly in her hand. There's blood dripping down between her fingers. Elizabeth guides Row towards a kitchen chair.

'What happened?' Bry hadn't noticed Rosalyn join them. She starts tearing open sachets of antibacterial wipes at the table with Elizabeth; she's one of them already.

'They were playing pirates,' Row explains. 'Clemmie pulled out an old piece of wood from behind the shed so they could walk the plank, and poor Lily caught her foot on a nail I didn't see sticking out of it.' Lily wails as Row pulls her bloodied hand away. Bry strokes Lily's hair and Elizabeth coos as she starts to wipe Lily's trembling little foot. Bry feels a sudden moment of connection to the other women, a maternal solidarity; one of their little ones is in pain and it's as if all their little ones are in pain. Nothing else matters; together they will soothe and repair Lily.

They soon stop the bleeding – the wound is a small but deep puncture. They clean it as best they can and then, with Rosalyn's help, Elizabeth wraps a bandage around Lily's foot. Elizabeth checks that Lily can wiggle all her toes, and she slowly quietens enough to drink the sweet elderflower and eat a meringue between heaving sobs. They sit Lily on the sofa in the playroom with another meringue, her foot propped up on a pillow, and Row puts cartoons on the TV. Clemmie and Alba slink quietly in to join the treat. Back in the kitchen, Elizabeth starts to boil the kettle and Rosalyn, turning to Elizabeth, says, 'Are you a medic?'

'Who, me?' Elizabeth pretends to look perplexed but Bry can see she's delighted by the question. 'God no, I'm actually a complete wimp when it comes to blood and that sort of thing.'

'Well, I thought you handled that brilliantly, like a pro.'

Elizabeth shuffles in the cupboard and pulls out a little teapot; she's trying not to smile.

'Elizabeth has been on so many courses she's probably more qualified than most doctors,' Bry chips in, and Elizabeth shakes her head modestly, her smile widening.

'That's a total exaggeration,' she says to Bry, before turning back to Rosalyn and adding, 'I had to go on a few courses, that's all.' She lowers her voice a little. 'Clemmie wasn't very well as a baby, you see, so I wanted to be prepared in case things ever got scary, which they did, a lot, so yeah . . .'

Row comes back in from the TV room and Elizabeth looks over to her.

'I'm making you tea, Row.'

Row smiles gratefully at Elizabeth but shakes her head. 'Thanks, but I'll stick with my wine.'

'Um yes, of course.' Elizabeth pauses, flicks the kettle off. 'I just thought tea would be better in case you need to drive.'

'Why would I need to drive anywhere?'

'Well, to hospital, to get Lily a tetanus booster.' Elizabeth says the words as if they're obvious, as though she can't believe Row needs her to spell it out. Row looks away from Elizabeth, and in the pause that follows, Bry feels them all falling away from each other again.

'She's all right, Elizabeth, she doesn't need to go to the hospital,' Row says, sitting back in one of the old oak chairs. Bry passes Row her own glass of wine. Bry feels Elizabeth's eyes on her and she's careful not to look back. Elizabeth turns again to Row, her eyes narrowing.

'She needs a tetanus shot, Row. The nail that went into her foot will be rusty and God knows how old.'

'Elizabeth,' Bry warns gently. Elizabeth's eyes dart towards Rosalyn, searching for the support that she isn't getting from Bry. But Rosalyn has taken a step away from the other women.

'If she has any sign of fever or infection, I'll take her to Emma for a homeopathic treatment straight away.'

Elizabeth groans audibly. 'People still die from tetanus,' she says under her breath.

Row shoots Elizabeth a look that says, *Shut the fuck up.*

'Tetanus isn't contagious, Elizabeth,' she says through gritted teeth.

'I know it's not contagious.' Elizabeth spits the words, her voice getting higher.

'So why are you getting so worked up about whether I take Lil for a shot or not?'

Elizabeth shakes her head at Row before replying, 'Because – believe it or not, Row – it's not just my kids that I care about.'

Bry gets up from the table.

'OK, OK, this is being blown way out of proportion. Look, Elizabeth, of course Row is going to keep a close eye on Lily. Any signs of infection, any problems, she'll go straight to the doctor, won't you, Row?'

Row takes a big sip of wine and nods, her hand raised heavenward for emphasis. 'God, of course I will, I'd never be reckless with her health.' Thankfully, Row misses Elizabeth raising her eyebrows dramatically, as if Row's the biggest hypocrite she's ever met. Bry puts a hand on Row's shoulder to remind her, silently, that she's not alone.

'Well, look, the kids seem happy and I for one was loving my burger – how about we go and finish our food?' Rosalyn talks as though she's been here before, as though she's used to defusing bombs thrown between women.

A fragile peace is brokered as Row puts an arm around Elizabeth and says, 'Thanks for your help, Elizabeth, I really appreciate it.'

And Elizabeth puts her arm awkwardly around Row and says, 'Of course, any time,' and Bry notices how quickly they drop their arms away from each other as they walk back outside.

*

Bry assembles a burger and carries it along with her wine to Rosalyn's end of the table. She sits on the grass close to where Rosalyn is eating her own burger. Bry wouldn't have had meat if she'd sat with Row; it wouldn't have been worth the aggro. Rosalyn smiles when she sees Bry and kicks her legs over the bench so they're facing each other. Bry smiles back apologetically as she takes a bite of the burger.

'Sorry that all got a bit intense in there.'

Rosalyn shrugs. 'You don't need to apologise. Poor Lily, it did look painful.'

'I mean about the whole going to A&E thing.'

Rosalyn nods. She can't have missed the tension, surely, Bry thinks, but her expression is impassive. Bry, emboldened by wine, keeps talking.

'It's just, you know, Row and Elizabeth have different ways of doing things and sometimes that can cause a bit of tension.'

'There's always tension when friends have different ideas about how to bring up their kids. I remember it when my friends had little ones.'

'Oh, so you don't have kids yourself?' Bry tries and fails to sound nonchalant.

'Honestly, I've just never had that maternal urge that other women seem to have. I mean, I love other people's kids, adore my niece and nephew, but being a mother never felt like me. So when my friends were all having babies, I moved to Italy to study sculpture.' Rosalyn pops the last piece of burger into her mouth and wipes her face with her napkin.

Bry's burger is poised halfway between her plate and her mouth. 'You learnt sculpture in Italy?'

Rosalyn nods.

'Yes, then I fell in love and couldn't bear to leave, so I

decided to stay and lived just outside Florence for nineteen years . . .' Before she finishes talking, Rosalyn looks up; Row has come to stand behind Bry.

'Hi guys, mind if I join?'

Yes, yes, I do! Bry thinks, but Row is already sitting down, forcing Bry to budge up to make room for her.

'How's Lily doing?' Rosalyn asks, leaning towards Row in genuine concern.

'Oh, she's fine, happy to be watching TV – we don't have a TV at home so it's a big treat,' she tells Rosalyn, pride creeping into her voice.

Yeah, but what about your three iPads? Bry wonders unkindly.

'I'm still feeling pretty jangled by it all though.' Row looks around, checks Elizabeth isn't close, before she adds, 'I mean, who does Elizabeth think she is? Saying that shit about tetanus? So unhelpful. Ewww, Bry, are you eating a burger?' Row pulls a face at Bry as though her mouth has soured from the very word 'burger'. She shuffles a few inches away from Bry as Bry tries to emulate Rosalyn and appear not to care as she takes another bite. But now Row's so close the meat tastes too bloody, as if it could still be alive. She drops the half-eaten burger back on her plate and forces herself to swallow the mouthful.

'I mean, look, I know Elizabeth and I have different ways of doing things and I respect her, I do, I just think it would be nice if she could reciprocate and respect my choice not to inject my child's body with harmful metals and unnecessary toxins. Do you know what I mean?'

Row looks directly at Rosalyn, who looks down at her wine glass for a moment before she says, 'I believe in "my child, my choice", certainly, but—'

'Yes! That's exactly what I'm talking about – my child, my

choice.' Row is smiling now. She looks from Rosalyn to Bry and then back to Rosalyn as she says, 'You know, Steve – that's my partner – read an article recently about how they're going to introduce a vaccine against chickenpox. I mean, chickenpox! It's not even dangerous! It's all about money of course; the pharma companies make billions a year from a single vaccine.'

A loud shout from a small mouth blasts across the garden from the kitchen as Alba calls, 'Mumma! Mummy!'

Bry only needs to glance at her wriggling daughter for a second to know she's either already wet herself or is about to. She looks around for Ash, but he's busy filling up everyone's wine glasses again.

'Coming, Albs!' she calls back as she reluctantly gets to her feet, smiling at Rosalyn and feeling for a guilty moment a flicker of envy for the freedom of the older woman's life.

Row takes Lily home just as Elizabeth's finished putting the meringues, berries and cream into bowls on the kitchen table. Elizabeth doesn't ask Row to stay and Row keeps her thanks to a bare minimum. Bry takes a few bowls of pudding outside, giving them to Gerald, Chris and Jane, who are still sitting all together at one end of the table. Elizabeth sits opposite Bry, next to Charlotte, as the others cram in around the too-small table – Rosalyn pleasingly close. There's a brief silence as people crack into their meringues, then Charlotte turns to Elizabeth and says, too loudly for it to be a private conversation, 'So what was all that about in the kitchen when the little girl hurt her foot? I was going to come in but it sounded like things were about to erupt.'

Bry watches her friend as she scans her audience, as though

62

checking that she's talking to a home crowd, and deciding she's safe, Elizabeth takes a drink and says in a quiet voice, as though she shouldn't really be saying anything at all, 'Row's an anti-vaxxer – she point blank refused to take poor Lily for a tetanus shot.'

'Oh, honestly!' Jane says as others sigh.

'I know, I know,' Elizabeth says, shaking her head. 'I've tried to talk to her about it, but she's unbelievably defensive.'

Under the table, Ash lifts his hand off Bry's knee.

'So, Lily hasn't had any vaccines at all?' Charlotte's voice is always too loud. Elizabeth is about to reply when Jack – peaceful, kind Jack – starts talking before his wife.

'No, no, she had some, didn't she, Bry?' Bry wishes Jack hadn't got her involved but now everyone's looking at her, waiting for her to say something.

'Lily was sick after one of the vaccines, I can't remember which – really high fever, nothing was helping – so Row took some advice from Emma. She's a local homeopath' – she says this for Rosalyn's benefit. 'Emma gave her some bella-donna and the next morning Lily was fine again, so that's why she's cautious about some vaccines, but yeah, I think Lil's had most of them. This is really delicious meringue, Elizabeth, thank you, is it from that new—'

But Elizabeth, ignoring the praise, interrupts.

'Bry, what you're leaving out is that know-it-all-Steve read a couple of articles on Facebook and decided he knew more on the subject than millions of experts and hundreds of years of scientific research.'

'Come on, Elizabeth . . . that's not—'

But Charlotte is much louder than Bry. 'Sorry, but anyone

who doesn't vaccinate their kids is a bloody idiot in my book; they clearly don't care about their own children. Sterilisation and mandatory vaccination is the only way forward, if you ask me.'

'Yes, but no one is asking you,' Bry says, too quietly for anyone other than Ash to hear.

At the other end of the table, Jane turns to Gerald and Chris and says, 'Chris, you're probably too young to remember polio, but Gerald, you and I know how awful it was,' and the two men nod and mutter in agreement, as Jane adds, 'That's the problem with these young people – they don't remember,' but then Bry can't hear the rest of their conversation as Elizabeth speaks up again.

'Of course I'd love to have Clem vaccinated, but our brilliant GP Dr Parker said it wasn't worth the risk. You know he didn't retire as a GP until he was seventy-five? He's in an old people's home now apparently, with terrible dementia. We've never had a relationship with a GP like that since. We trusted him completely, didn't we, Jack?'

Jack nods, muttering, 'Yeah, absolutely,' as Ash uses the table to help him stand.

Bry smells the wine, stale and syrupy on his breath, as he whispers in her ear, 'It's getting late. I'm going to get Albs ready to go, OK?'

Then Elizabeth says to no one in particular, 'The problem is all those anti-vaxxers are conspiracy theorists, as bad as those insane flat-earthers. In fact, worse, because at least the flat-earthers aren't putting our kids in danger . . .'

'We're going to have to go.' Bry stands up a little too suddenly, disturbing her half-empty bowl. 'It's almost Alba's bedtime already.'

Bry blows kisses to the table and hugs Elizabeth, who says quietly into her ear, 'I sent you an email earlier – make sure you have a read when you can,' and as she turns to leave she glances one last time at Rosalyn, who is, Bry realises, along with Ash the only other person who hasn't said a word.

'Really?' Bry says critically, as Ash opens another bottle of red once Alba's asleep and it's just the two of them in the kitchen.

Ash ignores her and Bry realises she's too tired to pursue an argument now. Ash rubs his forehead before he starts talking. 'Bry, tonight, tonight was excruciating.'

'I don't want to discuss it now, Ash, not when you're so pissed.'

Bry would love another glass of wine but she needs to make a point. She pours herself some water instead as Ash pushes on.

'I can't keep lying to our friends, Bry, I really can't.'

'I'm not lying!'

'Two years ago, she stood right here in this kitchen and you wilfully let her believe Alba is vaccinated.'

Bry knows exactly what he's talking about. Elizabeth had been over for a coffee to discuss Ash and Bry's building plans when Elizabeth had seen one of the reminder letters from their new GP about Alba's vaccinations. She'd slapped her hand down on the letter and raised the other to her chest and said, 'I'm so relieved you're doing the right thing, Bry. I'm just so relieved.'

Bry had opened her mouth to say something, but Elizabeth started telling her about a minor altercation at the school gates involving a vaccine-hesitant parent and Bry had closed her mouth again. It wasn't hard; after all, she'd become expert at stowing away the uncomfortable, unflattering parts of her life.

Ash takes a gulp of wine and says, 'Correct me if I'm wrong, but you have never said the words "Alba isn't vaccinated" to your best friend.'

'Don't you dare paint me as some fucking awful friend because *you* don't bother trying to understand. Elizabeth's my closest friend – she knows what happened to my brother, knows he will never be able to speak because of vaccines, and yet still, *still* she's never asked me outright if we vaccinate. Why do you think that is?'

'Because she assumes we do. Because she considers us to be sane, responsible parents.'

'No, that's bollocks. She doesn't ask because she knows we don't – won't – ever vaccinate Alba.'

'Whoa, whoa, whoa. Sorry, but *you* don't vaccinate. *I* don't get a say – I'm only her fucking dad, after all.'

'That's it, I'm not having this discussion when you're drunk and totally irrational.'

'Fuck off and read your emails.'

Bry closes the door to the master bedroom behind her. Ash can sleep in the spare room tonight. He's been there so often recently, Alba called it 'Daddy's room' the other day. She slumps on the bed and opens the email from Elizabeth. She reads it once, twice, and then throws her phone across the room and immediately wishes it was back in her hand so she could smash it again and again against the window, and with every crack and splinter of the glass feel her own life shatter into shards all around her.

66

Farley County Court

December 2019

'*My child, my choice, my child, my choice!*'

The words beat through my chest like a drum. They feel more potent, more urgent every time I shout them. Next to me, Sophie grabs my hand. She has tears in her eyes again, but she's still waving the placard with the photo of her little boy, Seb, stuck to the front, the dates of his impossibly short life underneath his smiling face: 13 May 2017–8 June 2018. Seb died a week after his MMR. On his death certificate it says '*Sudden Infant Death Syndrome*' but that's a lie. It should say '*Death by Vaccine*' like it does on Sophie's placard. I squeeze her hand. She calls me her '*sister in arms*'. I smile and squeeze back.

On the news yesterday they showed a photo of the sweet girl in hospital. My heart broke for her, but I felt angry too – where are the photos of Seb and the hundreds of other kids and families who have been destroyed by vaccines? Phil, the founder of *Vaccine Freedom*, sent our group a *WhatsApp* message after he saw the photo. It has over one hundred members now – Phil adds more every day. He told us that this is history repeating itself – we are the small but courageous minority leading the way to a better future. Think about the brave people who overthrew the slave trade, the suffragettes, LGBT campaigners – weren't they all laughed at, called stupid, dangerous and delusional just like us?

We are the new history makers, the truth seekers; we are David standing up to Goliath. That's what Phil said.

There's a hush from the group as a black car pulls up and two police officers elbow their way to the kerb. The police hold their arms out to keep us from getting too close. One of the younger members of our group threw an egg at the dad yesterday, caught him on his arm. Phil told him not to do it again and the young guy mumbled he would have thrown something worse – something toxic – if he could get his hands on it. I'm relieved he isn't here today.

We shout louder as the little girl's parents walk past. They keep their eyes fixed forward. They are thin, grey, nothing like the healthy, laughing family in the photos the press keep printing. Once the mum and dad have gone inside, Phil stands on an upturned bucket, his kids in their 'My parents call the shots' T-shirts next to him. He punches the air with his fist and gets a new chant going: 'Stand up for medical freedom! Stand up for medical freedom!' Sophie drops my hand so she can throw hers in the air in time with Phil, shouting with him. I wonder, is Phil her 'brother in arms'? I hope so. That would make us siblings too. I'm starting to like this new family of mine.

10 July 2019

Alba stares out of the car window on the drive to the care home to see her Uncle Matty. It's Matty's forty-second birthday today and Alba, who takes birthdays very seriously indeed, is wearing her blue taffeta ballet tutu with multicoloured stripy wool tights, a silver cardigan and a Batman mask that used to belong to Ash's son Bran.

'A superhero for self-expression,' Ash said as he kissed Alba goodbye this morning. Bry and Ash didn't kiss; they've barely spoken since the barbecue, apart from one tense exchange over coffee while Alba was preoccupied by some colouring. 'You read Elizabeth's email?' Ash asked.

'Yes, I read her fucking email.'

And that is all, so far, that they've said about it.

Bry is relieved Ash isn't joining them to visit her elder brother today. He has only visited Matty once with Bry, before they were married. Bry doesn't bother asking him to come with her any more; she knows from that one visit that it's more painful seeing Ash uncomfortable, fearful of Matty, than it is to keep Ash and Matty hidden from each other, like actors in a play who never share a scene. It's the same with Elizabeth. Her best friend has never even met her brother.

Elizabeth had asked once, years ago, if she could meet him, and Bry must have shut her down pretty conclusively because she's never asked again. Elizabeth has only met Bry's parents a few times – at occasions like Bry and Ash's wedding and Alba's naming ceremony – when everyone was on best behaviour and the talk was about beautiful things like love and babies and nothing inflammatory. Consciously keeping Elizabeth and her mum separate is the only way Bry can keep the peace.

Ash, perhaps out of guilt for being a drunken prick, or for not joining them today, has taken on most of the childcare the last few days – leaping up to give Alba her baths and put her to bed, dressing her in the morning, insisting that Bry go to extra yoga classes and encouraging her to make lunch plans with friends.

'Uncle Matty doesn't have a wife or a 'usband.' In the car, Alba asks questions disguised as fact to learn more about her strange uncle, as though she's teaching Bry about him.

'No. No, he doesn't,' Bry agrees, slowing for a roundabout.

'And Uncle Matty has to live in the 'ospital because he needs special medicine and special nurses.' Bry glances in the rear-view mirror at her daughter, who has turned forward, wanting the answer, the truth, from her mum.

'Well, it's not really a hospital. It's a special house where people who are like Uncle Matty all live together.'

Alba nods sagely and waves her hands in the air as she adds, 'And they're all friends.'

Bry smiles at her daughter in the mirror and says, 'That's right, darling, they're all friends.' The lies always come easily when she talks about Matty. Together with her parents and her younger sister Jessie, Bry has spent her life pretending to herself and others that she believes her non-verbal, severely autistic brother is OK, that he is happy, in his way. But his impenetrable silence is a mystery to Bry and has always seemed to be a tragedy for her parents. The only way she is able to alleviate some of their pain, Bry has learnt, is to pretend everything is fine. So this is what they all do.

Matty has lived in a facility since he was sixteen after he was caught trying to stop Jessie, who was six at the time, from crying by holding a cushion against her face. Jessie almost died and social services gave their mum, Sara, a choice: either Matty had to go into care or her daughters would be sent to foster families. As Sara said, it was no choice at all.

What social services didn't know was that fourteen-year-old Bry had been plotting how to get her brother taken away for a long time. Bry never had a single friend over to their house because Matty was doubly incontinent and Sara wouldn't put him in nappies because she felt it was degrading. Bry couldn't risk the horror of a friend finding a smeary shit on the landing; that would make the bullying at school a thousand times worse. Then there was the way Matty would shove his hands down his pants and masturbate whenever he felt the urge – it didn't matter where they were; in the supermarket or eating breakfast. The violence was bad too. Matty would start punching and thrashing if anyone upset an order or routine that only he understood. Sara's arms were always coloured a queasy blue with bruising. But all that was nothing compared to the fact that Bry felt her parents were always Matty's parents first and hers second. There was no parent shouting Bry's name at her netball games or clapping her performance in school plays. Bry had to take the bus to school on her own from the age of nine because Matty hated anything with wheels – which was also why they never went on a single family holiday. To Bry, it was as though their whole family was disabled. Her big brother had never said a single word, he'd never given Bry a hug or made her laugh. She knew, she *knew* it wasn't his fault, but she still couldn't help but wish he was someone else.

Bry spots her parents waiting in their twenty-year-old VW Golf as soon as she pulls into the car park. She feels her nerves twist and drop like cold pebbles in her stomach. As she parks, her parents tumble out of the car. Her dad is holding his wooden stick as well as two helium balloons – a number 4 and a number 2 – and a box wrapped in glittery blue paper. Matty loves anything shiny. Sara has put on make-up and a light grey cotton dress for the day. She fixes a bright red scarf around her neck and, with a wide smile, opens her arms ready to receive her elder daughter and granddaughter.

'Hi, sweetheart.' Sara smells sweet, smoky, as she embraces Bry. Bry can feel the tension in her mum's thin body; it's always there, a constant pulse. Four decades battling with her guilt, four decades of dutiful, anguished love. Alba is immediately hoisted up into her granddad's arms and wrestles one of the helium balloons out of his large hand.

'Gimme,' she says.

'Umm, what's the magic word?' Bry puts her hand on her daughter's upper arm to calm her.

'Ow, Mumma!' Alba says, batting Bry's hand away from her arm, unusually sensitive, before Bry kisses her dad's slack cheek.

'Hi, Dad.'

David is seventy-four and still working part-time as an accountant. Bry knows her parents worry about what will happen to Matty after they die. She needs to talk to Ash again, be brave and ask him whether they can take over paying for Matty's care – it's time for her dad to retire. Sara takes her daughter's arm and asks with a long breath out, 'OK, are you guys ready?' and Bry smiles, squeezes her mum's arm and says, 'Yes, we've been looking forward to seeing him, haven't we, Alba?' And another layer of delusion is added to their sediment of lies.

Victoria, one of Matty's carers, meets them just outside the visitors' room where Matty is curled in an armchair. There are bite marks on the armrests. Tufts of dark hair stick out of the cushioned helmet Matty's wearing to keep him from injuring himself.

'It's the same as the rugby players wear,' Victoria tells Bry proudly. She smiles at Matty, who is rocking and seems to be doing his best to look everywhere other than at his family. Alba balances on David's knee and Bry sits on a sofa in between her parents, feeling fourteen years old again.

'Happy birthday, darling,' Sara says. Bry can see how much she would love to touch her son's shoulder, but Sara knows this would scare him, that it's too soon, so she folds her hands together to keep them still.

Alba, encouraged by her granddad, offers Matty one of the balloons. ''ere you go,' she says, thrusting her chubby hand towards him. Matty looks at Alba, confused, empty. He ignores the balloon that bobs silently to the ceiling and instead starts shrieking and banging his fist against the helmet on his head, which makes Alba throw herself into her mum's lap. Sara reflexively leans in to help, but it is Victoria who is able to calm Matty by giving him a digital radio that makes him stick out his tongue and give little grunts of pleasure, absorbing him entirely. For the next twenty minutes Sara, David and Bry do their best to chat, to be positive.

'What was happening this time forty-two years ago then, Sar? Were we in hospital already?' David asks, and then there's the predictable argument about which child was born at what time of day. Bry tries, as always, to smile, to be fun, but it's as if there are weights attached to her heart.

'No, no, it was Bry, not Matty, who was born at 3 a.m., that's why she's such a night owl,' Sara replies, smiling at how well she knows her daughter. Bry doesn't bother correcting her; she hasn't been up past midnight for months.

At one point Alba moves towards Matty, who has uncurled one of his hands on the armrest of his chair. She turns her face towards him and says, 'You want to hold 'ands, Uncle Matty?' But before Alba can put her chubby hand in her uncle's large one, Bry swoops in, tickling her daughter and pulling her away. She knows too well how Matty can lash out.

Soon after, Alba becomes bored and starts twisting like a fish in Bry's lap, so David takes her off in search of plates, napkins and a knife for the birthday cake Sara baked last night, and Victoria bends towards Matty and asks, 'Matthew, your mum is going to brush your hair for you, isn't that nice?' before she slowly takes off his helmet. Matty doesn't take his eyes off his radio, determined to pretend none of this is happening, but eventually, on the second asking, he does twitch a finger towards his temple, which is all the encouragement Sara needs. She slowly pulls out the soft-bristled baby brush she keeps in her handbag and gently, gently moves towards her son. They keep Matty's hair almost shoulder length because he has always found having his hair brushed soothing. He has the same soft brown waves as Bry, Jessie and now Alba – the only clue that they share almost identical genetic material. As Sara places a gentle, maternal hand on her son's head, she smiles down at her boy, as if loving him is the easiest thing in the world. Bry thinks about Alba: would she, *could* she care for her daughter selflessly like this if Alba lost everything that made her Alba? The answer – *I don't know* – is almost more terrifying than the impossible question.

They sit there, the three of them in silence, Bry and Sara watching as the brush passes rhythmically through Matty's hair, making it smooth and glossy, Matty deadpan. After Matty has been still and comfortable for a few minutes, Sara turns to Bry and asks in a voice just louder than a whisper, 'Have you had a chance to talk to Jessie yet?'

Bry crosses her legs and refolds her arms in front of her.

'Only briefly, Mum, I don't want to overload her.'

'Did she say she'd got letters through from the surgery? They'll be starting to put the pressure on if she hasn't made an appointment yet.'

Sara is careful to keep her voice soft, her strokes rhythmic, so she doesn't upset Matty. Did she plan to have the chat now, like this?

'Maybe we should talk about this later, Mum . . .'

'No, no, darling, we have to talk about it now; Alba and Dad will be back soon.' Sara stops brushing and Matty starts fiddling with his radio again; sometimes Bry envies her brother his oblivion. Sara turns in her chair towards Bry. 'She doesn't want to talk to me about it, Bry. Being younger, she doesn't understand like you do how important this is, why I can't just sit by and keep silent about this. I can't, I won't risk my grandchildren, I can't let you go through everything Dad and I have been through.'

It wasn't only you and Dad, Bry thinks and then wants to kick her shitty self.

'She won't do it, will she, Bry? Tell me she won't take Coco for any shots.' Sara, like Bry's friends Emma and Row, always uses the more violent American term 'shots' rather than 'vaccine'.

She can't reassure her mum, so Bry leans forward and wraps her arms around her instead. She knows a part of her mum will always be stuck back in the summer of 1978, when Matty, a healthy, engaging thirteen-month-old, had his measles vaccine and a part of her son died. Sara is the one to pull away; she won't be placated by a hug.

'You need to tell her that injecting viral and bacterial particles does not create the same immunity as in nature . . .'

'I know, Mum.'

'They cause an abnormal immune response in some people – like your brother and highly likely Alba and little Coco – that results in neurologic dysfunction. I'm not just talking about autism, Bry, I'm talking about long-term auto-immune disorder, cognitive challenges, cancers and other stuff that may well not appear until adulthood. For whatever reason, our family does not respond well to shots. Look at your Auntie Lou with her asthma, and my poor dad with his Crohn's disease. Both undoubtedly caused by vaccines.'

'Yes, Mum.'

Bry didn't mean to sound so dismissive, it's just she's heard it all a hundred times before. She doesn't want to hear it again, not now, not so brazenly sitting here in front of the ruins of her brother's life.

'Look, look, Mumma! 'hocolate!' Alba has sped away from David and is jigging up and down, a piece of chocolate cake balanced precariously on a saucer, a tell-tale smear on her cheek, and at the sight of her daughter, Bry gratefully leaves the wreckage of her own childhood behind, for now.

Alba is uncharacteristically quiet on the drive home. She doesn't even protest when Ash takes her upstairs for her bath; she just hangs limply in his arms. Bry doesn't hear the usual laughs and chatter from the bathroom and when she comes upstairs, Ash is wrapping their daughter in a towel just as the tears start to come. Ash steps aside silently – he knows Bry needs to hold her and kiss her damp, sweet head. This, Bry notices, he understands. Alba curls up, foetal, pressing her body as close as it can be to her mother's. Once the intensity of Alba's sadness has passed and her sobs have become jagged breaths, Bry, still rocking, still kissing, whispers, 'I'm here, my darling, I'm here. Are you feeling poorly?'

Alba pushes herself against Bry's chest to sit up, closes her red eyes briefly as if checking in with her body and shakes her head. She keeps her brown eyes fixed on Bry as she starts to talk. 'When we went to Uncle Matty's bir'day party . . .'

'Yes, darling?' Bry strokes a dark, damp curl behind her daughter's ear.

'I asked Granddad why Uncle Matty has to live in that place that is like a 'ospital with his friends.'

The pebbles in Bry's stomach jump and behind her she hears Ash shuffle, but she manages to nod at Alba, to keep her talking.

''e said when Uncle Matty was a baby 'e had a shot that hurt 'im, hurt 'im very much. Granddad said after the shot

77

Baby Matty got sick and then 'e couldn't 'member how to walk or how to make baby noises no more.'

Alba's thin shoulders shiver as she takes another deep breath. She glances at Ash, shakes her head at him.

'Granddad said that's why Granny won't let me or Baby Coco 'ave shots, so we don't get sick like Uncle Matty.' She keeps shaking her head as the tears rise again.

Behind them Ash mutters, 'Fuck's sake, David.'

Bry, feeling heat gather behind her own eyes, tries to take Alba's body into her arms again, but now Alba struggles against her, she won't be held. Instead she looks at Bry, her almond-shaped eyes red-rimmed and serious, and she shakes her head hard as she says, 'I don' wanna be like Uncle Matty, Mumma.'

Bry strokes her daughter's face and lets her own tears fall freely. Gathering her daughter back into her arms, she whispers promises of safety and protection for both their sakes, promises she should know she could never keep.

Once Alba's asleep, Bry walks slowly downstairs, past the professional photos of the three of them, smiling and flawless in black and white, and into their large, open-plan kitchen. Tonight, unusually, Ash is sitting with his back to the door in the glass extension at their eight-seater kitchen table. Bry had pictured hosting dinner parties when they bought the table, each seat filled with an interesting friend, but it still hasn't happened. She thought the house itself, with its marble surfaces and under-floor heating, would somehow make her into the effortless host that she would inevitably become – more Elizabeth and less Bry – but no such luck.

Ash doesn't turn towards her as she comes into the kitchen.

'Tea?' she asks, but he shakes his head. She knew he'd say no. There's a bottle of wine on the table.

Bry puts her tea on the table and sits opposite her husband, pulling her legs up and tucking her knees under her chin. It feels as though the argument she knows is to come is already laid out between them. They just have to turn up to say their lines. Bry goes first. 'Dad shouldn't have said that to her. I'll ask him to apologise.'

Ash, who has been totally still since Bry entered the kitchen, slowly shakes his head. That's a new tactic. Usually he'd be demanding an apology, swearing at Bry's parents for interfering with their lives again. Instead he tugs at his beard and turns slowly to look at his wife. 'Remember when Albs was born?'

She'd been pink and loud, outraged by the shock of life before immediately taking comfort at Bry's breast.

'Of course I do.'

'Remember when that nurse came in with the injection for vitamin something just a few hours after she was born.'

Bryony doesn't know where this is leading but she nods and says, 'Vitamin K.'

'That's right, I remember thinking it sounded like a cereal.' He takes a sip of wine. 'That nurse, the fat one, came towards Alba with the needle, saying it was time for her injection. You picked Albs up, shook your head at the nurse and said, "No fucking way." You looked more terrifying than terrified – you looked like a lioness.'

Bry smiles. 'I felt awful after – it was the first time Alba heard a swear word.'

Ash nods. 'The nurse didn't stand a chance. Remember? She just backed away.' The feeling had been absolute, visceral – the needle was the toxic world trying to creep into her perfect daughter's bloodstream and only Bry could stop it. Ash keeps talking. 'I loved you so much in that moment. If I'm honest, I didn't want Alba to have that injection, I hated the thought, but I didn't have the balls to say no. You did though, and I loved you like fucking crazy for it.'

Bry smiles again and wishes they could always talk about the past, where Ash loves her like crazy.

'I remember thinking, that's it, that's motherhood, and I had this overwhelming kind of rushy feeling because Alba and I had you to look after us, so I knew we'd be safe.'

'Oh, Ash.' Bry wants to run to her husband, fall into him in gratitude for seeing her, for understanding, but then Ash's gaze suddenly drops away from her face and Bry readies herself for an attack.

'Then the lioness came out again when I mentioned her eight-week injections.'

Bry opens fire. 'Hepatitis B is a sexually transmitted infection, it's totally nuts we are vaccinating tiny babies . . .' But Ash's voice is louder.

'I know, I know, Bry. Then recently, I got another phone call from the GP about the MMR.'

Bry stops and breathes out. She lays her palms flat on the table and stares at them.

'You know I can never let her have the MMR.'

'Your brother's problems are not because he had a vaccine, Bry,' Ash says, as gently as his frustration will allow. 'Study after study has said the same – there is no link between vaccines and autism.' He seeks out eye contact but now Bry won't look up.

'You asked me once why I never talk about my early childhood. I didn't answer at the time, but you were right, I don't talk about it much. Why? Because it was fucking miserable, Ash. Fucking miserable.'

Bry feels herself released. She leans across the table towards Ash, smacking her hand down flat between them.

'You know what my first memory is? Trying to comfort Mum after Matty gave her a black eye. Do you know what my second memory is? Matty giving me a black eye. Matty's "problems", as you call them, have been my problems too, and you know what the worst thing is? I can't say any of this because it's selfish and ugly.' Bry hadn't realised that at some point she'd started crying, the tears hot and angry. There's so much more she's never been able to say to anyone. She can't tell him that she doesn't think she has ever loved her brother, not like she loves Jessie anyway, which is her fault. Always her fault, never his.

She reaches for Ash's wine and finishes his glass. Bry wishes he'd stand up and hold her. Instead he places his hand on top of hers, something at least.

'You know, at the barbecue Rosalyn said something that made so much sense to me,' Bry says. 'She said she believes in "my child, my choice" – I've heard it before, of course, but it was like the first time I really understood what it means, you know? It's like, where there is risk there must be choice.'

Ash squeezes Bry's hand and says gently, 'Yes, but what about Elizabeth and Jack? They don't have a choice, do they? They have to rely on other people doing the right thing to protect Clemmie.'

Bry pulls her hand away. 'I'd argue that Clemmie is safer just as she is—'

But Ash interrupts. 'Look, Bry, I'm sorry, I'm so, so sorry for Matty and your family. But blame life, get angry with how unfathomable, how unfair it is: don't cling to circumstantial evidence, don't blame vaccines when they've been proven unequivocally to be safe.'

Bry shakes her head. 'That's bullshit, it's not unequivocal. Some people have adverse reactions, severe, life-changing adverse reactions.'

'You sound like your mum.'

Bry flinches. 'Well, good, because she knows her stuff, way more than you.'

'She's a mum, Bry, a mum who wants to have something to blame for her son's disabilities.'

Bry leans in again, pointing her finger down at the table. 'Hours after Matty had the injection he had a fever, and then twelve hours after that he stopped walking, and this didn't just happen to us, it happened to thousands of families, Ash, thousands.'

'Look, it always gets out of hand when we talk—'

'I will never, ever—'

'I took her, Bry . . . I took Alba for vaccinations.'

Bry feels the world around her freeze and then start to boil. 'You fucking what?'

Ash looks briefly down at his lap, before placing his hands back on the table and looking directly at his wife.

'Meningitis and pneumonia.'

'No, no.' Bry shakes her head; he's fucking with her. It's a low blow, even for Ash. He's fucking with her.

'I read an article, Bry, at the Chamberlains', about a bloke – Mark Clancy – whose baby Rosie died from meningitis . . .'

She gets up from the table and is still shaking her head as Ash comes towards her.

'I knew him, Bry, I used to work with Mark. And then Jack on our run last week brought up all that stuff about Clemmie not being . . .'

Bry wants to roar, she wants to claw at his face, but instead she turns away from him and runs upstairs and closes the bedroom door behind her. Her cries rip through her chest and she thinks of her mum and she curls up on the carpet, gripped as the realisation tears through her. She's no lioness. She broke her one and only promise to her mum and to her daughter.

She's failed.

12 July 2019

Cleaning her kitchen feels a bit like putting make-up on someone far too old to worry about their appearance, but Elizabeth does it every Friday morning anyway. She would never admit it, but she secretly quite enjoys the simple task of getting down on her hands and knees to scrub the floor: she likes the simplicity of it, forgiving her family their muddy shoes, dropped Lego and stickers as she makes it clean for them again. Not that they'll notice, but there are so many things of course that children never know, should never know.

When she's done, she makes herself a coffee and opens her laptop on the kitchen table. Charlotte's emailed flight information and the hotel confirmation for their trip to Cornwall next week, the day after Clemmie's party. It's not ideal timing, but Charlotte is paying, so Elizabeth felt she didn't have any leverage to ask for a different date. Elizabeth types back, *Can't wait! Xxx*. God, it would feel good to treat a friend for once instead of feeling neutered by others' generosity. She will have to speak to Jack again; he needs a pay rise. She doesn't want her kids to be teenagers feeling down the back of the sofa for any dropped change, asking their mates to borrow a fiver. She needs to take control. Jack is many great things, but he is not an initiator, he does not *lean in*; so Elizabeth – like always – will.

Elizabeth opens up an email from Amanda, the mum of one of Clemmie's friends. She says they can't wait for the party, blah, blah. It's the second paragraph where Elizabeth finds what she's looking for:

Of course! I totally get it, and just so you know, I'd be the same if Mai couldn't be vaccinated – which she is, fully.

Elizabeth opens up her 'Clemmie's Party' document and puts a tick next to Mai's name in the 'Vac?' column. She looks at the spreadsheet. Nineteen responses out of twenty-six, all confirming their kid is vaccinated. She'll text the other seven – Bry and Row amongst them, of course – a simple reminder. It would be quite handy if Row takes this as Elizabeth hopes she will: the perfect reason to put distance between themselves and their daughters.

But Bry . . . well, Bry is different, Bry is always different. The way Bry patted Row at the barbecue after Lily hurt her foot, the fact Bry hasn't responded to her email, has been gnawing away at Elizabeth. Of course, neither of these things in isolation is cause for alarm – Bry is caring and always terrible at replying to emails – but the way Bry goes quiet whenever Elizabeth mentions vaccines is something Elizabeth fears, in the same way she fears drunk drivers and online groomers: she hopes it will remain an abstract, private fear, something she'll never have to face during daylight hours. Sometimes, late at night, she wavers, panics and tries to remember a moment when Bry has said explicitly that

Alba is vaccinated. She's fairly sure she did once, a couple of years ago when Elizabeth was over at Number 9 looking at their architect's plans. But now she needs reassuring again, especially since Alba is going to Nettlestone and suddenly the two girls have become close.

Furthermore, she went to the GP a few weeks ago when Charlie had that awful ear infection and the GP had told her that vaccination rates were falling both nationwide and locally, and were – around Farley especially – well below the herd immunity requirement. Elizabeth knows about Matty, of course, knows that Bry deliberately tries to keep her family and Elizabeth separate. Elizabeth is fairly sure this is because Sara has some wacky views about Matty and his disabilities that Elizabeth wouldn't be able to smile away and ignore like everyone else. Bry has always been cagey about Matty, and Elizabeth has, over the years, learnt to respect that it is simply too painful for Bry to talk about him and his life, and the impact on her family and her own life. All this and now that article by Mark Clancy has tipped the balance and punched the issue home: Elizabeth can't ignore it any more. Elizabeth loves Bry, but she loves Clemmie more. It's as simple as that.

Besides, there is no way Bry would risk losing Elizabeth over this, no way. If Ash hasn't made her see sense already and have Alba vaccinated, then Elizabeth will.

A ladybird lands on stout, jointed legs on the kitchen table. Elizabeth watches it for a moment, making its slow progress across the table towards her, before she flicks it into her hand and crosses over to the French doors to release it. Clemmie would be pleased with her. But as she opens the doors, she notices a huddle of little red, armoured bodies piled on top of each other, like bright buttons crowded in the hinge of the French doors. Something about seeing so many ladybirds makes them threatening suddenly, a slow, persistent invasion into their home. They start to separate, unpacking themselves like acne rash into the sparkling kitchen. *Where the fuck are they coming from?* The doors make a surprisingly loud crunching sound as she closes them, and she's about to get the hoover out again to clean up the broken red bodies when her phone starts buzzing on the kitchen table, Bry's name flashing on the screen.

'Hi, Bry' – Elizabeth places extra emphasis on the rhyme; she's answered Bry's calls like this for years – 'I was just about to text you.'

'Hey.' Before her friend has spoken another word, Elizabeth senses something isn't right.

'What's wrong?' Elizabeth says, forgetting about the ladybirds, even forgetting why she needed to speak with Bry.

'Oh, nothing, nothing really, I'm just feeling a bit low.'

'Want me to come over?'

'No, no, it's all right, Emma's coming over for tea. I wish I could cancel but we planned it ages ago and she'll be on her way now.' Bry pauses. 'I mean, obviously if you want to, you can join us.'

But Elizabeth wants to be with Bry, not with Bry and the annoying homeopath; she's got too much on this morning to sit listening to Emma drone on about stone circles and the power of the full moon.

'Do you know what's up?' Elizabeth asks, but Bry pauses, a little too long. Elizabeth suspects she does know but is hesitating to tell her for some reason, but then Bry blurts out, 'It's the baby thing.'

'Oh sweetheart, it will happen, it will. You just need to keep the faith and not put too much—'

'I know, I know. It's just, Jessie keeps sending photos of Coco, which is, you know, which is lovely but also just makes me feel . . . just a bit . . .'

'Yeah, yeah, I can imagine.' Bry's always had a more complicated relationship with her sister than she lets on.

'And you know what really pisses me off is the way everyone's kind of *congratulating* her for having the perfect home birth, like my mum's literally telling all her friends about it – twelve hours start to finish, birthing pool, no stitches, Coco born into her dad's arms. I mean, she did literally bugger all planning; she only had a home birth because I gave her our birthing pool.'

Bry's birthing pool had never been used. She'd ended up having a C-section after three days of labouring at home, Alba back to back for most of it. All the hypno-birthing, perineum stretching and doula sessions that Elizabeth took the piss out of for the full nine months, for nothing. Elizabeth can't understand why any woman would want a so-called 'natural birth'. You wouldn't ask a doctor to take your appendix out without anaesthetic, would you?

But her own body had had other ideas – her babies arrived so quickly, there'd been no time for the epidural she screamed for, so all three births had been excruciatingly, agonisingly 'natural'. Elizabeth is mystified that somehow 'natural' has become synonymous with 'good'.

'I know it sounds selfish,' Bry says, her voice flat.

'No, it doesn't, it sounds totally rational. You sound like me.'

Elizabeth feels herself lift as Bry laughs.

'I do, don't I?'

'Shall we go for a drink tonight?' Elizabeth asks, realising it would be better to talk to Bry about Alba and Clemmie's party in person. 'Ash mentioned they've got that nice red back in the Cellar. I could pick you up at eight?'

'Oh maybe, let me check Ash's at home . . .' And somehow Elizabeth knows they're not going to go out that night, but before she can try to persuade Bry, a couple of loud revs make the glass in the French doors rattle and a fat wood pigeon clatter out of the apple tree.

'Hang on, Bry, I can't hear, there's something . . . hang on,' Elizabeth says into her phone.

She steps out into the garden just as the revs come again, before they are drawn into one continuous mechanical moan. The noise rattles through Elizabeth's skull as if she's pinned back, the dentist's drill in her mouth.

'What the hell?' she mutters, stepping out into the garden where even the blue summer sky seems to vibrate with noise. She can just about hear Bry saying something, but she can't make out what as she moves quickly back into the kitchen, closing the doors behind her.

'It's coming from next door – that new woman, Rosalyn!' Elizabeth shouts into the phone.

'Could she be gardening maybe?' Bry says, her voice hopeful. 'I can't really hear it from over here . . .'

But Elizabeth isn't listening – she thunders up the stairs to the bathroom and throws open the window so she can lean out for a good view of Rosalyn's garden. There she is, her back towards Elizabeth in blue overalls, her hair held back by the protective goggles covering half her face. She's in a brace position, like a kung fu fighter, against the weight of the rotating blade she's holding in both hands, a huge rectangular

89

slab of stone before her. Elizabeth pulls herself back into the bathroom and slams the window shut.

'She's fucking *sculpting*,' Elizabeth says into her phone.

'Oh, that's so cool,' Bry says.

'It's not *cool*, Bry, it's fucking noisy and she didn't even warn us . . . it's, it's dangerous.'

Bry starts laughing. 'Elizabeth, it's not like she's cooking meth.'

Elizabeth ignores Bry as she leans in, close to the glass. She can just see half of Rosalyn as she sparks up the blade again. Metal screams against stone and a cloud of dust billows up around Rosalyn like smoke before being carried on the gentle breeze, spirited over the wall and into Elizabeth's life. This is worse, far worse than ladybirds.

'I mean, doesn't this woman think about anyone else?'

'Oh Elizabeth, come on, I think she's absolutely amazing – so confident, so, so poised, and she's had such an interesting life . . .'

'Ha! You only think that because she doesn't want kids.'

'Elizabeth, listen to me . . .' Bry's voice is a warning as Elizabeth runs, two at a time, down the stairs.

'I'm going to have a chat with her about this, Bry. I'll speak to you later.'

'Elizabeth, please don't . . .'

But Elizabeth's already hung up, and before she's thought about what she'll say, she's banging hard on the front door of Number 8.

The noise is muffled here at the front, but Elizabeth is surprised all the same that someone inside heard her and the door opens just as she raises her knuckles to bang again. She takes an involuntary step back on the Victorian porch tiles when the gorgeous man Rosalyn was with when she moved in answers. He's young, barefoot, his deep tan set off against a white T-shirt. He's holding a mug, like some kind of coffee advert.

'Hi,' he says, smiling from one side of his mouth, as if he's in no hurry, used to having to give people time to recover.

She should have showered, put some mascara on.

'Can I help you?' he asks, his Italian accent lyrical, thick as cream. Elizabeth thrusts her hand towards him, her fingers rigid; it gives her somewhere to fix her eyes.

'I'm Elizabeth, Elizabeth Chamberlain, from Number 10.'

'I'm Raffaele, Rafe, from Number 8.' He holds her hand as if he's trying to soften rather than shake it. It feels shocking, like a tiny infidelity, his warm skin pressed against hers. 'Nice to meet you, Elizabeth,' he says, releasing her hand and taking a sip from his mug before he adds, 'Would you like to come in?'

He opens the door wider and Elizabeth catches a glimpse of boxes stacked in the hall, the kitchen table busy with what looks like used glasses and plates.

'No, no, that's OK.'

'Rafe?' Rosalyn's voice is a song from somewhere deep inside the house.

Rafe turns his beautiful, dark head towards her and calls back in fast Italian.

There are footsteps down the hall and suddenly Rosalyn appears behind Rafe. The goggles are now propped up on her forehead; they've left marks around her eyes. Her skin is coated in white dust as though she herself is emerging from stone.

'Oh, Elizabeth, hi, how are you?' She smiles and even

though they're not touching, Elizabeth notices the way Rafe turns towards Rosalyn, how he moves, welcoming her, inviting her towards him.

'Do you want to come in? Rafe just made some unbelievably strong coffee . . .'

'Oh no, no, no, thank you. I've already had my cup for the day.'

They both smile at her as though they don't quite understand – one cup for a whole day?

Elizabeth scrambles. Why is she here? To complain, to tell Rosalyn that the noise, the dust, is not OK; worse – that it's *unneighbourly*.

But Rafe and his brown eyes and skin have made her priggish, shy.

'God, what is it with these things?' Rosalyn says as she flicks a ladybird off Rafe's arm. 'They're everywhere. Apparently the collective noun for ladybird is "a loveliness"; isn't that wonderful?'

'Feels like "an infection" of ladybirds would be more appropriate,' Elizabeth says, as the ladybird Rosalyn just flicked away flies like a tiny mechanical toy through the air and comes to land in Elizabeth's hair. She flaps at it, overreacting, making some of her hair kink. Rosalyn and Rafe look at her with patient amusement. Elizabeth thinks about stamping her foot on the ladybird as it hits the tiles in front of her, but instead she remembers why she's here.

'I wanted to ask you . . .' Elizabeth feels them waiting. 'I wanted to let you know . . .'

Rosalyn nods gently, encouraging her to keep talking. Is she resting a hand on his bottom? She could be, but Elizabeth can't see enough to be sure, because the front door is in the way.

'That it's Clemmie's – she's our youngest – birthday party next Thursday, so I'm sorry if there's a bit of noise from over the wall.'

'Oh, no problem at all.' Rosalyn smiles and asks, 'How old is she going to be?'

'Seven. She'll be seven,' Elizabeth says firmly. Then she nods, swallows and says, 'The schools will have just broken up for the summer so they're getting pretty excited.' Neither Rosalyn nor Rafe says anything and so Elizabeth nods again and says, 'OK, great. Thanks then,' and just before she turns clumsily to leave, ashamed by her own unusual timidity, Rafe says with a strong accent, 'Nice to meet you,' and Elizabeth has the sinking feeling that as soon as they close the door they'll turn to each other, eyebrows raised, and laugh at their odd new neighbour.

'Anyway, the whole thing was agony. I'm just relieved I didn't invite them to come over for the party. *That* would have been awkward.' Jack laughs around his toothbrush. Elizabeth watches him in the mirror as he sits on the edge of the bathtub. She tries to imagine what she would think of Jack if she didn't know him, if he suddenly appeared behind a door, the way Rafe appeared today. With his short red hair, pale skin and blue eyes, softened by decades of smiling, he's totally different from Rafe, but still, she'd think he was handsome, wouldn't she? Jack coughs against the toothpaste in his mouth and Elizabeth moves to the side so he can spit into the sink. If this was a different night, she might bring up the money issue again, but she doesn't want to now. She wants Jack to be annoyed at Rosalyn too.

'Anyway, this isn't about that, it's about the fact that Rosalyn is clearly dating – or at least shagging – this guy who is probably young enough to be her son!'

Jack wipes his face with a towel and moves away from the sink, allowing Elizabeth to reclaim her spot in front of the mirror. She looks down; he hasn't sluiced away his spit. She made the sink spotless this morning. How quickly things slide, become messy.

'So why are you acting pissed off? I thought you'd be all over it, older woman having her way with beautiful Rafe . . .'

'I'm not pissed off, Jack! I just think she comes across as, I don't know, a bit louche.'

A few half-bottles of mouthwash and antiseptic fall over as Jack picks out the dental floss; Elizabeth makes a mental note to organise the cupboard the next time she's in here cleaning.

'What does louche mean? I've always pretended to know but I've never really known,' he says, his stomach creasing into gentle folds as he sits back on the rim of the bathtub and starts to pluck at his teeth with the floss.

'Kind of erm . . . you know, irresponsible, irreverent.'

'You think she's irresponsible because she has a younger lover?'

'No, no, it's not that, it's . . . she . . . was chatting to Row for ages at the barbecue and . . . I . . . I just don't think it's fair that we all have to suffer for her bloody art.'

'Bry spent quite a bit of time chatting to her as well. What does she think of her?'

'God, predictably she's like a teenager with a crush.'

Elizabeth turns back towards the sink and splashes her face with water.

'Well, you have to admit there is something kind of interesting about her, don't you think?'

'Jack, don't, just don't.'

She closes her eyes and starts rubbing her foaming face-wash into her skin. Sometimes Elizabeth wishes that either her husband or her best friend would take her corner. Neither of them would understand how annoying it is that Rosalyn never apologises – she didn't apologise for being twenty minutes late to the barbecue for starters, and she didn't even notice that her 'work' could be disruptive to her new neighbours, and now there's this Rafe. She just doesn't follow the rules.

She rinses, and once she's dried her face on a fresh white towel, says, 'Jack, I mean it, this woman is a bit odd. I'll bet she has some strange views on things . . .'

'You sound a bit jealous, my love,' Jack says, in that soft voice that he must think is sexy but actually tickles, like some-thing creeping into her ear. She turns around to face her husband and tilts his jaw up, forcing him to look at her.

'I'm not jealous of her, Jack. I mean, she doesn't have any kids, I can't imagine a life without children. I've just made different and – I'd argue – better life choices.'

He stands up. His skin feels cool against her. 'Well, I'm pleased to hear you say that.' He kisses her full on the lips. She lets him kiss her before turning back to the sink and rub-bing some cheap moisturising cream she read was just as good as the designer brands into her face while Jack contin-ues flossing. Jack looks at her in the mirror, smiles from the corner of his mouth.

'What are you smiling at?' she asks, sounding more irri-tated than she knows is reasonable.

Jack spits again, a little bloody this time, into the sink.

'I think you're pissed off with yourself because you backed away from complaining about the noise.'

Elizabeth rolls her eyes at him in the mirror, so he doesn't see her grip the side of the sink.

'I've had a good response to the email about Clemmie's party, by the way. But nothing, predictably, from Bry.'

Jack's expression doesn't change, but she does notice the skin between his eyebrows form a pleat, a concertina of concern. This happens when he's reminded about something he'd rather not think about.

'I mean, I'm sure it's just Bry being crap and forgetful. I'm not really worried about it. I know she'd probably rather not think about it, but I'm sure Alba has been vaccinated. I saw the GP letters a few years ago, remember?'

Jack drops the used floss into the bin and, baring his teeth at the mirror, puffs air through the gaps between them and says, 'Yeah, and there's no way Ash would not have one of his kids vaccinated. I remember him telling me when Alba was a baby about how he was dreading taking her, that both his boys screamed the house down when they had their first jabs. Besides, I was talking about it the other day on our run and he didn't mention anything.'

Jack's thought about it then, Elizabeth consoles herself, *at least that's a kind of action.* Jack walks towards the bathroom door, but before he disappears Elizabeth calls out, 'Clothes!' and with a groan, Jack turns back and picks up his clothes from the floor and dumps them in the washing basket.

Two hours later, Jack is snoring softly and Elizabeth is lying next to him, trying to force her body to relax. It's like wrestling. Slowly, heavily, she kicks the duvet away and, pulling her dressing gown on in the dark, heads downstairs. Their ancient dishwasher is still groaning away, the shoes lined up by the back door, the breakfast things ready. How hopeful it all seems, how certain that Elizabeth would not be back down here until the morning, rested and ready for the new day. But here she is, exhausted and fretful having lost the battle against herself again. She makes a camomile tea and fires up her laptop on the kitchen table. There are two more responses following the reminder texts she sent earlier.

One from a mum who apologises for the late response and confirms that of course her little one is vaccinated, and another, who adds, *It must be so frustrating that you even need to worry about this stuff.* Both girls get their ticks in the 'Vac?' column. Just five more.

Elizabeth cups her hands around her tea and feels that wonderful tightening sensation she had this morning. It's a slotting-in feeling, the relief of being in control that nothing – not even Rosalyn or the fucking ladybirds – can take away.

Farley County Court

December 2019

There's always space at the front, in the disabled section of the public gallery. The nice usher at the door gives me a smile and his arm as I clatter in: step, step, stick, step, step, stick. I don't notice her until my stick clashes with her wheelchair: a woman, older than me, definitely older, with knitting needles and teeth all a-clatter. She must have smuggled those knitting needles in – no one checks old ladies too carefully. I stroke my hair. I had it set yesterday. The nice young man gently holds up his arm, a sign for me to let go, as if he's releasing a bird. I cling on. This old woman is in my space.

'Here you go,' the usher says, and my gloved hand – with some irritation – releases before he has to shake me off.

The old woman pauses her knitting and smiles up at me. She looks like a chatterer.

'Leave your stick here if you want, ducky,' she says. Ducky? I think. I nod down at her, prop my stick against her chair and, holding on to the wooden rail with one hand, I move my long grey skirt with the other as I squeeze past her chair into the space next to her. Most uncomfortable.

She starts knitting again and asks, 'Who are you here for then?'

A quick glance tells me she didn't bother to look at me, so she misses me not looking at her.

'I'm not here for anyone. I'm here to support the issue.'

'So you are here for something then. For or against?'

'If you mean do I believe in vaccination, then yes, overwhelmingly, yes.'

She stops knitting, looks at me with her soufflé face before casting her little winkle eyes down at my leg. The old and the young have so much in common – one of them is a distinct lack of subtlety. I cover my hands – a lifelong reflex – over my withered right leg, curled coyly as it always is towards its neighbour.

'My sister had polio too. She was in one of these things her whole short life, God love her.' She pats the side of her wheelchair. I stroke my hair. It's rare someone guesses nowadays.

''Course, her chair wasn't like these modern gizmos – no, it was wooden with a green leather seat and far too big for a little girl. Used to belong to an old Victorian gentleman, so we were told. It was the only thing we could get in Delhi those days. That's where we were, Delhi. Were you abroad with your family then?'

I shake my head, start to speak, but stop to clear my throat and say, 'London.'

'Ehh, you got polio in London?' she says, matter of fact, as if I've just told her about a bus service she didn't know about. Her needles start click-clacking against each other again. 'Bad luck, ducky.'

'Yes, I suppose it was rather.'

Strange to have the defining feature of my life so reduced. I was seven. I remember I was playing hopscotch with Nanny when the headache came on. Whispering in my bedroom sounded like thunder, light from a window like boiling water thrown in my face. The next thing I knew, I woke up screaming, paralysed, inside an iron lung; six other children, just heads poking out of their metal breathing caskets, around me. I was told I was lucky. Some of those children stayed in those torture chambers for the rest of their lives. Others became just a head, thorax and abdomen, all their limbs withered away like old fruit left too long on a branch. I never felt lucky though. I heard my aunt on the telephone just days after I was let home.

'Such a sadness; she was such a pretty little thing, and an only child to boot. Poor, poor sister.'

No one apart from me, and the odd doctor, has seen my right leg in the last seventy-five years and no one ever will.

'Well, I'm with you, ducky. Younger folk have no idea, no idea. My little friend in Delhi, nice French girl called Lucile, I'll never forget her, started coughing up blood. She and her brother died from TB just weeks later, and of course my own children have had the mumps, measles and all that. Then there's my cousin, who had the rubella when she was pregnant. Poor little baby born all deformed and died soon after.' She finishes her grisly roll call and then says, 'Mint?' while shucking a Trebor Extra Strong out of its packaging with a strong thumb.

I shake my head. Look around the court for any other seats with extra leg room, when a voice echoes.

'All rise!' And the nice usher opens the door for the judge, and me and my neighbour are the only two who ignore his command.

15 July 2019

Ash joins Bry, who is sitting outside drinking her morning coffee. She looks at him but doesn't say anything as he sits down at the far end of the table. She turns her chair towards Alba, who is on the grass laughing as a few ladybirds climb on their tripod legs up her arms like a creeping rash. They're everywhere now, dotted on the newly laid lawn like beads from a huge broken necklace.

Alba was supposed to be in nursery this morning in preparation for school in September, but Bry has kept her home. She'd sat up to watch over Alba that first night after Ash told her what he'd done, checking her temperature with a shaky hand and staring at her chest to make sure her breathing didn't change. So far, she seems perfectly normal – her usual wild, beautiful self.

'How about Albs and I go to the beach today – then you can go to a yoga class, take some time for yourself?' Ash asks, his voice gentle.

Bry shakes her head firmly and turns so she can look him directly in the eye as she says, 'No.'

She wants to wound him, like he's wounded her. She keeps her face impassive as she says, quietly so Alba can't hear, 'Jessie's coming over with Coco. I don't want you to be here.'

She knows this is how Linette used to be with him, that she froze him out of their sons' lives, and she feels cruel but glad for this targeted ammunition. Ash nods and after a brief moment picks his mug up and goes quietly back inside. Bry feels a fleeting spark of power. That's the only good thing to come out of this shitshow – that she's suddenly got the balls to say exactly what she needs.

But this one good thing is smothered by a mountain of crap things, the most unexpected being how very lonely Bry feels. Watching over Alba that first night, she realised she had no one she could talk to about Ash's betrayal. She didn't feel like opening up to Row or Emma or any of her other relatively new Farley friends, and her family would turn against Ash for ever if they knew. The only person she can imagine talking to is Elizabeth, but the repercussions of bringing it up with her – especially now with this email – feel too vast for Bry to wrap her head around. Her phone buzzes in front of her, and she glances at it expecting to see Elizabeth's name, probably reminding her again to reply to the email, but the text is from Rosalyn.

> Morning Bry, wondering if I can pop over later, I have something I want to ask you. Let me know. Rosalyn.

It's a brisk message, direct. Bry types her reply.

> Yes, beautiful morning! Hope you guys are well. We'd love to see you, why don't you come over for drinks later? Say 5 p.m.? Bry xxx

She rereads it. Shakes her head at herself, deletes it and instead types:

Hi Rosalyn, yes, Alba and I are home. See you later. Bry.

She sends the shorter message, and as soon as she does so, regrets not inviting Rosalyn for drinks. She'd be the perfect person to talk to about the Ash issue. Even though she doesn't know her well, Bry is sure Rosalyn would appreciate her candour, and Bry is pretty certain, judging by her behaviour at the barbecue, that Rosalyn is vaccine hesitant herself. It would be a way of bonding with this alluring woman, a way she could learn more about her, a way of learning more about how she, Bry, should be, how she could be. She types another message.

P.S. Why don't you come for drinks at 5 p.m.?

She takes a sip of coffee as Alba marches around the garden, collecting ladybirds in a jam jar as she goes.

'You definitely never told me I'd be this tired,' Jessie says a couple of hours later, leaning back on the rug Bry has laid out on the grass and squinting up at the sky, one hand on her forehead, the other on her belly. Alba is naked and busy filling up buckets of water from the hose on the side of the house – 'For the ladybirdy baths,' she told them, as though it should be patently obvious.

Coco, Jessie's newborn, is fast asleep in Bry's arms, her little mouth open and occasionally twitching around an imagined nipple. Bry holds her hand over Coco's eyes to shield her from the sun until a foamy cloud shades them all.

'I definitely told you you'd be knackered. You just chose not to listen.'

Jessie, ignoring her older sister, keeps talking.

'Honestly, last night was ridiculous. She'd only fall asleep if one of us was cuddling her. Joe had her until midnight but then she needed a feed so I took over and urgh . . . I was terrified all night I'd squash her so I didn't sleep at all, just kept doing that weird head-jerky thing. So how was it, last week?'

Bry knows her sister is talking about their trip to see Matty. She keeps her eyes fixed protectively on her beautiful niece.

'Just the same as usual. Dad seemed old, tired.'

'Mum?'

'Sad but being brave, like always.'

'Did Mum say anything about us?'

Bry rocks Coco in her arms, and thinks how strange it is that her sister asks after everyone apart from Matty. Bry wishes they didn't have to get into this straight away. She wanted a few sunny hours with her sister and Coco. She wanted, for a little while at least, to forget her fear, to forget about Ash, about Matty, about Elizabeth's email. To forget about how vulnerable everything feels.

'You know she did.'

'And?' Jessie props herself up on her elbows, her fingers gently raking her short, dark crop, to watch Bry's response. Bry decides to give it to Jessie straight.

'She's worried, terrified, that you're going to vaccinate Coco.'

Bry looks down again at Coco, imagines her perfect, blemish-free skin suddenly stabbed with a needle, her scream, the unknown fluid inserted into her veins, possibly to protect her, but also possibly to destroy her. The fact of the needle feels to Bry like a far greater risk than the vague possibility of an illness.

'Well, that's no surprise, of course,' Jessie says. The sisters had grown up with their mum's fear of vaccines. Neither of them had ever had one – even when they went abroad. It hadn't ever been a problem, not until Bry had Alba, and Ash and Bry started arguing about it.

'I've never caught anything!' she'd shout, and Ash would say, 'That's luck. Nothing more.'

And Bry would counter that it wasn't luck, it was proof that the risks of illnesses like measles and mumps had been grossly exaggerated by powerful corporations with a vested interest. They were caught in an endless wrestle – Ash fearful of the consequences of not vaccinating Alba, and Bry terrified of the consequences of vaccinating her. Eventually, motherhood and Sara won, and Ash agreed to wait for a few years until they spoke – argued – about it again. But evidently, he is a fucking liar.

'And you? Are you worried about what we decide?'

Bry can feel her sister's large brown eyes fixed on her as she waits. So she keeps her own gaze cast down on her niece. When Bry doesn't say anything, Jessie says, 'Well, that sounds like a yes.' Jessie lets her head fall back on to the rug again, arms splayed open in *savasana* now, and talks to the sky as she says, 'What I hate about this thing, the vaccination thing, is that no one seems to be OK with me not knowing what to do. The NCT girls actually grabbed their babies to keep them away from Coco when I said I had some doubts. They're all vaccinating, of course, so that's what they want me to do. I hate it when people do that, when they obviously want you to choose what they've chosen simply to make themselves feel better about their choice.'

Bry looks at her sister. With her bare feet and the small, dark features of her face scrunched up against the sun, Jessie looks exactly as she did when she was a little girl. For as long as she can remember, Bry has always felt a complex mix of feelings towards Jessie. She feels protective, like a big sister should, but simultaneously and privately jealous. Matty was safely away in The Rowans before the bullies could get to Jessie. Bry hadn't been so lucky. For all her school life, if she ever stumbled or coughed or did anything to draw attention, someone would push their tongue behind their bottom lip and curl their hands into fists and gurn and moan in Bry's blushing face, and everyone would laugh.

You're just like your brother the spaz!

Bry spent her school days trying to be invisible while Jessie was outgoing and popular. And that's not all Jessie was spared. She was too little to lie awake listening to their mum sobbing with guilt and grief; she didn't have to pack her own school lunch because Dad was busy with work and Mum was busy with Matty.

She doesn't blame either of her parents for their absence but it is something she knows Sara feels guilty about. Sometimes, after Matty had demanded even more of her than usual, she'd come into Bry's room, her face twisted in anguish, and she'd hug Bry as if she was going to suck the life out of her and she'd say, 'I love you, Bry, I love you so, so much.'

And Bry, holding her sobbing mum, would wish Sara loved her a little less.

Coco starts to squirm in Bry's arms, her little bud mouth puckered and sucking hopefully at nothing until, offended by the lack of nipple, she breaks into loud bleats. Bry carefully passes her back to Jessie and finds a cushion so Jessie can feed her comfortably. As Coco sucks at her mother's breast, she stares up at Jessie as if she's the sun, and Jessie, smiling, shines back at Coco as though her daughter is the world. Bry feels another twist of jealousy. Oh God, she wants that again.

The front doorbell rings. Bry looks at her watch; it's only half eleven. Rosalyn said she would come over 'later'; Bry assumed that meant the afternoon. She checks her phone: no text.

'Who's that?' Jessie asks.

Bry shrugs and winches herself up off the rug as Alba appears, dripping and muddy, from around the corner and bellows, 'Doorbell, Mumma, doorbell!'

Rosalyn is wearing blue workman's trousers, cinched together at the waist with a black belt, and a man's white shirt. Her skin is unusually matt, as if she's been baking; there are dust traces in her eyelashes.

'Hi, Bry,' she says, smiling and opening her arms. 'Beautiful day.'

'Rosalyn, hi,' Bry says, moving aside. Rosalyn's shirt strokes her arm as she walks past Bry and into the hall. Even though Rosalyn hasn't been to their house before, she leads the way, Bry padding behind. In the kitchen, Rosalyn looks around, but she doesn't say anything about the huge marble worktop or the glass extension or their designer Eames chairs. Instead Rosalyn moves towards a small blue painting of Ganesh, throwing gold leaf in an arc around his elephant head. Ash bought it for Bry on their honeymoon in Kerala.

Rosalyn looks closely at the Ganesh and says, 'What beautiful leaf work – so much more effective when it's restrained like this.' Bry is a little disappointed she doesn't ask where they got it from; she wants Rosalyn to know she's travelled, that she's had adventures too.

Instead she asks, 'Tea? Coffee?'

Rosalyn raises one slim, silvered hand, palm flat and facing the floor. It's shaking ever so slightly.

'Better stick to tea. I've had three of Rafe's coffees already.'

Elizabeth had rolled her eyes when she'd mentioned him to Bry: 'I just find it a bit, I don't know, a bit gross, like she's a teacher having sex with a pupil or something, do you know what I mean?' Bry laughed at Elizabeth but said nothing. She didn't find it gross at all, quite the opposite in fact.

'So I just wanted to check in to make sure the noise from my work isn't annoying.' Bry tries not to let her disappointment show – she'd been hoping Rosalyn wanted to ask her something more intimate, or maybe even invite her over.

'You mean from your sculpting?'

'Yes, Rafe pointed out that it can be quite noisy. He's aware of that kind of thing in a way I'm not, I'm afraid.'

'Oh, no, seriously, it's no problem. It just sounds like summer noises, like a lawn mower or something. Don't worry at all.'

Through the glass extension Bry sees Alba leaning on Jessie's shoulder, staring at her auntie's pale, engorged breast as Coco sucks away. Alba is transfixed, a little horrified. She's trailed muddy footprints across the rug. Bry feels Rosalyn looking at them too. 'Oh, sorry, that's my sister Jessie, and of course you've met Alba . . .'

But just then Bry's phone starts to vibrate – she usually keeps it on silent, ever since Alba and Ash made 'Crazy Frog' her ringtone. She's got no idea how to change it; Alba thought it was so funny she wet herself. Bry had turned up the volume this morning so as not to miss a text from Rosalyn. Rosalyn looks amused and says, 'Go ahead, I'll go and say hi,' as she steps out of the glass doors and walks towards Jessie, Alba and Coco. Bry hesitates when she sees who's calling – 'Row' flashing up on the screen – but she's already ignored two calls from her this morning and doesn't want to risk Row popping by, so she answers.

'Hi, Row. Sorry, this isn't a great time, my sister is—'

'That's fine. I'm busy too. I just want to say, what the fuck? Two emails and now a text?'

'I know, I know . . .' Outside, Alba waves to Rosalyn before pointing at Jessie's breast and starting to laugh.

'I just think it's so wrong that she's stigmatising our kids. I mean, I'd get it if they were sick, but they're healthy kids with robust, natural immune systems. Steve is fuming. He says he doesn't want Lil going to the party now.'

'So maybe just don't go then.' Rosalyn is bending over Coco now and Jessie smiles, enjoying the admiration as Alba starts rooting through Jessie's handbag.

'We can't just not go – Lil and Clemmie are like best friends, they'd both be devastated. And besides, I'm not going to let Lil miss out just because Elizabeth's mental.'

'But didn't Lil have most of the vaccines anyway?'

'I made it sound that way to keep Elizabeth off my case. She hasn't had the second MMR or anything, thank God.' Row pauses for a moment and adds, 'I think I'm just going to ignore the email.'

'Good luck with that.'

'What about you, what are you going to say?'

Row is one of the few people in Farley who knows about Matty and knows that Alba isn't – *wasn't*, Bry thinks with a pop of fury – vaccinated. She doesn't want to tell Row about Ash, not now anyway, so she says, 'I'm not sure, I'll probably have a chat with Elizabeth about it. We'll find a way. Look, I'm really going to have to go, Row. My sister will be wondering where I am.'

'Fine. Well, let me know how it goes.'

'Yup, sure.'

Bry hangs up quickly.

A few minutes later, Bry steps out to join the two women on the grass, carrying a pot of tea, mugs and biscuits on a tray, and a towel for Alba slung over her arm. Jessie is feeding Coco at her other breast now and Rosalyn is sitting on the grass, leaning back on her arms, her legs crossed in front of her, a ladybird walking up one brown leather sandal. Alba's skipped away to play with her buckets of water again. A telltale half-empty packet of chewing gum pokes out of Jessie's bag. Jessie's talking, animated, tugging at her short hair, a habit she formed during exam time at school; she says it helps her concentrate.

'Yeah, but you know, everyone used to think cigarettes were harmless – people even thought they were *good* for you – until everyone started dying of emphysema in their forties and getting all sorts of cancers.'

Bry puts the tray down on the rug with a little clatter. She feels as though the vaccine issue is infecting her whole life, wishes they would talk about something else, but as soon as there is anything on Jessie's mind, it's out of her mouth. Bry casts a quick glance up at Rosalyn, but she's looking at Jessie, her face impassive, as if she can't read what Jessie's thinking.

'Oh, tea! Thanks, Bry,' Jessie says, dabbing a muslin around Coco's mouth and manoeuvring her huge breast back into her bra before adding, 'What the fuck is it with all these ladybirds?' and waving the muslin to bat a couple away from Coco.

'My boyfriend looked it up – something about the climate, some sort of freak plague or something . . .'

Jessie, who wasn't looking for an actual answer, listens to Rosalyn politely before asking, 'Do you fancy a cuddle?' then adding with a scoff, 'Of the baby, I mean.'

Rosalyn beams – 'Oh, I'd love one' – so while Bry pours tea, Coco's tiny body is handed over, and Rosalyn rocks her gently back and forth, Coco frowning up at her as Rosalyn smiles down and says, 'Anyway, going back to the vaccine thing, I think you're right to question it, Jessie, I really do.'

'Thanks, Rosalyn,' Jessie says, sloshing tea as she takes a mug from Bry who is now kneeling on the rug. Bry remembers how inscrutable Rosalyn had been at the barbecue when they'd talked about vaccines. Her silence had spoken volumes.

Rosalyn keeps talking. 'And yes, you're right when you say improvements in our living conditions, sanitation, good nutrition and all that must really help keep the nasty stuff at bay, but—'

'So you looked into it for your own kids, did you?' Jessie asks, dunking a biscuit into her tea and drawing her knees up to her chest. Jessie has never had a problem with interrupting people.

Rosalyn shakes her head and says, 'Oh, I don't have children myself, but I have plenty of godchildren and a niece and nephew, so I remember my friends and sister having these same conversations. They sent me some articles about toxin overload, about social responsibility, that kind of thing.'

'And?'

'Well, I remember at the time people were especially concerned about aluminium in vaccines. But one article I read said we ingest more aluminium every day than is contained in any vaccine—'

'Uh huh. But then we're not injecting aluminium and other stuff straight into our bloodstream. Anyway, go on, what else?'

Bry frowns at her sister. *Jesus, let the woman speak, Jessie!*

'There is this other thing I remember, that I thought was interesting: whether you see your child's or your own body as something dangerous, potentially contagious to others, or whether you see it as something very vulnerable, something that needs to be protected.'

'Uh huh. Yeah, I feel that,' Jessie says, nodding and looking admiringly at Rosalyn. 'The thing is, I kind of agree with the theory of vaccines, I just don't know how relevant they are any more. I mean, there hasn't been a wild polio virus in the Western Hemisphere since 1991 – at some point, surely we have to recognise some diseases are no longer a threat.'

'In America, they even vaccinate against chickenpox.' Bry can't help chipping in; Jessie has taken enough of Rosalyn's attention already.

Rosalyn nods, thoughtful.

'I suppose in this country we see chickenpox as something inevitable, something kids just have to go through, just like our parents treated measles. But then you only need to hear one horror story about a child who is seriously affected by chickenpox and that might persuade you to have the vaccine, right?'

'Assuming the vaccine is safe,' Jessie says, holding up her hand, 'because that's not a given for everyone.'

Here we go. Bry feels coldness seep into her abdomen. *Here comes the Matty reveal.*

'Our brother Matty is in a home thanks to vaccines, and your neighbour Elizabeth, their little girl Clemmie had awful fits so she can't be vaccinated, isn't that right, Bry?'

Bry nods and feels a rush of panic as she always does whenever her family and her best friend are mentioned in the same sentence. She waits for Rosalyn's response to the Matty revelation, the pity, the sorrowful but intrigued expression that says, *I'm sorry; but tell me more, tell me more, tell me more!*

But instead Rosalyn just nods and says, 'That's sad.'

Then she turns back to Coco, who has started wriggling in her arms and lets out a damp-sounding fart. 'Oh, wow!' Rosalyn says, smiling at Coco. 'I think that is my cue to hand you back to Mama.'

Later, after Jessie and Rosalyn have both left and Alba's in bed, it's just Ash and Bry and the noises – cutlery against plates, corks out of bottles, the clearing of throats – that are suddenly so loud now they're not talking to each other. Ash is bent over loading the dishwasher as Bry says she's going to bed. It's only half eight, but she has a good book and a bed all to herself since Ash is still sleeping in the spare room, and besides, she wants to be where he is not.

Ash stands up from stacking their plates and says, 'I was kind of hoping we could talk tonight.' Bry stops in the doorway, turns towards him as he adds, 'It's been five days already.'

He looks so hopeful, his eyes pleading. Bry is struck by the thought that what is unfurling between them is his nightmare – another marriage possibly failing, another child who might grow up with parents who no longer love each other. But she won't be softened by his sad, brown eyes. He's done this, he vaccinated their child against her will – he's made Bry's nightmare her reality, and he's responsible for the consequences, not her.

'What do you want to say?' Her voice weary, cold.

'I want to say sorry. I shouldn't have gone behind your back.' His voice weary, sad.

'So why did you, Ash?'

'Because I was frightened. I was frightened of something happening to Alba and I was frightened of losing our friends.'

'Why would we lose . . . ?' But Bry doesn't finish the sentence because there's something more important she needs to say. 'But you were willing to risk losing me.'

'No, Bry, please, will you sit down with me? Just for a few minutes?'

She sighs; she sounds overly theatrical, like Alba when she's told she has to get dressed. Ash beckons towards the sofa in the sitting room, but Bry heads instead to the kitchen table. She mustn't be too comfortable, too relaxed; it might weaken her resolve.

He sits opposite her and she gestures for him to say whatever it is he wants to say. 'I told you already about my ex-colleague Mark whose little girl died of meningitis. Then there were those letters from the GP.' He shuffles his feet under the table. 'The final straw was when Jack asked me on a run about that email for Clemmie's party. I either had to lie to one of my best mates or basically stop being friends with him. I felt like I had no choice and I was pissed off about it. So I called the GP – they had an appointment just come up on Monday afternoon after a cancellation, so on a whim I took Albs after I picked her up from nursery.'

Bry pictures the nurses in their staff room, giving each other high-fives, thrilled they'd finally got her Alba. A clap of anger thunders through her. 'I've spent my life, my whole life, living with the consequences of vaccines and you decide to put our daughter, my Alba, at risk – *on a fucking whim?*' She shout-screams the last bit; she feels reckless, like she needs to smash something, but she swallows it and instead walks away from the table and says, 'I'm not ready for this, I'm not ready,' and she runs upstairs to their bedroom, *her* bedroom, and wishes there was still a lock on the door.

Alone now, Bry's not sure what to do with her anger and she's too wired to cry, so she runs a scalding-hot bath and lets her skin scream. She used to do this as a teen when the bullying was bad. It's not the same as cutting but the pain is helpful; it bleaches out her thoughts. She's tired of thinking. She only manages to stay in the bath for a few minutes before she gets out, her body dripping, red and pulsing. Still wet, she lies back on the bed to enjoy the numbness but her phone buzzes on the bedside table next to her. She doesn't move, just glances at the screen where the message is displayed. It's from Elizabeth.

> Bry, I know you're busy, but your silence is starting to worry me – Albs is vaccinated, isn't she?

Ha. Elizabeth's timing is always impeccable. At least now Bry knows what to say; the answer is clear and obvious. She picks up the phone and types:

> Sorry, sorry, thought I replied earlier. Yes, Alba is vaccinated.

Then she drops the phone and rolls into a foetal position to wait for the tears to come.

18 July 2019

Jack is awake but dozing when he hears Elizabeth muttering to herself from outside the bedroom window that frames the sherbet early-morning sky: 'So selfish,' and then 'Unbeliev-able.' He knows what Elizabeth's doing without having to open his eyes. She's done the same the last few mornings, while hosing the roses, the delphiniums and hydrangea bushes so that rivers of water would carry away the white dust that so offends her – the combination of the ladybird invasion and now the dust is too much for her. Jack rolls over, away from the window. 'Please let it go,' he'd begged when she got out of bed at 6 a.m.

But Elizabeth seems to think she can control the universe if only she tries hard enough. It was pointless asking, he knew, but he still hoped one morning she might shrug her slender shoulders, say 'Fuck it', and get back into their warm bed.

At the foot of their bed, on the floor, is Elizabeth's little wheelie case he bought her for their tenth anniversary three years ago. It's already packed, ready for Elizabeth's weekend with Charlotte in Cornwall. She's leaving first thing tomor-row morning for two nights. Jack has today and Friday off work and he knows the kids are already plotting what take-away they'll order, the beaches they'll visit and the films they'll watch. It's the start of the summer holidays and they're all fired up. Jack is looking forward to being with the kids – just him and them – more than he feels he can say aloud.

From the other side of the hall he hears a door open and little feet scuttle across the landing, before the old brass doorknob to the master bedroom starts to rattle. Jack pulls the duvet over his head just in time as the door bursts open, the room fills with poorly suppressed giggles, and suddenly there are warm, skittish hands under the duvet, tiny mammals trying to tickle his feet.

'Daddy! Daddy!'

Jack stays perfectly still for a few seconds.

'Daddy?'

He loves how she still falls for this trick. Suddenly, in a great roar, he pulls the duvet off his head and grabs his squealing daughter, singing 'Happy Birthday' to her and pulling her down on to his chest so he can wrap his arms around her and cover her neck and face in kisses, which always makes her whole body grip and twist with laughter.

'I can't believe today is today, Daddy!' She smiles her gap-toothed smile at him and sneezes hard three times before saying, 'I'm Happy with a capital H!'

She rubs her eyes and lies back, her red head on Jack's chest, and she plays with his fingers, plaiting them with her own and watching how the early-morning light dances between their palms. While Clemmie chatters about the magical day, the magical summer ahead, about popping candy and mer-maid tails, Jack kisses her forehead and thinks, *Yeah, yeah, all those hours on the train to work, the time away from the kids, worrying about money – right now, it's worth it. It's all worth it.* He only wishes Elizabeth were next to him so she could feel it too.

The morning passes quickly in a whirl of orders from Elizabeth. Max and Charlie help the bouncy-castle men before going back to their cricket stumps. Jack makes sandwiches for the kids while Elizabeth lays out glitter, neon paints and huge pieces of paper outside for a bit of entertainment between lunch and the magician. Clemmie is tasked with hauling upstairs into the boys' room their family coats and shoes that usually overflow into the hall. She sneezes hard, three times again, and Elizabeth – who is up a ladder hanging the 'HAPPY BIRTHDAY' banner that gets brought out for all the kids' parties – stops Jack on his way back to the kitchen from the loo as she spiders down the ladder.

'Jack, seriously. You've got to say something to Rosalyn; I'll bet she'll listen to you. It's her dust that's making Clemmie sneeze like that, it's got to be.'

Elizabeth's always tense before throwing a party, but even more so before a kids' party. Jack knows it's because she's desperate for it to go well for their sake, and it's exacerbated today because she's going to Cornwall tomorrow. She'd sent Jack an email at 1 a.m. that morning telling him exactly what food she'd left for the kids and reminding him of their snack preferences – an orange for Max, grapes for Clemmie. Her micromanagement makes him feel like he's at work when he's at home, constantly watched, assessed and always found wanting. He hadn't minded it so much when the kids were tiny, fragile things he was terrified of dropping, but now they're small people her instructions make him feel like a clumsy hired helper and not their dad. But Jack knows now is not the time for his feelings. Today it's all about Clemmie, and he wants this to go well for her just as much as Elizabeth does.

'Would you go and talk to her now, Jack? I'm just so worried we'll be in the middle of the magic show or something and she'll start making a racket and won't even be able to hear us telling her to shut up.'

'Elizabeth, she knows the party's today, she's not going to—'

'Jack, please, please.'

She's leaning in towards him, subtly pushing him towards the door. It's easier to do as she says than argue.

'OK, OK, I'll go.' And Jack suddenly finds himself standing outside Number 8. He knocks twice and is about to leave when the door slowly opens. Rosalyn is wearing an oversized man's white shirt, clearly just out of bed, and not at all the kind of thing Jack imagines Rafe would have in his wardrobe, but then maybe it's not Rafe's shirt – *Ha! Good for you, Rosalyn.*

'Rosalyn, sorry to disturb you early.'

'Hi, Jack,' she says, her voice still slurred with sleep. 'Isn't it about 10 a.m.?'

'Half past, actually.'

'Oh.' She half smiles, half grimaces, but she clearly doesn't care it's so far into a beautiful Thursday morning, she doesn't care at all. Jack wants to hug her for reminding him of this way of living; he wants her to tell him the secret so maybe Elizabeth would lie in bed with him until the sun was high and forget what she was wearing when she answered the door.

'How can I help?'

'Elizabeth just asked me to pop by to check whether you were planning on, um, planning on doing any work in the garden today?'

Rosalyn smiles.

'I have absolutely no plans to do anything today.'

'Lucky you,' he says, meaning it. 'Well, come over for a drink later if you fancy. I'm sure a few of the parents will stick around for a while.'

'Thanks, I might pop over.'

Somehow Jack knows she won't and feels, absurdly, like he's been rejected.

'Oh, there was one other thing actually. Um, Clemmie, our youngest, has been sneezing quite a bit recently, and we were just wondering whether . . .' He stalls, finds he can't ask what he's been told to ask, so Rosalyn helps him out.

'I'm the same. Does she have hay fever?'

'Of course.' Jack nods at her; why hadn't they thought of hay fever? Didn't Clemmie have it towards the end of last summer? Or was that Charlie? 'Of course, it's hay fever.'

'Hang on, I've got something that might help.'

Rosalyn disappears into the dark of the hallway and as she walks back, she's squinting at a little brown bottle in her hands.

'I don't have my glasses on, can you read the label?'

'Allium cepa, ambrosia and something else I can't pronounce . . .'

'Wyethia?'

'That's it.'

'Try her on this remedy for a couple of weeks and see if things improve.'

'This works?'

'Worked a treat for me, and it's totally side-effect free and won't make her feel like a zombie. Two pills in the morning before she has breakfast.'

'Wow, thanks, that's really kind. We owe you a drink for this.'

But Rosalyn just shakes her head and says, 'Consider it a little birthday gift for Clemmie. Hope it goes well today.'

She sounds like she wants to get back to bed, and Jack holds the brown bottle up to her and says, 'Well, thanks again.'

'Any time.' She waves before closing the door.

Elizabeth tries to smother her laughter when, back in the garden, he shows her the brown bottle.

'Oh, Jack.' She smiles. 'You actually think this will work?'

'Worth a try, isn't it?'

She kisses his cheek but he can feel her shaking, her mirth bubbling over.

She shakes her head and cups her hand over her mouth for a moment, trying to wipe her smile away before she says, 'Sorry, but I'm not giving these to Clemmie.'

'Why not?'

'We have no idea what else could be in it, no idea where Rosalyn got it from, if she put it together herself. We know nothing about it, Jack. I'm not giving it to her – end of.'

'And what about me?'

'What about you?'

'What if I want to give it to her?'

'Mu-uuum . . . we've finished the balloons. Can we check the score now?' Max is standing in the garden door, holding Elizabeth's laptop, Charlie's little face poking out behind him.

Without looking at Jack, Elizabeth starts walking quickly towards them and says, 'Hang on, Max, let me come and check the balloons,' and Jack is left standing on the grass on his own, holding the little bottle of pills and feeling like a ghost in his own life.

When the doorbell rings at half eleven, Max presses play on the playlist, and the first little girl arrives in a puff of pastel to the sounds of vintage Beyoncé, and everyone – even the boys – tense and then seem to reset into a new calm. Now the cake is decorated, the magician knows where the loo is and all the hundred balloons are tied up and bobbing about the house, the nervous anticipation – the worst bit, Jack hopes – is over. Max and Charlie slink away to their cricket stumps as it suddenly dawns on them that their house is about to be infiltrated by an army of seven-year-old girls. As soon as Ash arrives with Bry and Alba, the two men open beers and keep themselves looking busy by offering drinks as the guests shuffle in.

They haven't talked properly since the barbecue over a week ago, which is unusual for them. Ash had texted, trying to arrange a pint a couple of times, but Jack said he was too busy with work. He'd had to walk home carefully on those two balmy evenings, ready to hide in case he ran into Ash. But since Bry had at last responded to Elizabeth's text, confirming that Alba had been vaccinated, he felt easier. The whole thing had been like passing through a cool shadow, clammy and uncomfortable, and Jack was relieved it was over.

'Has work eased up?' Ash asks, already cracking open a second beer.

'Oh yeah, yeah, it's fine,' Jack replies, before Ash says, 'Shit, mate, that reminds me, I still haven't put you in touch with that recruitment guy. I'll get on to it later tonight – sorry, mate, totally slipped my mind.'

'No worries. We've all been busy . . .' Jack says, before adding, in a rush of camaraderie, 'I'm so relieved Bry finally got back about the vaccine thing. It was weighing on my mind, to be honest.'

'Oh yeah?' Ash clearly doesn't know what he's talking about.

'Didn't Bry say? She didn't come back for a while, you know, to that email. Anyway, it was just Bry being a bit forgetful. I knew, of course, that you believe in vaccination but, I don't know, it was weird, Elizabeth kept mentioning it. I'm just relieved, that's all, just relieved.'

Ash smiles as he lifts his beer bottle towards Jack, and the two men clink glass as Ash says, 'Me too, mate, me too.'

To Jack's immense relief, he doesn't hear anything else about the email until Row and Lily arrive, Row clutching a poorly wrapped gift in her heavily ringed hands – Steve is nowhere to be seen again. Lily explodes through the front door, throwing a quick wave towards Elizabeth. Row chastises her daughter: 'Lily, say hello to Elizabeth and Jack, please!'

But Lily ignores her and springs away, towards the bouncy castle.

'Lil's foot must be better then,' Elizabeth says, by way of greeting.

'Her foot?'

'From the barbecue, the rusty nail.'

'Oh, that – my goodness, I totally forgot. Yes, healed perfectly, knew it would.'

Elizabeth's face puckers slightly; it's Jack's cue to step in.

'Row, how are you? Can I get you a drink?'

'Hi, Jack. Oh, I'll just have an elderflower or something.

Where should I put this?' Row gestures down to the gift, which looks as if it's trying to burst out of its wrapping.

'That's kind, you really didn't need to—'

'You can pop it on the side in the kitchen,' Elizabeth interrupts, and just before Row starts to walk towards the kitchen, before his wife has opened her mouth, Jack knows what's coming and he wishes he could run out of the door.

'Row, you never got back to my email or texts. I know Lily had a few early vaccinations, but you have kept up with them, haven't you? I'm not asking for me, I'm asking—'

But before Elizabeth can finish, they all turn towards a loud commotion from the garden – a chorus of adult and children's voices, some calling for 'Mummy' but most calling 'Elizabeth', and through the kitchen window Jack sees the bouncy castle starting to deflate, a tower already flaccid and bending in on itself towards a little girl with pigtails. Jack doesn't recognise her; she must be a friend from school or ballet or one of the other hundreds of clubs his daughter attends that he has never taken her to, because instead of being with her he's in meetings about secure parking for his clients' Porsches. The little girl is falling dramatically and laughing, delighted by the attention of being the only one left on the castle.

'Oh, shit!' Elizabeth says under her breath, and Jack follows her as she rushes into the garden and tries not to care that no one, not even his own kids, called his name.

Ash stands alone, his back against the garden wall, and watches the magician over a forest of small heads.

'Who can find pink rabbit? What's the magic word – Abraca . . . !'

Things could be worse, Ash thinks; he could be that poor sod. The magician must be in his fifties. He has the haggard, haunted look of someone who has made a whole career out of fake smiling.

The beer bottle makes a satisfying hollow glug sound as he takes another big drink and searches for the familiar, dark figure of his wife. Most of the adults are huddled, chatting in small groups on the patio, standing close to the French doors, as though they are only half committing to being at the party at all. Jack, a bowl of Kettle chips in his hand, is talking to Mai's mum – Ash identifies the adults through the kids he knows from taking Albs to various singing groups, swimming and the park. Jack's looking around him, as though he's smelling the air, and says, 'You're right, they have disappeared, haven't they?'

They must be talking about the sudden departure – or death – of the ladybirds. They mysteriously vanished overnight but are still the main topic of small talk.

Next to them there's a larger cluster of parents, standing rigid as posts, chatting politely to each other. *Ahh, there she is*, in her red cotton dress, at the snacks table listening to Row, who'll no doubt be talking about something batshit crazy. Ash raises his bottle again as he stares at his wife. Yes, he still fancies her, no doubt about it. She has this undone look, as if she's just fallen delicately from a tree, that Ash finds incredibly sexy. She sits back in her chair, her cheeks dimpling as she smiles along with whatever hippie nonsense Row is wittering on about. There are a few screams from the kids, making the adults turn towards them as the magician pulls out a wolf puppet from inside his black cloak.

'AHA!' he howls as the wolf, guttural, as though he's about to hawk up from his lungs.

Alba – who is cross-legged in the front row, chin skyward, mouth agape – suddenly gets up and, balling her fists, runs her fastest run and crashes into Bry's lap. Bry immediately adjusts her body to contain her daughter's panic, her delicate fingers stroking Alba's hair, and she bends down to whisper something reassuring, loving, before she looks up quickly, her dark eyes on Ash, as if he's just said her name. He smiles, raises his bottle towards her, but she just frowns at him slightly, as if he's a stranger and she's caught him staring. Ash feels drawn towards them but also like a voyeur. He takes another long pull on his beer and his wife stops frowning as she turns back to her friend. He wishes he could be more like Alba, able to run to Bry, collapse in her lap, to feel her gentle hand on his head. Prone like that, he'd ask for forgiveness for going behind her back and she'd give it immediately and without reservation. He craves her forgiveness. He knows what he did was wrong, but he can't regret it. From his point of view, he'd had to choose between risking his kid's health and risking his wife's anger. He loves Bry, no doubt about it, but he'd choose her anger any day. No, she'd really given him no choice. He only hopes that in time, when her anger passes enough for her to admit that Alba is unchanged from the vaccines, she might come to understand he did it out of love. He'd left the Mark Clancy article, with its final plea (*For God's sake, I beg you to learn from Rosie's death. Vaccinate your children*), just by the kettle in the hope that Bry would read it properly, soften, but their cleaner had tidied it efficiently away before she'd had a chance to see it.

He feels foolish now, standing by this wall behind the kids, who are twitchy and distracted from having to sit still. He looks about for Jack, but he's become one of the shadows Ash can see moving around inside the kitchen. Ash takes another deep gulp of beer. He's thought about talking to Jack about what happened between him and Bry. But he's not sure he'd be able to put the feeling, the fear of losing Bry and Alba, into words. He's fairly sure he wouldn't survive. The grief would suffocate him, like sand poured down his throat and into his lungs.

He finishes his beer in a final swig and is about to go and find another when Bry, with Alba in her arms, starts walking towards him across the lawn, Alba's legs swinging like undone shoelaces on either side. He pushes off from the wall and starts going towards them, opening his arms to his family. But Bry can't open hers back so Ash holds them both in a sloppy hug for a moment, aware that Bry is looking around at the other parents, nervous probably that they might be seen like this. He lets his arms drop and inwardly he says, *I'm sorry, I'm sorry.*

He stops his fingers from tucking her hair behind her ear; he won't let himself stroke her cheek. He says, 'Everything OK?'

She turns back to him. Her eyes seem to reflect his own expression; they are distant, lifeless.

'She's knackered, swimming must have taken it out of her this morning. I think I need to take her home.'

'I'll take her, you stay here and catch up with people if you like?' Usually Bry would jump at the chance to have some child-free time on a sunny day, to have a few drinks with her friends, float dreamily home whenever she felt like it. But now they are strangers again, she won't leave Alba with him in case, presumably, he finds someone else to jab her with a needle. She shakes her head.

'No, I'll go. You stay. I forgot my keys though, so can I take yours?'

Desperate for any scrap of opportunity to help, Ash fishes in his pockets for his keys. Bry jostles Alba's weight in her arms; she'll be getting heavy now.

'At least let me carry her home, then I'll go out again if you want space.' Bry looks at him as she considers whether this will work for her.

She nods her assent and then kisses her daughter's cheek before she starts to peel her hot, sticky little limbs away from her neck. 'Sweetheart, Daddy's going to carry you home.' Normally Alba would squirm, protest loudly at being taken away from her safest place. She must be really tired; all she can muster is a quiet moan.

She clamps her arms and legs around her dad and hides her little face in his neck, and Ash feels a flutter of hope because Bry doesn't shrug him away as he puts an arm lightly on her shoulders to guide his family home.

Ash doesn't want to go back to the party but he knows Bry probably wants him gone, so while she's putting Alba down for a nap, he pours himself a quick glass of wine. He opens the fridge, unloads the dishwasher, looks through some mail and glances at his watch. Bry should have been down by now, surely; Alba was asleep in his arms when they got home. He pours another wine and empties the recycling. He finishes his wine and walks slowly upstairs. It's quiet. He crosses the first-floor landing; Alba's bedroom door is ajar and he creaks it open. His girls are lying on their sides, curled towards each other in Alba's little bed, Bry's arm draped protectively around her daughter. Their breath is like rolling waves, rhythmic and vital. They are both fast asleep. He moves slowly, doesn't breathe. He wishes he could pull back the covers, lie behind his wife, but there's no room for him, so he sits on his heels next to them until his feet go numb and he's run out of words begging her to love him again.

Farley County Court

December 2019

I walk past the county court twice a day from the kids' school to my office management job and back again. I keep my head down as I walk. I know the pattern of chewing gum spat out and stuck fast to the slabs. There are always more cigarette butts, more sweet wrappers directly outside the court, as though people gorge themselves before going to court, just in case they don't come out again. Often there are more people as well – 'Excuse me, excuse me,' I say, too quiet for anyone to hear as I pass.

Today there are protestors as well as photographers. I stop to watch them, wonder briefly how it would be to feel that strongly about something. A man with a banner that reads 'Where there is risk their must be choice' stands on my foot, but he's too busy waving his banner to notice. I want a big black marker to correct his stupid spelling. But the woman next to him, carrying a placard, hers with a photo of a grinning toddler on the front, does notice.

'Did he just stand on you, love?'

It feels weird to be called 'love' by a woman who is about the same age as me. She puts her hand on my arm and I try not to step away as she says, exasperated, 'Men, eh?' like we've been friends for years. It's only been a few seconds, but somehow the group has enveloped me; I'm being swallowed by the jostling crowd, all fists and solidarity.

'You with us, love?'

The woman still has her hand on my arm.

'No, no, I've got to pick my kids up from school.'

'Oh, right,' she says. 'Here, let me help.' Still holding on to my arm, she breaststrokes through the crowd, away from the courthouse. When we're on a quiet patch of pavement she says, 'Phew, that's better.'

'Thank you.'

'How old are they?'

I must look dumb; she adds, 'Your kids, how old are they?'

'Oh, Bethany's eight and Freddie is six.'

'Lovely names.' She smiles. 'Are they vaccinated?'

I nod. No one's ever asked me that before.

I didn't even know it was a choice. I just did what I was told. Like going to the dentist, paying my taxes and getting through the working day.

'So was my Seb,' she says, looking up quickly at the photo on her placard. I see the horrifying dates underneath his face.

'Oh God, I'm sorry, I'm so sorry.'

'He died in my arms, a week after he had the MMR.'

My throat seizes. I can't talk about this. How can this woman still be alive? Privately, I always knew I'd have to kill myself if Bethany or Freddie died.

'You know there are things you can still do, to counteract the damage from the mercury, aluminium and all the other crap they injected into your kids' blood.'

I look up at her, feel my mouth open.

'Oh yes, sweetheart, there are poisonous metals in vaccines. Ever wondered why there are so many kids now with behavioural problems, anxiety, allergies, depression? Life is supposed to be better than ever before, so why are we so sick, so miserable?'

This woman is asking the question I can never find the right words to ask. I feel it, I just don't know how to say it. Both Gareth and I work hard to give the kids everything: a nice house, new computers and two weeks' holiday in Spain every year. We fixed grins on our faces and asked, desperate, 'Are you happy?' when they unwrapped their iPhones at Christmas. But still Bethany had to go and talk to that counsellor when she couldn't stop crying, and Freddie was put on medication for ADHD.

'What are we doing wrong?' Gareth asked, back from another twelve-hour shift, weary and ashen.

Before me, the woman keeps talking. 'Five pharmaceutical companies literally run the world. Why? Because they are making billions and billions a year from vaccines that are making us sick, which of course makes them more money, and on and on it goes.'

She pauses; I blink.

'I'm not alone. I know, personally, over a hundred families who have the same experience. The story is always the same – their child had a vaccine and then their child changed. Autism, loss of motor skills, behavioural problems, respiratory failure, you name it. Does it make sense to you that a ninety-kilo man will get the same amount of vaccine as a nine-kilo, one-year-old baby girl? No, of course it doesn't. Those toxins flood her little system; she can't detoxify the same way a ninety-kilo man can. But it costs more to produce different, safer vaccines and there's no profit in it, so the huge companies won't do it. And what's more, she's not just getting a few vaccines. No, by the time a child is five years old – just five – they'll have thirty-five different vaccines. That's a hell of a lot, a hell of a lot of toxins.'

She stops suddenly. 'God, sorry. Sorry, love, I'm doing it again, going off on one.'

She is going off on one but I don't care. I want to hear this. I need to hear this. I wish Gareth was here.

I feel like this woman is tuning my life, from the white noise of sadness, confusion, into quiet focus. Now I think about it, don't Freddie's mood swings get worse, almost violent, after he has the flu vaccine at school every year? And didn't we get Bethany's first pink inhaler from the doctor just a month or so after her second MMR? Why have I never made the connection before? I feel lightheaded but refreshed, awake. I take the leaflet the woman is offering me: 'Vaccine Freedom' is written across the top. I don't flinch as she kisses my cheek and asks, 'See you at the meeting then, OK, love?'

19 July 2019

Bry is fast asleep in her own bed when a cry rips through the house. Before Alba was born she could sleep through ambulance sirens, foxes barking and Ash snoring, but she is finely attuned to Alba's cry.

Bry's head feels light as she sits up in bed, her legs watery and unstable beneath her as she pads across the hall and into Alba's room. From the glow of the nightlight Bry can see that Alba has kicked her duvet away. Heat radiates from her and her head is damp with sweat. She's feverish, murmuring, but her eyes are still shut. Bry tries to think what she should do, but her mind feels sticky, unresponsive. She should take Alba's temperature. Yes, that's what she should do, but then she can't think where the bloody thermometer will be – it should be in the family bathroom cupboard, but wasn't Alba playing with it in the playroom the other day? Maybe Alba should have a drink of water? There's none by her bed – yes, she should go and get some from . . . Alba murmurs again and Bry turns to leave but it's as if she's turning in slow motion.

She almost screams when she walks straight into Ash, standing in the doorway of Alba's bedroom in his boxer shorts. Ash puts his hands on her shoulders. 'Hey, Bry, Bry, it's OK.' He says, 'What's going on?'

'Water, I need to get her water.' Even though she only had one glass of Prosecco at Clemmie's party the day before, Bry feels as if she's woken to a jangly, confusing hangover. Everything feels critical and yet totally insurmountable.

'Please, Ash, just move so I can get her water.'

'OK, OK.'

Ash steps aside and Bry's legs seem to walk of their own volition to the bathroom. The bright bathroom light feels like acid in her eyes. She finds a glass and pours it half full, then uses the wall to help steer her back to Alba's room. Ash is sitting on Alba's little bed, stroking their daughter's hair away from her ear, an electric thermometer in his hand. Bry propels herself towards them, offering the glass to Ash who puts it on the floor before inserting the thermometer gently into Alba's ear. It beeps and Ash leans towards the light to read it. His eyes grow and then shrink. He shakes the thermometer, then his head, and says, 'Thirty-nine.'

Bry grips her own head. That's high. She knows she needs to do something to help Alba, but what? Ash looks up at Bry but she wishes he wouldn't; she wishes he'd just focus on Alba. She feels giddy again and finds the wall. Ash leaps up and suddenly he's almost carrying her back to their bedroom. 'No, Ash – Alba! Alba needs us, we can't go—'

'Bry, you feel like a furnace. You need to be in bed. I'm going to help Alba.'

He eases her back into bed and immediately Bry feels herself melt, her eyes burn with relief as she closes them. 'You'll stay with her? Promise me you'll stay with her. Don't leave her alone.'

'I promise, Bry. I'll stay with her. You need to sleep now.'

And just before Bry does as she's told, she could swear she hears him say, 'I love you.'

Hours later, Bry opens her eyes. From the way the sun slices high through the curtains she knows it's late. Her eyes are slow to focus. She works out that curled up next to her, but turned towards the window, is her sleeping daughter. Alba's kicked the sheets away and Bry watches her back rise and fall through her pyjamas. She wants to move towards her, to shadow her little body with her own, but when she tries, her head starts to crash and scream, so she stays still. Beyond her daughter there's the ancient leather armchair Ash inherited from his uncle decades ago. Slumped asleep in the chair is Ash. He's still only wearing his boxers, his chin touching his chest and his hands laced over a hardback book open in his lap, which Bry immediately recognises as *The Natural Family Doctor*, a gift from Sara when Alba was born. He's asleep but still alert; Bry staring at him is enough to wake him. His eyes go from shut to wide open immediately. He sees Bry and is up and by her side before she's registered what he's doing.

'Morning, morning,' he whispers. He's whiskery, his face droopy with tiredness, but his eyes are alert. Slowly, heavily, Bry tries to lift herself up. Ash helps her, props up pillows behind her. She looks at the water glass on the bedside table and Ash helps her drink.

'How are you feeling?' he asks softly, kneeling down next to the bed, mindful of Alba still asleep so close to them.

Bry asks herself the same question. Her body throbs, she can feel every beat as the blood pulses through her veins, and she feels acutely, painfully aware of the sun, the texture of the sheets against her skin, the pounding in her head.

'Awful,' she rasps back at him.

'Where does it hurt most?' he whispers, urgent.

Bry touches her head – her hair is brittle with dried sweat – and then she realises that's wrong: everything, everywhere aches. But that doesn't matter now.

'Alba,' she asks, 'how was she last night?'

'You were both pretty unsettled, hot and feverish. I thought it best to bring her in here so I could keep an eye on both of you.'

'You were here all night?'

Ash looks away for a moment, suddenly made shy by his own dedication. Bry lifts a hand up towards him, rests it on his cheek, which feels both bristled and soft. He puts his hand over hers and in that brief moment, in that simple touch, they start to heal.

Apart from brief visits to the bathroom for the loo or a luke-warm bath, Bry and Alba stay in bed all day. Ash gives them ibuprofen, which Bry accepts without argument, and sits in the middle of the bed reading *Alice in Wonderland* aloud. He feels his whole world in this bed, safe. He was scared during the night when it was dark and he felt powerless, but in the daylight, nursing the people he loves most, he feels happier than he's felt in a long time. Ash only leaves their side to make toast or to get them a warm drink when neither of them eats the toast. It's Friday and he decides, while Bry and Alba are napping, a squiggle of limbs and curly dark hair, to call the doctor's surgery before they close for the weekend. The receptionist offers a telephone appointment, which in a way is a relief. Neither of them wants to get out of bed and Ash doesn't want to break the spell cast by their new togetherness by dragging them to the surgery. The locum doctor Ash is transferred to sounds tired, weighted down by the week. He says it sounds like a viral fever – there's nothing they can do apart from hope their temperatures decrease, drink fluids and rest.

'I see Alba recently had her vaccination for meningitis and pneumonia.'

'Yes, yes, that's right,' Ash says, keeping his voice down even though Bry's asleep upstairs. He chooses to ignore the thought that flits into his head like a mosquito – *But what about the others? What about the vaccines she hasn't had?*

'OK, good. Well, call again if they're not any better by Monday.'

Ash hangs up, unsure whether he feels reassured or not. But then Alba calls from upstairs, 'Daddy, where Fred got to?' and he realises the reassurance he is seeking was upstairs all along. It feels good to be needed, to be useful. He skips up the stairs and doesn't even grumble when Bry asks him to get the homeopathy box she keeps in the spare room. He can't imagine ever wanting to cast a snide remark or tease Bry again. He kisses her hand and feels reborn by her forgiveness.

Later in the afternoon, Ash drapes a duvet over the sofa in the TV room, makes sure they each have water and plenty of pillows, then tucks them up. They lie together, fingers interlinked, Alba resting against Bry, as they start to watch *Paddington*. Ash changes the sheets on their bed upstairs, airs the room and chucks out discarded tissues. Then he opens the fridge and makes a brief list of the things they need – ibuprofen, soup and tissues most vitally. He hates to leave them; it feels as though something awful is more likely to happen if he isn't there, watching, ready to spring to their rescue. He's about to triple check they're OK when he has an idea that would save him from having to leave them to go for supplies at all. He picks up his phone.

'Hi, mate.'

'Ash, you all right?' Jack sounds uncharacteristically stressed, a little out of breath. There's the sound of the TV in the background, but then Ash remembers that Elizabeth is away; the TV will probably be on all weekend, a small rebellion.

'You sound like you're feeling the pressure.'

'It's Clem, mate.'

Ash immediately regrets his teasing tone; Jack is serious. The mosquito starts to whine inside his head again.

'What's up? Is she sick?'

'Yeah. She's had like a crazy fever and says she has a headache and stuff. Anyway, I took her to the doctor and he said—'

'You spoke to the locum?'

'Yes, yes, that one.'

'And let me guess, he said that it's a viral thing and not to worry?'

'Yes. Exactly, how did you . . . ?'

'Albs and Bry are the same. Are the boys OK?'

'Oh, shit. Sorry to hear that. Umm, Charlie has a raised temperature and says he feels rotten but he's not as bad as Clemmie. Max stayed at his friend's place last night so I don't know about him.'

Ash slaps the mosquito dead and feels the muscles in his chest relax. Charlie is fully vaccinated. If he's sick too, then most likely the doctor was right; their temperatures will come down and they'll all be fine in a day or two.

'Mate, what shitty timing with Elizabeth away. Look, I'm going to go and pick up supplies for Alba and Bry – can I get you guys some stuff too?'

Jack reels off a few items that Ash adds to his own list.

Ash is standing in front of the refrigerated soup section when he feels a hand on his back. *Oh, please not now.* He wilts internally when he sees Gerald in an emerald green waist-coat, grinning up at him as if he's got the best gossip on the tip of his busy tongue.

'Soup?' he says, eyes round in mock horror. 'In July, Ash?'

Ash makes himself smile. 'It's for the girls – they're not well. They've rejected everything else I've made them, so chicken noodle soup is my last resort.'

'Poor loves,' Gerald says, 'miserable to be ill when it's so glorious.' Ash casts a quick glance over Gerald's shoulder where, outside, the world seems to sparkle. He hadn't even registered the weather on the walk to the supermarket. Gerald keeps chatting. 'Chris's been moping around all day too, convinced he's dying *again*. Silly bugger. He really is the biggest hypochondriac I've ever—'

'What's up with Chris?'

'Oh, a headache, feeling chilled, that sort of thing. I don't actually need any of this stuff' – Gerald gestures to his shopping basket, full of expensive cheese and white wine – 'I just had to get away from his moaning for an hour or so. Honestly, he acts like he's the only person who's ever—'

'Odd question perhaps, Gerald, but Chris has had all his vaccinations, hasn't he?' The whining has started in Ash's head again, distant but there. Definitely there.

Gerald frowns, tugs a little at the thin scarf around his neck, then laughs. 'Ash! He hasn't got the pox! He's just a great windbag who likes to have a moan.' Gerald stops laughing and says, 'God, you're serious, aren't you? Yes, yes, I'm sure he has. What with Chris's heart thing, Dr Whateverhisnameis is always on at him; yes, I'm sure.'

The whine in Ash's head recedes; he's paranoid, that's all. Tired and overreacting.

'Is there something going on, Ash, something you should tell me?' Gerald cocks his ear towards Ash; no news is ever too small for Gerald.

But Ash just smiles, shakes his head and says, 'No, no, I'm just messing with you, there's nothing to worry about at all.'

Gerald touches his chest with his fingertips and says, 'Well, thank *heaven* for that.'

The door to Number 10 is unlocked, so Ash lets himself in and takes the bag of shopping Jack requested towards the kitchen. It's jarringly quiet, the kind of quiet that doesn't suit family homes full of children. The kitchen is littered with used coffee cups and cereal bowls; Jack can't have had time to tidy up since breakfast – Elizabeth's absence writ large. He's impatient to be home with Alba and Bry but he can't leave the kitchen in this mess. He starts to stack the dishwasher, the cups clashing against each other, so he doesn't hear the gentle slap of bare feet on tiles as Charlie walks into the kitchen.

'Oh, hi, Uncle Ash!' Ash looks up from the dishwasher. Charlie's wearing pyjamas, his dark blond hair tufty on one side from where he slept. One look at his clear bright eyes, his healthily rosy cheeks, and Ash can tell he's not sick. Not like his girls.

'You feeling better, Charlie?'

Charlie nods, starts poking around in the shopping bags. 'Did you bring us crisps, Uncle Ash? I'm *starving*.'

'Um, no.' He reaches into his own shopping bag, finds the packet of popcorn he bought for Alba as a treat when she's feeling up to eating again. 'But you can have these.' He throws the bag at Charlie, who whoops and pulls himself up to sit on the countertop – never allowed when Elizabeth's home – opens the bag and starts munching.

'Clemmie's sick,' Charlie says through a mouthful of popcorn.

'Yeah, your dad said. Is he upstairs with her now?'

Charlie nods, sombre. 'Mum's coming home early from her trip. Dad promised us we could go to the cinema tonight but I bet we can't now, which is so annoying.' Charlie's face brightens suddenly with light cast by an excellent idea. 'Could you take us, Uncle Ash?'

'Oh, mate, no, I'm sorry. Alba and Auntie Bry are sick too – I'm going to have to stay with them.' Charlie lets out an exaggerated groan. Ash ruffles his hair and says, 'Sorry, mate. Tell your dad I'll call him later, OK?'

When Ash gets home, Paddington Bear has flooded the bathroom and Alba has fallen asleep, mouth slack and open, in Bry's arms. Ash notices the thermometer and *The Natural Family Doctor* open on the floor by the sofa. He kisses Bry on her hot cheek and whispers, 'How's her temperature?'

Bry points for Ash to get the remote control. He pauses the film and sits carefully on the ottoman opposite the sofa. Bry's eyes are darker than normal, despite her flushed cheeks. 'It's the same,' she whispers back. Her eyes aren't darker, of course; it's something else, something fearful, that makes them seem darker. Ash feels his pulse start to quicken.

'What is it, Bry? There's something else, isn't there?'

She nods, her eyes filling; now he's back, the anticipation of sharing whatever it is that's making her so afraid is almost making her cry.

'Look at this.' She tilts her head back and opens her mouth, keeping her tongue down, and Ash peers inside, unsure what he's supposed to be looking for. Bry points to the inside of her cheeks and Ash sees what she's getting at. On the inside of both cheeks there are some small, white spots. Bry closes her mouth.

'I think they're called Koplik's spots. They're one of the symptoms of, um . . .' Her tears break and Ash holds her hand. 'I looked it up. They're one of the symptoms of measles.'

'Measles?' Ash says too loudly; Alba twists in her sleep.

More tears fall as Bry says, 'Look,' and she gently smooths Alba's hair away from her forehead. Along the hairline, running down towards her cheeks, is a flame path of red pimples.

Ash squeezes his wife's small hand and whispers, 'OK, OK. She's going to be fine. You're both going to be fine.' Bry nods along but the tears still fall, splashing down on their sleeping daughter.

'I read up on measles last night – the vast majority of people fight it off without any complications. All our parents had it when they were kids, remember? It was treated just like chickenpox is now – it will be OK, Bry.'

Bry laughs, splutters through her tears.

'You sound just like Mum,' she says.

'God, I do, don't I?' He raises his eyebrows dramatically so

Bry can't tell whether he's taking the piss or not. 'Well, she's a very wise woman.'

Bry laughs again before starting to cry, harder now. Ash strokes her cheek, careful not to disturb Alba. She doesn't explain why she's crying and he doesn't ask, not now. Instead he carries Alba, lost in sleep, back to their bedroom and they all get into bed together, Ash stroking Bry's dark hair until she too falls asleep.

20 July 2019

The journey home was expensive and painful. The short flight from Newquay to Gatwick was twenty minutes delayed, which almost made Elizabeth scream; the slow walkers, the flight attendants with their painted, vacant eyes, all seemed to be moving against her, just when she needed the world to work well.

It's past midnight by the time she gets home. She runs through the chaos of the house, the trainers and coats scattered on the floor, the plate with curling pizza left on the sideboard. The house carries the smell of her family – their unique brew of muddy trainers, grass and old furniture. The bergamot and herby smell of the spa – Elizabeth had gone to town on the free products – that had seemed so heavenly now feels suddenly brazen and wrong. All wrong. Like a little girl wearing lipstick and false eyelashes.

Elizabeth runs upstairs; she'd called Jack from the cab so she knows he's in their room. She opens the door slowly. It's dim inside. One of Jack's T-shirts is draped over the lamp by his side, presumably to keep the room as dark as possible. Jack is half sitting, half slumped in bed, his hand on Clemmie's back, rising and falling. Elizabeth moves, magnetised, towards her curled, still daughter. Her red hair is splayed out on the bed, as though she's underwater. The light is too low to see much. She looks a bit flushed and she's gripping their thick, winter duvet – which Elizabeth had packed away in the attic a couple of months ago – under her chin, but apart from that, she looks normal. Jack dozily opens his eyes, watches Elizabeth, her hand hovering just over Clemmie's sleeping body, not wanting to disturb her but needing to feel her life warmth. *Thank God I'm home.* It seems insane now that she'd ever wanted to leave them, that it had been exciting to be away. Elizabeth glances at Jack, who looks like he's just got back from a stag weekend. 'Hi,' he whispers. She kisses his cheek. He smells like a dirty laundry basket. She puts her hand on his before turning back to Clemmie.

'When did she fall asleep?' Elizabeth reaches out to stroke the silky ends of Clemmie's hair.

'About an hour ago, just after we spoke.'

'You took her temperature?'

'It's still hovering around the thirty-nine mark.'

'And you haven't seen any spots on her chest yet?'

'Not since you asked an hour ago, love.' Elizabeth had refreshed her chickenpox knowledge on the way home. Max had it as a baby but Charlie and Clemmie haven't. She leans in towards Clemmie, tries to lift her pyjama top away from her chest to peer down.

'Don't, don't disturb her. She needs to rest.'

Elizabeth pauses. He's right, sleep is the best thing for her now. 'I'll call the out-of-hours surgery in the morning.' She starts to scribble a to-do list in her head.

'Like I said, the locum is convinced it's chickenpox and just keeps telling us to wait it out like any other virus.'

'Yes, but I want to double check. And you didn't tell the doctor that she isn't vaccinated, did you?' She doesn't mean to sound accusatory, not now, not when Jack's been looking after everyone on his own, but she can't help it – she can feel the old fear start to prickle behind her eyes. Now she's home she needs to take control.

'Elizabeth, like I said on the phone, he'll have seen that in his notes and besides, it isn't relevant because whatever Clemmie's got, Alba and Charlie have got too, just probably not so badly.'

'You said Charlie was better.'

'He said he was still achy and had a headache when he went to bed tonight. He didn't even fight for more TV.'

Elizabeth puts the back of her hand on Clemmie's forehead. It's damp, hot. A ripple passes beneath her eyelids. Elizabeth hopes it's a dream moving within her, a dream full of her favourite things – mermaids and ponies. Elizabeth's just about to go and check on her sleeping boys when on the bedside table, Jack's phone starts silently flashing – it's Ash. Jack glances at it and looks back at Elizabeth. 'He's called like five times tonight.'

'Well, shouldn't you answer?' Elizabeth's voice is too loud; Clemmie stirs then stills, her hair a river behind her. They both glance at her before turning back to each other.

'He'll just be calling to check in again. He's been really worried about Clemmie, which is good of him, considering Albs and Bry are both sick.'

'You didn't say Bry was ill too.'

Elizabeth picks up Jack's phone; it's flashing, urgent in the still room. That's why Bry hasn't answered Elizabeth's texts. But why would Ash be calling so late? Maybe something's happened, maybe he needs help. She stands up from the bed and, walking towards the door, answers the phone.

'Hello, Ash?' she says softly into the phone.

'Elizabeth!' There's a brief pause. 'You're home.'

'I cut my trip short, got in just a few minutes ago.'

'Ahh.' She hears one of their £620 chairs (Elizabeth had googled the price) scrape back across the polished concrete kitchen floor. 'How's Clemmie?'

'Fast asleep. Her temperature is the same, hovering around thirty-nine. I'm thinking it's probably chickenpox. I'm going to call the surgery again in the morning. How're Alba and Bry?'

He doesn't reply.

'How are the girls?' she says again, more slowly this time. 'Ash?' she says, louder.

When he does finally talk, his voice is muffled, restricted, as though he's laying his head down on the table.

'Elizabeth, I need to tell you something.'

'What is it? Is it Alba?' Elizabeth's throat seizes as hard and tight as it would for one of her own children. 'Ash!' she says, fear making her impatient.

Ash breathes out before saying, 'It's not chickenpox. They don't have chickenpox, Elizabeth.'

'What? How do you—'

'They have measles,' Ash interrupts, his voice clear for the first time.

'What? That's ridiculous, they can't have measles. Apart from Clemmie, they're vaccinated, they can't have . . .' But she runs out of words because a continuous, high-pitched note strikes up in her head and all those never-had conversations, all those times she tried to bitch to Bry about selfish, hippie parents who choose not to vaccinate, all those times

Bry squirmed away, now hit Elizabeth in a great flood of memory. Then she remembers, more recently, her friend's text, her own relief.

'But Bry said, she said in her text that Alba was vaccinated.'

'Pneumonia and meningitis.'

'What?'

'She hasn't had the MMR, Elizabeth, and neither has Bry. They have measles and I'm so, so sorry but Clemmie probably has it too.'

'But Charlie, Charlie is sick and he's had all the vac—'

'I saw him today. He's not sick. Not like these guys are sick anyway. I looked it up; sometimes vaccinated people can have very mild symptoms of the virus if exposed. It could be that.'

She drops her arm, the one holding the phone, to her side. She doesn't feel anything, not yet. It's as though everything is coming into focus, but this new clarity makes less sense than everything did a few seconds ago.

Jack comes out into the hall, mouths, 'What is it?' and, without saying anything, she hands him the phone and he says into the receiver, 'Mate? What's going on?' as Elizabeth walks quietly past him, downstairs into the kitchen.

Led by the thumping of her heart, she walks to the dresser and for the first time in her life, Elizabeth wants to break things. She picks up a huge mug – she could do it, she could just let it smash to the floor – but then she sees the faint painted outline of Max's baby feet. They made it when he was just a few months old, she can't break this one. She picks up another but it's the one her dad used to like when her parents came to visit. The plates? No, they only have ten matching plates; it wouldn't be worth it. By the time she's found a bowl that's bland and unlovely, perfect for a sacrifice, the urge has gone. Instead of throwing it down on the floor, she slumps to the ground herself. She wants to cry, painful, ripping sobs, but she can't. They fucking lied. *She lied.*

Through the creaky floorboards Elizabeth hears Jack moving around upstairs, his voice. She stands, the bowl still whole in her hand. She places it back on the dresser before she goes upstairs to lie next to Clemmie and silently beg her forgiveness.

She doesn't know how long it is before Jack comes and sits on the bed next to her. She feels empty, emptied. Jack clears his throat.

'I called 111, love. They said we need to keep Clemmie out of public spaces, that we should ask for a GP to come here tomorrow instead of going into the surgery on Monday; they'll do tests to confirm whether it's measles or not. She said the rash usually starts on the forehead and that Clemmie might have little spots with white bits in the middle in her mouth.' Elizabeth knows all this, of course, but she lets Jack talk. 'They said we need to keep her hydrated and to keep a note of her temperature every few hours. They said ibuprofen and paracetamol are fine. She was pretty reassuring actually; she says measles is uncomfortable but it goes away and Clemmie will be fine. Don't forget, just a few years ago measles was treated like a rite of passage, like we treat chickenpox. She'll be better in no time.'

She knows he's repeating verbatim what he just heard on the phone, that he's trying to soothe, but she wishes he'd just shut up. She can't, she won't be soothed. Not now. He seems to understand and at last he stops talking. They sit in silence for a moment before Jack pulls his T-shirt away from the lamp to let more light into the room. He gently bends over Clemmie, brushes the hair away from her forehead and squints down at her. Elizabeth raises herself up on one elbow. She needs to see. There, as if competing with her freckles, creeping down Clemmie's forehead is a cruel mist of red, a vapour of infection, staking its rights over her little girl's body.

Elizabeth lies sleepless next to Clemmie until the first rays stroke the curtains just before 5 a.m. She feels like she did that first morning after her dad died. She woke early then too, in her North London flat, but then Bry was the one in bed next to her; she'd barely left her friend's side until the funeral. Clemmie splutters, coughs and frowns in her sleep. Elizabeth gets up – she's planned what she needs to do and she wants to make a start before Clemmie wakes. She finds the baby monitor stored away in the attic with tiny baby grows and soft play mats. She sets up the monitor in their room and then goes to the kitchen. She loads, washes and wipes and then she starts cooking. She makes stews, pasta sauces and casseroles, stuff that will keep and stuff she knows the boys will eat. While the pots are bubbling she makes a list of all the things they need more of – painkillers, cold and hot compresses, fruit for juicing, sausages, potatoes, Epsom salts and Olbas oil for the humidifier – the list goes on and on. She'll give it to Jack as soon as he's up. Yes, yes, this is good. She can handle the sadness, as long as she keeps moving. She makes a big batch of beetroot, ginger and carrot juice – the boys will need their immune systems boosting too.

Clemmie stirs with a cry just before 7 a.m. and Elizabeth's foot is on the stairs before she can cry out a second time.

Clemmie is sitting up in bed. She's kicked the sheets away and is rubbing her eyes with bunched fists, but when she sees Elizabeth she holds out her arms towards her and says, 'Mummy!' and then she breaks into tears. Elizabeth gathers her daughter gently into her arms before perching on the edge of the bed.

'Hi, my poppet,' she says, kissing her cheek, her red hair, any part of her, before sitting back a little to look at her face. The rash has spread – it's already down below her neck – and her eyes are the colour of diluted blackcurrant cordial. She'll have to try her best to keep her away from mirrors for the next few days.

'Oww!' wimpers Clemmie and she starts rubbing her animal-red eyes, her voice growing to a wail as she says, 'My eyes hurt, Mummy, they hurt.'

'We'll ask the doctor when she comes over for something to help with them, OK, poppet? Here, try not to rub them so hard. Where else hurts?'

'My throat and my head and just everywhere, everywhere hurts,' she says, dissolving into tears again. Elizabeth gives her the last of the child paracetamol and rocks her back and forth, back and forth, until she feels Clemmie's grip soften and she lays her back, asleep again.

The out-of-hours doctor, a Dr Mayhew, rings the bell on the dot at 10 a.m. The boys are out on the lawn with their cricket bats and Elizabeth has just finished putting away the shopping Jack brought home. Clemmie is on the sofa in the sitting room with the curtains drawn against the sun. It hurt her eyes to watch TV, so now she's listening to the Harry Potter audiobook. Elizabeth opens the door to a slim woman with a short bob and fashionable thick-rimmed glasses. She shakes her hand and beckons her in with a smile, thinking, *Shit, she can't be more than thirty.*

'Can I get you a cup of tea or coffee?' Elizabeth asks but knows immediately Dr Mayhew will shake her head. There's something off about her; she's unsmiling. Isn't part of a doctor's job description to be good with people? She glances upstairs, looking for the patient, like a plumber eager to fix a dripping tap so she can get on with the next job.

'Clemmie's in the lounge, through here.'

As soon as they're with Clemmie, Dr Mayhew thaws, but still she hardly looks at Elizabeth and Jack.

'Morning, Clemmie.' She stops to listen to the audio. 'Oh, which one is this, is it *The Philosopher's Stone?*' she asks, pulling up an armchair. Elizabeth turns the audiobook off as Dr Mayhew listens to Clemmie's heart and lungs, looks in her mouth and checks the spread of the rash, all the while chatting about Harry Potter – 'Which house are you? I'm Gryffindor all the way.'

Elizabeth can tell Clemmie likes Dr Mayhew; between coughs and splutters she describes in detail the Harry Potter wand she got from Auntie Bry, Ash and Alba for her birthday. Even just hearing their names makes Elizabeth's heart punch inside her chest.

'Mummy said I have measles,' Clemmie says to Dr Mayhew, serious suddenly.

'Yes, it's looking very likely you have measles, Clemmie. There have been a few other cases reported locally too.' She answers without even checking Elizabeth's around to hear. *What's wrong with this woman?*

'What I'm going to do now is just use this little stick to get some of your saliva, which scientists will check in a lab. Is that OK?'

'Saliva means spit?'

'Yes, that's right.'

'OK then.'

Dr Mayhew pats Clemmie's hand and Clemmie waves goodbye, and Elizabeth turns Harry Potter back on before she follows Dr Mayhew back into the hallway. Dr Mayhew's eyes frost over again and she scribbles a prescription as she says, 'So, I'm sure it's measles. We'll have these tests sent to the lab today and we should have the results to confirm hopefully by the end of the day. Measles, as I'm sure you know, is the world's most contagious virus, so *they'll* take it very seriously indeed.' Why does she emphasise 'they'll' like that? As though implying they – Elizabeth and Jack – are not taking it seriously?

'Here's a prescription for vitamin A to help prevent the infection spreading to her eyes.' She hands over a scrap of green paper to Elizabeth. 'Public Health England will be in touch. They'll want to ask you some questions, probably today, to find out if Clemmie's been anywhere during the infection period, which starts about four days before the rash and lasts four days after the rash appears. So it would be helpful if you could try and think carefully about where she's been, so we can help contain the infection.'

'Well, I took her to the doctor's surgery, obviously,' Jack says, overly keen to help. Dr Mayhew sighs an irritated puff, which for Elizabeth translates clearly as, *You fucking idiots*.

'Sorry, *doctor*,' Elizabeth says, unable to stop the childish emphasis, 'but we've just found out our child is very unwell and I can't help but feel you're not being very empathetic during what is clearly a very stressful time.'

'Elizabeth . . .' Jack puts a hand on her arm.

'No, Jack, don't.' Elizabeth shakes him off. 'I don't think it's right that we're being treated with such blatant disdain while our little girl is—'

'Excuse me, Mrs Chamberlain. Before I accepted this job, I had been working in Kenya for a year in a health centre in a town called Nanyuki. I saw kids die from typhoid and rabies. I vaccinated the luckier ones, children who'd walk for miles and miles to get vaccinated. Why? Because they know; they've seen the devastation when kids aren't vaccinated. Did you know a measles outbreak this year in the Democratic Republic of Congo has killed more than six thousand people? That's far more than Ebola but measles isn't Ebola or SARS, so the deaths attracted relatively little international attention. Perhaps it is unprofessional but I am still finding it an adjustment, meeting families who have different views—'

'You think we didn't vaccinate out of choice?' Elizabeth's voice is loud, too loud for the small hall.

Dr Mayhew glances from Elizabeth to Jack and back to Elizabeth.

'It said on her notes that Clemmie is unvaccinated and that we shouldn't send any more reminder notices. I assumed—'

'Well, you *assumed* wrong. If you'd bothered to read our daughter's medical history, you'd know about her seizures as a baby, that we were advised by Dr Parker not to vaccinate.'

Dr Mayhew shifts from one foot to the other. She's uncomfortable, which is gratifying.

'I see,' she says. 'I'm sorry. I shouldn't have been so, um, so . . .'

'Rude?' Elizabeth offers.

'I shouldn't have been so short with you, yes.'

'Well, OK then. OK,' Elizabeth says, the pulse in her neck easing.

'Look, I should get these samples off as soon as possible. Just remember to keep checking her temperature and keep her on the painkillers if she needs them. PHE will be in touch for your interview.'

'But she will be OK, won't she? I mean, measles sounds scary now but . . .'

'She's a healthy little girl so there's no reason she won't recover in the next week or so. Just if anything changes dramatically, make sure you call the surgery. I'll be in touch about the results.' She manages to nod and smile at them both while struggling to open the front door, before Jack steps forward to help her out.

Public Health England call Jack and give a two-hour window during the afternoon when they'll come by for an interview. Elizabeth is bathing Clemmie and changing the bed sheets when the front door rings, so she misses the first half of the conversation. Once Clemmie's settled back in bed with Harry Potter again, Elizabeth joins Jack and a woman in her fifties at the kitchen table. The woman introduces herself as Angela. She's wearing a lanyard and has two thin horizontal lines for lips. Her eyes are small and quick, her hair mousy. Jack pulls back a chair next to him for Elizabeth.

'I've just been telling Angela all our movements over the last couple of weeks.' There's a piece of paper in front of him with a short list of places written in Jack's slanting capitals. Elizabeth sees 'Nettlestone Primary Fete' written at the top. He moves the list to Elizabeth and says, 'That's everywhere, isn't it?'

'Lansdowne Fish and Chips.' Elizabeth flushes; no one told her they got fish and chips while she was away. They must have all agreed to keep it secret from her. 'That looks right to me,' she says, and Angela nods and bows back over her paperwork.

'Dr Mayhew said there have been other cases reported locally,' Jack says as Angela's biro darts across the page. 'How many have you had?'

'I'm not really at liberty to discuss other cases . . .'

'No, I can see that, but it can't be that serious, surely?'

Angela puts her pen down with a little sigh and threads her fingers together. 'Farley and the surrounding areas have one of the lowest vaccination rates in the country. The vaccination rate around here hovers at about 83 per cent for the MMR. This figure does not include infants under one and people who can't be vaccinated – by whom I mean people who have cancer, or are having organ replacement therapy, for example – so the number will probably be close to 20 per cent of the entire population who aren't or can't be vaccinated. If you take into account that in a group of one hundred unvaccinated individuals exposed to the virus, ninety of them will catch the virus and seven of them will develop serious complications, then yes, it does become serious. It's even harder to contain when people are coming from abroad, having parties, going on holidays and so on, which of course at this time of year they are.'

She picks up her pen and continues writing.

'But measles isn't that bad, is it? I mean, it's not like polio or something, it's not—'

The writing stops again.

'In the UK, one in every fifteen cases will develop serious

complications like pneumonia or encephalitis, which is swelling of the brain. Most cases of course won't develop complications, but for the ones that do, it is very, very serious indeed.'

Elizabeth leans into Jack beside her. She feels exhausted suddenly, her head far too heavy for her shoulders. Jack puts his hand on her arm and neither of them asks Angela any more questions.

That evening, Jack drives the boys half an hour to the coast with their kites and a picnic. Elizabeth is almost broken with exhaustion, but the boys have questions and one of them needs to answer them. By 7 p.m. Clemmie is asleep again and Elizabeth has just finished the washing up, and all she can think about is crawling into bed beside her daughter when she sees a shadow pass in front of the stained-glass panel beside the front door. The shadow pauses for a moment and then starts to walk away. Adrenaline shocks through Elizabeth; could it be Bry? Would she really be so fucking audacious as to . . . Elizabeth opens the door to the warm evening. It's not Bry retreating through the little black gate but Rosalyn in an indigo ankle-length dress, barefoot of course. Rosalyn turns when she hears the door and both women stand for a moment, stunned by the other. On the doorstep is a large foil-covered dish.

'I didn't want to disturb you, but we were having tiramisu tonight so Rafe made an extra one for you guys.' Rosalyn gestures towards the dish at Elizabeth's feet but Elizabeth doesn't look down; she can't take her eyes off Rosalyn. It's a bit like falling in love only the exact opposite: she's falling in hate and it's just as intoxicating.

'How dare you?'

Rosalyn frowns, confused.

'You think this makes it OK, do you?' Elizabeth gestures down to the dish. 'Make us a pudding and we'll all forget your recklessness.'

'What's going on, Elizabeth?'

'What's going on?' Elizabeth laughs, and even she can hear the madness in it. 'My daughter has measles because people like you, people we thought were our *friends*, don't bother to stand up for what's right.'

'Elizabeth, I think you—'

'No, no, I was the only one who saw through your whole bohemian bullshit when you first arrived. I knew what you were talking about with Row at our barbecue, I could *feel* it – it's anti-vaxxers like you and her who have put my daughter in danger. You don't give a shit about anyone else. You think your ridiculous sculptures are more important than my daughter being able to breathe freely without dust damaging her lungs. You have no idea, no idea what it's like to be a mother, what it is to love someone more than yourself. You have no idea how *serious* these issues are, how hard I've tried to protect Clemmie. You jeopardise her safety every time you talk against vaccines – you're just as bad as them.'

Elizabeth points in the vague direction of Bry and Ash's house. She's panting now, surprised that Rosalyn let her vent without interrupting or shouting. Where's her anger, where's her fire? It's maddening.

Instead she just stands there. She's not smiling, at least. She's simply looking at Elizabeth, not in pity or anger, just plainly, as if they've been discussing the weather.

'Elizabeth, I know you're angry. I understand that.'

'Ha!' Elizabeth shouts. 'You have no fucking idea.'

'But you should know I fully believe in vaccines. I actually took my niece and nephew to get their vaccines when my sister couldn't face it. If I had kids they would be fully vaccinated.'

Elizabeth feels all her vital organs – heart, lungs, stomach, all of it – drop.

'But, but you gave Jack that bottle of homeopathic stuff for . . .'

Rosalyn nods, smiles briefly. 'Yes, I am into homeopathy for some things, but that doesn't mean I don't also believe in medicine.'

Just at that moment, the front door to Number 8 opens and Rafe's beautiful dark head appears. '*Tutto bene?*'

Rosalyn nods briskly at him. 'I'll just be a moment.' He casts a dark look towards Elizabeth, who has started shaking, her anger trying to find a new release.

'I'm sorry about everything, Elizabeth, truly. I don't think it's right that Clemmie is sick after you've done everything you can to protect her.'

A lump rises in Elizabeth's throat.

'It's fair enough you're angry.'

Elizabeth can't look at her any more. How is it possible that Elizabeth feels like the negligent one suddenly? Heat sears her throat and she turns and runs back into the house, only just shutting the door behind her before she sinks to the floor, the heat at last flaming out of her as she crumples into herself and sobs.

Farley County Court

December 2019

You could say I'm a bit like a superhero. Most of the time, I'm just Lisa from accounts with the gross skin, dumpy Lisa who always eats her lunch on park benches alone and checks her phone for no reason at all. Others have no idea who I am — they notice the carpet more than me.

'Who's Lisa then?'

'You know, the one with the glasses.'

Silence.

'The chubby one with, like, all the eczema.'

Silence.

'Bit of a weirdo, smells like Cheddar, definitely a virgin. Anyway, doesn't matter . . .'

Lisa Climp, that's me, but you'd be wrong to think that's all I am. When the mood takes me I transform myself into someone powerful, someone unafraid to say the things everyone else is thinking. I become WildMama.

Today I'm finishing my bag of crisps on the bench opposite the court and feel WildMama twitch inside. I smile and, wiping the salt off my fingers on my trousers, I take out my phone. I loosen up first on some of the nosier sites — join in with the crowds on Twitter for a while. A pop singer bit of fluff has filed a claim of sexual assault against a fan.

Lea Lande needs to put some clothes on and shut her ugly hole.
She wants to be raped.

Post.

*Not bad. A few other regulars get involved – liking and retweeting –
which is nice. I move on. A white politician has been filmed calling
Chinese people 'baked beans'.*

Hey, let's meet at Mr Evans's – we can chop him up along with his
ugly wife and brats – they'd be lovely in a tin with tomato sauce.
I'll bring the knives.

Post.

Ha. That felt good – politicians are always fun.

*Today though, I have a mission closer to home. I look up at the
crowds across the road outside the court room, stamping their feet and
waving their banners. When I heard about the measles outbreak, I
had to go to the bathroom and scratch till my arms bled and my nails
clogged with skin. Even the thought of a rash on top of my already
red, flaky skin makes me flare up. But WildMama doesn't have
eczema.*

*I click on the Farley Forum. There are pages of comments already
but no one else has the balls to get stuck in. I read a thread from some
patient recalling their beloved Dr Parker, who advised anyone suffering
with measles to take vitamin A to protect their eyes. This is Dr Parker
who, a few years back, prescribed me a cream that made my eczema
worse and told me to lose weight. I crack my knuckles.*

Dr Parker deserves to rot – I have proof that when he was a
doctor he used to touch up his own kids.

Post.

I don't have proof, of course. But this kind of work is all about confidence.

Some stupid anti-vax mums like the people outside the court are spouting off, saying catching the virus is better than getting a vaccine. I silence them with a reality check.

Silver lining: fucking stupid anti-vax offspring will be killed off – natural selection at work.

Post.

Time for one more before my lunch break is over, I think. I go for something well rounded, not too personal.

Anyone who doesn't vaccinate their kids out of choice deserves to watch them fucking die.

Post.

Right. Back to reality. Time for a cuppa.

23 July 2019

A ladybird ambles across the mirror as Bry stares at her reflection in the downstairs bathroom. She hasn't seen one in a day or two; most of them have vanished as mysteriously as they arrived. Bry flicks it away and it lands ungracefully on its back in the sink. She runs the tap and sluices it away before turning back to her reflection. She looks medieval – her hair is lank, unwashed, her skin chalky and her eyes small compared to the dark half-moons resting underneath them. Most alarming of all is the red rash that covers her whole body, as if she's been rolling in red paint. The rash is everywhere, on her eyelids even.

She leans in, closer to the mirror, and lifting her hair away from her forehead she can see that it's starting to clear; the skin is unmistakably lighter, like a break at the edge of a thick fog. It's leaving, four days after it arrived, like the ladybirds: an uninvited guest who has finally taken their cue. It's a good sign but she's not better yet – even after just a couple of minutes on her feet her head starts to fizz, so she reties her bathrobe and walks back into the TV room where Alba is propped up on the sofa, her thumb plugging her mouth, staring languidly at the television.

The room is a mess of untouched bowls of soup, beetroot-stained glasses from a juice Row and Steve left on their doorstep, and an upturned box of Lego – Ash whistled while he tidied this morning; he didn't mind that it was messy again. He doesn't seem to mind anything so long as Alba and Bry are improving. It's taking a while though. Alba only managed to play with the Lego for five minutes before she held her head and started crying again. Still, the fact that she's even trying to play is a good sign. Bry has become a magpie, a gatherer of good signs – sharp-eyed, ready to swoop in and add them to her precious trove. Alba eating toast this morning, for example, asking when she can go outside to play again: both good signs. Alba doesn't move as Bry strokes her hair away from her forehead. *Yes. Yes!* Her skin is paler here, it's definitely paler! Without moving her eyes away from the screen, Alba shrugs her mum off and Bry adds another good sign to her collection. But her own head still pounds like a drum and she holds on to the back of the sofa as she collapses next to Alba.

'I think we're getting better, Albs, I think in a couple of days—'

'Shhhh!' Alba says, frowning and sucking a bit harder on her thumb in irritation.

Bry lies back, closes her eyes and imagines Elizabeth and Clemmie, just a few metres away, doing exactly the same as they are, but in a tidier, more organised way. She sees Elizabeth taking Clemmie's temperature, smiling. *It's down to thirty-eight!* She pictures Jack refilling Clemmie's orange juice glass and laughing at the orange moustache around his daughter's mouth, sunlight allowed back in her bedroom. Yes, yes, this is how it will be, their way out. She's not so naive to think that she and Elizabeth will recover with rest and time from the virus infecting their friendship. No. Elizabeth will be angry, she'll be fucking furious. She'll need to vent and swear, she'll need to spit and hate Bry.

But, when Clemmie's fully recovered, trying desperately to play cricket with her brothers again, running to Elizabeth in tears when one of them calls her stupid, then maybe, maybe she'll soften enough to let Bry try and explain. She'll tell her everything she's never been brave enough to tell her before: the details about Matty, the bullying, her inherited terror.

Bry is lying back on the sofa but there's something hard digging into her. She reaches for whatever it is and pulls out Ash's laptop. She hasn't looked at her emails for almost a week. She opens up the screen and types in Alba's full name and birthdate – Ash's password for everything.

The screen flashes up; Bry squints away and presses the button to make it darker. Once her eyes have adjusted, she looks at the webpage Ash must have been browsing the night before. It's the Farley Forum. Bry has never been on it before, but Ash reads out extracts to her every now and then, laughing at how small-minded, how vitriolic, small-town issues like dog poo and rights of way can become. She's about to go to her email server when the bold words in the subject bar catch her eye: 'Farley Measles Outbreak'.

What? She hasn't heard it called an outbreak before – she's never thought of it like that, hasn't thought about people other than them and the Chamberlains getting sick, sitting on their sofas with fevers and liver-red skin. The first post is from nearly a week ago, the day before that first frightening night.

Hi, I haven't posted on here before but I have a nine-month-old son – too young for the MMR – and I overheard a conversation today in Farley that some local kids have been diagnosed with measles. I know how infectious it is and tonight my little one has a temperature. I'm hoping I'm overreacting, but I was wondering if anyone has heard anything about a local outbreak? Thank you.

The first reply, written just a minute later, says simply:

Yes. Be worried. Three of my daughter's friends – I'm guessing unvaccinated – were no-shows for their big summer play and I've heard of at least two confirmed cases. Thank God my kids are vaccinated. Call your GP.

As Bry scrolls down, the replies come either fast and angry or fast and fearful, the words shrieking off the screen, pages and pages of them.

MissyP: Ten cases reported at the school where I teach.

SkaterMan: Good. At least we'll know who the fucking arseholes are who aren't bothering to vaccinate their precious little brats.

Prue: @SkaterMan you are clearly very ignorant. I have the right to parent my kids and that means protecting their health from vaccine damage. Your name-calling isn't going to change anything.

SkaterMan: What about those parents who have a sick kid who can't be vaccinated or a baby too young to vaccinate? What about their rights? You're the ignorant one.

Bry flinches, keeps scrolling. She's numb with shock. Why hasn't Ash told her how far this infection has spread, how serious it is? When Jessie called three days ago and said she was taking Coco to visit her partner Joe's parents in Scotland, Bry thought it was a bit of an overreaction, but now, reading this, Bry can see her sister did exactly the right thing. The thought of a baby as young and vulnerable as Coco catching the virus is too much to bear.

> BossWoman: My son's longed-for summer school trip has just been cancelled because the place they were going has just heard about the Farley outbreak.

> TooMuch: @BossWoman oh your poor, poor son doesn't get to go on his school trip because so many kids are fighting a potentially deadly infection. POOR, POOR HIM.

> BossWoman: @TooMuch fuck you.

On and on it goes, with some saying the immunity from a natural infection is much stronger than from any vaccine, others pointing out the virus can stay in the body for years, ready to strike with seizures and comas at some unknowable future date, until one comment temporarily shuts them all up.

> WildMama: Anyone who doesn't vaccinate their kids out of choice deserves to watch them fucking die.

'How're my little zombies doing?' Bry snaps the laptop closed and shoves it back between the cushions before Ash kisses her red, speckled cheek and then turns to kiss Alba. She doesn't have the strength to mention the forum now, not when things are so good between them. He'll have kept it from her to protect her, of course, wanting her to focus on getting stronger, not fretting about other people. It makes sense – she'd have done the same, wouldn't she?

Ash is wearing shorts, a T-shirt and flip-flops: a cruel reminder that summer, with all its swimming trips, ice creams and picnics in the park, is happening right now, just beyond these walls.

'Daddy, don't call us 'ombies!' The credits are rolling on the TV screen, so Alba points a stern finger at him, her well-sucked thumb glistening. He sits down between them, pats Alba's leg and casts Bry a smile, but Bry can't smile back. She feels as though she's absorbed all the hatred online and it's now in her bloodstream, bitter and hot.

'Bry, love, you OK?'

'Yeah, yeah, I'm OK, I'm just suddenly feeling exhausted again.'

Ash's smile drops immediately.

'Why don't you go and have a sleep?'

'Yeah, I think I will.' She leans on his shoulder and pulls herself to stand. Her heart feels as flimsy as a plastic bag. She gives herself a moment to acclimatise to her new position. Ash strokes her hand and Alba says, 'Poor Mummy.'

'Just remind me what time Sara's arriving again?' *Shit, fuck.* Bry forgot her mum was coming to stay. She's been straining at the bit to come and nurse them, but Ash has repeatedly requested – to Bry's relief – that she give them space. It hasn't been easy, but Jessie unwittingly saved the day by stopping off to see their parents on the way to Scotland, and Sara has been on the phone to Bry at least twice a day since their measles diagnosis was confirmed.

'Her train gets in about four-ish, I think.'

Ash nods and says, 'OK, love. Try and sleep, won't you?'

As Bry walks away from them, she hears the plastic clatter of Lego being tipped out of its box again and Alba says, 'Let's make a 'ospital, Daddy!'

Two hours later, Ash is carrying Sara's bags upstairs. One of them, a tie-dye fabric thing, tinkles like a mini apothecary shop. As soon as she arrived, she was all over Alba, fishing for her glasses in her handbag before checking Alba's mouth, her forehead and lifting her pyjamas to see the rash, Alba giggling and squirming away from her granny's stroking fingers.

'Tickles, Ganny!'

It was so wonderful to hear his little girl laugh that Ash hadn't bothered to ask Sara to go easy.

He drops Sara's bags in the spare room and quietly opens the door to his and Bry's room. Over the last few days he's become a ninja at moving soundlessly around the house, never wanting a slammed door or heavy step to disturb his girls' precious sleep. Bry is still in bed, but she's not asleep. She stirs as the light from the landing enters the room.

'Ash?' she whispers.

'Hi, darling,' he says gently, approaching the bed, still in stealth mode.

'Has Mum arrived?'

'Yeah, she's downstairs with Albs now.'

Bry rolls over and reaches her hand out towards him. Her hand is clammy, warm.

'She won't stay for long, just a day or two, I promise,' she says.

'Well, judging by the number of bags I just carried in for her, I'd say she's got other plans, but don't you worry about that, love. Just rest.'

'You,' Bry says, her voice thick, 'you've just been incredible – thank you so much.'

Ash perches on the edge of the bed, still holding her small, blotchy hand. 'Bry, you don't need to thank me. I love you. Love you both so much. I'd do anything for you.' Although seeing them both so ill has been torture, there is also a part of Ash that feels grateful he's had this chance to prove his devotion. He's found a kind of masochistic relief in keeping vigil night after night, welcoming his own discomfort, exhaustion and anguish. He is, he's discovered, a fearful, loving and living person, just as much as anyone else, and he hasn't needed booze to prove it. He hasn't touched a drop all week in case he had to drive to pick something up or – God forbid – take one of them to the hospital.

But then all this positivity flies away because Bry starts crying, and through her sobs she asks, 'Do you think I'm a selfish idiot?'

'What, why would I ever think that?'

'Because of the whole vaccine thing.'

'Oh sweetheart, sweetheart.' He strokes the tears away before they can fall and dampen her pillow. 'I know you had your reasons and I don't blame you for that, I don't.'

A thought nudges to the front of his mind. He hasn't seen or heard from the Chamberlains. Jack's been ignoring his texts, which is fair enough – but maybe Bry's been trying to reach Elizabeth?

'Has Elizabeth been in touch?'

Bry shakes her head, closes her eyes and starts to cry harder.

'No. I've composed messages to her but haven't sent any.

Anything I say just sounds so fucking trite. She'll be furious. I don't know if she'll ever forgive me.'

Ash doesn't say anything because he's not sure he can imagine Elizabeth ever forgiving this either.

'Daddy! Ganny says I can have ice cream!' Alba shouts from the bottom of the stairs.

Bry manages to raise a small smile. 'It's good to hear her making a racket again, isn't it?'

Ash kisses her hand and says, 'Just try to rest, love. I'll tell your mum you're sleeping.'

Bry nods and snuggles back down into the bed, and just before Ash closes the door she whispers, 'I love you.' She hasn't said it in weeks and, for Ash, it feels better even than the first time.

That evening, Ash puts Alba to bed while Sara makes a vegetarian summer stew, and Bry gets up and joins them in her pyjamas in the kitchen. As soon as she sees her, Sara holds on to her daughter, eyes closed, in a suffocating hug, before running her through the same checks she performed on Alba – mouth, forehead, stomach. She looks carefully at Bry's rash, stroking, nodding and smiling as though it's a pleasing pet.

'Yes, this is good. The rash is receding well, the virus has almost passed through. Are you starting to feel better?'

Bry scrunches up her face and then widens her eyes to try and stop herself from crying, but the tears have already gathered and they start to roll down her red cheeks.

'Oh, my Bry-bug,' Sara says, taking up position for another crushing hug. 'Sweet love, I know it's not nice but you're both absolutely fine and even stronger for having gone through this.

This is just as nature intended.' While Sara tries to soothe, Bry looks at Ash over her mum's shoulder and he knows in one glance that Sara is wrong. Bry isn't worried about herself or even Alba; she knows they'll both recover fine. She's worried about Elizabeth and Clemmie. She's worried she'll never again drink gin and tonics in Elizabeth's kitchen and laugh at Elizabeth's impressions of the Farley mums; she's horrified they won't be godmothers to each other's children any more, that Elizabeth will no longer be the friend she can call when she feels fearful and alone.

Ash shakes his head at Bry, silently tries to tell her not to think like that, that they'll find a way: a way to apologise and a way to be forgiven. Bry doesn't respond. Instead she wiggles out of her mum's arms and Sara says, satisfied that her hug has done its work, 'Now, did that help?' before dashing over to the Aga to stir the simmering stew.

Before they eat, Bry goes upstairs and has a shower and Ash takes the opportunity to try and brief Sara, who is lining up little vials of ointments and pills on the table, occasionally stopping to read a label before shaking her head and returning the bottle to her bag.

'They're actually well past needing a lot of these remedies. I'd have been much more help if I'd been allowed to come earlier . . .' She looks at Ash, one eyebrow slightly raised so he knows she won't forget that he kept her away. Ash chooses to ignore her and she soon goes back to clinking her bottles. 'But I think some of the ointments might be good, just to help ease that—'

'Sara.' His serious tone makes her stop flicking through her remedies and turn to look at him.

'Can we just go easy on the vaccination chat tonight? I

don't know if Bry's told you, but our good friends the Chamberlains are upset . . .'

'Oh yes, Jessie told me about this. That Elizabeth sent a message requesting only vaccinated children play with her child, which is frankly prejudiced and short-sighted.'

'Be that as it may . . .'

'I mean, we know our family have very severe reactions to vaccines and so by not vaccinating them we are protecting them – just like she's trying to protect her child by not vaccinating.'

'Well, it was the doctors who said that—'

'All parents should try to protect their kids from illness, injury and other misfortunes but when they do occur – which they will, inevitably – it's about how we respond to them that matters. Don't you agree, Ash?'

'Yes, Sara, yes. Look, I agree with you, I do, I just want to ask, because Bry's clearly feeling wobbly tonight, that over supper we talk about anything other than vaccines and, you know, the outbreak. I just want her to feel stronger before telling her what's been happening around town.'

Sara looks at him, bites her lip and says, 'I think "outbreak" is a little dramatic but OK, I suppose it's your house, your rules.'

'Thank you, thank you, Sara,' Ash says, feeling more relieved than he anticipated.

Sara inclines her head, accepting his thanks before asking, 'Now, how about you open one of those expensive bottles of wine I know you have stored away?'

Ash smiles and nods, placing only one glass on the table before he says, 'Deal.'

*

Ash sits opposite Bry at the table, her hair wet around her shoulders. She looks stronger again, as though the shower has washed a little more of the illness away. Sara sits at the head, between Bry and Ash, and stands to ladle out the sinewy vegetable stew into the heavy bowls Bry made on a pottery course. Bry is quiet, distracted by her sadness. The atmosphere is tense.

'So Sara, how're Jessie and Coco doing?' he asks brightly, as Sara starts liberally buttering a piece of her homemade sourdough and Bry fishes her spoon around the lumps of aubergine and courgette in her bowl.

'Oh, Coco is just a little poppet! So like Jessie at her age, don't you think, Bry?' Bry takes a mouthful of something that looks like squash and nods her agreement. It's all the encouragement Sara needs. 'Of course, she's keeping Jessie up all night feeding, and you can really see it in her, she's got those sweet baby rolls around her wrists – you remember, Alba had them too.' The meal continues in this vein – Ash scrabbling around for a Sara-friendly question which, lubricated with wine, Sara answers in detail with Bry vacant, contributing as little as possible.

Ash feels he's on the homeward stretch when everyone declines the offer of seconds. 'Honestly, delicious, Sara. I don't think I've had a summer stew before.' He clears the bowls and is about to suggest that Bry get an early night when Bry picks up a copy of the *Neighbour* – the local Farley newsletter – on the chair next to her. She lifts it to the table and turns to the front page. Sara must have picked up a copy at the train station. Ash's heart drops. He's been so careful to keep the local papers out of the house.

The main headline reads 'Farley Quarantine Continues'

and underneath there are photos of two kids sitting on the beach in swimsuits, wearing blue medical face masks.

Bry stares at the photo, blinking and silent. Ash stands behind her, a hand on her shoulder.

'It's staged, sweetheart, they're trying to make out it's worse than it is.'

But Bry doesn't respond; she's too busy reading the article. Ash scans the words behind her, trying to pre-empt the worst bits:

> At least two elderly people and one infant have been hospitalised . . . Farley residents who are not vaccinated are requested to stay away from public spaces and to minimise contact with anyone if their vaccination status is unknown to them . . . Police have reported there's been a sharp rise in online abuse and threats of violence relating to the outbreak.

'It's all hyped up, sweetheart.' Ash tries to sound reassuring but Sara, who has now retrieved the half-empty bottle of wine from the fridge, sits back at the head of the table and says, 'At last! Something we can agree on!' Ash looks up at Sara but she doesn't see him shake his head, begging calm, because she's too focused on pouring more wine.

'It's all about education. Everyone is going bloody berserk because no one plans for these things to happen any more. Everyone's too busy staring at their phones, so when life does happen, they can't handle it. With good nutrition and the right support for the immune system, measles does not have to be a big deal, does it?' Sara looks around her, as though expecting a roomful of supporters, not just Bry and Ash, neither of whom is looking at or even listening to her.

Because Bry has a hand over her mouth and looks like she's either going to be sick or burst into tears again.

She turns to Ash; he reads her thoughts as clearly as though they were his own and starts shaking his head. 'This isn't your fault, Bry, it's not your fault.'

'Of course it's not her fault! Honestly, Ash, you do say the most ridiculous things sometimes!'

'Sara, please. You're not helping.'

'Ash, don't . . .' Bry murmurs, but it's too late. Sara leans forward on the table, her eyes two flames, and smacks her palm down against the wood.

'Ash, if it wasn't for me, you could be nursing Alba not just for a couple of weeks but indefinitely. I'm not trying to be helpful, I'm trying to save my daughters and granddaughters from the agony I've lived for over forty years. I know you find it hard to understand, but frankly, I don't care.'

That's when it strikes Ash in the heart and head simultaneously. This is how it's been for Bry. Her mother's guilt, her fear, travelling into Bry as neatly and efficiently as a needle in the arm. She has lived this every day for her whole life. He feels an overwhelming compassion for his wife; he wants to wrap her up in his arms and only let her go when she's strong enough to emerge on her own terms.

Sara, surprised that Ash hasn't come rearing back, arguments flying, decides to keep going. 'It's people like you, Ash, who don't stop to challenge the status quo – you just swallow whatever you're told to swallow because you want an easy life, and I understand that, I do, but what—'

But then Bry sits up straighter, puts a hand on her mum's arm to quieten her, and says, 'Shh, Mum, shh. Listen . . .'

All three fall into silence and listen as a wail, mechanical and urgent, fills the night. It's close and getting closer. It sounds like it's about to burst through the wall, and the kitchen is filled with an uncomfortable, eerie, flickering blue light, when suddenly the sound stops.

Ash and Bry move towards the front door, where the noise was coming from. Bry is first and before Ash can stop her, she's opened the door and is walking quickly, barefoot, down the steps and out of their gate to stand on the pavement. Ash follows. The air is too warm, the blue light too strange for this to be real. The yellow ambulance is parked directly outside Number 10 – the door is wide open and Ash catches a glimpse of Max staring at the ambulance before he turns towards something inside and moves away from the door. What comes next squeezes the air out of Ash's lungs and makes Bry lift both hands to cover her mouth and wail, 'No, no, oh no,' because coils of long red hair fall away from the stretcher as the ambulance workers carry their light load down the Chamberlains' front steps. There's an oxygen mask covering Clemmie's face and Elizabeth holds her daughter's hand, only releasing her when she's lifted into the back of the ambulance, Jack following a pace behind. Just before Elizabeth steps up to take her position by Clemmie's side, she looks over at them standing silently, watching. Jack stares too. No one raises a hand or acknowledges the other couple. They just stare for a couple of seconds, as if through a screen. Elizabeth's eyes are wide, desperate, liquid with fear, but Jack's gaze is like being bitten, full of venom, and Ash knows what he's thinking.

It should be you standing here, your girl in this ambulance, not ours. It should be you.

25 July 2019

Clemmie's eyelids are puffy and tightly closed, her breathing controlled by a ventilator, her nutrition from a drip in her arm, the machines a mechanical percussion accompaniment to their nightmare. There are others but Jack doesn't know what they're for. Her blistered lips are healing and Clemmie's skin, no longer swollen, has calmed down to translucent pale again, the rash almost gone. A couple of days ago they thought she was getting better, her rash easing, but they didn't know the virus had just moved, migrated to her brain, causing it to swell, a complication of measles known as encephalitis. Now she lies here in a medically induced coma hour upon hour, her small hands that love to tickle curled and still, her thin legs meant for skipping, jumping and the occasional kick lying lifeless, barely making a mound out of the bed sheets. Even her hair looks different, as though the light that usually dances, glossy in the red strands, has been turned off.

Jack would never – could never – say it aloud, but it's as though his little girl is present in physical form only, her heart, her voice, her light spirited away somewhere none of them can follow. Not yet anyway. It's as if she's slipped out from between the pages of their story and he can't do anything to pull her back in with them.

They've all been shipwrecked, their whole family clinging to flimsy pieces of driftwood, the vast ocean with all its mysteries and unfathomable depths stretching like an oil spill all around them. It's Jack's job to keep them all clinging on and the only way he can do that is to protect them from the darkness, to keep them treading water, their heads skyward, hopeful for the sun. Like his parents said when they arrived to look after the boys the morning after Clemmie was admitted, he has to 'stay strong, keep positive', protect his family from his fearful, bleak thoughts.

The door clicks quietly open and the nurse on night shift peers round it. He looks up at her, suddenly aware how his hair stands as if electrified away from his scalp, how his eyes must be red with fear, black with exhaustion. If she's appalled, she doesn't let on.

'Sorry, Jack, it's that time again.'

A nurse checks on Clemmie every hour, noting her respiration rate, her blood pressure, other things that Jack pretends to understand. With Elizabeth asleep on the floor, the nurse needs Jack to move so she can get close enough to Clemmie to do her tests. As he stands all Jack's muscles grip and twist, horrified by movement. The nurse smiles and holds the door open so there's space for Jack to hobble past.

'It's a beautiful sunrise – maybe you should go and take a look, get a bit of fresh air.' Jack's just about to shake his head at the nurse, explain that he can't leave Clemmie, not while Elizabeth's asleep, when the nurse adds, 'I'll be with her for the next ten minutes or so.' The concept of daylight – *sunrise* – seems absurd, but still, there's no space for him in the room, so he just nods, and the nurse moves past him towards the chair that still carries the impression of his weight. Jack squints as he steps into the bright corridor and, glancing through the window back into Clemmie's room, the nurse already scribbling her notes, he realises it feels good to be standing after all. He looks at his watch but doesn't register the time. *OK*, he thinks, *ten minutes. I'll be back with them in ten minutes.*

As he walks down the corridor, he avoids looking through the windows into the other isolation rooms. If the nurses are changing or washing a patient, they close the roller blind, but otherwise they're left at half-mast. He'd looked that first day and later wished he hadn't.

He walks through the double doors that open – via another long corridor – into the main reception for the hospital. All the lights are on, but it's eerily quiet so early in the morning; the space echoes, with no porters pushing wheelchairs or lost relatives looking for directions. Beyond the main reception desk, the glass panels to the outside frame the morning. Jack almost cries out in surprise. The sky is bright pink, a shield of vivid colour. Jack walks faster, propelled towards the morning, transfixed, already thinking about how he'll describe it to Clemmie later, whispering in her ear. He imagines the sweetness of the pink air in his lungs, giddy with anticipation, with longing, when suddenly something he spots out of the corner of his eye makes him stop.

There, in the Quick Stop Cafe to the right of the entrance, is a lone figure sitting at a small round table, a cardboard cup from a dispensing machine in front of him. The person is – maddeningly – sitting with his back to the sunrise, as though he doesn't want anything to do with magic, with beauty. He's looking directly at Jack, the two of them drawn to one another, this man spoiling the other's rare moment of solitude. The man isn't moving much but then, still staring at Jack, he lifts his hand up to his chin and tugs.

You fucking bastard.

Surprise speeds quickly into rage and before he knows what he's doing, Jack is almost running, long, wild strides, towards Ash. Ash stands up from his table; the disturbance makes the cardboard cup topple over, spilling whatever it was in a brown puddle.

'What are you doing here?' Jack shouts at his old friend, stopping directly in front of him, on the other side of the table. Ash looks as bad as Jack feels. He seems deflated, his shorts and hoodie at least two sizes too big for him. Combed by Ash's fingers, his hair stands up on its own; his face looks unwashed, unshaven. For a plunging moment Jack thinks that either Bry or Alba has been admitted, that somehow Jack's worst thoughts have been read by a higher power and that, right now, they're being hooked up to the same machines that are keeping Clemmie alive. But then he realises that can't be true because Ash wouldn't be sitting here on his own, he'd be with them.

'What the fuck?' Jack shouts again. He imagines overturning the table, picking up a chair and hitting Ash with it again and again. Instead he stands there, eyes blinking and incredulous as Ash talks.

'Jack, I . . . I couldn't sleep. I kept thinking of you here and I, I didn't come thinking I'd see you, I promise. I came because Alba asked me to give Fred to Clemmie . . .' Ash tries to give Jack the pink flamingo, but when Jack doesn't move to take it, Ash puts it down on the table and admits, 'I came because I couldn't think of anywhere else to go.'

'My little girl is in here, in a fucking coma, because of you and your lies.' Jack points in the direction of the isolation ward, tears pouring down his cheeks. He wipes them away with his arm. Ash hangs his head, his fingers reach towards the table for support, and then he sighs, and when he looks up Jack knows what's coming.

'Look, if there's anything we can do, any special care she needs, just say the word, I'd be happy to pay—'

'Fuck you,' Jack interjects. 'I don't want your guilt money.'

Ash grinds his teeth, clenches his jaw, and a steeliness grips his expression, a toughness Jack hasn't seen in him since he sold his company.

'I know you're hurting, mate, I can't imagine how much, and I'm so, so sorry this has happened. I've thought about nothing else for the last two days and I can say you're right, we should have done things differently, and if we could go back, change things, then we would.'

'Oh, my heart bleeds for you,' Jack says. He turns away but before he can leave Ash grabs hold of his arm, makes him stay.

'Please, please just listen to me.' Jack shrugs his hand away, but Ash keeps talking. 'But you can't say it's our fault that Clemmie caught measles.'

Jack's hand grips into a fist he wants so badly to swing, for his knuckles to land in Ash's eye socket, to feel his soft eyeball give way against the hard bone of his hand. He wants nothing more than for Ash to suffer, but instead he stands in front of him, mute with shock and anger, as Ash keeps talking. 'Think about it: over half of all unvaccinated kids in Farley have measles – it's spread like wildfire. Public Health England are saying it started with an unvaccinated Spanish exchange kid who stayed with a family who don't vaccinate.

Then, with all the summer term stuff, the school trips, the fete, the plays and sports days, it spread even faster than anticipated. Clemmie could have caught the virus . . .'

Jack starts shaking his head; he's heard enough. 'None of this changes a thing, *mate*. I've been thinking as well, remembering a time when I was ten and a boy I played football with was killed in a car crash because he wasn't wearing a seatbelt. His friend's dad was driving him home after a sleepover and he died two streets away from where he lived. Now, whose fault was it that he wasn't wearing a seatbelt? Was it the kid's parents? Was it all the other parents who don't make their kids buckle up? Of course it fucking wasn't. It was the fault of the dad driving him back home. He alone was responsible, no one else. Just like this is your fault – yours and Bry's – and somehow we're going to make you pay.'

His last words are a surprise even to Jack. He didn't plan on threatening Ash, he just wanted to relieve himself of some of his own pain and fear, but now he's said it he feels lighter suddenly – *yes*, his body and his mind chime together. This is the focus, the solution. It's as if a valve has been opened in his head and the pressure is whistling out of him. Once Clemmie's better and they're home, that's what they'll do: they'll focus on letting the world know what their supposed best friends did. He knows Elizabeth will be with him.

Ash stares sadly at Jack before leaving Fred on the table. He walks towards him and says, 'I'm so sorry.'

Before Ash can put his hand on Jack's shoulder, Jack flinches away and says, 'Don't come near me or my family again, you understand?' But Ash doesn't answer; he just walks, his steps heavy, into the blazing morning.

Farley County Court

December 2019

My teenagers laugh at me for coming here, sitting in the public gallery at the courthouse on my day off, but when I tell them how many millions of lives have been saved because of vaccines, how important they are, they roll their eyes, before they glaze over and say, ''kay, whatever,' and I call after them, 'Come and kiss your mother goodbye!'

Maybe I should sit them down, talk to them like I try to talk to the parents who come into my clinic. Those parents who arrive clutching their children, their decision flimsily protected by Facebook posts and propaganda.

'Look,' I say, 'I know being a parent is scary, but trust me, a vaccine is a lot less scary than watching your baby struggle to breathe because they've contracted whooping cough.'

Some of them go quiet, just shake their heads and mumble something about having the right to say no. Others look at me as if I'm the child snatcher, sneer at me in my nurse's uniform. They talk about the rise in autism, they say cells from aborted foetuses are used in vaccines, that the vaccines are more dangerous than the diseases they prevent — I try not to swear.

I remember one dad who came to the clinic because his son needed an inhaler.

'I see from your records your son isn't vaccinated. Can I ask why?'

The dad nodded and said slowly and clearly, as though he was revealing a great truth, 'Because of the corporate, life-sucking pharmaceutical companies who make billions every year out of vaccines and are totally invincible because they're protected by the government. I won't ever trust them with my kid's health.'

'Fair enough,' I said, 'but you know the inhaler he needs is made by the biggest pharmaceutical company in the world, so . . .'

The son looked at his dad and his dad felt him looking.

'Just give me the inhaler,' he said. I never saw them again.

In the court, the mum and dad take their seats. I don't know her, but I try to catch her eye so I can smile my support. She doesn't look up.

'Good on you,' I want to tell her. 'Good on you for going through this, to make others listen.' People might think I'm extreme, but I believe vaccines should be mandatory. Remember the days when no one wore a seatbelt? Well, I do. As a student nurse, I remember tiny twisted bodies, heads snapped back like broken dolls. But not now. Because we all buckle up, don't even think about it, it's automatic, the belt the first thing we reach for. Vaccines should be the same.

The court stands for the judge. Their solicitor whispers something into the wife's ear. She nods. People talk about their rights as parents, but I've never heard a parent with a seriously sick child talk about their rights. They just want us to make their child healthy again, to give them another chance. Just look at these two. What they wouldn't give to have their little girl back, smiling and happy again, as she was just a few short months ago.

28 July 2019

'Mumma! Take me with you!' Alba cries, punching her little fist into the sofa in frustration. They haven't been apart for more than a few minutes for ten days, and Alba is livid Bry's taking the step out into the world again without her. But all that crap online, everything that Ash has been slowly drip-feeding, the stuff that Row and Emma have been texting since Bry asked them for their take: Bry needs to see it for herself, know how bad it is before she can let Alba out. Ash whispers into Alba's ear – promises about ice cream and the paddling pool – and she takes his hand firmly in her own and steers him like a puppy on a lead, chanting, 'Ice cream, ice cream!' towards the freezer.

Leaving the house had been Ash's idea. Bry suspects he's getting worried she's turning into an agoraphobic, which perhaps isn't a totally unfounded concern. For five days now, since the ambulance took Clemmie away, she's felt physically strong enough to brave the outside but emotionally far too frail. She'd cough and clutch her forehead when Ash mentioned it before; the thought of seeing someone, anyone, who knew what she'd done, how she'd lied to her best friend, who was now paying the worst price, made Bry want to run straight back to her bed and never come out. But there is

187

something about this morning, the way the sun incubates the house, the way the birds call to each other in the garden, that feels inexplicably and quite unexpectedly like everything is going to be OK after all. Yes, Clemmie is still in hospital, but Ash told Bry that he went there when he couldn't sleep, that he saw Jack. He'd said Jack was still angry, but he'd reassured Bry that Clemmie was in for observation, a precaution, that she'd be home in a few days. Ash grinned and kissed her this morning when she said she was going to the 11 a.m. hatha class at the Good Studio and so, at 10.30 a.m., with Alba enthusiastically unpacking the freezer, she makes her escape.

As soon as she takes a lungful of fresh air, Bry feels giddy with freedom. It's like the first time she left Alba with Ash for an hour or so when Alba was a few weeks old – the world feels strange but exhilarating. The sky is a wide open blue, all the colours clear, everything in sharp focus. Her arms want to float up, she wants to spin round and round – *Sound of Music* style – but then she sees sweet, elderly Jane in her front garden wearing a sun hat, secateurs in one hand, a rose in the other. Jane is looking directly at Bry but she doesn't make any sign that she's seen her, so Bry waves to catch the older woman's attention and almost skips across the road towards her neighbour.

'Jane! What an amazing morning!' Bry smiles, pleased to see her friend. 'How are you?' she adds, putting her hand on Jane's where it rests on the little iron gate.

But Jane doesn't smile back; instead she moves her hand away from Bry's and says, 'To be honest with you, Bryony, I've been better.'

'You've been ill too?' She speaks before she thinks.

Jane's eyes shrink to slits as though she needs to focus

hard to understand Bry. 'No, no, I had measles when I was a girl. It's not me I'm worried about.' Jane glances behind Bry, and Bry follows as she looks towards the Chamberlains' house where all the bedroom curtains are still closed, as though the house itself has lost consciousness.

'I know, I know . . . poor Clemmie. But Ash says she'll be home soon,' she stammers and turns back to Jane, but Jane is looking at her as though she's a stranger and she isn't about to help Bry out. In that moment Bry knows that all her neighbours know. They know she and Alba hadn't had the MMR, and they know Bry lied to Elizabeth and Jack. Bry feels flayed, exposed. She can't guess what Jane thinks of her but her eyes are firm, their usual friendly glint snuffed out.

'You know Chris has been in hospital with it too? He'd been taking immunosuppressants for years apparently, I had no idea. He's home now but Gerald's been in bits.'

Jane turns away from Bry with a sigh and pulls at a newly opened pale pink rose, tracing down the stem with practised fingers to find the right spot to cut. Bry feels sick, unsteady, but there's so much she wants to say. It feels urgent for Jane to know about Matty, that ever since Bry found out she was pregnant with Alba, she has felt frightened for her daughter every day. That she believed – really believed – that measles wouldn't be that bad. That her lie wasn't really a lie; it was a quick, careless half-truth – a text, for God's sake. But the words won't come, so instead Jane says, 'You must be relieved Alba is recovered.'

Bry keeps her eyes fixed on the rose in front of her, tears rising. Her shame starts to harden; she sees Clemmie's limp little body in a hospital bed, red hair splashed over a pillow.

Bry can't respond. Jane snips the rose stem and the bloom falls into her waiting hand.

'Look, Bryony, my advice to you is just to give it time. Once Clemmie's home and the town has recovered, then I'm sure people will come round, but just now there's a lot of confusion, a lot of gossip going around.' Bry knows what she's saying: Bry shouldn't be seen smiling up at the sun or waving at neighbours as though she's in a Disney film.

'OK?' Jane adds, before taking another rose in her hand and raising her secateurs again.

Bry nods, tries to swallow her rising nausea down, but it floods her throat as she turns her head towards the pavement and walks slowly away.

Bry pulls the hood on her light grey top to cover her head, tears raining small bombs. She keeps her head down, careful not to make eye contact with anyone in case they recognise her. She doesn't know where she's going exactly but she knows she won't go to the yoga class now.

At first, everything feels unchanged. The woman in the health food shop waves to her from behind her till; there are children's shouts and happy screams from the lido; the busker is there as usual, cross-legged on the bridge, grubby cap in front of him, humming a song as everyone ignores him. 'All right?' he calls to her.

Bry walks on the opposite side of the street to the cafes, careful to avoid looking in their large windows, full of hanging succulents, the glass steamy from people chatting. She'll walk to the park and then she'll head home through the cemetery and woods. Yes, that'll be far enough, no need to go any further. She walks a bit faster past an elderly couple wearing face masks. Just outside the park is a small gathering of people. Bry pauses and stares; she won't, she can't go in if it's a kids' party or something. Ash is not here to make her. But the people aren't in a group, they're in a line outside the large double-fronted Victorian doctor's surgery. They're queuing up for what look like two large portaloos, except most of them are wearing blue face masks and many of them are either carrying or holding the hands of twitching, squirming, bored children. Bry edges closer. There's a woman and a man, each with a clipboard, asking people in the queue questions and noting their answers. A woman in a fluorescent tabard asks her, 'You here for a vaccine, love?'

'Is that what this is?'

'I tell people it's like a pop-up shop, just for your health, not for your wardrobe. So are you joining the queue then?'

'Why is it here?'

The woman lifts her arms to the queue, indicating it should be self-explanatory.

'One of the lowest vaccination rates in the country round here, love. Measles has put the wind up people – rightly so, if you ask me – and now they're all scrabbling to get the vaccine. The doctors are at their limit tending to the people who already have the virus, so Public Health England came up with this idea. Clever, isn't it? Now, are you joining the queue or not?'

Bry shakes her head and says, 'No thanks,' but the woman's already wandered off to a couple with a pram behind Bry.

Bry keeps walking, not looking as she crosses the road for the entrance to the park. Next to the park gate there's a trestle table decorated with bright flyers, two women sitting behind the table. Bry keeps her head down when someone calls, 'Bry? Brrrry!'

She's been caught. One of the women behind the trestle

table is waving at her. 'You didn't tell me you were heading out this morning, darling!'

Bry freezes, dumbstruck. 'Mum?'

Sara stands up and pulls Bry into her open arms.

'This is Marie.' Sara beckons towards the other woman, who smiles up at Bry as Bry manages a quick smile down.

'Oh, you must be Bryony,' Marie says, still smiling. 'Your mum's been telling me all about you and little Alba – what a sweetie. I'm delighted you're both feeling better.'

'Hello.' Bry is close enough now to read the front of a couple of the flyers strewn across the table. One says 'The TRUTH about Mercury' and another 'Natural Immunity vs Vaccines'.

'Mum, what're you doing?'

'Well, Marie was looking for helpers and I was free, so here I am.'

Bry frowns at her mum; she knows that's not what Bry was asking.

'We're just offering an alternative view to all these poor people who have been terrified by the media and the so-called National *Health* Service.' Sara places a scathing emphasis on 'Health'. Marie looks approving and Bry doesn't know what to say next, so she just stands between the table and the park entrance, her back muscles prickling, aware of all the people in the queue just across the road. She feels exhausted for all of them – herself included – suddenly overwhelmed and shattered by the endless choices, the relentless responsibility of simply being alive. She wants to scream in everyone's defence, *We just don't fucking know, do we? None of us fucking know what to do.* Instead she just stands there, dumb, while Marie continues.

'Yes, we've had a busy morning, your mum's been an absolute godsend – so generous with sharing your family's story. One woman was here with her three kids – three beautiful, healthy children – she'd been planning on joining the queue over there.' Marie points to the queue of people waiting for a vaccine. 'She was obviously in a pickle about the whole thing, but just a couple of minutes with your mum and she was calm and resolute again. It was quite beautiful really.'

Sara sits down again next to her new friend and shrugs. 'Oh, I just talked to her mother to mother. When I told her about Matty, I could actually see her instinct kick in. She knew it wasn't the right thing to do – she just needed a bit of re-assurance, that's all. She took the kids to the beach instead, so they were thrilled.'

The two women chuckle; Bry doesn't join in and Marie starts straightening out the flyers on the table.

'In fact, now that you're out and about again, Bry, maybe you could give us a hand this afternoon?'

Two middle-aged men in shorts glance at the table, shaking their heads. Bry is sure one of them mutters, 'Bloody idiots,' underneath his breath as they walk by.

Bry's thumbs and forefingers massage her temples as Sara keeps talking. 'Just for an hour or so, so Marie can take a well-deserved break.'

'Actually, Mum, sorry, but my head still doesn't feel right. I think I'm going to have to go home.'

Before she's even finished speaking, Sara turns to Marie.

'This is her first time out . . . yes, maybe it's a bit too much to ask. Don't worry, love. I'll manage.'

Sara stands again and beckons Bry towards her. She puts a

hand around the back of Bry's head and kisses her before saying, 'I'll be home about five, OK, love?'

Bry manages a brief smile at Marie and, raising a hand, more as a request to her mum not to follow than a wave, she walks gratefully away.

The park, usually a patchwork of rugs, crawling babies and picnics this time of year, is as green and empty as the bowling lawn. Bry hurries now, down the central path, over the little bridge, towards the exit that links the park with the sprawling cemetery. She just needs to make it to the cemetery – she's never bumped into anyone she knows in the cemetery. She turns the corner, the kids' playground on her right, when a voice from the bank of swings intercepts her.

'Bry, Bry! Yoo-hoo – over here!'

Lily leaps off the swing at the highest point and grabs hold of Row's hand before the two of them trot towards Bry. Bry stands, awkwardly waiting, wishing she could bolt.

Lily pulls a blue surgical mask down from her forehead to cover her nose and mouth; they must have told her that Bry's been sick, that she needs to be careful around sick people. But then Row whispers something into Lily's ear and she lifts the mask back on to her forehead again. Bry notices a small, round, pink plaster on Lily's upper arm.

'I knew it was you!' Row says, a little puffed.

'I'm Dr Lily!' Lily says, pulling the mask down again.

Row's eyes quickly scan Bry – checking for a rash, Bry thinks – before she pulls her in for a hug. It feels good, to be hugged by her friend.

'Shit, I've been worried about you,' Row says, as she pulls away a bit sooner than Bry was ready for.

'That's a bad word, Mummy!'

194

'How are you guys doing?' Row asks, stroking her daughter's hand between her own.

'We're OK, yeah. We've both been given the all clear. We're not infectious any more.' Bry imagines this is something she's going to hear herself say again and again in the coming days. 'Thanks for the juice by the way, it was really tasty. Albs loved it too.'

Row smiles.

'Oh good, good, I'm just sorry we couldn't do more.'

'Ash said you guys have been OK, that you didn't get it.'

Lily shakes her head and points to her mask before she shows Bry her upper arm. She pulls the mask down this time so Bry can hear her. 'Nope and look. This plaster is like a badge and it means that I won't ever get sick because I'm a doctor.'

Bry feels Row's eyes on her again, anxious this time for different reasons.

'That's so nice, Lil, well done you.' Bry smiles down at the little girl.

Row's face is flushed, embarrassed, as though she's just pledged allegiance to a rival gang.

'Yeah, so Steve and I just weighed up the risks, you know, with everything that's been going on. Lil was super likely to catch measles – we've been lucky that she hasn't already – and we can't keep her inside all summer, so we decided, yeah, like actually the risk factors have changed, so, you know, it kind of . . .'

'It's OK, Row.' Bry squeezes her friend's arm. 'Seriously. You're right. Everything has changed. I'd have probably done the same if it was Alba.'

Row's face falls with relief and Bry wonders whether she would have done the same. She pictures herself just a few minutes earlier, sandwiched, awkward, between the vaccination queue and her mum's trestle table.

'Really?' She lifts her free hand to her face and half smiles into her palm. 'I've been feeling so fucking anxious about it—'

'Mummy, worst word!'

'Like I've abandoned my principles or something, and everyone's going to think I'm a massive hypocrite.'

'Swear box!' Lily cries.

'OK, Lil, why don't you run and show me and Auntie Bry how high you can swing without being pushed?'

With a quick, 'Right then,' Lily fixes her face mask back over her nose and mouth and bounces back towards the swings.

As soon as she's gone, Row leans in closer to Bry.

'Emma emailed and invited Lil and me to her parents' place in Wales. She left with her girls last week but Steve said it was madness to go into hiding, and besides, it's like what people are saying online: actually that could just be spreading the infection, so it could be a pretty selfish thing to do . . . Of course, now we don't need to worry.'

As she listens to Row, Bry finds she wants to shake her friend. It's like listening to a transcript of her own thoughts – all she's doing is worrying about what everyone else thinks and all that noise is drowning out her own thoughts and feelings.

'How's Alba? We've all been so worried.'

Bry reassures her she's doing better, will be up to leaving the house in a day or two, and then Row asks, more quietly, 'Have you heard from Elizabeth?' Hearing her name is like being slapped. The shock comes first and then the pain swells until it starts to thump. All Bry can do is shake her head.

'No, no, me neither. She isn't replying to any of my messages. Apparently four kids have been hospitalised now, but Clemmie is the only one in a coma.'

The words seem to make the air vibrate around them.

'What did you say?'

'Oh shit . . . but you knew she was in hospital though . . .'

'Clemmie is . . .'

'Apparently, it's a medically induced thing. Steve said it'll help with the swelling . . .'

Row tries to keep her voice steady, soothing, which only makes Bry want to scream. Ash said everyone was confident she'd recover quickly, that she'd be home in a few days. He hadn't said anything about a coma – a fucking *coma*.

Row keeps talking, faster now, but Bry doesn't hear what she's saying, she just knows she needs to get away, she needs to get home to Ash, to hear the truth from him. She starts to run along the slick tarmac path, Row calling her name behind her, desperate, but with distance growing quiet. She's out of breath; a new pain starts to peck at her side. She holds on to herself and stumbles to a stop as soon as the wooden gate has swung closed behind her. She's on her own again, in the cemetery. She lets herself breathe hard, painful breaths. She feels her temple again, throbbing. Her head seems to tick, dull like an old, tired bomb. Ahead of her is another path, pockmarked either side with graves. She used to walk this way with Alba, before Alba started asking too many questions, questions that Bry could never answer to Alba's satisfaction.

'But Mumma, what does they eat down there?'

She remembers the last time they came here. Alba, wearing her Batman mask, swimming costume, tights and wellies, stopped in front of one of the smaller graves. 'Mumma, why this one so tiddly 'n' small?' She scrunched up her little face in confusion. Bry, at a loss, didn't answer quickly enough, so Alba suggested, 'P'haps they had no legs?'

At the time, Bry had nodded her assent.

'Yes, that's probably why,' she'd said. 'Come on, Albs.'

She'd taken the easy road as always, wiggling away from the heat of her discomfort, away from her daughter's curious, wonderful mind, retreating back to safety and trying to remember what was in the fridge for Alba's dinner. But now, at least now, she stops and looks at the little grave. The person with no legs was, of course, just a child. Bethany Lewis. 1912–1917. Underneath, inscribed in green moss, are the words 'Suffer the little children'. Behind Bethany's too-small grave is another, for Samuel Lewis. He died two years after his sister. 1915–1919. Next to his is yet another small grave, this one for Matthew Lewis. Bry can't read his dates, her vision blurred by tears. She imagines their mother, how she must have left a piece of her heart bleeding but somehow still beating by the graves of each of her little ones.

She stumbles on but now her eyes have become cruelly attuned to spotting the smallest stones. They pop up, left and right, demanding her attention. 'See us! Look at us!' they call in high voices. But she can't, she won't. Instead, Bry starts running again and she keeps going, through the wood and down on to Neville Road before turning into Saint's Road. She tries not to look, but she can't help a quick glance at the Chamberlains' house. The curtains are still drawn and on the doorstep is a small bunch of Jane's garden roses. They're beautiful but they feel like a sign, a sign something worse is yet to come.

29 July 2019

It's Monday morning, Elizabeth is told, when the anaesthetist and the consultant, Mr Brownlee, tell her and Jack that they're 'satisfied' that the swelling to Clemmie's brain is slowly decreasing.

'So, you're pleased with her progress then?' Jack asks, leaning forward in his chair, using the same language they've used so many times – the language of parent-teacher evenings, of spelling tests and piano lessons. It strikes Elizabeth as odd that the same words apply when you're talking about your child's swollen brain, but she leans in too; she wants to know. Have they, has Clemmie, 'done well'?

'We still won't know for a little while how – if at all – the encephalitis has affected Clemmie's brain,' Mr Brownlee replies. 'But we're both satisfied that she's ready to progress to the next stage: we agree that we can start to bring her out of the coma.'

That word again, 'satisfied'. While they all shake hands, Elizabeth silently begs, pleads Mr Brownlee or the anaesthetist to say something positive, something she and Jack can cling on to in the long hours ahead, but neither of them does; they just nod their heads and smile their performative, professional smiles, before walking away in different directions.

Elizabeth and Jack are left alone. Jack puts a warm hand on Elizabeth's knee and says, 'That's good news, sweetheart, that's fucking good news.'

Jack will want a whole chat about how positive this is, but Elizabeth won't be led this time.

Elizabeth pats his hand, as if he's a little dog she doesn't have time for just now.

'I'm going back to her.' She stands, but Jack pulls her back.

'Why don't you get a cab home for a bit, love?' His eyes are swollen red, like two infected bites.

'You said the boys are OK, that your parents have everything under control.'

'Yes, yes, they do, but they're still worried, they miss you.'

Elizabeth puts her hand over Jack's, squeezes reassurance for a moment before she pries his fingers away from her own.

'Don't make me feel guilty, Jack, please. I can't handle it if you make me feel guilty.'

'I'm not trying to, Elizabeth, I'm just worried, so worried about you.'

'Yeah, well going home isn't going to change that.' She opens the door to the corridor that will lead her back to her little girl. 'I'm not leaving. Please, go and see the boys, tell them I'll FaceTime them later and that I love them very much, but don't ask me to leave her again.'

Elizabeth pulls the visitor chair as close as possible to Clemmie. She's still lost, deep within herself. People – nurses, the anaesthetist and others – come and go but Elizabeth stays in her position, holding Clemmie's small, slack hand. Sometimes she leans forward to rest her forehead on her arm and sometimes her head tilts back against her chair. Hours pass.

She doesn't think about much; her head has become a blank space, full only of white noise. More hours pass. The rhythm of her heart beats in perfect time with the beep of the machines keeping her little girl alive. Do. Not. Stop. Do. Not. Stop.

Her foot moves first – well, at least that's the first thing that Elizabeth sees. Elizabeth hadn't noticed how still the room had been until it happens, the smallest twitch under the sheets. It happens again and again. It's as if she's been electrified. Elizabeth sits bolt upright in her chair and clasps Clemmie's hand tightly between her own – *Ow, Mummy! Too tight!* she imagines Clemmie complaining.

'Do it again, poppet, please, move again, my love,' Elizabeth whispers. This time it's both feet, as though something's itching her heels.

Elizabeth kisses her daughter's hand before grabbing for the alarm to call the nurses, then kisses her hand again and whispers, 'Thank you, thank you, thank you' – to whom, she doesn't know.

The nurses come, then a consultant Elizabeth doesn't recognise. More tests and checks. Clemmie starts to move her legs. Next her hands flutter, like birds frightened into life. Someone must have called Jack because suddenly he's back. He sits in the chair while Elizabeth sits on the floor in the corner, her elbows resting on her knees, the heels of her hands in her eye sockets. She's shaking too much to be any closer to Clemmie. Her whole body vibrates with the relief of love almost lost. She feels like she's just given birth to Clemmie again, that somehow, through all the blood and the agony, they've given life to each other.

Jack cries next to Clemmie and the nurse tells him to stop,

gently jokes that she doesn't need another bed to change, thank you very much. Clemmie's room is suddenly a room of laughter. Slowly, but so quickly, things develop. She moves her neck to coos of admiration; her mouth and lips twitch to life. It's like watching a great, beautiful thaw.

When Clemmie starts to move her head back and forth, back and forth against the pillow, Elizabeth comes over and takes her hand again, Jack standing directly behind her. Clemmie starts to moan and Jack says, 'She's always hated being woken up.' Elizabeth doesn't need to see him to know that he's smiling at the nurse; she smiles back.

'Don't we all?'

Then, incredibly, Clemmie lifts the hand Elizabeth isn't holding to rub her eyes. She moans again and then Elizabeth sees a ripple of life pass, backstage, behind her eyelids. Jack and the nurse crowd closer and the nurse presses a button. Elizabeth keeps her eyes fixed on Clemmie. She doesn't breathe; she tries to channel all her love, all her energy, through her hand and into her daughter. Clemmie's eyelids quiver; another groan and then Elizabeth feels what she's been waiting for. Clemmie squeezes back. Elizabeth's whole life rushes to her hand. The ripples below Clemmie's eyelids become waves and suddenly she starts blinking her eyes open, rolling her head around on the pillow, and Elizabeth hears her own voice through her tears: 'Clemmie, poppet, Mummy's here, I'm here, Clemmie.' Behind her Jack is crying and laughing. Two more people, doctors, walk into the already crowded room. Clemmie keeps a tight grip on Elizabeth's hand and silently her lips start to move, her eyes tracing across the ceiling, as though looking for something they expect to see any moment.

'Mummy, Mummy.' Her voice is tiny, dry. Elizabeth leans

forward so she's hovering right in front of Clemmie's eyes, filling her line of sight.

'I'm here, my love, I'm here, my Clemmie, Mummy's here.'

But Clemmie's blue eyes don't rest; they don't even seem to register Elizabeth. Instead they just keep scanning back and forth, back and forth across the ceiling. Tears spill out of the corners of her eyes. One of her machines starts to beep and a doctor steps forward.

'I'm here, poppet, I'm right here,' Elizabeth says, stroking the side of Clemmie's face, trying to get her to be still so she can focus, but Clemmie's eyes keep dancing away.

Clemmie starts to cry louder and through her own tears Elizabeth tries to shush and calm her, but Clemmie shouts, 'Mummy, Mummy, I can't see you. I can't see you!'

Jack doesn't touch Elizabeth's knee this time as they sit in the same chairs they sat in just a few hours ago. Neither of them talks. They just sit, heads bowed, like criminals waiting for their sentence. Elizabeth doesn't even look up when three men walk in: Mr Brownlee and an eye doctor she met earlier, and another she doesn't recognise.

'Mr and Mrs Chamberlain, this, you might remember, is Dr Edwin, the ophthalmologist who has been assessing Clemmie's eyes.'

Elizabeth glances up. The man is small, too young for his head of perfectly white hair. She nods and Jack wipes his face one more time before he looks up and says, 'Please call us Jack and Elizabeth.'

The men nod in acknowledgement before Mr Brownlee continues with the formalities. 'And this is the consultant neurologist, Mr Clarke.'

The three men sit. Elizabeth wishes she could hide or, better yet, run out of the room. Somehow she thinks if she can only stop these men from saying whatever awful things they're about to say, then this won't be happening, none of this will be real.

'I know you're both anxious to know what has been going on since Clemmie regained consciousness, so we'll get straight to it. Dr Edwin, do you want to start?'

Dr Edwin shuffles forward so he's perched on the edge of his chair. His hands are gently clasped in his lap, as though he's opening a negotiation.

'I'll be brief. It is, I'm glad to say, good news as far as the workings of Clemmie's eyes are concerned. As you'll know, we've been giving her vitamin A, which has protected her from some of the complications commonly caused in the eye from the measles virus. Her eyes are healthy and working well.'

'So why can't she see?' Jack asks.

'I'm afraid this is where I must come in.' Mr Clarke stares at a spot behind Elizabeth's shoulder as he talks. 'I've been reviewing the results from the MRI we performed since Clemmie regained consciousness.' The nurse had injected a sedative into her IV to keep her calm before she was wheeled away, Elizabeth still clutching her hand.

'It looks as though Clemmie might have something called cortical blindness. This is caused by damage to the occipital cortex in the brain. Essentially, as it currently stands, the part of her brain that registers sight has been affected by the encephalitis. This means she has a neurological visual impairment.'

'She's blind?'

'She's visually impaired, yes.'

'But this will – this will get better, right? I mean, she's not going to be blind for ever, is she?' Jack sounds like he wants to laugh with the absurdity of the question.

'It's far too soon to tell exactly how much damage has been caused and whether there will be any improvement. We'd hope to see at least some, but it's impossible to say how much that will be at this stage.'

The men keep talking but Elizabeth doesn't hear what they say, because somehow she's become detached from her own body, loose and unbound, standing just beside herself sitting quietly in the chair. All she hears is a high-pitched whine and all she can see is the men's faces before her, moving silently, like plasticine models. She feels wonderfully blank; maybe the kind nurse gave her a tranquilliser too? There'll be such a lot to do when they all go home; beds to change, laundry, meals to make. How good it will be, all that activity, that usefulness again, and then she'll sit back with a glass of wine and watch the kids playing outside, knowing the house smells good and the carpets are clear of fluff. But back in the hospital, the men are standing, looking awkward because Jack's crying too much to take their hand, so she knows she must step up. Her body lifts and Elizabeth beckons herself on, offers each man her hand – shake, shake, shake – before she turns, an automaton, to leave, but before she makes it to the door, her legs start to dissolve, and before she can say anything she's on the floor, staring at three sets of shoes and wondering what the hell she's doing down there before everything goes black.

Farley County Court

December 2019

*My ex-wife will tell you that the reason I break great stories before any
other reporter is because I don't have one moral bone in my body. I prefer
to think of it as an instinct, a sixth sense. Once I know the outline of
the story, I'll add a little colour. If I hear about a politician caught with
his trousers round his ankles, I'll add a cross-dressing fetish, for example,
because our readers like spice. But then every now and again you get a
story, a story like this one being played out in this court room, a story
that comes to you so crammed full of delicious ingredients — deception,
tragedy, revenge — that I don't have to add much at all.*

*When I first saw that photo of the Farley Foursome, I felt like I'd
been handed a wad of money and ushered into a casino. I mean, look
at them. They're just so perfectly cast: the statuesque, cold bitch wife and
her unlikely best mate — the dark, rich, thick-as-shit hippie — and their
two lolloping husbands. The kid who went blind is perfect too — skin
like a porcelain doll, and those unseeing blue eyes that still give me the
shivers. The story was a wriggling newborn in my arms — perfect and
full of potential. We laughed in the office about the four of them. We
laughed at how stupid entitled middle-class parents can be — as though
there aren't enough problems in the world. They shake their shiny hair,
sip their turmeric lattes, and say their kids are too good for the vaccines*

they're so lucky to have access to, the vaccines that have saved literally millions of lives. Makes my blood boil, it really does.

Then I found out about the autistic brother and that opened things up very nicely. I found myself writing all over again about the bullshit science unleashed on the world by Andrew Wakefield. Our readership numbers went up; my boss was buying me drinks. So I added a few flourishes here and there, just to keep our readers snacking on the story before they can really pig out on the court case. I found a few photos of the thick little hippie with the ice queen's husband — the two of them with their arms all over each other, laughing, under the heading 'Love versus Virus?' I let our readers use their own imaginations on that one. Then we were anonymously sent a photo of the hippie, her face twisted and scary, trying to carry her daughter, kicking and crying, having a right paddy. I splashed the words 'A Mother's Love?' above that one.

So yeah, I did a proper job on them. Why not? Someone had to take them down a peg or two and if I cause offence, like my ex delights in telling me I do, then so be it. It's how I earn my keep and, what's more, if my stories get a few other parents to wake up and vaccinate their kids then I reckon that gives me a nice shiny halo above my head.

3 September 2019

It's another month before Clemmie comes home. A month of scans, tests and waiting for results. A month of trying to keep the tears out of their voices, of painful phone calls, plastic sandwiches and comforting others. A month of holding Clemmie while she shakes with terror as they have to tell her that, no, still nothing has changed. Trying to explain to a seven-year-old that, if anything, there'll be even less light as the tests conclude that the worst of the damage is permanent. A month of learning about sticks, special assistance and alarms. Of watching their daughter cling to the wall in terror, as if she's about to drown in the darkness. Of learning how language can fail feeling. Of watching her tiny hands, shaking with fear and courage, feel for her brother's familiar face, as he blows a raspberry that makes her jump and scream instead of laugh.

'Morning, beautiful – you look like a girl who's ready to go home!' Jack closes Clemmie's hospital door slowly behind him, making sure it clicks loudly, as he's been told, to help Clemmie place him.

Clemmie is sitting on the edge of her bed, in the yellow dress Elizabeth bought especially for today. Her red hair is brushed and loosely plaited, her legs kicking back and forth.

'Daddy!' She looks just past his shoulder; he's still not used to it, as if she's addressing another daddy, his own shadow just behind him. He kneels in front of her and she lifts her hands to his face, their new greeting.

'How am I today, Clemmie?' he asks his little oracle.

'Hmmm, oh Daddy, you're feeling ummm . . .' Her hands press against his eyes, his nose, his grinning mouth. 'Happy with a capital H!' she says, clapping her hands and rocking backwards on the bed. He steadies her automatically, even though he's been told to try to let her take the odd bump.

'Think of it as like having a toddler again,' one of the assistants told him. 'She needs to learn her new boundaries, how things have changed, for herself.' But Jack doesn't think he'll ever be able to stop himself, ever leave things to chance again.

'You're so good at this, Clemmie! You're right, I am Happy with a capital H.' He reaches towards her and she reaches down to him and slips off the bed, confident of his arms. She still smells as she always did, of strawberry lip balm and pencils, her little hands linking behind his neck.

'Aha! Here you are!' Elizabeth emerges from the tiny bathroom, Clemmie's packed wash bag and a see-through bag of pills in her hand. She doesn't kiss Jack hello – Clemmie won't see, after all – but she does keep the bounce in her voice, to reassure Clemmie all is going well, very well, on this special day, that they're all Happy. She offers Clemmie her 'seeing' stick and touches her shoulder so she knows it's time to stand.

'Right, come on, let's go and give all the nurses a great big hug goodbye.'

*

When they get home, Jack carries Clemmie into the hallway on his back, Elizabeth by their side, holding Clemmie's hand and her stick, as though still keeping vigil. Max stands up from where he was sitting on the stairs and Charlie uncurls his arms from around the banister. Jack's parents were dispatched back to Surrey that morning; they understood, they said, it hadn't been just the five of them for so long. Jack feels Clemmie turn her head up to the air, searching for comfort, for the smell and feel of home. She doesn't say anything, but her legs grip Jack's back a little tighter.

Max breaks the silence, comes forward first, strokes his sister's leg and says, 'Hey, Clem.' She looks down with her unseeing eyes towards him. Then Charlie joins his big brother and strokes the top of her hand, which makes her jolt before she reaches for him.

'Do you like your banner, Clemmie?' Charlie lisps. He's been working on his big surprise for the last few days; no one has been allowed to know anything about it: 'Top secret,' he'd called it. Jack looks up. Above each step up the staircase, Charlie has fixed a careful, glittery letter, each a different colour, spelling out 'Welcome Home Clemmie!' His heart drops for Charlie and then drops again for Clemmie. Charlie's still looking up at his sister, eager for her to clap her hands and laugh. But she doesn't; she isn't even looking at the banner. Instead she starts to whimper, confused, turning her head in all directions.

Elizabeth kisses her hand and says in an overly bright voice, 'It says "Welcome Home Clemmie!" Well done, Charlie. Now, who wants some of Granny's special chocolate cake?'

*

Jack moves Clemmie from his back to his front, and she clutches fast to him, so he sits at the table with her clinging to him like a koala, her knees purple with bruises from where she keeps bumping into things in her dark world. Elizabeth buzzes around for plates, milk and cake, and in the same too-bright voice says, 'Max, tell Clemmie the funny story about your cricket match with Tembury the other day?'

They moved the knives the night before, along with the bleach and the matches, so it takes her a moment to find a knife to cut the cake. The boys take their places, quiet and slow, as though an unknown but important guest has come to visit and they don't know how they should behave.

'So someone brought this huge dog, like an Alsatian, to our cricket match, Clem, and this dog loves balls, like really, really loves balls . . .' As Max talks, Jack gently lifts Clemmie to face the table and guides her hands to feel the little china plate Elizabeth places in front of her. Everyone watches as her hands feel for the fork. Her forefinger runs across the prongs and, holding the plate steady with her other hand, she takes a gentle stab at the cake on her plate. Finding it, she gets a bite-sized amount on to the fork. Max gamely keeps trying to tell his story but he's running out of steam and no one's listening; they're all transfixed by the little piece of chocolate cake on Clemmie's fork as she lifts it slowly, slowly towards her – *please, please*. But the icing has made it top-heavy. It wobbles on the fork, topples, and just as Clemmie opens her mouth, the cake drops, leaving an ugly brown smear on her pretty yellow lap.

From the kitchen, tidying after dinner, Jack watches them through the baby monitor. Elizabeth lies next to Clemmie, who is at last asleep in their bed. They've pushed it from the middle of the room up against the wall so Clemmie won't fall out. Clemmie's sleeping with Elizabeth and Jack's in Clemmie's room until she's properly settled. Elizabeth has moved all Clemmie's cuddly toys and dolls on to their king-size bed, hopeful that now she's home she'll reach for something other than Fred, but no, Jack can just see the flamingo's beak, clamped under her arm in a choking grip. Jack knows he probably shouldn't, but he can't help but watch them through the little screen. His girls, turned towards each other, Elizabeth stroking Clemmie's hair, Clemmie's mouth a little open, slack in deep sleep. Elizabeth's shoulders are shaking slightly, but the image is too grainy to see whether she's crying. She rolls her face into the pillow for a moment, then whispers something into Clemmie's ear before slowly peeling herself up from the bed.

Jack turns the monitor over so it's facing the countertop and busies himself, wiping down the kitchen surfaces as Elizabeth walks quietly into the kitchen. He turns to look at her. She's thinner than ever before, her jeans flapping around her legs, her cheekbones and clavicles pushing out of her like exposed roots, her eyes bruised. Unsure what she wants, Jack decides to move towards her, slowly opening his arms. She doesn't respond but she also doesn't turn away. She lets him hug her, the bones of her body softening, just a little. They stand there in the middle of the kitchen, the slosh of the ancient dishwasher and the occasional shout from the boys on their computer game upstairs part of the comforting sounds of home. Jack's stopped telling her, in rare moments of connection like this, that everything's going to be OK. He'd been telling her mostly to hear her agreement, to feel his own heart ease slightly with the reassurance, but when she'd stopped being able to say, 'Yes, yes, I know,' and then stopped being able even to nod, he'd stopped saying it, because he couldn't believe it either. But now that all their children are upstairs, now that they're together, the five of them – changed certainly, but nevertheless home together – he says, 'I know we're going to be OK, I know we are.'

And he feels her head nod against his shoulder and he holds her a little tighter.

He's about to suggest he opens a bottle of wine – one of the oddly celebratory gifts from neighbours and friends, most sticking safely to a cake or flowers – when the doorbell rings. Elizabeth flinches in his arms; she's successfully avoided all but essential contact with the outside world for weeks. She looks up at him; her eyes, so like Clemmie's, seem strangely still. They don't wander about, as if they're sure to see something if they only look hard enough.

'I'll get the door,' Jack says, holding Elizabeth's thin biceps. 'How about you open that bottle of red and then I'll get the boys to bed.'

He makes it sound like a fair deal. Elizabeth nods and says, 'OK then,' just as the doorbell rings again. They've put little bells over all the doors so Clemmie can hear when someone is coming or going; the front door jingles and Jack almost laughs with surprise when he sees who it is waiting. Standing in their little porch, a wicker basket of stuff at his feet, is Ash, and just behind him, looking like she's about to throw up, is Bry.

Jack opens his mouth but finds he can't say anything, so instead he just shakes his head in disbelief.

Ash raises a hand and starts what sounds like a well-rehearsed speech. 'Look, Jack, we don't want to come in or even expect you to talk to us, we just wanted to drop these things off so you know that we're thinking about you so much and that we're here if—'

But Jack doesn't want to give Ash the satisfaction of finishing his sentence.

'So leave this shit on the doorstep like everyone else. I thought I was clear when you ambushed me in the hospital – we don't want to see you.' He glances at Bry. 'Any of you. So leave us the fuck alone.'

He pulls the door towards himself, ready to slam it closed, when suddenly, 'Jack? What's going on? Who's . . .' He spoke too loudly, wasn't careful enough; Elizabeth's by his side. The sight of them standing outside their door makes her stop perfectly still, and even though they're not touching, Jack feels Elizabeth's heart crash about inside her. Her eyes lock on to Bry and they don't let her go.

'Elizabeth, I . . . I'm so, so . . .' Bry's lips quiver around the words she can't finish; she dips her head and lifts her palm to her mouth as she starts to cry. Elizabeth doesn't flinch.

Ash takes over. 'Elizabeth, we were just telling Jack, we wanted to drop these things over to you. Alba's been busy making things for Clemmie, so . . . And there's a letter in there, and gifts for you and the boys too. Anyway, here they are.' He gestures to the wicker basket at their feet, but Elizabeth keeps her eyes fixed on Bry. When she speaks at last, her words are for Bry, only for Bry.

'Why are you sorry?'

Bry's eyes skip over Elizabeth's face, checking to see if she's serious.

'I mean it, Bry, I want to know why you're apologising. Is it because our daughter's blind – is that why you're sorry – or are you sorry because it's your fault she won't ever see again?'

Bry's eyes widen in horror and she looks like she's about to run away, but Ash takes her hand to steady her. He keeps his voice calm, ever the negotiator, as he says, 'Elizabeth, this wasn't anyone's fault. No one can prove Alba or Bry passed on the virus; there are so many different places she could have—'

'I wasn't asking you, Ash. I was asking Clemmie's godmother. The person who swore to protect her.' Elizabeth's voice drips with disdain as she turns calmly back to Bry. 'So?'

'I'm just sorry for everything, Elizabeth. I'm sorry that I wasn't strong enough to tell you the truth, I'm sorry I wasn't a better friend, and most of all I'm sorry that this has happened to Clemmie.' Bry keeps her head bowed, her eyes fixed on a spot on the ground. Elizabeth doesn't react; she just nods and looks as though she would like to stamp her heel, hard, on Bry's face.

'But what you don't seem to understand is that if this didn't happen to Clemmie, it would have happened to some other poor kid. You know what I find most abhorrent about you? It's your selfishness. You've proven that you think your child's rights are worthy of more protection than my child's life, and I fucking hate you for it.'

The word 'hate' comes out as a breathy hiss. Bry tries to pull away again; her eyes are almost closed and her free hand is covering her mouth – whether to stop herself from shouting or puking, Jack can't tell. Ash tightens his grip on her, a vein bulging in his temple, as he says, 'Elizabeth, that's not fair, we're here to offer help, we want to help . . .'

'You want to offer money again, do you, Ash? Great. Find

me a surgeon that can make my daughter see again and then we can talk. Until then, get the fuck away from my family before I call the police.'

Ash opens his mouth to reply but Elizabeth slams the door shut before he has the chance.

The silence that follows rushes in Jack's ears. He feels as if he's just been injected, straight into the heart, with a huge needle. Elizabeth is shaking but she's not crying. She won't want him to hold her, not now, not yet, so they just stand side by side in the shock before Elizabeth takes his hand in both her own. It feels solemn, sacred. Once Elizabeth's breathing has calmed a little, she says, 'I was going to tell you tonight, but I talked to a lawyer, Jack, someone Charlotte recommended.' Her eyes are silver, full of sharp, determined light. 'I have to do something, Jack. I want the world to know what they've done, and I want to stop it happening again. It feels like the only thing we can do for Clem now.'

Jack nods slowly, taking it in, surprised he's not more surprised.

'OK, Elizabeth, OK. If that's what you want.'

'It is. I've been thinking about it so much. I think it's the only way I can move on, the only way *we* can move on from this.'

'OK, look . . .' Jack leads Elizabeth into the kitchen, pulls a chair back from the table for her and takes two wine glasses out of the cupboard. The opened bottle is sitting on the table, and he pours them both a large glass before he sits down opposite her. The wine feels like acid down his throat but his brain immediately recognises the sweet, numbing effect.

'I've thought it all through, Jack.' Elizabeth reaches across the table for his hand. 'The solicitor I spoke with – Beth Ingram – says the CPS would be really unlikely to pursue the case because – strictly speaking – Bry and Ash haven't done anything criminal. So it would be down to us to take out a personal injury claim against them on Clemmie's behalf. She thinks the magistrates' courts won't touch it as there's no precedent for this kind of case, so they'd pass it up to the High Court, which means it'd be heard by a judge not a jury, which Beth thinks would be better for us. She thinks it's likely to be a very high-profile case, with a lot of media interest, and I'm sure she's right.'

Jack takes another long gulp of his wine. He nods, squeezes Elizabeth's hand as though he's fully on board, and wonders when the hell she had time for all of this. He's been run ragged learning how to give Clemmie baths safely, comforting Max and Charlie, arranging meetings with occupational therapists, not to mention negotiating a six-month unpaid sabbatical from work. He still hasn't figured out how they're going to survive financially, but that's a worry for another day. Then he thinks of all those long nights and mornings when Elizabeth stayed with Clemmie in hospital, when Clemmie was still on the tranquillisers that made her sleep for fourteen hours at a time, and he feels another irrational urge to laugh out loud. Will he always underestimate Elizabeth? Probably. He was worried she'd retreated so far within herself that she'd be lost to him for ever. Had he got her so wrong that when she was apparently mute with sadness she was really gathering reserves, plotting a fight? He looks at her across the table, her hands still, her back straight, and her eyes, God, her eyes seem to spark and spit like a new, unsettled fire and he realises she's back, the woman he fell in love with is back, and the whole kitchen seems to wake up, brush itself off and lift into colour – she's back.

'I'm going to email Beth now, arrange a time for us both to sit down with her and talk it all through.'

She stands to get her iPad from the kitchen worktop and as she sits back down, fixed to the screen, a small cry comes from the bottom of the stairs. Jack instinctively goes straight towards the sound. Charlie, wearing the pyjamas Jack put in the dirty-washing basket this morning, is precariously balanced on the banister, arms flailing above him, straining towards a page of Clemmie's glittery welcome home banner. In two long strides, Jack has caught hold of his legs. Charlie cries out in surprise and Jack says, angrier than he intended but not as scared as he feels, 'What the hell are you doing?' He lifts his son off the banister and adds, 'You could have broken your bloody leg, Charlie, for God's sake!'

It's only when he's put his son back down on the ground that Jack sees how red Charlie's eyes are, that he's been crying and is about to start again thanks to Jack. Jack breathes out and bends down, wraps his arms around his son, whose body feels smaller, shrunken with sadness.

'I'm sorry, mate, I'm sorry, you just frightened me, that's all. I shouldn't have shouted at you.'

Jack feels Charlie nod against his neck. He sucks some snot back into his nose and says in heavy breaths, 'Max called me an idiot for making the sign, said that I was a moron for forgetting that she wouldn't be able to see it.' Charlie pulls away from his dad, wipes his arm under his nose and, still shaking his head, his forehead creased, says, 'I didn't mean to, Dad, I'm sorry, I didn't mean to do it.'

Jack pulls his boy towards him again so he can't see the

tears that have started running down his own face. He thought he didn't have any heart left to break but a new piece splinters, sharp shards into his chest for his boy. He strokes his son's dark blond hair, marvels as he always does at the perfect shape of his head, and whispers into his ear, 'We know you didn't, mate, it was an accident, that's all. You made a beautiful banner for your sister. She loves you very much, we all do.'

'Not Max, he doesn't.'

'Oh, he does, but you know Max, he just has a funny way of showing it sometimes.'

Charlie clamps his legs around Jack's torso as Jack stands and turns towards the staircase.

'Come on, mate, bedtime.'

Just as Jack lifts his foot for the first step, Elizabeth calls from the kitchen table where she's working on her email to the lawyer.

'Everything OK out there?'

'Yeah, yeah, we're fine. I'm just taking Charlie up to bed.'

Jack pauses, hopes Elizabeth hears his silent request to come up and kiss her boys goodnight, but instead she just says, 'OK then, love you, Charlie Boy.'

Charlie keeps his face nuzzled into Jack's neck. Usually Jack would nudge him to say goodnight to his mum, but not tonight. Tonight it's Elizabeth who needs the nudge, but Jack doesn't have any heart left to make the request. He starts his slow, heavy way upstairs, his arms burning with the weight of his precious boy and his broken heart alive suddenly with a new fear for what their lives are about to become.

8 September 2019

Ash opens the front door cautiously, like a rabbit that senses foxes close by. But it's just after 9 a.m. on a Sunday, so the road is still blessedly quiet. Yesterday, he'd opened the door and there was the basket, ruined by rain, they'd left for the Chamberlains, dumped back on their own doorstep. The paint from the card Alba had lovingly made for Clemmie staining the front step. The presents they'd carefully wrapped for each of them, the letters they'd written, the cakes they'd made, all a pulpy mess and silvered by snails. He'd had to throw the whole basket away, told himself he wasn't going to let such a small thing get to him as he slammed the bin lid closed as hard as he could. He understood they were livid with him and Bry, but shunning Alba's homemade gifts made Ash's pulse quicken. Still, this morning there was nothing on the doorstep and no one around.

The night before, Ash had called Sara, who agreed to look after Alba for a few nights. She didn't ask why Alba needed to stay with them, so he didn't have to tell her that Bry couldn't get out of bed during the day, that he heard her pacing the house at night. That he'd had to attend Nettlestone Primary on his own to meet with the headmaster and discuss delaying Alba's entry into reception because Bry wouldn't leave the house. He doesn't, if he's honest, love the thought of Alba spending long, unchaperoned hours with Sara, who is still preaching and righteous, but Bry's absence has started to upset Alba and he can't focus on helping Bry with Alba racing around. So his plan this morning is to drive Alba the two hours to Sara and David's, and be home in time to make lunch for Bry and try to coax her into talking to him.

He calls back into the house, 'Come on, Albs, time to go,' before lifting the bag he hastily packed for her over his shoulder. Just as he opens the boot and is about to call for Alba again, a delivery van stops on the road and a man walks energetically towards him.

'Asheem Kohli?' Ash nods and signs before the delivery man hands him a white envelope, calling, 'Have a good day, mate,' over his shoulder as he skips back to his van.

The front of the envelope is marked with a name Ash recognises as a London-based solicitor's practice, Edmund and Worth, and suddenly he knows exactly what it is. He stares at it for a moment, the paper soft, expensive, between his fingers. These firms always want you to think they're richer, more powerful than they actually are. The car starts beeping, letting him know he's left the boot open. He silences it with a click and, still stroking the envelope, between his fingers, walks down the middle of the road a few paces until he's standing outside the Chamberlains' house. Their place is still in night mode, all the curtains upstairs drawn, but there are no curtains in the front room and, although Ash can't see in, he's certain Elizabeth will be watching him, that she'll have closely tracked the delivery of the envelope, not wanting to miss the moment of no return. He doesn't say anything, just waves the envelope a couple of times at the house. He thinks of Bry, crippled with guilt for something that wasn't her fault; he thinks of Alba's paintings ruined in the stinking bin, and it's as if someone's thrown a bucket of freezing water over his head. He feels the vibration of his blood through his body. The envelope crumples in his hand as he clenches his fist and waves it in front of the Chamberlains' sitting room window, whispering, 'If it's a fight you want, then a fight you will fucking well have.'

Edward Armitage QC – or 'Ed Arm' as he used to be known over twenty-five years ago at University College London when Ash and Ed were good friends – arrives fifteen minutes late for their lunch appointment the next day. Ed had suggested a discreet bistro close to his office to discuss 'informally' how to proceed. Ash spots Ed through the bistro window, waving to a black cab that pauses to let him cross the road, which he does in three long strides. He's one of those tall, lanky blokes who only needs to shave once a week, a baby face in a suit. Ash stands as Ed scans the dark restaurant for his old friend. They give each other a pat-hug before sitting down either side of the small table.

'God, I'm starving,' Ed says, as a waiter pours him water. Ed waves away the waiter's offer of a menu and orders chicken. Taken aback by Ed's pace but not wanting to show it, Ash asks the waiter for the same. Ash asks after Ed's wife, another lawyer called Ellen. Ed replies vaguely, before checking the time on his phone and saying, 'Right, mate. So, like I said on the phone, time is especially tight for me today. But I did read the email you sent over last night.'

At Ed's request, Ash had spent Sunday afternoon writing

in painstaking detail everything that had happened in the last few weeks. How he'd taken Alba to get some vaccines without Bry's knowledge, how Bry had finally replied to Elizabeth confirming that Alba had been vaccinated – when she wasn't, not fully – how sick they'd been but how much worse the virus had affected Clemmie, and how their closest friends were taking them to court on a personal injury claim for gross negligence. He was drained afterwards, emptied by the day, and he didn't have the heart to approach Bry that evening, to tell her about the court summons. Instead, he just got into bed next to her and tried to hold her.

'I think you're right. The charges they have against you are flimsy. We'll have to look into it all in detail, of course, but it sounds like it'd be hard to prove that either Bry or Alba passed on the virus to Clemmie given that they all started showing symptoms at the same time, and that they were all at the same fete along with the infected Spanish kid.' It's as though Ed's slowly lifting a heavy weight off Ash's chest.

'Yes, yes, that's exactly what I've been saying . . .'

Ed holds up one long finger to Ash.

'However, I bet they'll go down a duty of care route – that is, try to convince the judge that you and Bry had a duty of care towards Clemmie – which I don't think will be hard.'

'Duty of care?' Ash asks, feeling the weight lower once again on to his ribcage.

'Yeah, you know, like how a teacher has a duty of care towards their students, for example. But this is murkier. Bry's Clemmie's godmother, you're neighbours and very close friends – is that right?'

'Well, yes, we were . . .' But Ed's no longer listening to Ash.

'So that will prove proximity and, as you said in your email, you both knew Clemmie wasn't vaccinated, and as educated, thoughtful people who have, by your own admission, discussed vaccination in depth many times, you were able to foresee the harm arising from choosing not to vaccinate Alba.'

'If we'd ever had any idea that it would—'

'The judge will also look at whether it's fair and just to impose a duty of care in line with policy considerations – which again, in my opinion, won't be a problem.'

Ash doesn't understand, but Ed either doesn't notice or doesn't care, so Ash decides it's best not to interrupt his thought process.

Ed pauses to take a sip of his water, his eyes still on the solicitor's letter on the white tablecloth in front of him.

'The gross negligence part will be about failing to disclose Alba's vaccination status, evidenced in part by Bry's misleading and inaccurate text.'

The waiter approaches and smiles at Ed, calling him 'Mr Armitage' as he places a plate of chicken and pasta in front of him, Ash whipping the solicitor's letter away just in time. Ed nods a smile at the waiter and fixes his white napkin into his collar, then starts eating before Ash has picked up his cutlery. Ed keeps his eyes fixed on his food as he talks. 'One thing I'm not clear on is their reasons for bringing it to court. You said you'd already offered them money?'

'Yes, yes, of course . . .'

Ed looks up at Ash, his eyes round in his thin face, but his voice suddenly crackles with excitement as he says, 'So they'll be after revenge then. That's worse than money – for you, anyway. You should prepare yourself for media interest in this, I'm afraid, mate. Vaccination is a hot topic, and if it is revenge they're after, then they're probably the kind of people who'll get the media involved. They'll want to harness public sympathy.'

Ash nods, the weight now pressing hard, bruising his chest.

'It's already pretty bad online, to be honest. People are saying all kinds of shit about us.' The comments – that the people he loves most are evil, that they deserve to die painful deaths – hurt him deeply. He thought he'd be hardened to it, but sitting alone reading threats against his family with the armchair next to him empty, where either Bry or Jack used to sit, has made him hollow, weak.

'Yeah, well, that's unsurprising,' Ed says casually. 'Just try to ignore it.' He pauses briefly before adding, 'Where does Bry stand on all of this, the case and everything?' He glances up at Ash and, seeing that Ash doesn't know where to look or what to say, Ed guesses. 'She doesn't know, does she?'

Ash takes a sip of water, eyes settling at last on the food in front of him.

'I wanted to figure out what the options were with you before talking to her. She's, umm, she's . . .'

'Not in a good way, huh?' Ed talks around a mouthful of pasta.

'Not really, to be honest, mate. No, she's not at all, and I'm worried this is going to tip her over the edge.'

Suddenly Ash wishes he could be sitting with Ed the friend and not Ed the lawyer, but they've hardly seen each other since Bry and Ash's wedding, and Ed's phone pings with an email which he opens and scans quickly before saying, 'Sorry, mate, I'm going to have to wrap this up soon.'

They spend the next ten minutes discussing the terms and conditions of Ash hiring Ed as their lawyer, then Ed gives Ash a pile of documents to sign. He's expensive, far more expensive than Ash had been prepared for, but *Fuck it*, Ash thinks, *war always comes at a price*.

After lunch, Ash takes the train straight back to Farley. It's a beautiful afternoon, the air sweet and plump with autumnal warmth. Things around town appear to have returned to normal. He doesn't see one person wearing a face mask and the only anti-vaccination flyer he notices is caught in a hedge where dogs often pause for a sniff and a piss. He buys a loaf of sourdough and some French cheese he knows Bry loves, and stops at the florist's where he points to the biggest, brightest bunch of flowers they have in their display. As he walks through the park, he thinks about taking Bry on a surprise trip to Paris; they hadn't got to celebrate her fortieth after all and they'll both be due a treat once this is all over. He sees a couple of mums whose kids are friends with Alba, the kids in their blue Nettlestone reception uniforms chasing each other while the mums sit on a bench sipping from brightly patterned coffee cups. He hasn't seen them since Clemmie's party, so, over the huge bunch of flowers, Ash waves at them and, pausing, says, 'Hi guys, how're you . . .'

But one of them stands, turning away from Ash to call for her son, and the other looks down at the cup she's holding, cowering away from him as she stares at her hands and tries to suppress a nervous laugh. Ash shrugs and keeps walking. *Fuck 'em*, he tells himself, and tries to remember all those boring, stilted conversations he used to dread, tells himself it's a good thing he doesn't have to fake smile his way through them any more. So why does he feel bruised, like the shunned kid in the playground?

As he crosses over the bridge adjacent to Saint's Road, he sees Chris and Gerald walking side by side on the pavement ahead of him. Chris's eyes dart around when he sees Ash and he whispers something to Gerald, whose mouth and eyes pop open with surprise as he registers Ash just a few paces away. They're too close to cross and ignore him completely. No one smiles as Ash forces himself to take the first step. 'Hi, Gerald, hi, Chris.'

'Ash, hello,' Chris says before looking at his shoes. Gerald is hardly recognisable without a broad smile on his face.

'How was Croatia?'

'It was good, just the tonic we needed after Chris being so ill and with everything going on here . . .'

Still smarting from those women ignoring him in the park, he wishes he could shout *It's not our fucking fault!* into their faces, but he knows that won't help. So instead he takes a long breath and says, 'Look, I know it's difficult at the moment with everything that Elizabeth and Jack have been going through, but Bry and I are doing everything we can to try and ease . . .'

But Gerald shakes his head as though he can't believe what he's hearing. He moves closer to Ash and says, 'A little girl is blind, Ash. Clemmie's blind because of you.'

'No, Gerald, that's not right. What has happened is a tragedy, but you can't blame us. There's no evidence that Clemmie contracted the virus from either Bry or Alba.' Gerald listens, but his face is still stony as Ash keeps talking. 'Please, I'd like things to remain civil between us while we all try to get through this very difficult time.'

'But you lied, Ash, you lied. I mean, what were you thinking not getting them both vaccinated? You could have protected

Clemmie and you didn't . . .' Gerald's face flushes with emotion, his voice on the verge of cracking.

Chris moves forward, pulls Gerald's arm gently away from Ash and says, 'Come on, Gerald, we should be getting on.'

But Gerald keeps staring at Ash, looking for an answer or at least an apology. Ash has nothing to offer, so Gerald just shakes his head again and lets Chris pull him away.

Bry is facing away from the door when Ash slowly enters their bedroom an hour later, the air so warm and thick it's like a third presence in the room. Bry stirs under the duvet but doesn't turn around as Ash opens the door precariously with his foot, balancing Bry's flowers in a vase in one hand and a cup of tea in the other. He walks around the bed; her eyes are open but she's staring, her gaze vacant, at the wall.

'Hi, love,' he says, his voice just above a whisper as he moves towards her. 'I thought these were pretty,' he adds as he places the vase on her bedside table, next to a little pot of pills that makes Ash's heart leap in panic. He puts the tea down next to the vase and picks up the bottle of pills, shaking it to make sure there are still some left.

'Don't fuss, Ash, they're just sleeping pills, I'm not going to do anything stupid.' Her voice is a thin rasp, aged from lack of use.

His is the voice of a frightened kid as he asks, 'Where did you get them from?'

'You were prescribed them, years ago when you were going through the divorce.'

Ash thinks about putting them in his pocket but Bry reaches her hand out to take them and he's not here to argue.

He'll come back later, he reassures himself, when she's asleep, and he'll take all but one pill away.

'There's some tea for you here, Bry.'

'Thanks.' But she makes no sign of sitting up to take a sip.

Feeling lost, clumsy, Ash turns to open the curtains but Bry calls out, 'I heard you on the phone last night, I know you were talking to Ed. They're taking us to court, aren't they?'

Ash feels like he's spinning, mid-air.

'You don't need to say anything, Ash, I know they are. I read the letter from their lawyer, you left it on the kitchen island last night.'

He's free falling.

'I know you're trying to protect me but you have to stop. I don't care what happens now; I don't have room to care about anything.'

He hits the ground with a thud.

'I don't believe you, Bry, I don't believe that you don't care.'

'Please, Ash, please leave me now. Thank you for the flowers, but I need to sleep. Those pills . . . I . . . I need to sleep.'

Ash searches, desperate for some way to soothe her and some words to cool the panic quickening through him. A part of him wants to run downstairs, lose himself in a bottle and pretend he was never here in this room, crumpled on the floor, powerless, pathetic. But he can't leave her, not now, not when he's terrified of what she could do. So he just shuffles back until he's leaning against the wall, and watches as the light drains out of the room and his wife drops into a heavy, chemical sleep.

Farley County Court

December 2019

I try, I really do try to stay impartial. You have to as a social worker, if you don't want the job to kill you, but now that I'm here, sitting across the court room from her, looking so beaten and weak, I can't help but feel a little stirring of pity. 'C'mon, you silly old thing,' I scold myself, and I remember when I visited her at home. How I lost sympathy for her as soon as I stepped into her gleaming kitchen. It was huge with one of those islands with a marble top and fancy flowers in a fancy vase. I asked if I should take my shoes off and she said, 'No,' but I still caught her looking suspiciously at my black slip-ons like they could be covered in dog shit. I sort of hoped they were.

That morning I'd been at the Wilsons' again – five kids and their mum squeezed into a two-bedroom flat, mould on the walls and one toilet between them – and then I came into this palace. She started crying as soon as we sat down at the huge table and I thought, 'Yeah, the papers were right about you, weren't they, love? You are spoilt and stupid.'

I started asking the questions the court wanted me to ask about drug use and mental illness, and while she shook her dark head at me and told me about her charmed life, I asked myself silently the questions I wished I could ask: 'Did you think you were better than the rest of us? That viruses were something for the likes of the Wilsons and not for you in your cashmere cardigan sipping your posh coffee?'

'How much did this table cost? How much was this silk cushion?'

I moved on to the questions about Alba, her health, her weekly activities. She was dabbing her eyes again as she told me about Alba's Montessori childminder, the holidays they take her on, the bloody riding lessons she got for her fourth birthday. We carried on like this for an hour until I'd filled in my forms.

She opened the door for me, but hid behind it like she was frightened of who might be out there, which is fair enough. I gave her my professional stare, the one that scares my kids, the one I usually save for the drug-fogged dads who forget to feed the baby while their teen girlfriend's out looking for work – the look that says, 'I'm in control here. I'm on to you.'

I don't usually get a reply when I stare at someone like that, so I was surprised when she said, 'You think I'm a shit person, don't you? You think I deserve this.'

I paused and tried to imagine a scenario where I could tell her that yes, honestly I have no time for people like her who have everything the rest of us spend our lives struggling for but never get, for people like her who have it all and still manage to fuck up. Instead I let my silence answer for me, and the last thing I heard was her sob before the door clicked closed behind me.

14 September 2019

Jack is still getting used to the way Clemmie's loss of sight marks every corner of their lives. Even this morning's trip to the supermarket, for example. He's had to time his visit for when it's at its quietest – which is now, at 7.30 a.m. on a Saturday morning. It isn't just friends and acquaintances he wants to avoid, but since the story in the Farley *Neighbour*, 'Local Measles Girl Blind!', last week, and then another this week insinuating he's been having an affair with Bry, Jack has avoided everyone. Gossip, he's realised, is even more contagious than the virus itself. When someone does recognise him, mostly they're sympathetic, but the online abuse – accusing them of fabricating the whole thing to make money, that Clemmie never got sick, that she can see perfectly – has tainted every glance from a stranger, every kind smile from an acquaintance.

But this morning, so far, is a successful morning. He was the first customer through the supermarket doors and has gathered their usual list – as well as the fresh pastries, flowers and expensive coffee Elizabeth requested for the interview with a Sunday newspaper magazine supplement this afternoon – without anyone recognising him.

He's at the self-service checkout in less than half an hour. His fingers dance over which card to use for payment; the total is close to two hundred quid and none of his bank cards evoke any sense of confidence. He tries his current account first; it's rejected, which means they've already burnt through the grand his mum quietly transferred to him last week. There's no point trying his Visa credit card – he's already receiving warning letters about that one – so he tries the Mastercard he took out for emergencies, the one they've been using to pay the lawyers, but that too is rejected. *Shit.* He looks around briefly for help, realises no one can help with this, and takes out his phone. He logs on to his bank account. He was right; they're just forty quid from their overdraft limit for the current account. He clicks on to the tab with the three savings accounts – one for each kid. Being the eldest, Max has the most money at almost six hundred quid. Mostly it's from his grandparents – gifts given when he was born and for birthdays. In front of him, the supermarket checkout machine starts beeping, wanting to know what's taking him so long. He presses a button for more time before returning to his phone.

'Can I help you, sir?'

The man working at the machines is much older than the students usually serving the self-checkout area.

'No, no, I'm fine, thanks,' Jack says, keeping his face fixed down towards his phone. Can he do this? Can he steal from his own son?

'Only if you leave it too long, you see, it'll wipe your whole basket and you'll have to rescan everything.'

'Just one moment,' Jack says, without looking at the other man.

The machine begins beeping again, and on the screen a timer starts ticking down the seconds.

Max never has to know.

He taps to transfer two hundred from Max's savings into his own current account and then changes the amount to four hundred before making the transaction.

'Sorry, sir, but it is company policy to try and encourage our customers to use their phones *after* they've used the checkout machines.'

The man stands close to Jack, too close; he's holding on to Jack's machine with one hand to remind Jack who's top dog in this corner of the supermarket. Jack looks at him briefly. His skin is covered in tiny wrinkles, but his eyes are as sharp as any twenty-year-old's. Jack mutters an apology but the man stares at him, comes even closer before his fingers click together. 'Hang on, I know you, I know you from somewhere.'

'No, no, I don't think you do.'

Once the bank transfer's complete Jack shoves his card into the machine, but the clock on the screen keeps ticking, just ten seconds now.

'Please can you . . .' Jack gestures towards the machine, starts mashing buttons on the screen, but the clock keeps ticking down; it's as if even his own fingers are against him. The screen is frozen.

'Wait, are you a footballer?'

'No, no, I'm not. Please, my shopping . . . I just need to—'

'Oh God, you're the dad, aren't you? The dad of that poor little girl who went blind from measles, bloody awful business. I'm right, aren't I?'

The machine starts flashing red before it resets back to the resting page – 'Please scan your first item' – and Jack has to grip on to its metal sides to stop himself from screaming.

'Oh, Jack, there you are! What took so long?' Elizabeth is sitting at the kitchen table, her laptop in front of her. She's still wearing her dressing gown and the breakfast things have been washed up by hand, which means that Jack's mum – who doesn't trust their ancient dishwasher – must have done it.

Jack hauls five straining bags of shopping on to the stained wooden work surface, his hands stiff and bloodless from the weight.

'Are my folks still here?' he asks, slightly out of breath.

'I sent them to that National Trust place they've been going on about. Thought it best if it was just the five of us for the interview.' Jack winces at Elizabeth, but she's already turned back towards her screen, so she doesn't notice. Jack's parents have been staying as B&B guests in Jane's tiny annexe for the last two weeks, his dad doing his best to entertain the boys and his mum baking cakes, hanging up laundry and wiping up after them all. But for all her in-laws' kindness, Elizabeth still treats them as though she is paying them for a service and not as family doing the best they can.

For the second time this morning, Jack feels like screaming. But instead he goes to the sink, swallows his scream with a glass of water and looks out into the garden. Clemmie's out there with Claude, a golden retriever guide dog specially trained to support children, and the only living thing that makes Clemmie smile these days.

'God, have you seen this?' Jack moves towards the French doors. 'She's getting so much better, it's amazing.'

He's about to open the doors, to whoop and tell his little

girl how brilliant she is, but behind him Elizabeth looks up sharply from her computer and says, 'Jack, don't, you'll distract her.'

Jack spins round to look at his wife but she's already turned back, towards the screen. Upstairs, he hears shouts and calls from the boys on one of their computer games. They used to have football club on Saturday mornings, but they hadn't been for weeks.

'What're you looking at?'

'Oh, it's one of the court transcripts Beth sent through, the one she mentioned about the guy who was found guilty of transmitting HIV knowingly to three other men.'

Jack doesn't remember their lawyer saying anything about an HIV case; he just stares at Elizabeth. She's leaning towards the screen, her eyes flickering, her brow furrowed, as though her whole world, all her future happiness, depends on her reading whatever's on the screen. When Beth had estimated that the court proceedings would cost anywhere upwards of £40,000, Elizabeth hadn't blinked. Instead she'd calmly told Jack that most of that money would be spent on barrister fees and that she wanted to represent them as a litigant in person. If they used their savings, they could afford to pay Beth on an hourly basis to oversee the more technical elements of the case, but Elizabeth as an LIP would take on the lion's share of the work. Beth nodded her agreement. It was settled already. Jack wasn't being asked, he was being told.

'I've thought it all through,' Elizabeth had said lightly, as though they were talking about what to have for dinner that night.

'Elizabeth, we need to talk.'

Her shoulders tense in irritation.

'We can talk later,' she replies.

'No, now.' Jack walks over to her and closes her laptop, Elizabeth only just pulling her hands away before they're trapped between the screen and keyboard.

'Jack, that's important!'

'I'm sure it is, but I reckon the fact that we have absolutely no money is more important.'

Elizabeth blinks at him. 'What about that new credit card?'

Jack shakes his head.

'Beth's invoice took care of most of that.'

Elizabeth frowns, chews her bottom lip. She looks more irritated than troubled.

Jack sits opposite her, rests his elbows on the table, rubs his face between his hands before he says, 'I've been thinking about setting up a crowdfunding page, you know, asking people for support.'

Elizabeth looks at him as if he's just slapped her. 'But isn't crowdfunding for charitable stuff?'

'Elizabeth, we have literally nothing. After that shop I just did, we have forty quid left.' He stops himself from telling her they now also owe their twelve-year-old four hundred pounds.

'You know, people keep asking what they can do to help – well, this is it, this is how they can help.'

Elizabeth sits very still. He knows she'll be desperately trying to think of other options, but they've already been turned down for a second mortgage and he can't ask his parents again.

'Could you go back to work, maybe on a part-time basis?'

He looks at her; there's so much he could say in response. He could ask her who will help the boys with their homework, who will learn Braille with Clemmie, make sure she doesn't fall down the stairs while Elizabeth's doing whatever it is she's doing on her laptop for hours on end. Or he could finally come clean, tell her he can never go back to that office, to that life. Besides, he's read a couple of emails that the company is looking to make redundancies in the New Year and he's certain his name will be top of the list; due to the three months' salary he received while he wasn't working over the summer, they'll do everything they can to avoid paying him a redundancy package.

'You know the agreement: three months paid, three months unpaid. There's literally nothing else we can do, Elizabeth, this is it.'

She breathes out, cross with Jack for distracting her, cross with money for getting in the way.

'OK, but I think we'd better keep any of the legal stuff out of it. Maybe it could be to raise money for Clemmie to have additional help learning Braille, a counsellor, for the new carpets so she doesn't trip up, all the house adaptations – stuff like that.'

Jack nods, relieved to find a solution, albeit an imperfect one.

'OK, well, we do have to pay for all of that. I'll work out how much and set our goal as that amount – it'll probably be a few grand.'

'That sounds sensible.' She looks at her phone. 'Shit, the reporter is going to be here in an hour. I've got to get ready.' She glances at the shopping Jack left on the worktop and says, 'Those flowers need to go in some water.'

Alice Ranton is smaller than Elizabeth expected, her body thin in a way that does not seem natural. She's wearing tight jeans and a loose light grey silk blouse, and as soon as Elizabeth looks into her eyes she knows Alice is an expert at getting people to like her. When they were planning the interview, Elizabeth hoped for a natural ease between them, a female camaraderie. *Bry would call it 'sisterhood'*, she thinks, before she can stop herself. But as soon as Elizabeth sees Alice, she knows that's not possible. Yes, Elizabeth thinks, Alice is one of those disingenuous, controlling types, but she's also the person who's going to tell the world about Elizabeth's family, so Elizabeth will smile along, pretend she hasn't clocked who Alice really is.

'Elizabeth, hi, so great to meet you.' Alice is full of compliments as soon as she walks through the door: 'Such a beautiful road,' and 'Are these tiles original?'

While Elizabeth makes tea, Jack introduces Alice to the boys and the dog trainer, Clemmie and Claude finish their session, and Clemmie walks into the kitchen holding Claude's harness. Elizabeth beams at her daughter and says sotto voce to Alice, 'That's the first time she's done that on her own.' Elizabeth studies Alice's reaction to Clemmie, but she's such a pro; there's no pity or sadness in her expression, just the same carefully arranged smile.

Everyone makes a fuss of Claude, and Elizabeth feels Clemmie's relief. With Claude by her side she's no longer just the blind girl; she is, as the dog trainer keeps telling her, Claude's best friend, his mistress, the person he loves best. She clings on to Claude's harness, her knuckles white. Elizabeth passes her bone-shaped treats and Clemmie tells Claude to 'lie down' and then 'roll over' as Alice claps her hands and says, 'Wow, that's brilliant, Clemmie!'

It couldn't be going better, Elizabeth reassures herself.

The boys disappear upstairs back to their computer game and Jack sets Clemmie up in the sitting room with her headphones and a new audiobook, Claude curled like a golden shell by her feet.

'They're great kids,' Alice acknowledges, as the three adults settle back around the kitchen table.

'Thanks, yeah, we think so,' Jack says, pouring three glasses of water. 'I mean, it's not easy but they're adjusting well, all things considered.'

'We're so proud of them, especially Clemmie, of course. But Jack's right. It's not easy. It's undoubtedly the hardest thing any of us have ever gone through, and to think it could all have been avoided . . .' Elizabeth reaches out and cups her palm around the back of Jack's hand, but it feels unfamiliar, her hand over his, and she can't pull away because Alice will see. 'That's why we're going ahead with the case and why I approached your magazine about this article. It's not about winning. We know there are no winners here – we only want to raise awareness about the importance of vaccinating, to try and stop other little ones from going through everything Clemmie's gone through.'

Alice nods and says, 'I understand, I do, but as I said on the phone, Elizabeth, it's best if we don't mention the court case or the Kohli family in the article; we don't want to risk any libel action. So why don't you tell me more about the impact Clemmie's illness and visual impairment's had on the family. I mean, it must put a huge strain on you emotionally?'

Alice's eyes flicker as Jack pulls his hand out from under Elizabeth's and takes a sip of water before he says, 'I mean, a big thing has been the financial strain.' Elizabeth narrows her eyes at Jack; she knows he can feel her staring but he chooses to ignore her. 'You see, I've had to stop working for a few months, so things are pretty stressful in that regard. I don't suppose you can mention our crowdfunding page in the article, can you? I'm going to set one up to help us pay for all the expenses – the NHS have been great – but there are some extras Clemmie really needs. We've got to make the house safe for her, for one thing.'

Alice nods and says, 'Let me ask my editor about that one and come back to you.'

What's Jack thinking? They don't want to come across as charity cases!

'Yeah, but Jack,' Elizabeth interjects smoothly, 'Alice asked us about the *emotional* strain, which has been huge. Clemmie got really upset yesterday – she said she couldn't remember what her hair looks like – and Charlie's definitely become a bit withdrawn.' Alice nods, but her eyes are dull; she wants something else from them, something more.

'And what about you guys? How are you both doing emotionally?' Her eyes are on Elizabeth and it's as if Alice is trying to look up her skirt. She wants to slap her away but she can't, so instead she looks to Jack. But Jack just looks back at her, as though he's just as interested as Alice to hear her reply.

Elizabeth feels that the two of them are trying to crowd her into a corner, and, opening her hands to them both, she nods and makes herself laugh a little as she says, 'I'm fine! Absolutely fine!'

The newspaper photographer is with them for the last half-hour. He asks the five of them to pose with Claude in the sitting room and outside in the garden, before Alice glances at her watch and casts a look at the photographer, who starts packing down his tripod.

Elizabeth feels weary as she shows Alice and the photographer to the door, as if she's just given blood. But Alice's smile is just as spritely as it was when she arrived, and so Elizabeth forces herself to keep up the charade, smiling broadly as Alice offers Elizabeth her bony hand and says, 'So good to meet you, Elizabeth. Thank you so much for sharing your story with me. I'll be in touch when I'm back in the office next week?'

But suddenly Elizabeth can't hold on to her smile any more because, beyond Alice's thin frame, Rosalyn is standing on the pavement, looking directly at her. Rosalyn's not smiling and she doesn't look away in pity or embarrassment when Elizabeth meets her gaze. Instead she just looks plainly at Elizabeth. The photographer glances over his shoulder, tries to see what's suddenly caught Elizabeth's attention.

What is Rosalyn doing? How dare she just stand there, staring at them? Stopping herself from running over to her neighbour, telling her to mind her own business for once, takes as much effort as it does for Elizabeth to haul the smile back on to her face, a smile Elizabeth hopes will somehow tell Rosalyn to fuck off and simultaneously convince Alice that she's had a great time too. She says, 'Thanks so much for coming all this way to talk to us. I can't wait to read the article!'

And it takes every ounce of strength to keep smiling until at last they're gone, and before she's even closed the door behind them, she lets her smile wither and die.

17 September 2019

Bry lies awake, blinking into the night as Ash breathes softly, fast asleep at last next to her. Since he found those pills he's insisted on sleeping in their room again; it's as though he trusts her less when it's dark. She wakes every night now at about 3 a.m. When Ash was in the guest room, she'd just sit in the chair by their bedroom window and stare at the inky sky until morning. Sometimes she'd go downstairs. But now, with him in the way, she moves quietly into Alba's room. She sits on the floor, her back pressed against Alba's little bed so she can stare out of the window. Ash is wrong; he shouldn't be worried about her at night. The night is her ally. During the night, she can drop the exhausting pretence and it's as though she is finally allowed to feel, properly feel, that which is really always there. She has blinded Clemmie. She is guilty and she will never be innocent of anything again.

But as daylight starts to lift the sky, she feels herself exposed and creeps back, reluctant, into her empty body. She moves her leaden legs, adjusts her position on the floor, and her eye catches on another nothingness. There, on the wall at the foot of Alba's bed, there used to be a framed photo of Clemmie and Alba taken last Christmas, but it's gone. The photo was a close-up, the two girls clutching each other, laughing into the camera. Where is it? Ash must have moved it – maybe he thought it would upset Alba, that it would remind her what her mum has done to her friend. But now she's thought about that photo, Bry needs to see it. She opens a few of Alba's drawers, but the photo isn't there. Nor is it in the spare room or any of the cupboards in Alba's bathroom.

She goes downstairs, wired now. Maybe Ash hasn't hidden it from Alba, but rather taken it to stare at himself? It's tidier than normal downstairs, better without her. She opens the drawer under the island – Ash calls it the 'misc drawer', for all the homeless household crap: old chargers and last year's birthday cards. Bry steadies herself; there it is. On top of an old magazine. She pauses for a moment before she picks it up. Clemmie lost a front tooth just before Christmas and she'd been a bit shy about the gap in her mouth, but in this photo she is laughing too much to care. She glows with joy, her eyes bright, as though she is lit from within. Bry feels herself start to quicken, panic, her heart lifted from its leaden state. She's about to close the drawer, take the photo back upstairs, when she realises that Clemmie's gappy smile is also printed on the magazine beneath the frame in the drawer. Bry snatches up the magazine. In the photo, Clemmie's lost another tooth. She's smiling at the camera but it's as though the internal light has been snuffed out. Her eyes are fixed a little away from the camera, dull and vacant where all that light used to be. In her lap she's holding on to a large, sandy-coloured dog, the dog's tongue lolling out of its mouth. Bry opens the magazine, her heart falling like a leaf as she real- ises it's a full article, the headline 'Our Battle Against Measles' above a photo of the whole family, pressed up against each other on the sofa. Clemmie is sitting on Jack's lap, Elizabeth behind them and the two boys either side.

Bry clutches the magazine and it twists in her grip as she shuffles towards the table. She's just sat down when suddenly all the kitchen lights flick on, making her wince. Ash is tying his bathrobe around his waist, no longer asleep but not yet fully awake either. He holds on to a chair to keep himself steady.

'Bry, there you are.' He places his hand above his heart in relief.

'I just found this.'

Bry waves the magazine at him and Ash rubs his face with his hands, nods grimly and says, 'I was going to tell you about it, Bry, find the right time . . .' Bry shrugs and starts reading the article while Ash sits sadly by her side until she's finished. Afterwards, Bry stares into a corner of the room and neither of them says anything until Ash mutters, 'They don't mention the text message and they don't use our names, which is something, I suppose.'

Bry blinks but doesn't move. They may not have mentioned either of those things but the article states that a court case is set to start in December, and it's the work of a few seconds online to find their names. But that doesn't matter either. Let people know it was her. Their hatred is easier to take than her own self-loathing. Suddenly Bry says, 'They've set up a crowdfunding page.'

'Yes, yes, I saw that, but you know I've offered money already. They won't take it from us.'

Bry nods. Her hand falls limply away from the table and she gathers it back into her lap. Before he goes back upstairs, Ash holds his warm hand against her face for a moment and strokes her brow, his fingers gliding over her eyelids, nose, mouth. And she remembers those times in his London flat when he was broken and there was nothing she could say to put him back together. She doesn't know she's going to do it, but on an impulse, she holds on to his hand, presses it into the side of her face for just a moment, before she turns away from him and retreats into her silence.

She doesn't wake again until late morning and then only because someone, somewhere, is calling her name. The caller, a woman, is getting closer, coming upstairs. For an exquisite split second Bry lets herself believe it's Elizabeth, that none of this ever happened, but then the caller knocks quietly at the bedroom door and says, 'It's Rosalyn. Bry, sorry to wake you, but there's a supermarket delivery for you downstairs, says he'll charge if he's turned away.'

Bry pulls herself to sit up in bed; her head thumps with the sleeping pills she took that morning. She puts her feet on the floor and wobbles like a toddler as she forces herself to stand and go downstairs.

Rosalyn is wearing jeans and a colourful, oversized blouse. She's fishing in the cupboards as the kettle whines to boiling on the Aga. There are supermarket bags dotted around the kitchen.

Rosalyn turns to look at Bry but she doesn't seem to notice Bry's stained, worn T-shirt or her saggy leggings. Instead she looks into Bry's eyes and it's as if she's shining a torch directly into her. Bry squints and looks at the floor.

'I hope you don't mind, but I thought I'd make us both a coffee,' Rosalyn says before adding, 'but I can't for the life of me find your mugs.'

Bry shuffles, still mute, and opens the cupboard next to the Aga, before she opens her heavy lips to ask, 'What are you . . . why are . . .'

Rosalyn moves in front of Bry, takes two mugs out of the cupboard and, turning to Bry, says, 'OK, I admit it. The supermarket delivery was just a convenient excuse to come and see you.'

Bry can't think of a single good reason Rosalyn can have to want to see her. Noticing Bry's confusion, Rosalyn says more gently, 'Just sit down, Bry. I'll make us a drink and then I want to tell you something.'

She doesn't have the strength to question or argue, so she just sits and watches with heavy eyes as Rosalyn buzzes around the kitchen for a few minutes, before she places two steaming mugs on the table and eases herself into the chair opposite Bry. They sit in silence. Bry stares at her mug and has the odd sensation that Rosalyn is not only occupying the same physical space as her, but that somehow she is also sharing her emotional space as well. It's as though she's squeezed herself on to the same chair as Bry, but somehow, it doesn't feel uncomfortable. Quite the opposite in fact.

'Do you want to talk?'

Bry shakes her head.

'Do you mind if I talk?'

She lifts her eyes to Rosalyn. She shakes her head again.

'OK. I want to tell you a story, something I did when I was in my twenties at art college in London, if that's all right with you.' Rosalyn takes a sip of coffee, twists a silver ring on her forefinger. 'I haven't talked about it in a long time but the last few weeks have reminded me of that time, or more accurately, you remind me of myself back then.'

Rosalyn tells her story gently, her voice soft and forgiving, as though she's comforting her younger self.

'I was a bit of a partier back then, into the whole bohemian artist lifestyle cliché. Anyway, I was at a party with a friend. I wanted to take LSD but Zara – my best friend – didn't want to.' Rosalyn exhales a deep breath through gently pursed lips, as if the memory still carries heat and she needs to cool it before she can continue her story.

'I gave her loads of shit for it, telling her she was being boring, all that kind of crap. I basically forced it on her, if I'm honest. I didn't know where I was or who I was with for the next twelve hours. I basically remember nothing from the trip, but when I came round the next afternoon, Zara was missing. She'd vanished. Zara's boyfriend called the police and they said she was in hospital. Some bloke on his way to work found her half naked and mumbling by Westminster tube. Anyway, Zara recovered physically but she was never the same after that trip. Six months later she was sectioned. She killed herself the day after they released her from the psych hospital two years later.'

She closes her eyes briefly, gives out another long exhale.

'Zara's boyfriend and her family all blamed me. They said I'd basically murdered Zara. I was banned from her funeral and they sent horrible letters. But they didn't need to; I was punishing myself worse than they could ever punish me. I didn't get out of bed for weeks, I was fired from a gallery I worked in, I lost friends. Then I started to drink and party again. I was reckless, taking everything I could, using drugs to get me out of bed and using drugs to get me to sleep again. But then I went too far, ended up in hospital and then rehab. I could hardly remember my own name, I was so full of sadness. One day my aunt barged into my room, and gave me the talking to of my life.'

Rosalyn's eyes glaze over, as though she's staring directly through a window and watching herself back in her room at rehab.

'What did she say?' Bry whispers.

Rosalyn smiles suddenly and looks up to the ceiling before she answers.

'She never took any bullshit. She agreed with me. Called me an idiot, said that, yes, Zara's death was partly my responsibility. But then said that I was in danger of doing exactly the same thing again. I was in danger of poisoning myself and destroying my own life. She said I owed it to Zara not to let her death destroy me. That was the moment I started to change.'

Neither of them says anything for a long time. Bry's mug grows cold. At last Rosalyn says, 'I believe in grieving, I do, and I think you have a right to grieve, Bry. Yours is a horribly hard situation and I can see how much pain you're in, but don't let it suffocate you, because it's not just you who's suffering. Alba will be suffering too, as is Ash, and they will both drown with you if that's what you choose.'

At her daughter's name, Bry feels herself sharpen. She hasn't been able to speak to Alba for two days; she didn't trust herself since the last time when she'd started crying at the sound of Alba's voice. Alba, panicked, had started wailing herself, pleading, 'Mumma, Mumma, please don' cry, don' cry.'

Ash had taken the phone off Bry then and managed to calm Alba down, but no one had suggested another call since. She hears those words again: *Alba will be suffering too.* Slowly, Bry becomes aware of a new ache deeper even than her guilt. It comes for her in a great wave, breaking into her heart and sending ripples through her whole body, and Bry feels herself, at last, begin to wake up.

When Bry hears Ash pull into the drive an hour later, Rosalyn has just left and Bry is still in the kitchen. He'd called as he was driving home from another meeting with Ed about the case. Ash's voice was higher than normal on the phone, surprised Bry had answered. As soon as he opens the front door he stops still, taking in the fact that Bry's washed, dressed and sitting quietly on the stairs in front of him. He starts breathing hard, looks up to the sky before looking back at Bry, shakes his head before glancing at the sky again, as though there's something up there he needs to thank, and then Bry opens her arms to him as he begins to cry.

They still don't talk much over the next twenty-four hours. Bry is still so weary and Ash is awed, a little intimidated by her recovery. During the day Bry naps downstairs on the sofa and eats all the food Ash lays in front of her; at night they spoon in bed. Ash never knew relief could be so much like bliss. They agree to collect Alba the next day. Bry stares out of the car window, watches the world flash by as though it's the first time she's seen autumn turning the landscape to rust. At one point Ash turns to her and says, 'I've been thinking. Maybe it would be good for us if we rent somewhere in the countryside, just for a few months until all this is over? You know, have a bit of space from it all.'

And Bry nods and says, 'I'd like that, I really would.'

And Ash smiles out at the wide road ahead of them.

They make good time, and once Ash has parked outside

her parents' house she puts her hand on Ash's leg, feels his muscles flex, surprised by her gentleness, and says, 'I might go in on my own, if that's OK? I just want to have a quick chat with Mum. I'll say you're on the phone. Just give me twenty minutes and then come in.'

Ash looks at her; the change over the last two days is so great he can't fully trust it, not yet, but he nods and says, 'Sure,' before she kisses him and goes into the house she used to dream of escaping.

The house is surprisingly quiet but as soon as she opens the door, Sara emerges from the kitchen and pretends she wasn't waiting for her, as Bry knew she would. Bry feels her mother's eyes sweep over her, making their assessment about Bry's mental wellbeing, before she says, 'Oh, my Bry-bug, we've been so worried about you.'

And she holds Bry's thin body tight, as if she's trying to donate some of her own strength to her daughter.

Bry gently eases Sara's grip and says, 'Thanks for having her, Mum, you've been amazing.' She glances up the stairs towards her old room, which is now Alba's room when she stays here.

She's desperate to go and see her, but Sara's already walking away, beckoning Bry to follow her back into the kitchen as she says, 'Alba's just getting her things together with Granddad. Come and fill me in on how you're doing; they'll be down in a moment and she'll be so excited to see you, we won't get another chance to chat.'

Sara clearly has things she wants to say, just like Bry. She flicks the kettle on. The window's open to the garden and Bry can hear the ghostly song from one of Sara's wind chimes outside.

'I've been so worried about you, Bry,' Sara says again.

Bry squeezes her hands together in her lap. 'I know, I'm sorry.'

'Don't be sorry, love. I know it's hard for you – you're not used to all the attention, all the different opinions.' Sara pours hot water into two mugs and puts a herbal tea on the table in front of Bry. The tea has a faint farmyard smell.

'How are you guys? How's Alba been?' Bry asks, but Sara ignores both questions.

'I hope you know that amongst our community people are really behind you, singing your praises, in fact. Ash's too,' she adds with a surprised little flick of her eyebrows. 'I'll forward you some of the things they are posting online.' She pauses before she says what she really wants Bry to hear.

'I do think though, Bry, that it's time you embraced the amazing opportunity you've been given.'

'Opportunity?' Bry repeats, the word clumsy and strange in her mouth.

Sara looks up from blowing on her tea, her brow furrowing at Bry's confusion.

'Yes, darling, the golden opportunity you've been given to raise awareness nationally about vaccine injury.'

Bry cups her forehead in her hands before she looks at Sara and says, 'Mum, my goddaughter is blind. She's seven years old and she's blind.'

'I know that, darling!' Sara opens her arms, exasperated, as if Bry is asking the impossible of her. 'It's sad, very sad indeed. But I can give you a hundred names right now of children who have lost more than their sight because of vaccines—'

'I won't do it, Mum.'

Sara stops talking and looks at Bry with a strange mix of irritation and curiosity.

'You won't do what, Bry?'

'I won't be the poster girl for your cause.'

Sara's knuckles glow white against the handle on her mug.

'That's a crude way of putting it,' she says primly, before adding, 'and I've never thought of it as *my* cause; it's our family's cause, or at least it should be.'

'Well, maybe that's where we've all gone wrong,' Bry says as gently as she can, standing now.

'What are you saying, Bry?'

'I'm saying that I don't want to feel guilty any more. Nothing and no one is to blame for Matty's disabilities,' she says firmly, before adding, more gently, 'They are just a part of him.'

'You weren't there, you weren't even born when he had that shot, you haven't been through what I've been through . . .'

'No, I wasn't there. But I've lived every day of my life as though I was.'

Sara's face falls. It's as though a mask, lovingly made and carefully worn, but a mask nonetheless, cracks and falls away. Underneath Sara is exhausted, raw.

Bry wants to move forward, to touch her mum's arm, to tell her she still loves her, but the fear that Sara will turn away makes her stop.

Bry looks up as suddenly, upstairs, Alba starts running along the landing, making the old floorboards thunder above their heads. Sara turns away from Bry, towards the window so Bry can't see her face.

'Mumma! Mumma!' Alba shouts, her voice an explosion of joy.

But Bry ignores the instinct to run to her little girl; instead she chooses to listen to an older, dormant instinct and says, 'Mum, Mum, please, I don't—'

'Go to her, Bry, we'll speak soon,' Sara says, without turning to look at her daughter.

It is as though an invisible kite string connecting them has at last snapped. It hurts but as Bry turns round, opening herself to Alba, her face like a star, as she runs with all her might into Bry's arms, she feels the relief of no longer being tethered to so much old pain, and she smiles as Alba presses her lips close to Bry's ear and asks, 'We going back 'ome now, Mumma?'

And she whispers back, 'Yes, my darling, we're going home.'

Farley County Court

December 2019

The waiting is the worst bit. Even though I know the questions I'm going to be asked, waiting to walk up to the witness box is still interminable. I rub my thumb into my moist palm and try to control my breathing. It was hailing this morning and now the heating in the court room, combined with all our damp clothes, has made it musty like an unaired bedroom – a strangely intimate smell, a reminder of how much we all share. Damp clothes, smells, the air we breathe.

I look down at the notes in my lap. Ben, my husband, listened to me practise this morning while he ate his bran flakes.

'Smile!' he said before looking at me and saying, 'No, no, too much. No one likes a desperate-looking scientist.' I tried to calm my face into an authoritative but friendly expression. Ben nodded. Better.

'OK, so what are you going to say when she asks whether vaccines cause autism?'

This question – about vaccines and autism – is the key bit. It's why I've been called as an expert to this first-of-its-kind court case. I look at the huge list of in-depth studies, each and every one disproving the damaging claims made by Andrew Wakefield in the late nineties. How extraordinary that one man – one bad study – can still do so much damage more than two decades later, that his terrible science has – albeit indirectly – led to a little girl going blind and to this court case. It's easy to forget sometimes what a huge responsibility it is, being a scientist.

My leg starts twitching again. I shuffle my feet to try to get my leg to still as Elizabeth, her husband and solicitor enter the court room. Elizabeth looks around until she sees me. I lift my hand to wave, reassure her that I'm here, ready to help. She nods at me, offers the faintest smile before finding her seat at the front of the court.

I start to recite my lines in my head again; the facts help alleviate some of my nerves.

'We now know that autism,' I tell myself, 'is a naturally occurring form of neurodiversity. An analysis of studies involving over one million children found there was no link between vaccination and the development of autism. In fact, there have been so many studies that have disproved any link between vaccines and autism that the only thing we scientists can state with any degree of certainty is that autism is not caused by vaccines.'

Yes, good.

Ben, in my head, asks, 'What do you say when they ask about the risks associated with vaccines?'

I answer silently, 'Vaccines are proven to be safer than the illnesses they protect against. For example, one in five thousand children develop encephalitis as a complication of measles, but less than one in a million develop encephalitis as a complication of vaccines.'

The door to the court opens again and this time it's the Kohli couple who shuffle in. Unlike her ex-friend, Bryony keeps her eyes down, too afraid to look around the court. Poor woman. The truth is, I feel for her just as much as Elizabeth.

'Don't get emotional,' I imagine Ben telling me. 'You're there to report the facts, nothing more.'

I take another deep breath and reread the section in my notes about why people should continue to vaccinate against diseases that are no longer common.

'Infectious disease is only a few hours' flight away. Travellers to countries which still have diseases like polio and diphtheria can bring back these diseases to the UK. Since 2015, for example, two unvaccinated children in Europe have died of diphtheria. Once a disease is wiped out in every country in the world, vaccination is no longer necessary, but so far this has only happened in the case of smallpox.'

A separate smaller door is opened by the court usher and the judge walks, robes flowing, into the court.

Oh God. This is it.

'You'll be all right once you're up there,' Ben reassured me this morning.

I swallow, fold my notes away and hope he's right.

18 November 2019

It's raining. The boys are fighting in their attic room directly above where Elizabeth is sitting on Clemmie's small bed, her laptop in front of her, trying to understand a report and a series of brain scans from Clemmie's neurological consultant. Clemmie's bedroom has now become Elizabeth's room. She works on the case in the little pink room most of the time now, even when the kids aren't home, and she sleeps in here too since Clemmie still wakes every night. But now when she wakes, Clemmie calls for Jack, not Elizabeth. So without saying anything to Jack, she'd simply moved herself across the landing.

The first night she moved, Jack poked his head around Clemmie's door. Elizabeth was sitting in her usual position on the tiny bed, her back pressed against the wall and her face bleached by the light from her laptop screen. Jack crouched on the floor next to her, held her hand and said, 'It's only because I'm spending more time with her in the days, Elizabeth, that's the only reason she's calling for me.'

Elizabeth had squeezed his hand, made herself laugh gently and said, 'Oh Jack, you think I'm worried about that when I'm writing my opening comments for the case?'

He'd pulled his hand away from her then, scalded, and he hadn't come to say goodnight again. It was petty, really.

The problem is, he still doesn't understand how important the case is. They have one chance, just one chance, to get it right, and that heavy weight rests entirely on Elizabeth's shoulders. Jack is never going to step up to the plate, offer to take on the work or the immense pressure and represent their family in court. But then he's taken to his new domestic role with a lightness and energy she'd never anticipated. He hums while he irons the kids' school uniforms and has started reading around their school topics so he's informed when he helps them with their homework. She'd peeked out of Clemmie's room one afternoon and heard him laughing with the kids over a revolting bolognese he'd made for their supper. She couldn't remember the last time they'd laughed, all of them together, like that.

Suddenly there's a loud thud followed by a howl from upstairs, as the boys' argument escalates into violence. With a groan, Elizabeth snaps her laptop shut and walks stiffly towards the stairs to shout a reminder that she's trying to work, when she almost crashes into Jack who is already springing up the steps. He doesn't see Elizabeth so she just stands and watches as Jack opens the door to the boys' room and asks in a calm voice, at normal volume, 'OK. What's going on in here?'

Back at her computer, Elizabeth listens to the boys' mumbled explanation before, a few minutes later, they all trudge downstairs, talking animatedly now – about what, Elizabeth doesn't know. She turns back to the warmth of her screen and hopes for the excited but almost fearful feeling she gets in her chest when she's fully absorbed in the case, like the first flush of nervous love. Well-wishers and supporters keep saying that the case will be over in just a few months. Elizabeth knows they're trying to say the right thing, to be reassuring, but the thought of going back to a life without the case makes Elizabeth feel vertiginous. She can't imagine a time, a life *after*, and if she's honest, she doesn't want to. She glances at the pile of legal books she borrowed from the library, her notebook full of ideas and questions – there is still so much to do, she reassures herself, and feeling a little comforted, she squints back at her laptop screen and soothes herself in abstruse, sprawling words.

Elizabeth is already awake, staring at the glow-in-the-dark stars on Clemmie's ceiling, when the alarm from across the road shocks the silence. She doesn't need to look out of the window to know it's coming from Bry and Ash's house. It whoops and wails like something in pain. It's happened once before, a couple of years ago, when Bry and Ash were away and some kids tried to break into their shed. The fancy alarm system called the police automatically but Elizabeth, who had a spare key and the code for the alarm, was over in less than a minute; the kids had already disappeared into the woods. It took the police ten minutes to arrive, by which time Elizabeth had disabled the alarm, made a pot of tea and reassured a couple of neighbours that it wasn't anything to worry about.

Tonight, she stands up, pulls her bathrobe over her pyjamas, shoves her feet into her old trainers, grabs her phone and the keys to Bry and Ash's, and it's not until she's outside, the freezing November air almost painful in her lungs, that she remembers. This isn't her job any more. Bry and the wellbeing of her family are not her concern. She shouldn't care. She should go home, let the police deal with it. But then she notices Jane's bedroom light flicker on; the alarm will wake the whole street if she doesn't move quickly and, besides, she's already out here, freezing in the dark. She may as well just go and shut the thing up for everyone else's sake; no one will thank her for doing nothing. Gerald told her last week he'd heard from Row that Bry and Ash are renting a cottage a few miles outside Farley; she can easily stop the god-awful noise and be back home before either of them arrive.

The alarm keeps screaming into the night and Elizabeth's almost at the front door when she feels a grinding under her feet, before something sharp bites her toe. She's too surprised to call out – she looks down and realises she's standing on broken glass. The light from the alarm makes the shards glow a strange fluorescent red, and she realises there's shattered glass all around her. Some of it has just pierced her old trainers and lodged itself into her big toe.

'Elizabeth, careful!' a woman's voice shouts at her. Elizabeth turns, dazed, and sees Rosalyn, bulky in a thick winter coat, a few paces behind her. The red light is glowing on her skin. She's wearing heavy boots, the ones she wears when she's sculpting. She crunches over the glass towards Elizabeth as though the shards are nothing but a thin layer of ice. Elizabeth's foot starts to throb in time with the alarm. Rosalyn reaches for her hand and, leaning in so close that her lips graze Elizabeth's ear, she says, 'Hold on to me.'

Elizabeth, placid with pain, light and noise, grips on to Rosalyn and the two of them hobble to the side of the front door, away from the glass, where Rosalyn eases

Elizabeth's grip on her coat and, leaning in again, says, 'I'm going to turn the alarm off.' Using her own key, she opens the front door and disables the alarm. The sudden silence swells in Elizabeth's ears, as loud for a moment as the piercing noise. Elizabeth rests her foot on its side; she can still put some weight on it and it doesn't feel wet, so the cut can't be that bad.

Rosalyn turns on the outside lights and now Elizabeth can see that one of the long panels of glass she helped Ash choose to flank the front door has shattered. Across the road, a couple more upstairs lights have turned on and Elizabeth recognises Chris's anxious face peeking out from behind the bedroom curtain, but she turns away from him to face Rosalyn, who crunches back across the glass, shaking her head.

'Some idiot put a brick through the window,' she says, her voice bouncing with anger and surprise as her phone starts buzzing in her hand.

'Hi, Ash.' Rosalyn answers her phone and Elizabeth feels as if she's been sliced for a second time. She can hear Ash's voice through the receiver but it's just a mumble. The alarm company would have called him straight after calling the police.

'No, it's fine. Really, we're fine,' Rosalyn says into the phone, looking at Elizabeth for confirmation that she is OK. 'Yes, Elizabeth's here but she hurt her foot, I'm afraid . . . She cut it on some glass. Some arsehole put a brick through the front panel . . . Yup. I think she's OK. You want to talk to her?'

Elizabeth shakes her head, waves her hands furiously at Rosalyn. No, she doesn't want to fucking talk to him, has the woman no sense? Rosalyn dangles the phone towards Elizabeth but she doesn't take it.

'She doesn't want to talk. Look, Ash, the police will be here soon – can you deal with them and I'll take Elizabeth back to mine and have a look at her foot?'

Rosalyn hangs up and, looking at the glass, glistening, beautiful, on the ground, says, 'Thank God they weren't home. It would have terrified little Alba.'

An instinctual relief warms Elizabeth before she kicks herself again – Alba isn't her concern any more. Without thinking, she says, 'These things happen. She'd have got over it.'

Rosalyn grimaces and Elizabeth looks away from her.

'This didn't just *happen*, Elizabeth. Someone put a brick through their window, probably because they've read something untrue in the media about them. We both know that.'

Elizabeth looks sharply at Rosalyn.

'What are you saying – you think I'm to blame for this?'

Rosalyn breathes out a cloud of cold air.

'Look, we're both in shock. Come to mine, I'll take a look . . .'

'No, no, you've started this now. The least you can do is have the decency to answer me. Do you think I'm to blame for someone putting a brick through their window?'

Rosalyn stands perfectly still as she replies.

'I don't think you're to blame but I think, indirectly, you're partly responsible, yes. But honestly, it doesn't matter what I think.'

Elizabeth can't decide whether to laugh or scream. Instead she just says, 'You're unbelievable.'

'Elizabeth, you knew, especially with all the media interest, that by pursuing the case Bry and Ash would be vilified. That some nutters would take it to the extreme. You knew something like this was a risk, but rightly or wrongly you've decided to keep going with the case anyway.'

Elizabeth limps towards Rosalyn, ignoring the slicing pain in her toe.

'I know exactly what you're trying to do. You cannot compare what they did to Clemmie with this. It's not the same. It's not.'

Rosalyn nods and replies as gently as she can, 'What happened to you was much, much worse, of course it was, but I think the principle's the same. There's risk inherent in every decision we make, in everything we do.'

Elizabeth stares, scrabbling, desperate for words that fit the white rage that fills her whole body. She feels liquid, almost ecstatic with anger.

'Please, Elizabeth – look, I'm sorry, I probably shouldn't have said anything. Please let me help.'

Rosalyn reaches forward, touches Elizabeth's arm, but Elizabeth whips her hand away and says through clenched teeth, 'Don't you touch me.'

'Everything all right?' a voice calls from across the road. Elizabeth doesn't need to turn around to know it's Chris, calling to them from his doorway.

Rosalyn glances at Elizabeth again and calls back to Chris, 'We're fine. The police are on their way.'

'What happened?' Chris calls again, and Rosalyn, with a reluctant glance at Elizabeth, moves across the empty road to reassure him. Elizabeth turns, numb with cold, her solar plexus tight. She presses her bleeding foot into the hard road, and the pain almost makes her scream, but at least she doesn't feel her heart any more as she stumbles into the darkness, telling herself she will make it home.

Ash had been right; even though the entire footprint of the cottage they're renting in a tiny hamlet ten miles outside Farley is roughly the same size as their downstairs at home, there is more space here. It is as though Bry had been living with something covering her airways, eyes and ears for months, and it has finally been ripped away. There are long hours when she still can't think because of the pain, but at least when she emerges and finds herself here, exhausted and broken, she still wants to breathe. Three days a week Alba goes to a local childminder who runs a smallholding, and she lets Alba help her feed the pigs, goats and chickens. The childminder – who says she is too busy for the internet – either doesn't know about the case or she doesn't care, because she hasn't asked either of them about it. Ash has started jogging again, and surprisingly his consultancy work has picked up, so he's busy every morning strategising with small media companies, guiding them through acquisition bids. He still protects her from a lot, she knows; he still hasn't told her why the alarm went off at home the other night, and she has decided she doesn't want to know. Not yet anyway.

Bry spends her days going for long walks, talking online with her new therapist Caterina, and sitting quietly with Matty. She visits him almost every day now at The Rowans. She'd never visited him on her own before and she's been surprised to feel a fellowship in the quiet afternoons they spend together. For the first time she simply sits with her brother; she no longer stares at the clock and wonders how long she has to stay. He is the only person who doesn't demand an explanation from her; he has no expectations and his acceptance is like a balm. She feels a gentleness grow between them that perhaps has always been there but she's been too full of her own fear and shame to notice.

On her fourth visit, Victoria, his carer, had passed Bry Matty's hairbrush and she'd brushed his hair for the first time. The next day, Matty pointed to his head as soon as he saw his sister, which made Bry laugh.

'He likes you,' Victoria said with a smile. Bry had to bite her lip to stop herself from crying as she picked up his hairbrush. It was the first time Matty had made her laugh, she now knew, because it was the first time she'd given Matty the chance to make her laugh.

Last week she'd taken Alba with her, and Bry didn't flinch when Alba started walking her dinosaur figures across her uncle's lap as Matty sat perfectly still, peacefully absorbed in his little niece's game. The only thing Alba didn't understand was why the two of them playing silently with her toys had made her mum cry. For the first time in her life, Bry feels as though she has a brother, not a burden.

She only turns her phone on a couple of times a week now. Last week Row texted, asking her how they were, saying she'd love to come and visit. Bry hasn't replied yet. Jessie had been more forceful in her message, telling Bry she was leaving Coco with Joe and coming to see them the next day. Briefed by Ash, no doubt, Jessie hardly mentioned the case or the Chamberlains. Bry asked after their mum and Jessie said she would be fine, that they would be fine, but just like everything else it would take time. That was all Bry needed to hear. Jessie stared at Bry closely, watched her every move, as though the way Bry stirred the soup or laced her boots could reveal something important about her sister's inner world.

She talks to Rosalyn every few days; twice now Bry has called her on one of her long walks and Rosalyn just listens, quietly, as Bry cries into the phone. Last time they talked, Rosalyn told Bry she was going back to Italy at the end of November. Rafe has just got a job in Milan working for an art gallery and Rosalyn has decided to go with him. She said she worked better over there, that the lifestyle suited her, that she'd forgotten how gruelling British winters could be. Bry will miss her new friend but the news hadn't really come as a shock; somehow it feels right that Rosalyn should roam again.

Bry still hasn't talked to her mum; she's heard nothing from her and Jessie was resolute that she didn't want to get involved. Bry finds she cares less than she probably should. Her life – broken as it is – feels freer now she is no longer tethered to Sara's paranoia. There will be a time, Bry knows, when they will find each other again, but not now, not while they are both still so full of fear.

Bry feels like a stain on the blue morning sky as she drives – cajoled by Ash and her therapist, Caterina – into Farley for an appointment with her GP. She'd been careful to book in with a new doctor after she'd finally conceded that a low dose of antidepressants was probably a good idea. As Caterina said, 'Just as extra support for the next few months.' It is part of Caterina and Ash's campaign to get Bry to accept that the court case is happening, no matter how much Bry tries to ignore it, and that she needs to be emotionally prepared. For Bry, thinking beyond tomorrow is like trying to envisage a world before she was born. But still, here she is, trying to do the right thing.

She arrives a few minutes early, parking close to one of Elizabeth's favourite cafes. She sits in her car for five minutes, making herself late so she can avoid hanging around in the GP surgery and risk being recognised. When the GP calls 'Bryony Kohli?' into the waiting room, Bry notices one of the receptionists lift her head and, frowning, whisper, 'Bryony Kohli,' a couple of times before turning to her colleague to ask where she's heard the name before. Bry keeps her head down and walks quickly towards the tall GP, into her small, white room.

'Hi Bryony, I'm Dr Fisher.' Dr Fisher gestures to the chair opposite her own for Bry to sit, which she dutifully does. 'I'm still fairly new here. It's good to meet you.'

'Hello,' Bry says. Dr Fisher crosses her legs. She must know who she is, surely?

'Right. How can I help?' So that she doesn't need to look directly at Dr Fisher, Bry stares at a couple of smudgy pictures by young children pinned to the wall as she starts to recite the words she practised during the drive.

'Well, I've had a difficult few months and have been low, very low indeed, as a result. This difficult period won't end any time soon, and my therapist Caterina Kennoy – you should have got an email from her – recommended I start a course of antidepressants. But a low dose, just a low dose, please.'

Bry only looks towards Dr Fisher once she's finished her little speech. After the stares, the comments online and whatever happened the other night on Saint's Road, Bry prepares herself for a battle whenever she steps outside the cottage.

So it's a surprise when Dr Fisher doesn't scowl or smirk. Instead, she looks at Bry carefully without accusation or pity, but with a gentle acceptance that reminds Bry of Rosalyn.

'Yes, I did read about you and your family. What an awful experience for all of you.'

Ah, here it comes. Bry bows her head and waits for the recrimination. But it doesn't arrive. Instead Dr Fisher turns back to her computer and types something before she speaks again.

'Right, let's take a look.' Bry recognises the letter from Caterina on Dr Fisher's screen. She nods as she reads and then turns back to Bry. 'I just need you to fill out a couple of forms for me and then I can write a prescription. But before we do that,' Dr Fisher says, making Bry flush and twist her hands in her lap.

Here it comes: the judgement, the repulsion.

'I just want you to know that you can come and talk to me any time. Even though I'm a GP, I still found it hard to vaccinate my own kids; I was up the night before, questioning whether it was the right thing to do.' Bry feels her jaw soften and loosen as Dr Fisher keeps talking.

'My mum always says it must be harder than ever before, being a parent these days. All the choices we're constantly faced with, all the different opinions, and on top of that we're made to feel that it's our fault if something doesn't go to plan – people always want to blame the mum. Anyway, I just wanted to say that if you have any questions, about vaccines or anything medical, then just make an appointment and I'll help as much as I can. OK?'

Dr Fisher's words are like a warm breeze moving through Bry, and her eyes fill. She wishes she could stand up and hug

Dr Fisher, but she's already turned back to her screen and says, 'Righto, I'll just print out these forms and then we can get you on your way.'

That night Ash and Bry eat leftover stew and baked potatoes, sitting cross-legged on cushions as close to the black-iron wood burner as they can get without burning themselves.

'Aha! Proof that there are more decent people out there than shit ones, don't you think?' Ash says, when Bry tells him about her meeting with Dr Fisher that morning. They finish their food in contented silence before Ash says, 'I got a call from Ed today.'

Bry accidentally bangs her cutlery against her empty plate. She always gets clumsy whenever their lawyer or the case is mentioned. She makes herself speak.

'OK, and?'

Ash drinks his water down in one go before he looks directly at Bry. It's something Caterina suggested: that instead of looking away from each other when they have something hard to say, they practise looking at each other instead. She can feel how badly he wants to look away, poor Ash, but he doesn't give in.

'Apparently the CPS has withdrawn a case that was scheduled before ours. It's been decided to bump up ours because of all the media interest. Ed said we might not get quite so much attention with Christmas and everything coming up, so he seems to think it'll work in our favour. He's happy, so I said I'd talk to you and come back to him tomorrow.'

'When will it start?' Bry's voice is almost a whisper. Ash cups his hand around Bry's crossed ankle. She presses into the warmth of his palm.

'They're suggesting Monday 9th December. Ed says that it'll be over before Christmas.'

'Shit, that's, what . . .'

'Three weeks away,' Ash says. On Ash's instruction, Ed has tried twice to settle the case outside court and both attempts have been flatly rejected, as Bry knew they would be. Elizabeth never settles; she fights.

Bry exhales, her lips pursed.

'Yes, it is much sooner than we expected.' Ash talks carefully, as though the wrong word could cause Bry to detonate. 'But like Ed said, the sooner it starts, the sooner it's over and we can move on, properly move on with our lives.'

Bry doesn't say anything for a few minutes before Ash asks, his voice weary but patient, 'What do you think, Bry?'

But Bry isn't really thinking anything, she's just aware that she's still sitting here, in front of Ash, that she hasn't run for the nearest small, dark hole. Instead she finds she actually means it when she says, 'OK. Fine. Three weeks. Let's call him together tomorrow and confirm.'

Ash squeezes her ankle again and says, 'OK, OK then.'

Ash clears away their plates and Bry makes them tea, and without saying a word to each other he sits down on his cushion with his back resting against the little threadbare sofa and Bry lies in front of him, her head in his lap while he strokes her hair, the wood burner glowing like a heart in front of them.

9 December 2019

Elizabeth's almost disappointed; the crowds outside the court sounded much bigger from down the road, before she could see them. There are probably only eight people here, bulky in hats and gloves, half of them sharing a thermos of steaming tea, their signs propped up on the bench outside the grey court building. Their solicitor Beth had prepared them to expect many more. But it's a freezing day and still before 9 a.m.; Elizabeth guesses many of them will have kids to deliver to schools, jobs that need some attention, before they can get out into the knife-cold air and start spouting their anti-vaccination bullshit.

Jack next to her turns and asks, for what must be the tenth time this morning, 'All right?'

Elizabeth nods automatically, straightens the designer camel-coloured wool coat on loan from Charlotte, and rolls her gloves into a ball so she can take Jack's hand. Beth hadn't had to tell her that it was important for them to put on a united, loving front, and of course any one of those sad people outside the court could be a reporter. The small clutch of protestors nudge each other as they approach, but their leader has been held up in traffic and they're not sure what he'd want them to say or do, so they just stare as Elizabeth leads Jack up the grey steps and towards the heavy oak doors of the court.

It was absurd of Jack to ask Elizabeth if she was OK so many times, really; he must have seen her clear eyes, her relaxed smile, the vigour in her movements. She is better than OK; she feels fantastic. Why wouldn't she? She would never admit it out loud, but she carries within her a small, hard certainty, like a pearl hidden deep inside, that she is about to change the world. That Clemmie will know, for the rest of her life, that her mum might not have been able to make her see again, but she changed the world for her, that she saved countless lives for her. How many little girls can make a claim like that?

They are met at the door by the court usher and shown to a small room with a table and some lockers, where they are told they can leave anything they don't want to take into court with them. Elizabeth takes off Charlotte's coat, folds it into a locker along with her handbag, checks her hair in a tiny mirror and then turns to Jack, who is standing in the middle of the room still in his scarf and coat, texting.

'What are you doing?' she asks; she can't believe what she's seeing.

'Mum can't find Clemmie's headphones.'

Elizabeth sighs. Jack has been nothing but a liability so far this morning.

'Didn't you pack them last night?'

'Yes, but Clem had them out this morning and now she can't remember where she left them.'

'Oh, for fuck's sake, they must have spares at school she can use?'

At last Jack looks up from his phone; his eyes are watery, dull.

'Don't swear like that, it's not her fault.' Elizabeth recoils; he just spoke to her not like he talks to the kids, but like *she* talks to the kids. Doesn't he get it that this morning, of all mornings, she needs to stay focused, that she mustn't be distracted with anything? His phone buzzes in his hand again.

'It's fine. Mum's found them.'

She forces herself to smile at Jack – she needs to keep the peace this morning. An argument now wouldn't help the case.

'Good, that's great,' she says stiffly, and she picks up her dad's old briefcase full of her carefully arranged, colour-coded notes, and says aloud but mostly for her own benefit, 'OK. Let's do this.'

Elizabeth tries to follow Beth's advice and not look at Bry and Ash, who are already sitting ramrod-straight in their front-row seats in the large, wood-panelled court room, but she can't resist a quick glance. Their skinny, wolfish barrister is beside them and in the pew behind them sits – Elizabeth guesses – their solicitors. Ash looks older, his complexion almost as grey as his beard, his face lined by deep vertical wrinkles. Bry – God, Bry looks like she did when she used to dress up for Halloween. She has thick black circles under her eyes and her skin is blotchy and raw across her protruding cheekbones, even though she must, surely, be wearing make-up. Bry turns around, towards the side doors through which Elizabeth and Jack have just entered. She used to say she could always sense when Elizabeth was close; she called it her very minor superpower. Elizabeth looks sharply away and instead notices the face of a social worker, a medical ethics academic and a child psychologist, all of whom have interviewed her family over the last few months, each one entrusted with a piece of their story. Elizabeth clutches the handle of her briefcase with one hand and grabs Jack's hand with the other. She doesn't want anyone to see that she's shaking, in case they mistake the adrenaline coursing through her for fear.

Court room six, refurbished in the nineties, is, in Elizabeth's opinion, badly designed. They have to walk past Bry and Ash to get to their seats on the other side of the judge, where Beth is standing in a pale grey suit, waiting for them. But even so, she already loves this place, this place of right and wrong, the clarity of it. Walking into court feels like a homecoming of sorts. But of course, it's not the same for Jack. She feels the reverberation through his hand as all his muscles tense and his skin grows damp against her own.

They make it to their seats and Elizabeth smiles vaguely towards the back of the court, where she glimpses Charlotte, Chris and Gerald and a few other supporters, as Jack sits down immediately. The press benches to the right are full already, most of the journalists leaning over phones and notepads. Beth smiles warmly as they approach and instead of a greeting she holds on to Elizabeth's upper arms and whispers, smile unbroken, 'Confident and resolute, remember?'

That's the mantra they've agreed on to help Elizabeth through any tough moments. Elizabeth nods and smiles as she sets her briefcase down and takes her seat between Beth and Jack. It was a sweet idea, but Elizabeth doesn't need mantras. All she needs is to remember Clemmie, her eyes wide open, screaming into her endless darkness, and she feels every muscle, bone and fibre of her being rise up to fight. She's ready.

District Judge Bower must be well past normal retirement age. He holds on to the wooden railings as the court usher calls, 'All rise!' and he walks unhurriedly up the steps, a skinny crow in his black robes, towards his seat. He wears thin-framed, thick-lensed glasses; the tight curls of his judge's wig sit too far back, revealing a shiny, bald head and giving the impression that his face is falling away from his skull, drooping in soft folds an inch or so below its presumed starting point. Beth had told Elizabeth that he was old, though she'd also warned, 'But don't let that fool you.'

The judge pulls his glasses away from his face and, address-ing the court, says, 'Please take your seats,' and Elizabeth knows immediately what Beth was getting at. His voice is the voice of someone thirty years younger. It is clear, strong and cuts through the warm, soporific court air like ice water. Only the judge remains standing behind his large desk. He glances down at some papers in his hand and, putting his glasses back on his face, looks at the benches to his left and then at the bench to his right, directly at Elizabeth. He nods and then smiles at the court room.

'Good morning, everyone. As you know, we are here this morning to hear a personal injury claim brought to court by Jack and Elizabeth Chamberlain of 10 Saint's Road, Far-ley, who are representing their daughter, a minor, against Asheem Kohli and Bryony Kohli of 9 Saint's Road, Farley. The claim against Mr and Mrs Kohli is of gross negligence, and I will decide whether the Kohlis were negligent in choos-ing not to vaccinate their daughter, also a minor, and whether that led to the Chamberlains' daughter contracting the measles virus and her subsequent severe and permanent visual impairment.'

Taking his glasses off his face again, he briefly taps them against his cheek before his tone softens, and without looking at his notes he adds, 'Whatever the outcome, this is a tragic situation. A young family has been forever altered, and we are, I'm sure, all too aware of the high emotion and intrigue surrounding this case beyond the confines of this court. We can expect interest to intensify as these proceedings get underway. We will, of course, all encounter the demonstrations just outside the court and there will be much coverage in the media as well. We will be pressed for details and information about the case, but I implore you to remember this case has at its heart two minors; leave the supply of information to the press, who also have a presence in this court, and trust them to do their job. I have decided to allow a public gallery but I will not hesitate to change my mind if I feel the authority of this court is being disrespected in any way. I hope I make myself clear.'

The judge nods, satisfied that he has been heard, and Elizabeth feels blood rush to her face as he turns towards her and says, 'I understand, Mrs Chamberlain, that you are representing your case as a litigant in person?'

Elizabeth grips the table in front of her, a shock of energy passing through her as she stands, and, keeping her eyes fixed on the judge, says in a clear voice, 'I am, sir.'

'Very good. If you need clarification on any legal terms or require any extra procedural support, please let me know.'

Elizabeth nods.

'Thank you, sir, I will.'

'Very good. Well, without further ado I invite you to deliver your opening statement, Mrs Chamberlain.'

Elizabeth nods again but before she starts, she spends a moment picturing Clemmie back in hospital, rubbing her eyes red raw, desperately trying to make them see again. She feels the flame of her anger leap and spit. She curls her short hair behind her ear; it's a new affectation, minutely observed, making her look feminine but strong. She clears the heat away from her throat, takes a sip of water, and from behind her bench starts to speak, slow and steady, the words she must have practised a hundred times already.

'This case poses the question – if a parent knows the dangers of a contagious disease but still chooses to put other, vulnerable children at risk, should the parents be exempt from the consequences of that choice? If I choose to drink and then get in my car and hit you, it is my responsibility. If I fail to maintain my property and a brick falls from my wall and injures a passerby, it is my responsibility. Negligence holds us all to a community standard and if we deviate from that standard, we are correctly liable for the harm we cause to another, whether we believe our conduct was reasonable or not. Why should failing to vaccinate both yourself and your child be any different?'

She pauses, looks up at the judge, whose watery blue eyes are fixed on her, just as she knows the hundred or so other eyes in the court room will also be staring at her. She doesn't pace as she did at home. Instead she's very still, letting her words and her voice do the work. She takes another sip of water before she starts to talk again.

'I'd like to turn the court's attention now to some facts we will prove over the next few days. Fact one: Mr and Mrs Kohli were made aware on numerous occasions that our daughter could not be vaccinated due to the severe seizures she had as a very young baby.

'Fact two: My husband and I were falsely led to believe by Mr and Mrs Kohli that their daughter was fully vaccinated and would not pose a risk to our daughter's health.

'Fact three: Both girls as well as Mrs Kohli contracted measles – a strain of the virus that has been traced to a Spanish student who was visiting Farley as part of an English-language programme.

'Fact four: Mrs Kohli and her daughter recovered from the measles infection without any medical complications. Our daughter developed encephalitis, a rare but serious swelling of the brain as a result of which part of her brain – the occipital cortex, the part that understands sight – was irreparably damaged.

'Fact five: Our seven-year-old daughter will only be able to see shadows for the rest of her life. Never again will she see the faces of the people she loves. Her life and her future have been altered beyond all comprehension.'

Elizabeth feels Jack shift in his seat next to her. He's staring up at Elizabeth, his eyes wide, almost fearful, on the verge of tears. Elizabeth turns away; it would probably be a good thing if the judge sees one of them cry, but she can't be that person. She clears her throat again.

'The defendants will claim that no law has been broken as Mr and Mrs Kohli have a legal right in this country to choose not to vaccinate their child. They will say that it cannot be proven that either Mrs Kohli or their daughter passed the virus on to our daughter. Indeed, they will go so far as to suggest that our daughter could have contracted the virus first and passed it on to them.

'But all this is immaterial, as we will demonstrate that they had a duty of care towards our daughter that they failed to uphold. They willingly misled my husband and me, letting us believe our daughter was safe when she was not. They will correctly state that we have already refused private remuneration outside court for the damage they have caused, and they are right – my husband and I did refuse their money. Why? Because financial compensation is only one small part of the issue. It is about recognising that in a community, we have a duty not to cause each other harm. It is about casting real light on this difficult issue and refusing to look away. It is about protecting all those other children who cannot be vaccinated, from the same dark, uncertain future our daughter now faces.'

Elizabeth can feel the admiration of everyone in the court room. This case is going to be even better than they hoped, with Elizabeth, the tragic but inspirational mother, in the starring role. She tucks her hair behind her ear again and reminds herself not to smile before she continues, 'This case is unknown territory – there is no legal precedent – but it is my sincere hope that a guilty verdict will encourage other so-called "vaccine-hesitant" parents to re-evaluate their decision.'

Elizabeth pauses again, for another sip of water. The court is pin-drop quiet. She turns back to the judge as she starts to talk again. 'We are lucky that most parents no longer have to watch their children choke to death from diphtheria, be paralysed from polio, break ribs and bleed from their eyes because of whooping cough. But our family, despite my husband's and my own best efforts, has not been spared. We have had no choice but to watch our daughter's agony as she struggles to come to terms with her sight loss caused by a vaccine-preventable virus that Mr and Mrs Kohli, our closest friends and neighbours, exposed her to through their negligent and reckless choice not to vaccinate. I am looking forward, sir, to stating our case to you and this court, and we hope very much that this case will set a precedent to protect any future parents and children who risk having their lives brutally and tragically altered because of another parent's choice not to vaccinate their child. Thank you, sir.'

Elizabeth almost anticipates applause as she sits down, but this isn't the theatre. Jack smiles dutifully next to her and nods his head and mutters, 'Well done,' before Beth squeezes her arm and whispers, 'Excellent, Elizabeth. I'd say that's one-nil to us.'

Bry always knew Elizabeth should have been a barrister rather than a solicitor. Elizabeth's debut was masterful. Just homespun enough that the judge was constantly reminded that it was this woman right before him who'd suffered so much, but practised and professional enough to prevent him from becoming frustrated. He looks impressed, his eyebrows lifting as he makes a few notes with his fountain pen after Elizabeth has finished talking. Bry looks over to Ed, who is shuffling his papers together, preparing to make his opening comments, and suddenly it feels as though they've hired his robes and wig as a costume they can hide behind because they're either too scared or too stupid to do what Elizabeth just did – defend their family themselves; they have to pay someone to do it for them instead. Ed had been pleased when he found out Elizabeth was acting as a litigant in person; he told them an LIP always makes at least one major mistake. To which Bry replied, 'Yeah, but you don't know Elizabeth.'

To the court, Bry knows that Elizabeth must look great. She's wearing a pinstripe pencil skirt Bry recognises from when they used to live together fifteen years ago, and a light pink silk blouse that must be new. She appears elegant and upright, her hair recently highlighted and cut to her chin; as always, she's in control. But Bry still knows her better than anyone. She knows that her posture only looks perfect because all her muscles are so tight they start to spasm if she relaxes for too long. She knows that the way her eye pulses occasionally means she hasn't been sleeping, and she knows from the way Jack stares at her, as though she's someone he used to know but can't quite place, that things aren't good between them. But none of this knowing matters: everything they learnt in friendship feels irrelevant now they are, to all the world, enemies.

Bry starts to pick at her scabbed fingernail with her thumb and Ash puts his hand on hers to try and stop her from doing more damage. He squeezes, his hand warm, and smiles at her – 'OK?' – and she wishes he would lift his arm around her like a wing and make her invisible. But she knows she can't hide any more. She has to sit here, let herself be seen and judged.

At last, Judge Bower nods towards Ed.

'Good morning, Mr Armitage.' His tone is familiar; Ed has appeared before Judge Bower before, but Bry can't remember now whether he won then or not. Judge Bower gestures with one hand for Ed to begin his opening comments when he's ready, and Bry recognises a sort of paternal gentleness pass from the judge to Ed, as though he sees his younger self in their thin, serious barrister.

'Thank you, sir.' Ed steps away from their bench to stand directly in front of the judge in the narrow space between the two sides, no man's land. He turns briefly, nods first towards the public gallery then to the row of experts and even towards Elizabeth and Jack, and says, 'Good morning, everyone.'

He exudes confidence and calm, as though the court is his natural habitat and he's relieved to be home. Suddenly Bry understands why they're paying him £600 an hour.

'Thank you, Mrs Chamberlain. You certainly raise some interesting points, but I fear the issues brought to light by this case are rather more nuanced and complex than your comments allow. You talk about community and responsibility but you seem to forget that our society is built on a liberal, individualist tradition – whether you agree with it or not – and freedom is the very cornerstone of this tradition. Bryony and Asheem Kohli were simply exercising their legal right to only partially vaccinate their daughter.' He turns to the judge. 'Just like Mrs Chamberlain has exercised her legal right to refuse their offers of financial support and bring this case to court.'

He's unhurried; his voice carries just a little swagger.

'Let us be under no illusion here: this case carries significance far beyond these two couples sitting here today. It could pave the road for activists to pursue mandatory vaccination in this country. This means that our children – in order to benefit from state education and to be accepted within our society – will have to undergo over twenty-seven forced medical procedures by the time they're five years old, according to the NHS vaccination schedule. The State would have control over our children's bodies – whether it harms them or not. The same State that accedes that there are risks inherent in vaccinating, as evidenced by the existence of the government-funded Vaccine Damage Payment scheme, which seeks to compensate people who have been – and this is a direct quote from the NHS website – "severely disabled as a result of a vaccination against certain diseases".

'The State itself recognises that, for some, vaccination will cause severe disability. It recognises that there is risk in vaccination – and where there is risk, there must be choice.'

Ed pauses for a moment, places his papers back on the bench so it appears as though he's so enthralled by his own argument that he doesn't need any prompt.

'Life is inherently risky. There is risk in absolutely everything we do. The person who dies choking on a piece of food, the child who slips and breaks their neck playing football. If we are to live freely, then we need to accept there are some things beyond our control. And so it follows that we must not penalise parents – in this instance Bryony and Asheem Kohli – for refusing to expose their child to a risk they deemed unreasonable. Informed by their own experiences and histories, they made a perfectly reasonable, legal choice for their child. This is not negligence. This is parenting.' Ed pauses, his chin raised, his gaze fixed somewhere far beyond the court for a moment, before he seems to return to himself and says, 'Parenting is hard and parents are liable, of course, to make decisions they may later come to regret. I think this is a point most parents' – Ed casts a pointed look towards Elizabeth and Jack – 'even Mr and Mrs Chamberlain, will identify with at some level.'

Beth whispers something into Elizabeth's ear but Elizabeth shakes her head in response.

Ed returns briefly to his notes before continuing in a more casual, almost slightly bored tone.

'Mrs Chamberlain will say that Bryony and Asheem lied to them about their daughter's vaccination status. But at no time over the years of their close friendship did either Mr or Mrs Chamberlain – these great vaccine advocates – ask either Bryony or Asheem whether their daughter had had the MMR vaccination. The question Mrs Chamberlain asked in her text message on which much of the claimant's case rests, "Is your daughter vaccinated?" is vague, just as Bryony's reply, "Yes, she is," is equally vague. But being vague is not the same as lying.

'Of course all of us wish, most sincerely, that neither of the girls nor Bryony ever contracted measles. We wish even more that the Chamberlains' daughter never developed complications and that her sight was not affected. But we are not – as you made clear, sir – here for emotion. We are here to look at the plain facts within our long-established legal framework and ask ourselves – has a crime been committed here? To which, you must agree, it has not.

'Thank you, sir.'

Ed sits back down next to Ash and accepts his 'Well done' with a fleeting smile and a quick incline of his head. While the judge takes his notes, a lone voice from outside the court shouts, the words too muffled to be heard clearly in the court room, before a small army takes up the chant again and again. Bry feels as if she's running too fast down a steep hill, her feet no longer connected to the rest of her, the hard ground rushing up to meet her where she will either fall and break or somehow regain control and at last slow down.

It has begun.

Farley County Court

December 2019

People ask me how it started and the God's honest truth is that I never saw this happening either. It was seeing all those protestors on the telly, right where we are now, outside the court here, waving their banners, shouting about choice, that forced me off my sofa. Honestly, I didn't come here for a fight or even to try and get them to change their minds. I've never protested anything in my life, don't usually vote, none of it. I came because at that time, this pavement on the other side of the court doors was empty. Yeah, I suppose you could say I came here for Molly.

I didn't know what to do at first – I just sort of loitered, hands in pockets, probably looked like I was about to be called up in court on some shoplifting offence. Then one of them anti lot came over to me, Sophie she said her name was, she's here most days, nice-looking woman but a bit crazy in the eyes.

'You look lost,' she said. A quick look at her sign told me all I needed to know. But her kid is one half of the story; mine is the other. She saw me looking and said, 'He was the sweetest little boy. I keep thinking he would have loved all of this, the noise, the shouting and stamping about.'

I nodded.

'He looks like a good kid.'

She smiled and came closer. I took out my phone – she probably thought I was being rude but I wasn't, I just needed to show her someone too. I showed her the one after chemotherapy. 'This is my little one, she's called Molly.' The photo was taken a week before her fifth birthday, three years after her diagnosis. Her nappy is the only clue that she's a little girl, otherwise you could mistake her for a tiny old person. She's gripping the sides of the toilet with both hands, bald head bent, trying to catch her breath before the next wave of puke. The notches of her spine stick out like marbles. Her ribs are little sticks.

I felt Sophie flinch next to me; I think she said something like 'Oh my'. I flicked on; in the next one Molly's in her pram, again only wearing a nappy. Her arms and legs are swollen, red from steroids, the plastic port access in her chest secured by tape. Her brown eyes are turned away from the camera. I remember she kept whimpering that day; she didn't have the strength to cry. God, what I would have given to hear her cry.

'Acute lymphocytic leukaemia,' I told her. 'Platelet transfusions, chemo, blood transfusions – you name it, she's had it.'

Sophie blinked and I thought, 'Aha! She doesn't like hearing about other people's heartbreak.'

'I'm sorry to hear that, I really am,' she said, quiet like. 'How is she now?'

And I told her about Molly wanting to go to Cornwall, to visit the white beaches, but then the doctors told us we had to lock her in, that she couldn't go: after three years of agony she couldn't go and do the one thing that kept her spirits up. Why? Because of the measles outbreak.

I remember Sophie's sign wavered a little when I said that.

We couldn't rely on herd immunity to protect her any more – she was too sick, too vulnerable, and there was too much measles about. The doctors said if she got it, it'd kill her. And you know what Sophie said? And this I'll never forget. She said, 'I'm sorry, but that's not our fault. We're just protecting our rights.'

And she sort of turned, gestured towards the other antis to show she wasn't alone. She wanted so badly to run back to them by this point, I could tell, but I wasn't going to let her.

Which is when I asked her, 'What about Molly then? Is she just collateral damage? Worth less than your precious rights?'

That's when I lost her. She ran back to her lot and I watched them for the next hour or so talking amongst themselves, casting me the odd worried look, but I didn't give a shit about them, did I? I think I hung around that first day for an hour or two and then, I dunno, I just knew that wasn't enough. So the next day, I made my first sign. Molly said it was OK for me to use the photo of her in hospital, chemo needle in her arm, bald and grey as a January sky but still trying to give a thumbs up. Underneath I asked my question again – 'Collateral damage?'

A couple of folks just walking by stopped to shake my hand, show their support, and then the next day two other people came to join me with their own signs and, yeah, we just grew from there, so that's how it started.

12 December 2019

The crowds outside the court have at least tripled in size over the last few days. Ash lifts the collar of his navy wool coat up towards his ears, adjusts his scarf and pulls Bry as close to him as he can without actually lifting her off the ground. He kisses her clumsily on the temple and she turns her big brown eyes up to him and says, 'OK. Ready?' and the two of them clutch each other as they hurry towards the court building and the demonstrators from both sides fold in around them like a human net. It's so loud, so confusing; it's almost impossible to tell which arms are trying to pat them on the back and which would punch them if they could. As though all the pent-up energy of the court, stoppered and concentrated, is unleashed here on the cold, grey pavement – snarling, angry and human. Fuck, it would feel so good to shout back, but instead Ash burrows his chin deeper into his scarf and lets himself be pulled along by the two security guards who are shouting at the crowds to get back, trying to make a safe passage for Ash and Bry so they can scuttle up the steps and into the contained, more polite fury of the court building.

The case is starting half an hour later than usual this morning at 10.30 a.m. Judge Bower didn't say why, which suggested he had something personal he had to attend to. Like the way he viewed a teacher when he was a child, Ash finds it odd to think of Judge Bower having a life outside the court, almost laughable to think of him flicking through an old magazine in a dentist's waiting room or attending a grandchild's nativity play.

Ash and Bry are using the extra half-hour to have a meeting with Ed before Bry is called to the witness box, where she will be questioned by Elizabeth. They know the drill now; the usher unlocks their little locker room with a friendly smile and they both take off their coats, hats and scarfs, silently folding them into the same locker before Ash goes and buys them both a cup of tea from the vending machine. By the time Ash is back in the room, Ed has arrived, already dressed in his robes and wig and bent over the small table, Bry looking tiny but upright, listening carefully as Ed says, 'Right, Bry, I don't want you to feel you have to be a certain way today. I just want you to answer the questions honestly. If you get emotional, so be it – it won't hurt for Bower to see for himself how distressing this has been for you. Elizabeth will really try to push your buttons, but I'd like you to avoid getting angry or appearing dismissive – neither of which I've ever seen from you before, so again, I'm not worried.'

Ash walks towards them and puts the two cups on the table so he can shake Ed's hand. 'Sorry, mate, I should have got you a tea as well.'

Ed shakes his head to show he doesn't want tea.

'Take a seat, Ash.'

Before Ash has sat down, Ed starts talking again.

'I was just telling Bry that Elizabeth might try and make her appear a bit unhinged, make it look like Bry is the sort of person who could behave recklessly.' He turns back to Bry as he says, 'But don't worry. If you tell the truth, that you were raised to be sceptical of vaccines – feel free to talk about your brother, by the way – that will help our defence.'

Bry's eyes are wide, locked on to Ed, but her hand doesn't shake as she takes a sip of tea and her voice is steady as she says, 'OK, I'll do my best.'

Ed bends towards his briefcase and slides a thin folder across the table towards Bry and Ash. He keeps one hand on top of it, not quite ready to reveal the secrets inside.

'So, this is a copy of the paperwork submitted to Bower outlining my plans for the defence.' Ed looks from Ash to Bry and back again to Ash. His eyes flash, excited, like light reflected in small mirrors. 'Now, I know you have had some queries about my approach to date.' Ash rearranges his feet under the table. 'Queries' is a bit of an understatement. 'And I think this' – he taps the folder with his long fingers – 'will give you more questions. But please, you have to trust me and let me do my job, OK?'

Another thing that has kept Ash blinking into the thick December nights is that, apart from his opening statement, Ed hasn't contributed anything beyond, 'No questions from the defence, sir,' when the judge has invited him to cross-examine Elizabeth's witnesses. Sometimes, when the court is stuck on some legal detail, Ash sits in his hard seat and works out how much Ed has cost him so far – almost fifteen thousand is his reckoning. Ed has attempted to reassure Ash, in exactly the same way as this morning, telling him that it's better if he doesn't reveal too much about his plans and imploring Ash to trust him. He says he knows exactly what he's doing and is pleased with how everything's going. Ash can't see how he could be, given that the judge has heard nothing from the defendants. Every time Ed says his line about not having any questions, Judge Bower lifts his eyebrows and purses his lips as if he's faintly irritated or amused; Ash can't tell which, but neither feels positive.

Elizabeth's case – and he does always think of it as 'Elizabeth's' – on the other hand, seems to Ash to be meticulous and well planned. Over the last two days she's called to the stand an intimidating list of professionals, including Clemmie's neurological consultant, an infectious disease expert, a representative from Public Health England, a child psychologist and a social worker. They have all been impressive, answering her questions clearly and coolly. The medics confirmed that nothing – short of a radical and unprecedented advancement in brain surgery – can help Clemmie regain her sight. The other two scientists confirmed that had Clemmie not been exposed to measles she would still be able to see, that the significant drop locally in herd immunity – mainly due to rubbish posted on social media – is, in their view, to blame. Clemmie's time at the school fete on that Saturday before the Chamberlains' barbecue and how close her contact with the Spanish boy had been was only given the briefest review by the PHE official, and Ash couldn't help himself lean over and whisper to Ed, 'You are going to question this, aren't you?'

But Ed infuriatingly replied with his stock answer: 'Please, Ash, you have to trust me.' The hardest part was listening to the child psychologist's report. There were a few murmurs and stifled sobs from the public gallery as the court listened to the psychologist read from a transcript about how much it hurts Clemmie when she bumps into things, how she's already starting to forget what her brothers look like, and how frightened she is now of things that never frightened her before.

The next round of witnesses were personal connections rather than professionals. Gerald took to the stand, telling the court in a voice vibrating with emotion how at the barbecue back in July they'd all discussed vaccines, that Elizabeth and Jack had made it clear that they needed to be extra careful to protect Clemmie, and that Bry and Ash knew 'without question' that Clemmie was vulnerable. At one point Elizabeth passed Gerald a tissue to stop his tears splashing on to his yellow waistcoat. Then she'd called two mums – Amanda and Jenny – who smiled at Elizabeth, awed and humbled by Elizabeth's bravery, as they confirmed that, yes, Elizabeth's email about their children's vaccination status ahead of Clemmie's party had been very clear, that they'd respected and understood why she'd felt compelled to send it. One of them kept casting quick, furtive looks at Bry, like Alba, Ash thinks, when she's told not to stare at someone but still she can't resist.

Now, here they are. Just one more witness left on the claimant's list – Bryony Kohli – before it's Ed's turn to take the stage.

In front of him, Ed lifts his fingers away from the top of the file. Ash looks at Bry but she doesn't move, so he leans forward, opens the file himself. He blinks down at the photocopied piece of paper in front of him. Ed's written only one name. Elizabeth Chamberlain. Ed must read the shock and then the worry printed across Ash's face.

'Ash, I know what you're thinking, but there's nothing I can do but ask you to trust me.'

'You could tell us what you're planning . . .'

'We've discussed this. If I did tell you, then I would be

294

worried that one of you might – unwittingly of course – behave differently or do something that might somehow influence things. Trust me, I've seen it happen. Things are going well, I don't want anything to jeopardise that.'

Ash had forgotten what a patronising, smug bastard Ed could be at uni, but it's coming back to him now, hard as a punch in the gut. Perhaps he'd been too hasty hiring his old friend; they hadn't even got a mates' rate on Ed's fee. But Bry is looking up at Ash, her eyes seeming to have grown even bigger in the last few moments. 'I'm OK with it if you are,' she says, and Ash reminds himself that in a matter of minutes Bry will be walking up to the witness box and facing questions from the woman who for two decades she called her best friend, a woman who will do everything in her power now to destroy her.

He needs to stay calm and resolute for Bry, but he doesn't smile as he nods at Ed and says, 'OK, it seems we don't really have a choice. We have to trust you.'

Judge Bower pulls his glasses away from his face and looks directly at Bry. His voice is gentle, as though he's worried for her, as he says, 'Mrs Kohli, please approach the witness box.'

Bry feels hot at the sound of her name, a burning feeling gripping her solar plexus. Ash's hand falls away from her leg as she makes herself get up. She keeps her eyes on the witness box, just like Ed advised, as she walks towards it. Her voice is small as she is sworn in but she doesn't shake and she looks directly at the solid, upright figure of her dearest and oldest friend. For a moment the whole court stills. There are no shuffles or coughs from the public gallery and even the press stop tapping at their devices as the two women face each other. Externally, Elizabeth looks like Elizabeth – the well-kept blonde hair, the thin face, the quick, blue eyes – but to Bry, the person before her is a mannequin. Her eyes are hard, set, and with one look Bry feels the whole world between them and she knows, deeper than she's ever known anything before, that this woman who has comforted, loved and always prioritised their friendship now despises her.

But then Elizabeth does something unexpected, something that unsettles Bry far more than her statue-like absence. She smiles. Elizabeth smiles and says, so quietly only Bry can hear, '*Hi, Bry.*'

Bry holds on to the witness box to steady herself because there she is, there's a glimpse of the old Elizabeth – changed, yes, but it's the same voice she's heard every day for all her adult life. But her eyes – no, Elizabeth's eyes are still full of rage and Bry knows that despite the smile, despite the soft voice, this Elizabeth mannequin isn't her friend but a dangerous construct, created to unsettle Bry, to make her seem unstable, like the kind of person who could intentionally hurt a child.

Bry grips the stand harder, nods at Elizabeth to show she's ready, and the smile, like a bird shot mid-flight, falls from Elizabeth's face.

'Mrs Kohli, can you please tell the court, in your own words, why you chose not to vaccinate your daughter?'

Bry opens her mouth, the fire from her chest licking up into her throat. When the words come, they're painful but there's also something purifying about at last telling the world – this new world that thinks she's stupid, uncaring and reckless – the simple truth. She was scared.

'I have a severely autistic, non-verbal elder brother. He has lived in a home for almost twenty-six years. My whole life, I was taught that my brother's autism was the direct result of him receiving the measles vaccine as a baby. There are other conditions in my family – Crohn's disease and some asthma – that I also grew up believing were caused by vaccines. Not vaccinating my daughter wasn't so much a choice, but rather something I knew I could never risk. In the same way we'd never let our daughter play with knives, I'd simply never allow her to be vaccinated.'

Elizabeth looks at Bry, her eyes unseeing, as though Bry's explanation is so dull she's close to sleep.

'Who was it who "taught" you as a child that vaccines were a risk?'

'My mum, mostly. She was, and still is, adamant that they cause far more harm than good.'

'Do you think of yourself as a responsible parent, Mrs Kohli?'

'I'm not perfect, I can be disorganised—'

'I'm not asking how organised you are, I'm asking whether you see yourself as a responsible parent – yes or no?'

'Yes.'

'So when you became an adult and then a *responsible* parent yourself, you didn't think to do your own research, to look into the vaccine issue yourself?'

Out of the corner of her eye, Bry sees Ed make a note on the empty pad in front of him.

'My husband, Ash, wanted to . . .' Bry glances at Ash, who is watching her, perfectly still, not even blinking.

'Again, that wasn't my question. I wasn't asking about Mr Kohli, I was asking about you. Did you do any research into vaccine safety and efficacy yourself as an adult and *responsible* parent?'

'You know I didn't.'

Judge Bower turns to Bry and says, a hint of warning in his voice, 'Please address the court in your answers, Mrs Kohli.'

Bry clears her throat, nods an apology at Judge Bower, and looking out beyond the public gallery, says, 'No, no, I did not.'

'Do you know how many accredited scientific research studies have concluded that there is a link – or even suggested there could be a link – between the MMR vaccine and autism in the last twenty years?'

Bry shakes her head.

'No? No, of course – you haven't done any research. The answer is none. Not one accredited scientific paper of the hundreds published in the last two decades concludes there is even a tenuous link.'

Bry's head suddenly fills with noise, arguments shouting about the dangers of aluminium, toxic overload, vaccine shedding, but it's not her own voice screaming at her, it's Sara's.

'If I could go back and change things, I would.'

Elizabeth's eyes snap up, clash with Bry's, and she hisses, 'Oh, trust me, if we could go back and change things you'd never have come anywhere near my family.'

'Mrs Chamberlain!' Judge Bower's voice quivers; he is outraged that events in his court have momentarily spiralled into the familial rather than remaining safely in the legal. 'This is an official warning. If you let things become personal again I will have to prematurely dismiss your witness. Do you understand?'

'Yes, sir, I apologise.'

Elizabeth looks down, chastised, and the press gape as their fingers fly across keyboards and notepads. But Bry knows from the flicker at the corner of Elizabeth's mouth that she wanted things to get personal, that she wants to remind the court and the people beyond the court reading their papers and scanning headlines online how deeply she was betrayed. That she is the brave mama-bear rearing up, fighting for her little cub, and Bry is the cruel hunter who caught her baby in a snare. It is very personal indeed. Elizabeth curls her hair behind her ear; the gesture seems to settle her back into her new lawyer persona.

'What happened on 20th June 2017, Mrs Kohli?'

Bry's eyes crease. She has no idea; her memory rarely reaches back beyond July 2019 any more. All she can think of is ladybirds.

'You look confused, Mrs Kohli. Perhaps I can help refresh your memory? You were in a park in London having a picnic with some friends and your toddler daughter. You were drinking wine – a *responsible* adult might say that you drank too much wine, because you lost your daughter, didn't you, Mrs Kohli?'

The fear had been like liquid lava as Bry ran, screaming Alba's name, around London Fields. Alba was found by a friend twenty minutes later sitting on a wall and eating her first ever ice cream with a dreadlocked woman whose dog she had decided to follow. It was only when Bry had screamed, 'What the fuck are you doing?' at the woman that Alba had started to cry.

'Was that what you'd call responsible behaviour?'

Elizabeth had been the first person, before Ash even, Bry had called, sobbing great lungfuls of air into the phone.

'What about the time you locked her as a baby in your flat

in London on her own? Or the time you left her in the car while you paid for petrol at a service station? I believe a member of the public complained about that one. Do any of these bear the markings of a responsible parent?'

'No. No, obviously they don't.'

'You are aware, are you not, that people who have not been vaccinated are more vulnerable to contracting some infectious diseases than vaccinated people?'

'Yes, of course I am.'

Elizabeth raises an eyebrow in a way that suggests that when it comes to stupidity, on Bry's level, even the simplest facts cannot be taken for granted.

'And when were you made aware that our daughter could not be vaccinated and was therefore more vulnerable?'

'When she was just a baby, a few months old, I think.'

'She was a year old when we were told not to vaccinate her. I called you that evening.'

Bry swallows, frightened of where this might be going, but she forces herself to nod. 'OK, I knew when she was one.'

'So you had six years when you knew you were intentionally putting my daughter at risk. Is that correct?'

'I . . .'

'Seven years of sharing her life: taking her for walks, joining us for meals, Christmases, birthdays, holidays . . . the list goes on and on, and during all that time – all those baths, hugs and special treats – you never thought about the fact you and then your own daughter could be exposing her to a potentially deadly disease?'

Bry hangs her head. She feels her body demand more and

more oxygen but she also feels weightless suddenly, untethered, as though gravity has decided to let her off and leave her to float around.

'Did you love my daughter, your goddaughter?'

'Yes, of course – I, I still do.'

'But not enough to not put her at risk?'

Bry's chest starts to thump and her throat starts to close, as though it too is giving up on her, and Bry thinks, *OK, Elizabeth, you can have it, here it comes, here's your moment.*

'I . . . I'm not sure . . .'

'Did you, for example, talk to either me or my husband – keeping in mind the fact that you saw one of us most days – about the issue?'

Bry clutches the witness box.

'No, no, I didn't.'

'Did you try to encourage some distance between our daughters, and between my daughter and yourself, in order to protect her?'

Bry's hands slip with sweat.

'I'm sorry, I'm so, so sorry . . .'

'Just answer the questions, please, Mrs Kohli.' Bry feels Elizabeth's eyes on her as her throat closes smaller and smaller while her panicked lungs fight for oxygen, sweat prickling against her neck. There are tears running down her face now but she doesn't wipe them away.

'So, over the course of seven years you were fully aware of the serious risks you were exposing my daughter to, but you chose to do absolutely nothing to alleviate those risks. Is that right, Mrs Kohli?'

'I was scared, I was—'

'I don't care whether you were scared or not, Mrs Kohli — did you do the responsible thing and try to alleviate the potentially serious risk you were exposing my daughter to — yes or no?'

Bry will say or do anything now to make Elizabeth stop; she'd leap off a building if it meant this moment would end.

'No.'

Elizabeth lets the syllable reverberate around the court. She doesn't need to point out that doing nothing can be just as negligent as doing something. She moves closer, looks at Bry, and in that moment everything falls away and Bry sees for a second a dimness creep into Elizabeth's eyes. She recognises that look; Elizabeth seems disappointed. She's disappointed that Bry, for some reason, hasn't been able to give her what she wanted, disappointed perhaps that the revenge she has chased like a rabid dog is finally here and yet, with Bry bloodied and quivering before her, nothing has changed. Her daughter is still blind.

'No further questions, sir.'

13 December 2019

Jack is getting dressed for court. Across the hall Clemmie is in the bathroom brushing her teeth, humming to herself, overseen by Claude, who is lying down, eyebrows moving as his eyes follow her every move from his position on the landing floor, his head propped on his front paws. Jack buttons up his white shirt and puts a blue-spotted tie into his trouser pocket for later. Without consultation or acknowledgement, getting the kids up and ready for the school day has become Jack's domain while Elizabeth preps for the day ahead in court. He doesn't mind, quite the opposite in fact; helping Clemmie pull on her tights or listening to Max recite gruesome facts about life in Ancient Rome, these moments are like brief spells of sunshine in his otherwise overcast days. Elizabeth is downstairs already, of course. The sound of her moving about boiling the kettle, emptying the dishwasher, suddenly makes her seem lonely, vulnerable, in a way no one in the court room would ever recognise. By now, at half seven in the morning, she'll usually be practising her lines for the day ahead, her voice carrying up the stairs, stopping and starting again if she stumbles on a word or if her tone isn't quite right. But today is the first day for the defendants; she can't practise her lines because she doesn't know what they are yet.

Last night Jack was eating a bowl of pasta on the sofa, the TV glimmering but ignored in front of him, when Elizabeth had come into the sitting room and perched on the arm of the sofa, next to him. As soon as the kids are in bed she's got into the habit of reading all the supportive press and social media she can find about the case at the kitchen table while Jack stares for an hour at the TV – 'buffering', Elizabeth calls it – so her coming to see him last night was unusual.

'Everything OK?' he'd asked, automatically picking up the remote, thinking she was going to tell him the TV was too loud.

Elizabeth didn't look at him but stared somewhere beyond the TV.

'Why do you think they've only called me as a witness?'

It felt like the first time she'd ever asked his opinion, and although he'd been taken aback, he'd been wondering the same thing.

'I was thinking maybe they aren't going to put up a fight, maybe they just want this all to be over so they can figure out how to move on with their lives.' Jack felt the little pinch of a home truth as he spoke.

'I was thinking the same,' said Elizabeth. 'Maybe that lawyer has made Ash realise they don't have a defence.' But as she went back to her laptop in the kitchen, Jack knew she was wrong, very wrong. He felt suspicious, unsettled. Since they'd found out that Elizabeth was the defence's only witness, it had been like existing in that strange extended silence that usually precedes violence in films. He didn't trust it, but even if he could do something about it, it was too late now, so he sat and stared at the TV and waited until it was time to go to bed.

From the bathroom Clemmie stops humming and spits into the sink, and Claude immediately stands alert and pads into the bathroom so he can escort Clemmie back into the bedroom, where Jack's laid out the jeans and pink jumper she said she wanted to wear today. They've become a bit of a crack team, Clemmie and Claude, and every day their confidence in each other seems to grow. Yesterday at breakfast Clemmie had made toast with Claude by her side, and the two of them walk down the stairs now as though it's the easiest thing in the world. Hard to believe that just a few weeks ago Jack had to carry Clemmie whenever she needed to go up or down. Jack strokes Claude's back, his coat as sleek as a fish through Jack's fingers. Claude guides Clemmie safely into the bedroom, making sure she's close enough to touch the bed so she can orientate herself before he flops back to the carpet a couple of feet away and, catching Jack's eye, sweeps his tail across the floor a couple of times, acknowledging another job well done. Since living with Claude, Jack finally understands why desperate people get dogs. Their love is so pure, so reliable, and so completely different from human love.

'Daddy, I can't hear the boys,' Clemmie says, wiggling out of her pyjama bottoms and feeling on the bed for the clothes she knows will be exactly where Jack left them.

'Oh God, you're right, Clem, I bet they've gone back to

sleep,' Jack says, picking up her hairbrush. 'What do you think – karaoke box?'

Clemmie giggles and nods; from the floor lifts his eyebrows. And as the three of them go upstairs to the boys' attic room, Jack holding Clemmie's purple karaoke box, which they'll turn to full volume once they're in the boys' room, he pretends not to notice Elizabeth carrying her coffee and her laptop and slipping, silently, back into her new room.

At 8 a.m. exactly, Jack's dad beeps his horn and the three kids plus Claude bundle out of the door, Charlie still cramming toast into his mouth, to be driven the short distance to school. The frantic pace of the early morning always makes the house feel emptier once they've all left. Jack loads the dishwasher and wipes the table, wondering whether Clemmie remembered to pack Claude's treats, when his phone makes a high pip-pip sound. Jack's heard the alert enough recently to know it means they've received a donation on their crowdfunding page. He opens up the app as he sips his coffee. At first he thinks the donation is for five hundred pounds – their second biggest yet – taking them well over their target. He squints at the screen and splutters, rubs his eyes and looks again. But this time his spluttering becomes a full chesty cough, forcing him to lean against the kitchen units and pull his shirt collar away from his neck. No, no, this must be a mistake. Once he's caught his breath he picks up his phone again. It's still there. It's still fucking there. The anonymous donation isn't for five hundred, it's for fifty thousand pounds, and there's only one couple Jack knows who have that kind of money readily available.

*

For the first time, it is Elizabeth and not Jack who asks, 'You OK?' as they walk through the cold cemetery and into town towards court. It is Jack who keeps his hands wedged into the pockets of his thick coat and his hat drawn over his ears, a sign that not only does he not want to talk but he also doesn't want to listen. So they walk at last in the silence that Elizabeth has been craving and Jack has feared. Like the last two days, they hear the chants from the demonstrators well before they arrive outside the court. As they walk past the war memorial, with its sparsely decorated Christmas tree limp with last night's rain, Elizabeth tucks her arm into Jack's, just in case someone recognises them. Jack's decided, for now at least, not to mention the donation to Elizabeth. It would only distract her, make her angry, which is probably precisely why Ash decided to make the donation the night before she was due to be called as a witness for the defence. He knew pulling a stunt like this would make her angry and that she wouldn't be able to conceal her anger on the stand. Jack thinks Ash is many things – self-serving, arrogant – but he never thought he'd be capable of such calculated manipulation. The pale grey court building comes into view, and Jack wonders whether he could find a moment on his own with Beth and ask whether Ash's donation is even legal, considering they're in the middle of a court case. But every morning so far, Elizabeth and Beth haven't left each other's side – running over the plans for the day, answering last-minute questions. It is unlikely Jack will have the chance to talk to Beth without making Elizabeth suspicious. He doesn't know what to do, other than delete the app and close the fundraiser, which he'd already done before they left the house. Once they've made it through the crowds with the help of the court guards, Beth meets them in the foyer, and Elizabeth releases Jack's arm and pins herself to her comrade.

'Morning, Beth, did you get my text?'

The two women talk as the three of them start to move towards their waiting room. Jack is just about to indicate that he's going to get a coffee from the machine when across the wide hall, out of the corner of his eye, he sees Ash disappearing into the men's toilets. It's too good an opportunity to miss. Elizabeth nods vaguely but doesn't take her eyes away from Beth when Jack tells her he's going to the toilet, that he'll meet them in their waiting room.

There are just three urinals along the wall. Ash stands at the one on the far right; he doesn't look up when Jack enters and Jack decides to stand next to the sinks and wait for him to finish. Jack has no idea what he's going to say, so instead he fantasises about hitting Ash square on the jaw, but the repercussions wouldn't be worth it and, besides, Jack's never hit anyone in his life before; he probably wouldn't do it right. As soon as Ash turns away from the urinal, he stops suddenly, shocked to find Jack so close. The two men stare at each other. Ash looks wounded. The flesh around his eyes is discoloured and swollen; his cheeks are gaunt hollows. Jack feels Ash looking at him in just the same way, gently and with more curiosity than anger, and in that brief moment it feels to Jack as though the two men could just as easily open their arms to each other as they could clench their fists. But then he remembers the provocative, huge donation, the manipulative timing, and he thinks about Clemmie and his hand starts to curl.

'Why'd you do it?'

Ash doesn't say anything, he just keeps looking steadily at Jack.

'You honestly think money is just going to make this all go away, don't you?' Jack feels his mouth twist into a smile. 'You think that's what we want from you, don't you? You're such a capitalist prick you think it's the answer to everything.'

Ash doesn't flinch but his eyes drop to the floor for a moment, and once he seems satisfied that Jack doesn't have anything else to say, he looks up at Jack again, his voice low, calm, as he says, 'Tell me then, Jack, tell me what it is you want from us. You've made it clear you don't want money. What then? A public shaming? Open any paper, talk to any neighbour and you'll have it. We are well and truly disgraced. You want a pound of flesh? It's yours. I'll do whatever it takes. Just tell me what it is that will make this better and we'll do it.'

Jack takes a step back. What *does* he want? He wants . . . he wants . . . No, no, this is all wrong. Ash is twisting things.

'You made a fifty-grand donation the night before Elizabeth's called as a witness for the defence.'

'Bry and I agreed we'd make the donation. If you don't want the money, then you can donate it to a charity of your choice. We don't want it.'

Ash looks again, briefly, at the floor. Jack remembers reading an article years ago that guilty people have a tendency to look either up or down. He just can't remember which one it is. Ash breathes out.

'Look, Jack, you're right. None of us can do the one thing that would make this all go away – none of us can make Clemmie see again. But one thing we can do is save you and Elizabeth from public humiliation . . .'

'What are you talking about?'

309

Ash takes a step towards Jack. His eyes don't flicker any more but are fixed tight on Jack's face.

'Ed has only called Elizabeth as a witness because he's got something damning on her. I don't know what it is exactly but I have no doubt it's going to eviscerate the case and both your reputations along with it. Please, Jack, please talk to her about dropping the case now before she gives evidence.'

From outside in the foyer, a recorded announcement says court room six will convene in five minutes. Jack pictures Elizabeth and Beth talking hurriedly, Elizabeth pacing their waiting room, still trying to second guess the questions Edward Armitage will throw at her, which direction his defence will take. Jack wonders whether Elizabeth has noticed he's not there, whether she even cares.

'You tell me this now?'

'We only found out yesterday. Jack, please. I promise we have no ulterior motive: see this as our final act of friendship. I'll make something up and ask Ed to request an extra hour now before we start so you can talk to Elizabeth. But please, you have to talk to her.'

'And tell her what, Ash?'

'Tell her exactly what I've told you. Tell her if you want money you can name your price and we'll pay it, but please, please tell her to end the case before she enters the witness box.'

He's bluffing. He must be bluffing.

'No, Ash. I won't do it. This is what she wants. This is what she needs. I won't take it away from her.'

Ash hangs his head and he doesn't raise it as he tries one last time. 'Jack, please reconsider . . .' But Jack's already

310

turned away from Ash, and as he re-enters the commotion of the busy hall a tiny hammer starts beating deep in the back of his head, chipping away like a warning, that a truth he has always known but has never whispered even to himself is about to be exhumed and brought back to life.

13 December 2019

Elizabeth knows she's earned the respect of the court; she can feel it, a great warm swell of admiration behind her. One of the journalists smiles faintly at her before quickly looking away, and Judge Bower nods subtly as though already in agreement with whatever she's about to say as she walks to take the witness box. As she's sworn in she glances around the court to drink it all in – the little old ladies clacking about in the disabled bay, the guard standing quiet but alert by the door – and already she feels a sense of nostalgia for this place and with it a quiet panic that soon, when the case is over, she'll lose something vital that she has found here. She wishes there were more witnesses for the defence, simply so they could all stay here a few days longer, but then that skeleton in a gown and wig approaches her.

'Good morning, Mrs Chamberlain.'

She replies, her voice firmer than that of this cocky, over-paid lawyer whose job she has proven is simpler than he'd like the world to believe.

'Mr Armitage.'

'I'd like to start by asking you, in your own words, why you believe Mrs Kohli chose not to vaccinate her daughter?'

Elizabeth smiles gently. Despite all the eyes scrutinising her, a wonderful sense of ease fills her as she replies, 'In my view, Bryony Kohli didn't vaccinate her daughter because she was ignorant and scared.'

'And when did that translate into reckless negligent behaviour, as you claim?'

'When – knowing both she and her daughter posed a threat to my daughter – she allowed and even encouraged very close and very frequent contact.'

'Thank you, Mrs Chamberlain.' A collective sigh seems to ripple through the court; this is old tired ground, and the expensive lawyer who has stayed quiet for so long is disappointing them all. Elizabeth smooths her hair behind her ear, and on behalf of the whole court raises an expectant eyebrow at the lawyer, who glances down at his notes before addressing Elizabeth again.

'I'd like to ask you a little more about your relationship with the GP Dr Parker.' Elizabeth, unlike so many other over-keen first-time witnesses, resists the urge to talk before she's been asked an actual question, so the lawyer continues.

'Can you please tell me what you thought of him as a practitioner?'

'He was our family GP for almost seven years. He was already towards the end of his career when he took our family on as his patients. He was very experienced; I trusted him completely.'

The lawyer nods his wigged head as though he's in complete agreement with Elizabeth and asks, 'Can you tell me, please, Mrs Chamberlain, what it was about him that you trusted so implicitly?'

For the first time Elizabeth feels something twist, tiny but sharp, like a needle, deep in her stomach, but her voice doesn't waver as she answers.

'He listened to his patients, really listened. He was always very respectful and seemed to take a real interest in our well-being. By his own admission, he was old-school – he took notes by hand and didn't care about targets and box ticking, he cared about his patients. I remember, for example, once he called us at home on a weekend to find out how our second son was responding to some antibiotics he'd been prescribed. I always felt Dr Parker went above and beyond.'

'And he was the doctor all five members of your family were registered with until the time of his retirement five years ago, when your daughter was two years old – is that correct?'

'Yes, that's correct.'

The lawyer's head is cocked to one side, a studied affectation, no doubt, to make him seem like he's both listening and unsure of the truth of what he's listening to.

'I'd like to remind the court that sadly Dr Parker is now cared for in a nursing home where he is living with advanced dementia, so he was not fit to be called as a witness.'

He turns back to Elizabeth and the needle starts to dance, pricking deep inside her.

'And can you please tell the court what Dr Parker, your experienced and much-trusted GP, advised when you discussed your daughter's infantile fits?'

'He said that she could not be vaccinated.'

The lawyer makes a quarter-turn to address Judge Bower directly as he repeats what Elizabeth just said. 'Dr Parker said that she could not be vaccinated.'

The needle pricks deeper now, sharpened by years of suppression. The lawyer turns back to Elizabeth, the tiniest smile rippling his thin lips as he says, 'But that's not true, is it, Mrs Chamberlain?'

Someone in the public gallery coughs, and out of the corner of her eye Elizabeth sees Jack shift in his seat – can he feel the needle too?

'Dr Parker may have been – to use your words – "old-school", but he was fastidious and would stay after his shift ended to type up his notes on the NHS system. With thanks to this court for special dispensation, I was able to acquire the notes he wrote on 12th July 2013 pertaining to your appointment with him when you discussed your daughter's vaccinations. To refresh your memory, I will now read the exact words Dr Parker wrote about this appointment six years ago.'

Elizabeth forces her expression to remain impassive while her organs start to slip and liquefy. All the people in the court, from Judge Bower to the old women in the disabled bay, seem to move as one body, collectively holding their breath as the lawyer starts to read slowly and clearly from a printed page.

'"Engaged in a long and frank discussion with patient regarding her fears about vaccinating her daughter following febrile seizures which were caused by repeated infections to the middle ear, see notes above. I made it clear that while there is some evidence that vaccination can increase the risk of febrile seizures in infants who have already had seizures, there is no cause for alarm and her daughter can be vaccinated safely. She expressed her fear that her daughter would have more seizures following vaccination. I reassured her it was her choice and that her daughter would most likely, due to current high vaccination rates, be protected by herd immunity. Advised patient to take her time to consider the matter, to seek further advice and consult with me again should she wish."'

For a moment everyone is perfectly still; the whole great body of the court doesn't even move to draw breath. But the lawyer is paces ahead of everyone else. He repeats a couple of lines as though to help the rest of them shift what they've heard from ear to brain.

'She expressed her fear ... It was her choice ... Her daughter can be vaccinated safely.'

The silence is long and layered. The press gallery breaks it first with small, excited intakes of breath followed by vigorous tapping, before the public, realising the magnitude of what they've just heard, start to rumble with gasps and someone, possibly Gerald, shouts, 'What the—?'

Elizabeth looks wildly around the court; everyone is, of course, fixed on her, apart from Jack, who's dropped his head in his hands. He can't watch as, smile broadening and without any warning from the judge, who looks as shocked as everyone else, the lawyer approaches Elizabeth and asks, 'Tell me, Mrs Chamberlain, did you take Dr Parker's advice? Did you consult other practitioners about this most vital decision?'

Elizabeth's thoughts run wildly into each other as though they're on fire.

'Did you consult other practitioners, Mrs Chamberlain?'

'No, no, I didn't, but I—'

'And yet in that same year you took your son to three different specialists to look into a very minor skin ailment – is that right?'

Elizabeth frowns at him. Now the eyes on her don't feel so friendly any more; she feels them all widen and narrow.

'Answer the question, please, Mrs Chamberlain.'

'Yes.'

'You chose not to vaccinate your daughter, didn't you, Mrs Chamberlain?'

She feels stripped naked, exposed, and those eyes, God, all those eyes on her. She never knew eyes could be so much like mouths; they all seem to bite and gnaw.

'Answer the question, please, Mrs Chamberlain.'

'Yes.'

'You chose not to vaccinate your daughter for precisely the same reason my clients didn't vaccinate their daughter. Because you were scared. You were scared and so you made a special exemption of your daughter, just like my clients were scared.'

This time no one hears Elizabeth answer because everyone in the court is either shouting at the judge, Elizabeth or the lawyer, or they're quietly involved in their own mini crisis as they try to digest what has just happened here. The usher holds his hands up in a hopeless appeal for calm. Instinctively, like an animal whose throat has already been cut making one last, useless struggle for life, Elizabeth looks back towards Jack and Beth, but Beth is just staring straight ahead, her face a fixed mask of shock, and Jack next to her has crumpled in on himself, his back heaving, his head still in his hands. So she turns the other way and then she sees her, she sees Bry. Bry is standing behind her bench, tears streaming, her eyes fixed but gentle on Elizabeth, and Elizabeth knows she needs to get to her, that her only safety is with her friend, but then suddenly a guard starts telling her and Jack that they have to go back to their room outside the court, and when Elizabeth doesn't move, he holds her upper arm and all she can do is call Bry's name as she is led away.

23 December 2019

From the kitchen window of their tiny cottage, Ash watches Bry and Alba as they gather ivy for the Christmas wreaths Alba has decided she wants to make for everyone she knows, including their neighbour's dog. There's a huge amount growing here, twisting green tentacles around the shed, suffocating a wizened apple tree. Ash takes a sip of his coffee and through the window returns Alba's thumbs up before he clicks the Wi-Fi on and sits at the kitchen table to check his emails for the first time in over a week. After the collapse of the case, he'd decided, with encouragement from Bry, to turn the Wi-Fi and his phone off until things quietened down. Unplugging was easier than he thought; life is more peaceful this way and has given him the space to focus on the only thing that he cares about – his family. He has grown quite ambivalent about the world outside the cottage and is relieved they've been able to cut themselves loose from Farley, that they rented the cottage through an online agency and paid for it upfront in Bry's maiden name. The press can't get to them here, while according to Row, who drops off their mail occasionally, Saint's Road is still a carnival of cameras.

It takes a few minutes to organise his inbox – to delete the junk mail, mark the few work-related emails and figure out how many of the messages from press and friends he has the energy to read. He scans a couple of messages from old friends of his in London. It's incredible the way people have crept out like woodlice from under a stone now that they are – legally at least – vindicated. All of them stayed well hidden, of course, when the newspapers were calling them child abusers. He deletes their saccharine, creepy emails without replying. He opens one from Rosalyn sent to them both. It reads like a postcard.

> Thinking of you all. I hope you can start to look to the future now that this painful time is almost at a close. It's cold but still sunny here – do visit soon, the hills are so beautiful in the winter. Much love.

Next he opens one from Ed, sent six days ago with the subject 'End of representation':

> Dear Ash and Bry,
>
> As promised I'm attaching a scanned copy of the legal documents that confirm your case has been dismissed as agreed by Judge Bower and both parties. A hard copy is in the post to Saint's Road but I imagine you'll want to avoid that show for a while yet.
>
> I know you said you're not interested in any financial recompense, but I do want to reiterate that should you change your mind we would have very good grounds to reclaim all your expenses from the Chamberlains – including my fees – relating to the case. Think about it.
>
> We followed your instruction in relation to the press and I'm also including in this email a few examples of articles and news

clips where I've acted as your representative. I hope you are satisfied with them.

Let's go for drinks in 2020 to finally celebrate such a great outcome.

Merry Christmas to you all,
Ed

'Prick,' Ash whispers to himself. In the mad confusion following Elizabeth's revelation, Ash, Bry and Ed had been hurried back into their locker room before they were told that Judge Bower had dismissed the court until further notice, presumably so everyone could recover and he could spend some time considering how to proceed.

While Ash tried to comfort Bry, Ed sat on top of the little table, still wearing his wig, a broad smile slick across his glistening teeth as he said, 'What did I tell you, Ash? She was always going to make at least one huge mistake. Any decent barrister would have got a copy of those GP records and realised there was no case to answer.' He leaned back in his chair, smiling as though sated, and had it not been for Bry still sobbing in his arms, Ash would have delighted in telling Ed what an unfeeling arsehole he'd become.

In the cottage, Ash clicks on one of Ed's video links. The screen opens to a brightly lit news desk where a newsreader is turned towards an image of Ed, floating on a screen next to a woman identified as Dr Margaret Cross, Clinical Psychologist. Ed's Adam's apple bobs, jovial, in his throat as he smiles his thin smile and tells the newsreader that his clients are 'relieved that the case is over and request that the public and the press respect their desire for privacy during this difficult time'.

When the newsreader asks him whether he thinks the case will open a debate on mandatory vaccination, Ed cocks his head and says, 'I believe it has already paved the way for a necessary and—' Ash scrolls the clip forward. He heard enough of Ed in the court room; he would pay never to have to hear him again. He stops the clip as the newsreader turns to address Dr Cross.

'Dr Cross, one of the questions that has been repeatedly raised on social media platforms is this issue around whether Mrs Chamberlain actually believed she couldn't vaccinate her daughter or whether she is, as one newspaper bluntly stated, "a bare-faced liar"?'

'Yes, this is something that has come up a lot. Mrs Chamberlain was, in my opinion, suffering from undiagnosed postnatal depression following the birth of her daughter. She was terrified for her daughter's wellbeing, especially following her seizures, and she felt herself unable to make decisions on her daughter's behalf. By choosing not to vaccinate her daughter she was recusing herself from one such debilitating decision. It is my belief that, as she started to recover from PND, she reframed some of her memories in order to make sense of everything that had happened. I think she then started to repeat what she now believed to be true, something we psychologists call the illusory truth effect, fairly common in cases of PND. Which is the theory that the more a person says something, even if they know it to be false, the more they, too, will start to believe it.'

'Brrrrr!' Bry and Alba bustle in through the back door with a cold puff of wind, each carrying a bucket of ivy, tendrils of the stuff falling out of the buckets as if it's trying to escape. Bry notices as Ash quickly shuts down the video but she doesn't say anything. They don't talk about the case when Alba's with them. They will have to talk to her one day, of course, but not yet, not when it's Christmas and she's only four years old. With gloved hands, Alba grabs an armful of ivy and tickles Ash on the neck, and he lifts her into his arms and tickles her until her face turns red and Bry, with a smile, tells him to stop.

They don't talk about anything more important than whether Santa prefers mince pies or Christmas cake until Alba's in bed and they lie together again, back on the old sheepskin rugs in front of the wood burner. Tonight, for the first time since the case was dismissed, Bry is dry-eyed and looking at him in that slightly searching way of hers that means she wants to talk. He nods to show he's there to listen to whatever she needs to say. She keeps looking at him as she says, 'I've been thinking about next year and I think maybe we should go back to London.'

Ash feels his surprise ripple across his face. Like Bry, he doesn't want to go back to Farley. It's too claustrophobic, they'd never be able to escape the case, and more importantly, it could make settling in at school harder for Alba. But he'd expected Bry to suggest Cornwall or Scotland – somewhere she could walk for miles without seeing another person. Anywhere but London.

'I just think London makes sense. We know it for one thing, we can be closer to your boys, to Theo and Bran, there are lots of great schools for Alba and work options for both of us, plus of course it's anonymous so that'll be good too . . .'

Ash nods. The ability to disappear, for their faces to become unremarkable and immediately forgettable, has become a new prerequisite to any discussion of their future plans. Ash strokes her arm and repeats what he's said before.

'I just want us to be together, to take time and figure out how we move on. But, yeah, London is an option. Definitely an option.'

Bry looks away, nods, and Ash knows there's something more that she needs to say but she's not quite ready, so he just waits and stares at the orange flames as they slowly lick the inside of the wood burner a deep black, and then she turns back to him.

'I think I need to see her, Ash.'

24 December 2019

The night opens from darkness into thin light like a great door slowly creaking open. There are no birds this time of year; they've been replaced with journalists who have been standing outside their house for days now, calling Elizabeth's name as though they too are lost and expect her to find them. She'd looked at a few comments online a couple of days ago. She'd been called everything from a media-hungry bitch to a psychopath. Strangely, the more twisted comments were like glancing blows. It was the ones from women mostly, who empathised, who shared their own stories of PND, who blamed a societal lack of care for new mothers, that really hit Elizabeth in the heart. 'Elizabeth Chamberlain,' wrote one journalist, 'like all parents, was just trying to do the best for her family. She was trying to protect them. She got it wrong, really wrong, because she was unwell, not because she wanted to cause any harm.' She didn't know why but compassion hurt her more than cruelty.

Today though, for the first time, there are no journalists outside. Jack had told her that today was special though now Elizabeth can't remember what he said, but it doesn't matter, it won't change anything. She will still just lie here hour after hour, rigid on her side, curled and hard in her daughter's soft bed, waiting for night or day to arrive, whichever is next. She shouted at Jack when he tried to turn a light on; it's the only thing she wants, to be left in the dark, as though the blackness itself will somehow bring her closer to Clemmie. As if the two of them might, fumbling as they are in the vast darkness, somehow find each other there, and Elizabeth will clutch on to her little one and she'll be the first to hear the truth of what happened to them both over seven years ago.

Memory tugs at Elizabeth like a small hand demanding to be held. She sees herself propped and still bleeding in a hospital bed, holding Clemmie's fresh, red body. That was when she first felt the dark nudge. It was as though in giving birth to Clemmie she'd also given birth to her own heart, and now it lay, beating and oh so vulnerable, outside her own body, and where it once rested behind her ribs was nothing but a hard knot of fear. She never felt the soft melt of new motherhood that she'd felt with the boys. No, she felt like a spitting cat, hackles raised, ready to sink her teeth into anyone who came too close to her daughter. She told herself it was because Clemmie was her longed-for girl, that's why it was different. Bry and others said it was natural, instinctual, to be protective, but when Elizabeth's back was turned she knew they rolled their eyes and said, 'Typical Elizabeth.' Typical Elizabeth to micromanage her newborn, typical Elizabeth not to let her out of her sight, to lie awake, counting her breaths while she slept.

Then Clemmie had her first fit and in its wake, after the noise and the terror had quietened, Elizabeth felt vindicated. She'd been right to be vigilant – didn't everyone say a mother should trust her instincts? From then on, Elizabeth was her daughter's bodyguard, her only protection against the horrifying, unpredictable world, and she'd never, ever stand down. So when Dr Parker told her that warm Friday morning in July that having Clemmie vaccinated could increase the risk of more fits, she'd heard something different. The encroaching darkness, the fact she hadn't slept for longer than two hours in weeks, the fact she had to smile at everyone and say, 'So well!' when they asked, 'How are you?' meant that when Dr Parker spoke to her, she heard something else entirely. All she heard was risk. It was as though Dr Parker had handed her some dice and asked her to throw for her daughter's future. She couldn't do it. So instead she slipped the dice into her pocket and walked away. But of course, the game still went on; she was still gambling whether she wanted to or not. When Jack asked her later that evening how the appointment had gone, she spared him the suffering of choice, told him what she felt to be true. They could not safely vaccinate their daughter.

Outside her door she hears a shuffle before there's a gentle knock. Jack knows he'll be waiting a long time if he wants to be invited in, so he opens the door a crack. Elizabeth feels him close in on her before he sits on the edge of the bed.

'Morning, Elizabeth.' He talks more slowly now, as though she is no longer a grown woman but something that can only handle life in whispers. Sometimes she thinks it'd be better if he screamed. She opens her eyes just enough to let him know she's awake.

'Here,' he says, and she opens her hot palm to take the pills. She doesn't know what they are but that, like everything else, doesn't matter. They are chalky on her tongue, chemical, as though designed for machines and not for something living.

'Did you sleep?'

It's not a real question; she doesn't have to answer.

'I'm going to get the kids today, Elizabeth – remember, we talked about it. It's Christmas Eve and they're excited to be coming home.'

Since the court case the kids have been staying with Jack's parents in Surrey, Jack driving between the two houses every day because he too is frightened. Frightened to leave anyone he loves on their own for too long.

Christmas Eve. That's why today is special. Elizabeth tries to feel something, some stirring of joy, no matter how distant, but there's nothing. She just feels panicked.

She has to force the voice out of her throat as she says, 'But they can't, they can't see me like this, Jack.'

'We talked about this, remember, Elizabeth? The doctor said that at some point it would be worse to keep them away, that they'd feel like they were being lied to or ignored. They're begging me to come home. They know you're not well, they'll give you space, but let them come home, Elizabeth, please.'

She feels herself nod because he's talking too much, and she longs to slip back down into the comfort of the cool darkness she knows will be waiting for her as soon as she closes her eyes again.

She's lying with her hands turned up, empty, when she hears the scratch of a key followed by the tingle of the bell on top of the front door as it rattles open. Her chest tightens as she braces herself to hear one of her children calling her name, but where there should be running feet or raised, excited voices there's just more silence, until someone with slow, plodding steps starts walking upstairs, turning the lights on as they pass through the landing. Elizabeth ignores the crash in her head as she lifts herself up to lean against the wall. Maybe Jack changed his mind about bringing the children home after all. But then from across the landing a voice calls, 'Elizabeth?' followed by a gentle tap at the master bedroom door. Through the chemical fug another memory demands attention. It's years ago and Elizabeth's dad has just died and Elizabeth is crying in the early morning. She's hiding her face in Bry's shoulder, Bry's hand stroking her hair and reassuring her that she's not alone. That Bry will never let her be alone.

Bry calls again.

'Elizabeth?'

But Elizabeth can't reply because her voice is jammed by a thick plug of fear, so she just sits in the darkness and waits.

She hears the little bell to Clemmie's door ring before Bry appears, backlit, in the doorway. Elizabeth's eyes crease, assaulted, as Bry turns on the main light. Even though she must have expected to find her somewhere in the house, Bry still lets out a startled 'Oh' when she sees Elizabeth cowering in the little bed. For a moment the two women just stare at each other, and in that moment every human emotion seems to flow between them. It's too much; Elizabeth can't take it. She drops her head to her knees and braces herself for Bry to say or do whatever she's here for. She feels Bry move into the centre of the room, hears the soft thump as she sits down on the carpet.

She hears her shuffle to get comfortable, her breath, and then she hears her say, 'I want you to know I don't expect you to say anything or do anything. I'm here for me.'

Elizabeth doesn't move.

'I did exactly this, after Clemmie lost her sight. I couldn't get out of bed, I felt like I'd bled every good thing to death. I felt if I moved in the world again, I'd only cause more suffering and I couldn't, I just couldn't bear . . .' She can't finish her sentence but she doesn't need to.

'Then I realised something, Elizabeth. I realised that even though I hated having to exist, I had no choice – I have to exist.'

Elizabeth doesn't move but she feels her face wet with tears.

'You cannot abandon your children, Elizabeth. They need you to show them that recovery is possible, that no matter how much sadness, guilt or shame they feel, no matter how many times they fuck up, it's all surmountable, that they have survival in their DNA. We all carry shadows. But if you sink too far, Elizabeth, if you go to a place where no one can reach you, then you'll be dragging them down with you and, just like you, they may never get out.'

There's a small fracture to Bry's voice, but she limps on.

'It's time to get up now, Elizabeth. It's time to stand in the shower and be downstairs when they come home. They need you and you need them.'

For the first time, Elizabeth looks up at Bry. They are both crying freely now but neither woman reaches for the other. Elizabeth feels like she's dissolving, as though layers of herself are melting away with every tear that rolls, plump, from her eyes. She feels ancient and brand new, raw and flawed. But she also feels the hard ball of fear release and she knows, for the first time, that she's going to have to survive.

Clemmie falls asleep on the drive home, Claude next to her on the back seat, his yellow head and shoulder her cushion.

The boys stare, grave as monks, out of their windows as Jack whispers careful words of instruction, of reassurance.

'Just give your mum space, OK, boys? She needs lots of rest at the moment so she gets better quickly, OK?'

They wanted to come home but now he can feel their hesitation; the air in the car is thick, troubled. Jack pauses for the hundredth time, wonders whether he should turn around and drive them back to the cheery Christmas lights, tinsel and pine-scented air of his parents' house, instead of towards the unfathomable depths of their mum's desolation. Jack wishes he could tell them the truth, wishes he could tell them that he's frightened too. That he's terrified Elizabeth will rebuff or, worse, ignore them, or that having them close could cause her to sink even deeper. It has been months after all, all the way back in that lost world of ladybirds and sunshine last summer, since she last tucked them in or kicked a ball with them, since she's been the mum he wants them to remember. They've adapted, as kids do, but the cracks are starting to show. Jack had been called in at the end of term to Max's school after he hit another boy in the playground. Charlie had become uncharacteristically withdrawn and moody, and then Clemmie had burst into unexpected tears yesterday. It had almost broken Jack when her small hands wiped away the tears that had also started to run down his own face, as he tried to convince his little girl that it most definitely wasn't her fault that Mummy was so tired and needed so much rest.

If anyone has mistreated Elizabeth, Jack knows it's him. He's known since the beginning that the case was never about setting a precedent or helping others. It was instead the only way Elizabeth knew how to live with her pain. Anger, he now knows, is so much easier to feel than sadness.

He should have stopped her then, he should never have let her take it so far. No, no, he's still getting it wrong. He should have stopped her seven years ago when, in a high, tense voice, her face blank, shadowed with exhaustion, Clemmie a tiny baby at her breast, she'd promised that she was OK, that of course he should go to work, she was absolutely fine. For seven years she's been in perpetual motion, always doing something useful, whether it's sharpening the boys' pencils for their art class or campaigning against the development of another supermarket site. Sometimes he found her busyness admirable and sometimes he found it intimidating, but it should always have been a warning. He should have got her to stop but he never did, because he never took the time to figure out how to get her to stop. Sometimes being still and sad is the hardest thing.

He has no idea how the next few hours, let alone the coming months, are going to work out. The few friends who haven't withdrawn their offers of support since the case was dismissed have advised him to use the money from the Kohlis to get them through financially and to take one day at a time. There's no other way, they said, and they are right of course. Eventually they'll have to move – somewhere cheaper, somewhere with space to rebuild their lives – but not today. Today he just has to get his children home and make sure his wife doesn't slip – seen but unreachable – beneath the impenetrable ice of her sadness.

Clemmie stirs as Jack parks the car outside their house. Number 10 along with the unlit Number 9 are the only houses on the road not to have any fairy lights or Christmas cards on display. Even the new tenants next door have put a small silver tree in their front window. The boys look curious and a little shy as they stare at their home while Clemmie, her hand on Claude's head, asks, 'Are we home, Daddy?'

Jack's relieved – as he knew he would be – that he left the downstairs lights on so the house wouldn't look too bleak when they arrived. Everyone turns towards him for an answer, so Jack opens his door and forces brightness into his voice as he says, 'We're home!' And as he gathers Clemmie up, yawning, into his arms, Charlie suddenly grapples to undo his seatbelt and kicks open his door in a rush, and as soon as his feet touch the ground he starts running, with a little yelp of joy, towards the front door.

With Clemmie in his arms and Claude now circling his feet, Jack can't see what's got him so excited. But then Max, his head craning and bobbing to see what his brother just saw, shouts, 'Mum!'

And before he's even seen her for himself Jack starts running too, Clemmie laughing now in his arms because she doesn't need her eyes to tell her that her mummy is there, standing in the doorway, her arms wide and aching to hold them all again.

13 January 2020

The removal men don't stop for a chat or even a cup of tea; they can sense the urgency, Bry's need to leave quickly and cleanly. They've been paid extra to start so early, while it's still dark, with the hope of avoiding as many watchful eyes as possible. This place that once represented freedom has become a panopticon, somewhere Bry and Ash feel constantly observed, a place where people will always mutter and point. It can never be home again. Light the colour of dirty water starts to bleed through the dull sky just as Ash comes out of the house, helping the removal men carry the huge rolled-up rug from the sitting room. Apart from Rosalyn and Row, they've heard nothing from their old neighbours. It is as though they've all agreed to pretend they never sipped wine in each other's gardens or babysat for Alba. The two years they spent on the street are like a stain they all want to ignore. But her family have lost too much to worry about the neighbours. They've become a juicy footnote in the history of the street and the town. So be it.

Alba has spent the last hour moving solemnly from room to room, stroking the walls and saying goodbye to the creaky stair, the wall in the loo where she used to scribble with her crayons, and other secret places. Bry was worried it could confuse or upset her, to see their old home emptied and lifeless, but she's too interested in the future to bother much with the past.

Just as the grey morning starts to blanket the sky, Bry notices Jane's curtains quiver open. If she's watching them, she's doing so from a safe distance. Bry turns away and, as the men feed the carpet into the van, Ash dusts his hands on his jeans and says, 'Well, I think that's it. That's everything.'

He puts his arm over Bry's shoulders and they stand silently watching as the removal men make sure all their possessions are secure and packed safely for the drive to the flat, which is still just a flat but will somehow magically become their home. They both turn towards the front steps to watch as Alba skips down them for the last time.

'I've done goodbye,' she tells them firmly before sliding her hand into Bry's. 'Can we have pancakes now?'

Bry squeezes her daughter's hand and is about to lead her to the car when someone from down the road clatters their recycling bin out of the side gate and away from them along the pavement where other green bins are congregated, waiting to be emptied. Bry's new instinct is not to look up, to keep pressing Alba towards her car seat, but Alba isn't afraid. She lifts her hand to point at the man who has now turned around to walk back to his house, the man who used to blow raspberries on her stomach and gave her her first scooter. She shouts, her voice high and excited, 'Uncle Jack! Uncle Jack!'

Quick as a fish, Alba's little hand wiggles out of Bry's and, ignoring Ash and Bry calling her name, her hands fold into fists and start to pump the air as she runs towards her old friend. Jack, in bathrobe and slippers, just stands and stares, frozen and uncertain like Bry and Ash. What will they do? Jack watches Alba blankly for a moment before he turns and calls something inside his house. Alba slows before she reaches Jack and Bry clutches Ash's arm as Clemmie, using the recently fitted rail, starts to walk slowly down their front steps. She's taller and her hair has grown in even thicker waves down her back. Bry moves to go to them but Ash stops her.

'Just watch,' he whispers.

Alba has reached the steps now, Jack still some way beyond, but she's not so interested in him any more. She gives a little hop as Clemmie reaches the bottom step just as Elizabeth appears at the top, hugging a mug with her hands. It's the first time the girls have seen each other since Clemmie's party in July. Alba, still fizzing with excitement, moves closer to Clemmie and Clemmie tilts her head, thoughtful for a moment, before Alba says something, something that makes Clemmie smile, and she moves closer to Alba and places her hands on Alba's face. They stand like that for a brief moment before Alba starts to shake with laughter, which makes Clemmie giggle, and then Alba turns away from the girl she used to call her sister and calls out, 'Bye, 'lemmie!' and waves at her, before she turns around and starts skipping again towards another ending and another beginning.

Author's Note

I can remember the exact moment I felt the first spark of an idea for *The Herd*. It was the sweltering summer of 2018 and I was bouncing on a birthing ball, crotchety and swollen, nine months pregnant with our first son in our overgrown garden, watching my husband James and Sophie, our birth doula, argue.

I'd pushed for us to choose Sophie – she was the kind of mother I wanted to be. Strong, unafraid and incredibly kind. Alternative, yes (she had a yurt in her garden where she'd perform rebirthing rituals), but her life choices were rooted in experience and her shelves were heavy with books about birth and parenting. They were arguing because Sophie had just asked us whether we intended to vaccinate our baby. Honestly, I hadn't thought about it properly yet, but was eager to hear Sophie's wisdom, while James scrunched up his face as though her question had released a terrible smell.

'Yes, absolutely we are. One hundred per cent yes,' he said, without even looking my way. Sophie smiled her calm smile at him, the one I'd seen her use with her young kids.

'Did you know, James, the UK has one of the most concentrated vaccine schedules in the world? By the time your little one' – she placed her warm hand on my bump – 'is four months old, they will have had twenty-three vaccines? At eight weeks old their immune system will be flooded with aluminium – over two hundred times the recommended weekly intake, in one injection.' I felt our baby twitch.

James's eyes widened. Sophie's opinion, I knew, riled him. But James is a history buff, so he came back with: 'So we should leave our child vulnerable to the diseases – diphtheria, polio, measles – that maimed and killed so many of our grandparents' generation?'

'When was the last time you heard of someone contracting polio in this country?' Sophie asked, still calm, still smiling.

James almost shouted, 'That's because of the bloody vaccines!'

That was it. That was the moment. I stopped bouncing and stopped listening to the row. The choice was terrifying. If we vaccinated, we were – according to Sophie – risking damaging our baby's nervous system, or, if we chose not to vaccinate, did we cross our fingers and hope they didn't contract meningitis? I was entirely responsible for this new little life, but also helplessly out of control. And that was the moment the idea for *The Herd* was born.

I had to wait another two weeks for our son.

I started my research a few weeks later, chatting to parents at baby groups and in the park. I heard stories about best friends who no longer speak because one did vaccinate and the other chose not to. I heard of relationships pushed to the brink. I spoke to my ninety-two-year-old friend who shared memories of the night her sister died from polio, and to a father whose one-year-old stopped making eye contact a couple of weeks after he had the MMR. I sat at dinner tables where the topic is banned. For some, it's just too painful.

I spoke to anyone who'd talk to me about vaccines. And

beyond the noise of the anger, the outrage that people could be so ignorant, so selfish, so stupid, I'd noticed the same quiet panic I'd experienced that humid day in our garden. We all just want to do the right thing for those we love and we are terrified of getting it 'wrong'. I hope I've managed to convey this in the novel.

We have chosen to vaccinate our sons and I believe it was the right thing to do; both for us and to help protect others. That doesn't mean I didn't dread the moment the needle entered their soft bodies. But I knew it would be infinitely worse to watch them contract measles, meningitis or whooping cough – knowing I could have prevented their suffering.

The timing of this novel has been extraordinary. I wrote the lion's share during the first 2020 lockdown. I've never known a time when our individual choices could directly and catastrophically impact others so profoundly. Learning about all this in theory and watching it play out in practice across the world has been the education of my life.

I really hope you have enjoyed reading *The Herd* as much as I enjoyed writing it.

With thanks,
Emily Edwards

Acknowledgements

There may only be one name on the cover of this book, but, really, there should be many. Firstly, I'd like to thank my sons for making me live some of the tough decisions faced by my characters and for making writing a book feel easy. I love you very much. I'm also deeply grateful to my husband, James Linard, for looking after our toddler every day during the first, longest and, for us, toughest lockdown, so that I could write. His enthusiasm for digging up worms knows no bounds.

I'm forever thankful to my agent, the indomitable Nelle Andrew, for her wise counsel, unfailing support and for refusing to bullshit anyone, ever.

Huge thanks to Frankie Gray for her dedication and vision for *The Herd*. It has been an incredible experience working with Frankie and the whole Transworld team, which includes, but is by no means limited to: Imogen Nelson, Viv Thompson, Josh Benn, Phil Evans, Laura Ricchetti, Laura Garrod, Emily Harvey, Gary Harley, Tom Chicken, Louise Blakemore and my copy-editor, Claire Gatzen. Thank you.

Big thanks to Beci Kelly for her wonderful cover design and to Becky Short and Louis Patel for being the best cheerleaders for the book.

Thank you to Kate Lynch and Chloe Mortensen for their sage advice and guidance on the novel.

Thank you to my friend Jane Whistler who always listened, shared and laughed. I miss you.

In deep gratitude, as always, to my incredible parents, Sandy and Edward Elgar, for always loving and never giving up.

Thank you to my friends, my circle and my sisters.

Thank you to each and every person who talked to me about their experiences and views on vaccines – from strangers, to health professionals, to close friends – you helped and inspired more than you probably know.

I also want to salute everyone who has had to make hard decisions for others. It's not easy – but know that you are not alone.

Finally, thank you, reader for making it all possible.

ABOUT THE AUTHOR

After studying at Edinburgh University, Emily Edwards worked for a think tank in New York, before returning to London where she worked as a support worker for vulnerable women at a large charity. She now lives in Lewes, East Sussex, with her endlessly patient husband and her two endlessly energetic young sons.

Reading-group guide

1. *The Herd* follows Elizabeth and Bryony — two women with very different viewpoints and perspectives. Did you identify more with one character than the other? Why?

2. Think about the events leading up to the birthday party. Could the drama that develops from that moment have been prevented? Which characters are to blame for the way in which the tragedy unfolds?

3. Discuss the theme of responsibility in the novel. Do you think the characters are justified in acting in the way they do? Would you have made the same choices had you been in their place?

4. Were there any moments you found unexpected or shocking?

5. Think about the perspectives we are shown from people in and around the courtroom. How did these voices affect your reading of the novel? Did they make you consider any points of view different to your own?

6. Were you surprised by how the final chapters played out? While you were reading, did you have any different ideas for how the novel might end?